T0149340

Feeling
in the
Dark

Victoria Rene'e Manley

iUniverse, Inc.
Bloomington

Feeling in the Dark

iUniverse books may be ordered through booksellers or by contacting:

iUniverse
1663 Liberty Drive
Bloomington, IN 47403
www.iuniverse.com
1-800-Authors (1-800-288-4677)

ISBN: 978-1-4759-0771-1 (sc)
ISBN: 978-1-4759-0773-5 (hc)
ISBN: 978-1-4759-0772-8 (e)

Printed in the United States of America

iUniverse rev. date: 5/11/2012

Contents

Chapter 1
All About the RIDE!

Tory was waiting for her flight to board. She had spent the entire week in Las Vegas attending her cousins wedding that ended in disaster. See, her cousin Vera had been dating Raymond her ex-boyfriend. Tory and Raymond had broken up when she decided to move to South Carolina in 2008. Some months later, Vera called to explain to Tory that Raymond had wanted to date her. Tory didn't pay it any mind because that was the kind of cold hearted, small minded bastard that he would become when he wouldn't get his way. Tory had explained to Vera that his motives might not be to the best of her interests, but Vera thought that she was saying that because she may have been jealous and scorned. Tory figured she would just back off and just continue to support her cousin. The truth was Vera and Tory weren't just cousins, they were like sisters. They were each others best friend and they were inseparable. The two of them would do almost everything together. Tory never had a sister so Vera was like the sister she never had. When they were kids they would dress alike and the even used to get drunk together. Their friendship came to a halt when Tory told Vera she was leaving Las Vegas. Vera didn't take it well. In fact, Vera stop contacting Tory and the only time they would speak is if Tory would contact her. Ultimately, they lost contact altogether; until one day Vera called to tell Tory that she and Raymond were engaged. She hadn't realized they were dating. So now Tory had the tedious task of pretending to be happy for them. Now the big day had arrived and it was the most dramatic wedding she had ever been to. Tory's other cousins, Vera's sisters were acting out throwing themselves on the floor like the dramatic diva's they were. Vera's mother came to the wedding drunk as a skunk. Tory got the impression that no one wanted this wedding to go down. She remained low key the entire time. The only time she showed face was at the beginning and when it was over, she didn't even stay for the reception. "Good ridden to all of them." She said as she regained her consciousness. Finally, she heard her flight boarding, "now boarding flight 432 to South Carolina boarding at gate 8A." Those words were like audio gold to her at that point. Plus, she had been looking forward to her upgrade to first class.

Que`Shuane was coming from a connecting flight from France. He had another one of his treacherous board meetings where he had to convince his investor's to stay interested. The meeting wasn't hard but at some point there was always one investor who would challenge him. See, Shaune was an oil tycoon. His father was the sole owner but, some five years ago he had given his son full run of the family business. This meant that he now had to run back and forth out of the country to keep the business running and his father happy. And that included trying to appease the investors as well as the share holders. Nonetheless, he had won them over. "Once I get on the plane I'm going to get myself a nice stiff drink." He said to himself after hearing his flight boarding. After he checked his bags in, he headed straight to the gate.

As Tory got on the plane, she made her way to the first class section. Her seat was center 12 and when she got to her seat, she realized it was soiled with what could only be described as vomit. At least that was the smell it gave off. She checked her ticket and looked at the seat and checked the ticket again hoping that it might be a mistake or maybe it would even change. "OH COME ON!" she yelled. The stewardess came to Tory and introduced herself. "Hello Ma'am. My name is Sonya. What is the problem?" Then Sonya caught a whiff of the problem. "Well, I guess you can understand exactly what the problem is." Sonya was looking around and realized that it was a full house on the plane and Tory's seat was what was left. Or so it seemed. Then the stewardess said "Ma'am, I'm sorry but you're going to have to wait for the next flight to South Carolina." Tory became indignant. "I don't think so. I paid for this flight. It was your job to make sure that these seats are supposed to be passenger ready. I'm sure that when the plane pulled up to the gate to let people off, someone had to see this." She was getting worked up about having to wait for another flight after the week she just had. Then Sonya said "Ma'am could you stay right here?" "I would gladly." Tory replied with sarcasm. As she watched Sonya leave, she looked around the plane and saw everyone looking back at her. All she could think to herself was "Of all the people on the plane this had to happen to, it had to happen to me." She looked to her left and she had seen this well dressed, handsome, caramel complexioned man in a suit trying to get her attention. Tory turned to look behind her; that he was possibly waving to someone else. With confusion in her eyes, she said" Are you talking to me?" Then the man got up and walked over to her. He moved in close to her and whispered, "My name is Que`Shuane Guadau. And I see that you are in need of a seat. It appears that I have an extra seat of my own that I purchased for my comfort. If you don't mind I would be happy to give you my extra seat if you don't mind the extra paper work?" Tory looked at her vomit filled seat; then she looks back at him and she thought to herself, "No brainier." Then she answered, "I would love to take that seat. Thank you." As they walked towards her new seat, she asked, "So how do you say your name again?" He responded "It's Que`Shuane Guadau. Just call me Shaune." "Fair enough." She shrugged. "My name is Torianey Heckstall." As she reached to shake his hand, instead of shaking it he kissed her hand.

Tory thought to herself, "Damn! This brother is smooth." Tory was curious to know so she asked, "Anyone else would have would have let me stand all the way back to South Crack. Why would you be so generous to a total stranger?" Shaune replied, "You needed a seat. I had one and I didn't want to see a lady get dragged off the plane." Tory giggled and asked, "How did you know if they were going to take me off the plane?" He pointed and said, "Turn around." She turned and saw the stewardess pointing at her with two TSA Officers to come and drag her off the plane. She turned to him and said, "AW HELL NAW!" Tory thought for sure her fait was going to be spent through out the night being held in an airport cell waiting for the locals to book her all over a misunderstanding. So then Que`Shuane grabbed her hands and said, "Don't say anything. I'll handle it." Deep down inside Tory was prepared to get dragged off the plane. She thought to herself "Seriously, what could this guy do to help me and who is he to stop them?" As the TSA Officers approached Shaune and Tory, the first Officer said, "Ma'am could you please come with us?" Que`Shuane asked, "Is there a problem Officers?" The officer replied nervously, "We were informed that this woman was causing a disturbance on the plane and according to FAA code, any disturbance must be removed for the safety of the flight and its passengers." "Well does she look like she's causing any disturbances now?" "No but, the…" Then Que`Shuane cut in and said, "Ms. Heckstall is my guest and this is her seat. Do I need to speak with your superiors?" With shame in his voice the TSA Officer replied, "No sir. However, if she causes another disturbance, we'll have to remove her." As they walked away, Tory thought to herself, "Damn! He must be related to the President or something." Shaune turned to her and asked, "You won't cause another disturbance will you?" "Nope; I'll be a total angel from here on out."

From then on, they talked and joked from the duration of the ride. Shaune thought she seemed quite attractive and at certain times while she was talking, he would manage to steal a glance at her voluptuous body. He even admired how smooth and natural her brown skin looked without makeup. "Not a lot of black woman can pull that look off." He thought to himself. Also, it was something about her ability to be vulnerable to him that attracted him to her. She would tell him everything from where she worked at Carrapellies to the wedding that she just came from. When Tory stops talking, she realized that she had told this stranger everything he wanted to know not knowing anything about him. "I really love my job at Carrapellies but…" Then she stopped in mid sentence. But Shaune tried to keep the conversation going. "But what?" "But I must seem terribly selfish talking about myself and not giving you a chance to tell me about you." "I have a very boring life. I like hearing about you more then I like talking about me. Please go on." "Surely you have something that you have to say about yourself." "Well, I am a traveling business man that travels most of the time. How interesting is that?" "Well, if you put it that way." After sometime had passed, dinner time came around. Tory couldn't afford the food because she had spent most her money on her upgrade seat. Sonya, the Stewardess was coming around with the dinner cart. As she asked Shaune for his order, Tory jumped up and grabbed her purse and headed for the vending machine. While he watched Tory approach the vending machine, he gave Sonya his order. At the vending machine, Tory realized she only had enough for a bag of fruit snacks, a bag of Doritos and a can of sprite hoping that would hold her till she got home. When she got back to her seat, she noticed that Shaune had his meal and on her table, there was another meal. Tory tried to flag Sonya down to let her know that she may have delivered to the wrong seat, but then Shaune asked, "Is there a problem?" "Yeah, I think she gave away someone else's food." Taking a sip of his wine, Shaune replied, "No she didn't." "How do you know that?" "I think she realized you might have wanted dinner." Then she held up the three items she had in her hand and said, "But I already have dinner." They looked at each other of a second and both busted into laughter. As she sat down in her seat, just before she commenced to eating she leaned over and gave Shaune a kiss on the cheek. He turned to her and said "Wow! Thank you." Then she said, "No, thank you."

After they had finished their meal, Shaune purchased another bottle of wine. He asked Tory to join him and she accepted. While they were sipping away, Tory asked, "Would you be interested in playing a game with me?" "How does it go?" "Well I call it the "Mile High Game" it's kind of like who done it, where and with who. See, we look around the plane, we see who may have had a mile high moment and with whom they may have. For example, do you see that woman over there in that well dressed suit?" "Yeah I see her." "Do you think she may have had a mile high moment?" Not really getting the point, Shaune was sought of loosing interest. So then he answered, "No. I don't think so." "Why don't you think so?" "She seems too conservative; too closed in." "Exactly, keep your eyes on her as the Stewardess passes by. See, every time she walks pass her, she looks at her with this seductive look. Maybe she might have had one with another Stewardess at another time or so. But it looks like she wants this one. And that conservative look she's exhibiting just might be a cover up of the freak that she really is." "How do you know about these things?" "I like to study people some times. Moments like this it help the time go pass faster." So to pass the time they would look around the plane to guess who might have or might not have had a "Mile High Moment." It was fun for a while, but eventually they grew bored with it. Then they became quiet. Shaune turned to Tory and asked, "What about you?" "What about me?" "Don't act coy with me. You know what I'm talking about. Have you ever had a mile high moment?" Tory started to stutter. "Oh, what, who me? Oh no." Now the scene was really silent as she looked around to try and divert the conversation. But Shaune kept it going. "Are you interested in one?" "Well, it sounds interesting." Now Tory started to get nervous. But Shaune was determined to get an answer. So he continued "But are you interested?" "I just wandered about other people. I never wondered about myself." Although she was trying to evade the question, Shaune wasn't buying it. So again, he threw it out there, "Right, but are you interested?" Tory Finally gave in and said "Maybe I thought about it, but I didn't think I would follow through with it." This was her most honest but safest answer she could ever give aside from laying it bare. "You know it's actually a really great experience if you try to enjoy it." Then she laughed and said, "I knew you had a few. Probably you had a few more then that." Then there was that uncomfortable silence again. Tory felt she had to change the subject. So she asked, "So, do you have to travel outside the country much?" "I have to travel outside the country all the time. I actually have a home in France that I travel back and forth to." Maybe he might know a few phrases in French. "So do you speak French?" "It's actually my first language." "Wow! Are you serious? So, English is your second language then?" "Yes it is." "How did you learn to speak English so well?" "I was always exposed to the English language growing up. While in college I decided to study it extensively." "So say something in French?" "What would you like for me to say?" Tory always thought of the French as a sexy culture, so she asked him, "Say something sexy." Shaune figured that she wouldn't notice what he was saying or how it was as long as it seemed sexy. So he started "Pardon Me vous vous asseyez dan mon siege!" "I don't get the feeling that was supposed to be sexy." Then Shaune giggle and said, "Nope, it wasn't. I actually said excuse me, you are in my seat. Look, I don't want to offend you. You might smack me." "No. I appreciate your ability to be a total gentleman but, we're grown, so you can bring the sexy." He paused for a few seconds then he drew closer to Tory's face and with a seductive whisper he said, "Okay, you asked for it. Vous avez un corps tre' sexy." Then she smiled and asked, "And that means?" "Your body is very sexy." He was so close to her that she could smell his cologne and his natural body scent. Along with being tipsy, she started to feel turned on. Then she got bold and asked "What if I was interested in a mile high moment, how would that happen?" Tory couldn't believe she had said that. So Shaune answered without as much as a blink or a smile "That could easily be arranged." She was expecting him to turn her down. Then he said, "We could go into that room there." He was referring to the room that was about eight feet away. "But what if we get caught?" "Let me worry about that." Tory looked around the plane to see what was everyone else doing at this time. People were sleeping, reading, or scanning through their PDA's. She looked back at him and said, "Am I supposed to go now?" "Yes, you go now." Tory got up and made her to the little room. Of course with all his clout, Shaune manages to get the key from Sonya and slip her a couple of cee notes.

Tory was in this little room that actually was a mini baggage room. It was dim with a few bags. Perhaps, bags that were left on the plane or maybe they belonged to the Stewardesses. There stood a crushed velvet, armless black comfort chair. She sat on it and it felt warm as opposed to the drafty room itself. As she sat there for a while, she thought to herself, "Maybe he's not coming." Then she laughed and said, "He's not going through with it. He was kidding." So she thought until the door opened and Shaune entered through it. As he closed the door, he locked it behind him. Tory's heart started to pound. She was about to have sex with this stranger. "The perfect stranger." She thought to herself. As he walked closer to her, she backed up and said, "Wait!" Shaune stopped and put his hands in his pockets. See, he knew that if he applied too much pressure, she just might not be down for it. Then Tory said "I have one rule." Sarcastically, Shaune replied, "Oh, only one?" "Yes, after this is all over, I don't want to see you anymore. No phone calls, nothing." "Why is that?" "Because, I'm not really into hit and runs; plus, moments like these always end with no emotion involved. That if we continue to see each other this way, then the sex will always be meaningless. This is not what I want for my life. Do you understand?" Shaune tilted his head and said, "Agreed." Shaune walk towards her. He leaned in to kiss her on the lips. Tory could feel his lips against hers. They were soft and sensual. His kiss was a little off; maybe even mediocre. In fact, his kisses weren't good at all. Then she opened her mouth to taste his tongue. His breath was like a unique fragrance. It was like a hint of raw meat, plus a hint of wine and food that he had eaten which wasn't bad at all. Although, she smelt worse breaths, his by far his was nothing to deal with. Shaune started to get swept up in her kiss. So then, he grabbed her by her face so that he could kiss her deeper. Tory was loosing control and started feeling all over his body.

She felt the urge to take control and she did. As she was kissing on his neck, she was unbuckling his belt. Shaune was amazed at how quick she recovered from the scared chic to dominant chic. But he liked this side of her. Tory whispered in his ear "Do you have protection?" Shaune went into his pocket and pulled out a condom. "At your request Madame." "Very good." She said. She stood up and she pulled him up onto his feet. Then she pulled down his slacks. After his slacks came off, she pulled his boxer briefs down. She opened the condom and slid it on to his penis. She even played with it to see how he would react. While she was doing all that, Shaune's arousal became heightened. His eyes started to roll back into his head and he started to breathe deeper. He had realized that it was time to remove some of her clothing but she was already wearing a skirt. And in Shaune's mind, that meant easy access. He reached under her skirt to remove her underwear and noticed she was wearing thong underwear; which was more of a turn on for him. As he removed her underwear, he couldn't resist the urge to fondle her thighs. They were soft and smooth like caramel wrapped in silk. Then Shaune did an unconscious, unthinkable thing. He leaned in to kiss her thigh and when he did, he bit into her and immediately it startled Tory. When she looked at Shaune, he said "I'm sorry, I couldn't help myself." Then she sat back in his lap and whispered "No worries." As she sat back in his lap, she had decided she wanted him inside her. She started to ease him in but, she was met with resistance. It had been sometime since she had been with anyone. So over the years, she had tightened up a bit. She tried to laugh it off while she would continue her painful process of trying to mount him. "I'm sorry, just give me few seconds I can just…" Shaune wasn't buying it, he knew the only way to break the tension was to take it. So he grabbed her tight and in one motion he thrust himself into her. At that point, she reacted by trying to pull away from him but he was too strong. After he was in, she stopped struggling and held on to him. Then he whispered in her ear, "The worst is over now." And he was right because shortly after she started to ride him; and it felt so good. Now she started to grind him. Tory felt like she just wasn't getting enough of him. In fact, she was feeling like she could take him in whole. Then she started to grind faster and faster and as she moved faster, her thighs tightened around his waist and Shaune loved that. Her moans were getting louder and she was breathing in Shaune's ear which was turning him on more and more. Then they stared each other eye to eye and that's when Shaune knew he made a bad deal. He hadn't had sex like this before in his life. Of course he's had plenty of women, but there was just something about her that made him feel he wanted more of her then just this moment. In fact, he knew he would want her more then just once. She whispered in his ear and said, "Daddy this feels so good." Hearing that blew his mind. He thought to himself, "She called me Daddy? Damn that sounds so sexy." Tory started to loose control. She was grinding deeper and deeper on Shaune. Then she said, "Daddy, I want to cum for you." Then Shaune whispered, "Cum for me now Baby." As she started to climax, she grabbed him closer and her thighs began to grip him so tight that he started to loose his air, but he didn't care. He loved her thighs around him and the more she squeezed, the more he love it. With all that action going on, he felt her muscle contracting on his throwing him off his rhythm. So he grabbed her tighter and started to cum. While the both were cumin, they looked at each other again. This time Shaune had felt something he had never felt before while having sex with a woman. But he couldn't explain it to himself what it was. Feeling scared about such a feeling, he looked away. They were breathing and grinding in synch. Now the plane was about to land and the "seat belt on" light came on which means they had to stop. Shaune told Tory "We have to stop now." He gave her one last kiss. Then there was a light tap at the door. Tory asked, "What was that?" "It was the Stewardess. She's letting us know we have to get back at our seat." "You told her?" "How else was I supposed to get the key to the room?" "Damn! You got clout like that?" "Look, you better go out first and then I'll be right behind you." Tory eased off of Shaune. Then she left to go to her seat. As Shaune started to fix his clothes, he realized that Tory left behind her underwear. He picked them up and giggled to himself.

Then he shoved them in his pocket. After he got himself together, he left the room and went to his seat.

As they sat side by side, they had looked like they ran laps around the plane several times. Shaune turned to look at Tory but she would not acknowledge him. See, Tory made a deal with him and once she was done with him, she was completely done with him. But he didn't get it. Shaune being the rich man that he was, he thought all women could be swayed, but not Tory. She'd been in this position before and promised that she would not allow her heart to be broken that way again. The plane had finally de-boarded in South Carolina. Tory was walking in front of Shaune heading for the baggage claim. His instinct was to go after her but he was met by his driver. "Mr. Guadau, may I take your bags sir?" "Yes please. Wait for me in the car. I'll be there shortly." Then Shaune walked over to Tory. He was standing behind her so she didn't see him. As she turned, he startled her causing her to drop her suit case. As they both went to pick it up, Shaune said, "I'm sorry, I didn't mean to scare you." "It's okay. Are you waiting for your luggage?" "No. My driver took it to the car. But do you need help or a ride somewhere?" Tory laughed and said, "No. I think I have had more then enough of a ride from you. Plus, my car is in the parking lot somewhere." Shaune snickered behind Tory's joke and he found himself doing something that he had never done with a commoner before. He reached into his pocket, pulled out his wallet and pulled out his business card with his private cell number on it. "If you should need anything, don't hesitate to call me." Then Tory said, "Thank you and it was really nice knowing you." Tory didn't want to seem rude while brushing him off so she took the card in one hand and shook his hand with the other. He still didn't get it though. Shaune was so self assured that he could still pull her from that deal they made. Not taking no for an answer, he pulled her in to kiss her on the lips; But when Tory turned her head, his lips landed on her cheek. As she backed up, she pat him on his shoulder and said, "Really, it was nice knowing you." She grabbed her suit case and left for the parking lot. Shaune watched her leave. And although he was hoping that she would look back, she never did. For once in his life the great Que'Shuane Guadau was feeling his heart break and he didn't take it well. Deep down, Tory wanted to look back. She even wanted to kiss his sexy lips for the last time. In fact, she wanted to see him again. But the rules were the rules and she could not deviate from them or she would be back to where she started from; painfully alone.

Tory found her Jeep and loaded her suit case in the back. As she got in, she strapped herself in and paused for a second. Then she said to her self out loud, "Was I being too rude brushing him off like that? He sure did look sincere." Finally, she shook her head and said, "All for the best Torianey. Hell, you ain't gonna see him again anyways." Putting full confidence in that thought, she tried to start her car. But the engine started to stall as it would many times before. "Please baby, I swear I'll get fixed shortly." Upon her bargaining with her car, it started up. She hugged the steering wheel and headed home. Then she said out loud, "Damn, I left my underwear on the plane!!!"

Que'Shuanes' limo had pulled up to his vanity style QG gate waiting for it to open. Shaune had forgotten he was even in the limo heading home. In his mind, he was still on the plane with Torianey Heckstall. Then the jerking motion of the car stopping woke him out of his thought. He shot such a look at the driver like if knives were coming out of him. Noticing the look through the rear view mirror, the driver said, "Sorry sir." Shaune was visibly upset. As they pulled up to the steps of his two winged mansion, Shaune got out without waiting for the driver to open the door for him. He walked up the stairs but then he stopped and turned to look up at the moon. He had wandered what she might be doing at this time. It was a little after ten pm and the night was still young in his mind. He thought to himself, "was she thinking of me like I'm thinking about her?" But the way she snubbed him at the airport he thought to himself, "Possibly not." Then he turned to proceed up the steps. Gregory Duvain, Shaune's assistant and publicist, was awaiting his arrival. Greg had been working with Shaune for five years and they had built up a friendship as well as a working relationship. Greg knew Shaune well enough to know when he was bothered by something. He just had to pry it out of him. In a tip toeing voice, he asked, "So how was your flight?" Both Shaune and Greg took a seat in the den. "Is it that obvious?" Greg let out a sigh of relief and said, "Yeah man, since you got out of the limousine, your driver has been putting everyone on high alert. Now we're all walking on egg shells. What happened between our phone call and you being on the plane? Before you got on the plane, you said the meeting with the Share holder went well. Hook, line and sinker was the phrase you used. Now did they call you back and renege on the close?" "This has nothing to do with the deal. It still stands. This is something way left field from that." He felt uneasy telling Greg but he figured he would give it a shot anyway. "Have you ever met someone that you couldn't stop thinking about?" Then Greg laughed and said, "Yeah, I married her. Remember my wife?" "Greg I remember your wife but, what I'm trying to get at is, remember the feeling you had when you had to leave her after you met her?" Not really getting the point, Greg answered, "And that's why I got her phone number and called her that night. And it was bliss ever since. So who did you meet and why didn't you get her phone number?" "I met this woman on the plane. I gave her my extra seat because hers was badly soiled. I wasn't really thinking of her as anyone but after getting to know her, I started to like her. After we played this ridiculous game she had concocted on the plane, things started to change. We had so much wine that we both became overly fond of each other. Then we ended up having sex on the plane; but just before we did, she made me promise that we would not see each other again after the fact. I had agreed since I didn't know too much about her. After having sex with her I felt different. I couldn't understand why. It was like I was under a spell or something. I just couldn't shake it." After hearing the total story, Greg still couldn't understand what his hang up was. Then he told him, "Shaune, you've done this before man. Okay, there might be some differences in the way it went down but I don't get it." Shaune realized he had to take Greg to his level. "See, we met and it was totally innocent. Unforced, unpredicted. It was the agreement that destroyed any chance of me trying to get with her ever again. What's so strange is any other woman would have never let me go…" Cutting him off, Greg said, "Yeah, but your Que`Shuane Guadau. She had to know that." With a burst of energy, Shaune yelled "That's the thing. I don't think she did." Sounding skeptical, Greg said, "She could be playing you to." "As true as that might be, I really don't think she was. By the time we got off the plane, I gave her my business card and told her that if she needed anything to call me. Do you know what she did? She patted me on the shoulder and said, "It was really nice knowing you." I never felt like shit in my life before that moment." Then Greg came over to pat Shaune on his shoulder and said, "Hey one thing I know about women is if they look back after leaving you that means they just might want to see you again. Did she turn around?" "Not so much as sides glance." "So she's the one woman under a rock who doesn't know who you are. So what? You forget about her and move on." Shaune heard his words but they were proving to be more easily said then done. Greg and Shaune moved their conversation into business and two hours later, it was time for Gregory to head home. As he left the den, Greg turned to Shaune, who was staring out the window and yelled, "Worse case scenario, if you miss her that much then you can pay her a visit at Carrapellies. You can book one of your Father's fund raisers. It would be the perfect reason to see her again. That is if there is anything worth salvaging." Que`Shuane thought that would be a perfect idea. As he ran up stairs to his bedroom, he opened the door to realize that his bedroom still looked like he had been married. After he left for his business meeting he had forgotten to change all the floral crap his wife Lisa had put all over the room. Even the bathroom had matching floral designs all over. He never liked it and since he was divorcing her, he didn't have to put up with it anymore. He had decided to allow it because he did it all for her. He figured that was the order of things when it came down to marriage. Getting slightly distracted from his mission, he called Marta his Lead Care Taker to get rid of the furniture and have it refurnished with something more fitting for a bachelor since he was on his way to becoming one again. Marta had been with Shaune since he was a child. She practically raised him after his mother passed away in a terrible boating accident. Shaune always looked at her like a mother always coming to her for her advice on certain personal affairs. He had always respected her opinion and like any good mother, whether she had opposed his decision or agreed she would support him. Therefore, they got along well. As Shaune removed his clothes in his floral filled bathroom, he put a towel around his waist and walked over to the mirror. As he took off his glasses he realized a small red gash on his neck. He rubbed it to make sure it wasn't lipstick. Sure enough it was one of Tory's love hickies. Perhaps as she was loosing control while nibbling on his neck, she couldn't tell she was doing it. Upon seeing the blemish, he closed his eyes and drifted into the memory of when she was biting into his neck. It felt so good that he didn't realize she was going in on him that hard. By now Shaune was deep in thought. He could literally feel her again; like she was in the bathroom with him. He had imagined her hands all over him and the feel of her lips and the taste of her tongue. He had remembered the feel of her smooth thighs and the way the felt when they tightened around his waist. Then he found himself getting aroused again. He had started to imagine her whispering the word "Daddy" in his ear. And the look in her eyes while she climaxed. Then that feeling that he got in the pit of his stomach that he couldn't shake came back. "Why do I feel this way?" he thought to his self. Suddenly, his cell phone rang loudly waking him out of his deep erotic thought. Aggravated, he grabbed his phone and yelled, "Hello!" "Hey man, what's going on?" It was his best friend and hanging buddy Marcus Swain. Marcus was another trust fund baby. But unlike Shaune, he never had to earn one dollar a day in his life. He was a spoiled Afro-Euro grown man with an arrogant behavior. It would be his father who would supply him with his lavish life style. They were like night and day. Shaune was the good guy while Marcus was the bad guy. Shaune only tolerated Marc because at times, he felt sorry for him. Then Marcus asked, "Are you busy? You sound like I interrupted you or something." Shaune thought to himself, "Hell yeah you interrupted me." Then he said to Marcus, "Naw, I was just about to take a shower. Hey, what are you doing tomorrow?" "I don't have any plans at the moment. Why?" "Why don't you come with me to conduct some business tomorrow?" "Sure, why not?" "Great, meet me at my house tomorrow by noon." Then Shaune hung up the phone. His plan was to throw Tory completely off guard and let her know that he was not going to give up so easily.

Tory got out of her shower and threw on her silk black robe. She had felt a lot better after the day she had. As she lay across her bed, she had started to think about the stranger she had sex with on the plane. She started to re-imagine the way he held her in his arms. She felt a sense of security; and his arms were so strong and muscular that she felt that he just might be able to carry her. Tory hadn't had sex that good in a long time. In fact, she hadn't had sex in a long time and Shaune was the much needed release for her. "I sure wouldn't mind having him again." She said out loud to herself. Then she thought about the deal they made that they wouldn't see each other any more. She started to feel like maybe that wasn't the right thing to do. Perhaps, she should have considered it after the sex was over so that if it was as good as it was, she might have been able to hold back and not make the deal at all. Then she thought to herself, "Yeah fool and we would be having meaningless sex. We've been down this road before." But she still couldn't get him out of her mind. As she started to rub her thighs, she remembered where he had bit her and how it startled her; but as she looked back, as she thought about it, it kind of turned her on again. Then she remembered how she left things with the kind hearted gentleman who gave her his seat and fed her no doubt. Now her guilt started to play with her. "Maybe I should call him and apologize. He was only nice to me." Tory was going back and forth with her thoughts on whether or not to call him and apologize for her rudeness. "But he got what he wanted. He wanted sex and that's what he got. I said no more sex. He agreed and case closed Torianey. HE AGREED!" Finally, she turned off her lamp and went to sleep.

Chapter 2
Can't Get You Out Of My System

The next morning Tory stood on her couch looking at the "Redliner Oil Rig" business card. She hardly slept the whole night. Conflicted with the option to call Que`Shuane and apologize for how bad she treated him, she picked up her phone and dialed the number; then she hung it up. Tory had never treated anyone that bad before when he was only being kind to her. Now all she had to do was just pick up the phone and say she was sorry. As she picked up the phone and thought came across her mind. "If we engage in a conversation, he might want to come over then we'll be having meaningless sex. Not that I wouldn't enjoy it, but this is not what we want. RIGHT?" Then she put the phone back down. Finally, she came to the conclusion to call him just to get the guilt off her mind. As she dialed the number, she prayed in her mind that he would not pick up the phone. She just wanted to leave her message and move on with her life. The phone began to ring. One ring went by, and then it was two rings, then the third ring it went to voice mail. "YES!" she yelled as she listened to his voice mail message. She couldn't help but realize that his voice sounded unhappy. Then when the beep prompted she started, "Hello, Mr. Guadau. It's Torianey Hecktall. You probably don't remember me. Of course you do, we met on the plane just yesterday. You gave me your seat. Any how, I just wanted to apologize for being so rude to you when you were only nothing but nice to me. Okay, I just want to say that. You be well, and take care." She hung up the phone and she actually started to feel better. She went up stairs to get into her school work. She had been gone for a week and hadn't touched her work. There was a paper due next week and she needed to get started immediately or risk failing. For two hours, Tory worked on her paper. When she looked up at the time, she realized it was time to get ready for work. Before she jumped in the shower she pulled out her clothes to wear to work. After she got out of the shower, she put on her makeup and went down stairs to toast her English muffins and make some coffee. She took her breakfast to go because time was winding down. As she got into her car to no avail, it stalled again. "Come on baby, don't do this now." She pumped the gas a few hundred times and eventually it started. "THANK YOU!" she yelled and she was off to work.

Tory made it to Carrapellies where she was the manager and while Louis Carrapelli was the owner. Lou was also her surrogate Father. Tory had lost her family 15yrs ago, and it was only 5yrs ago she decided to move to South Carolina. She had felt there was nothing else keeping her in Las Vegas, so she figured she could move and start all over again. When she came for a job that was posted for the restaurant, they hit it off instantaneously. Now after 5yrs, Tory and the entire Carrapelli staff were all like family. Whenever anyone would need anything they would all step in to help each other. Lou's staff was a mix of misfits from Italy and some locally. But they all seem to get along and made the lavish reservation only restaurant a well oiled machine. Because of the high end clientele, they had to keep it reservation only. Lou's restaurant was featured in more then several magazines and news papers across the globe. He would frame every photo of a big shot that donned his restaurant as well as any column that was printed in the paper and magazine. He was proud of himself and his staff; so every now and then he would shutdown and just let them let their hair down or if it were any special events, Holidays, or birthdays they would eat and drink till they were drunk and give them all the next day off. As Tory walked into Lou's office, he immediately asked, "How was the wedding?" "Dysfunctional. First of all, let me tell you about the family. My two cousins, her sisters, they were acting a fool. My aunt came to the wedding drunk out of her mind. And everyone was talking about how Vera was going to end up divorced in at least 6months. It was a regular Jerry Springer moment. See, that's why I can't get married. I would end up on an episode of "SNAPPED" shortly." As they both chuckled, Lou replied, "Yeah and I can see how you women can snap. I was married for 5yrs and from the minute she said "I do." She was snapping my head off. Thank God I don't have that problem anymore." As she got up out of her seat, Tory joked, "Yeah right, she didn't want to wheel your old butt into a corner while she head out to the club. Wasn't she like 20yrs your junior?" "Yes, but we were in love. You don't know anything about that." "Exactly, and that's why I haven't been on "SNAPPED" yet. Didn't I tell you that?" After she kissed him on the forehead, she ran off to her office to see what her work load was like. She walked into her little office that held her computer, menus, paperwork and mail all over her desk. Her desk also had framed photos of her and the Carrapellie family during happier times. She sat at her desk to listen to her voicemail of all the events that she would have to plan for the month and next month. Although she tried to pray that she would not have any conflicting schedules, she ended up with several. This meant that she would have to haggle and sometimes battle with these rich people to try to opt for another day or to see whose money would be able to buy them the chosen time slot. Ultimately, this meant massive stress and headache. Just as she was finishing up on her voicemails, Fernardo came in. Fernardo was a young 25yro chef straight from Italy and he was extremely talented in the kitchen. He was another one of Lou's favorites. Tory would always joke with him that if he would continue to cook the way he did she would marry him. His English was poor, but when it came to Tory he knew how to get his point across. As he sat down he said, "I find our song, yes!" "You did?" Fernardo had gone back to his country on vacation and since they shared a love for specific house music group, he managed to find the one song that they could not find in the States. "We hear it now no?" He asked in his broken English. "Let me knock out this work and we'll meet in the VIP room." "Very good." Then he left and Tory got right to work.

Shaune was in the bathroom getting dressed. Marta walked in to get yesterdays clothes. "Good morning Shaune." She said as she curtsied. Then Shaune bowed to her and said, "Good morning Madame Marta." Marta noticed that he was exhibiting a very happy demeanor about him that she normally doesn't get to see on any other occasion. And Que Shuane had a good feeling about today. All he had to do was deal with his lawyer and see his Father, and it was off to Carrapellies to sweep Tory off her feet. Marta was checking his pockets for anything that might be important so that it wouldn't get destroyed at the dry cleaners. She had found a pair of red thong under wear that was in the pocket of his slacks. She turned to Shaune and cleared her throat. Shaune turned to realize that those were Tory's underwear. As he walked over to Marta, he took the underwear and said, "Sorry." When Marta left the room, Shaune couldn't resist the urge to take the time to analyze Tory's underwear. Then he decided to smell them. They smelt like a hint of her perfume and her body scent. Then he was taken back to the plane. He started to remember himself kissing and caressing her thighs. The more he smelt them more captivated he became. While in the middle molesting Tory's underwear in his hand, Marta walked back into the room without knocking. Shaune tried to quickly hide them behind his back looking like a 6yro who just got caught. And although she had seen him, she pretended not to and said, "Marcus Swain is downstairs." Nervously, he replied, "Uh, yeah, tell him I'll be down in a minute." Then he took the underwear and tucked them in his underwear draw and headed downstairs. As he met with Marcus at the bottom of the stairs, Marcus asked, "So what business are we going to do today?" "I'm scouting for fund raiser spots." Shaune was wearing his lucky tailor made caramel suit with matching tie. This was the suit he would wear to most of his heavy hitting meetings and would walk out victorious. "So what country are we traveling too?" Marcus asked. We're staying locally. In fact, we're not leaving the state." "Oh great." Marcus said unenthusiastically. While in the limousine, Shaune had tried to explain to Marcus about how he met Tory. He didn't take the conversation too deep with Marcus as he did with Greg. See, the problem with Mark was that he didn't respect women like Shaune did. Sex to him was just sex. Marcus never loved anyone other then himself. Every time they would travel abroad, he would just throw money around to get women to do what he wanted; then throw them out like trash. Shaune always had respect for women. Even when he was married and found out about his wife's infidelity, he still handled it with grace despite how he felt. "First stop is my Dads'." Shaune dreaded seeing his Father. It wasn't that he didn't love him; after his mother died twenty years ago, his Father changed. He still lived in the three winged mansion they all used to live in. He never changed the furniture or repainted the house. Although he had the money to pay for it all, he would never consider changing anything in the house. When Shaune Jr. was just 17yrs, he couldn't wait to leave the house. He had decided to move back to France to go to college where he would major in business, finance and English. His Father would always tell him that he would someday take over Redliner Oil Rigs; which is one of the reasons why he took up business and finance. Plus, as he got older he would hear his Father sounding more and more tired. Que`Shuane Sr. was a 57yro Afro-European Frenchman who was proud of his roots. He had started Redliner Oil Rigs with his own money and sweat. Since then, he hustled Redliner to be to the top of it's' mark making the Guadau's billion dollar oil tycoons. Now it was up to Jr. to carry on the mark. When Mark and Shaune entered the den, Shaune told Marcus to stay behind in the living quarters while he chatted with his Father. Shaune Jr. knocked on the door and cracked it to look in. His dad motioned for him to come in. Almost immediately his Dad noticed his sons' mood. "Ah, you seem light in your spirit. Perhaps you and Lisa have reconciled?" "No Pare, the divorce still stands. About the meeting, everything went well…" As his Father interrupted he said "I already know how the meeting went. If I wanted to know anything about it, all I have to do is pick up the phone. Now what or might I ask who has you a cloud?" "What makes you think it's someone?" "You just told me." Shaune knew that his Father would never let up. So, he decided to play along. "Alright, Fine. I met this woman on the plane coming home last night. We kind of hit it off and I would like to see her again." Sr. was no fool. He could always read between his sons lines. Even though he was a business man, he studied law as well. So when ever his son danced around his words, he would catch him. "Kind of hit it off. Explain that to me." "Pou qui Pere?" Shaune asked his father. He started to get frustrated with his fathers line of questioning. He also started to feel guilty for no reason. He wanted him to mind his own business, but he couldn't tell him that though. He would never disrespect his father. Sr. thought it to be amusing how he could play on his sons' guilt to make him tell the truth. Then Sr. Started, "Well, as I listen to Mon files tell me a story about how he met a woman and the both of you "Kind of hit it off." And "You" would like to see her again." Feeling edgy Jr. said "What are you getting at Dad?" "Sil vous plait, you tell me? It sounds as though your chance meeting went well but somewhere around the "Kind of hit it off" portion it sounded like it started to fall apart. Eh Pou qui?" Jr. started to unravel under his fathers' pressure. Feeling nervous and embarrassed he felt compelled to tell the whole truth. As he started to stumble over his words he said "We had sex on the plane." "Ah! And upon that happening, you stated to me that only "You" would like to see her again. Explain to me why not she and you would like to see each other or the two of you are going to see each other?" Now Shaune Jr. started to feel like he was on trial "We made a deal that…" Before he could finish, Sr. interrupted "Ah! Ah! Ah! Bon! Now we get to as they say here in the States, "The meat and potatoes" of the story. Now what was this deal?" "Dad, do we have to do this?" "Qui mon fils, I would not be your father if I were not interested in your well being. Please continue." With a deep breath; sounding defeated Jr. said, "She made me agree that after we were done, we would never see each other again." Shaune father could see in his eyes and hear in his voice that his heart was breaking. He walked over to his son and said, "She made a deal that was nonnegotiable. You have to abide by the terms." "But you said that all deals are negotiable. It's what we bring to the table." Jr. tried to fight his father, but really he was no match for his fathers' wisdom. As Sr. sat back at his desk he said, "Les affaires sont des affaires; but when it comes to affairs of the heart, those deals are non negotiable. In her eyes you could have made a different choice but you chose the easy way, which may have been hard for her or did you ask?" "No Pere. I didn't." "Did she at least explain why she made this deal with you?" "She felt that if we continued to see each other it would always be sexual with no emotion involved. She said she didn't want that for her life." "Very well, your fait is sealed. The ball now is in her court." "So what do I do? Just sit and wait for some act of God to happen?" "Exactamon, you open the door and wait for her to come to you. Now if you don't mind, I have some phone calls to make." By the time Shaune left his fathers den, he felt like he had his ass handed to him. "This day is not going as well as I anticipated." Although he knew his father was right because Tory did spell out the terms and why she made the deal, he was still eager to give it one last college try. Then Shaune and Mark jumped into the limo and headed to Carrapellies.

Chapter 3

They Always Return to the Scene of the Crime

I t was 9pm that Tuesday evening. Tory's eyes were hurting with all that scheduling and rescheduling, not to mention the haggling and arguing she had to do with the people to situate the month of September. She went into her draw and pulled out a bottle of Excedrin's and took two. She remembered that she was supposed to see Fernardo about their favorite song they were supposed to dance to. She called Fernardo and told him to meet her in the VIP room.

The limo pulled up to Carrapellies. Before they got out Shaune was listening to his voice messages. "Hey Marc, she left me a message." As he listened on, he couldn't help but feel that giddy feeling he had prior. Then Marcus asked him, "What is she saying?" "She was apologizing for how she treated me." "How did she treat you?" "She kind of blew me off when I gave her my business card." Marcus started to laugh uncontrollably. "Wait a minute, Que`Shuane Guadau, billionaire to the Redliner Oil Rig Corporation was blown off by some random chic and you're turned over by that? I fail to understand the logic in this situation." "As my father would call it I'm trying to get her to walk through the door." As they walked into Carrapellies, they were met by the hostess who knew exactly who he was. She stuttered her words to greet him "Hel... Hello Mr. Guadau. How can I help you?" "Yes I would like to meet with the owner or manager about booking an event here?" "Sure, give me a minute and I will get one of them here." While she picked up the phone to call Lou, Marcus turned to Shaune and said, "Don't you have an assistant that does this for you?" "Yes but there are something's I can do on my own. Plus, Greg has the day off. I left him on call." Then Mark said with an attitude, "you should give him a call." "Look, I asked you if you wanted to come along and you accepted. So pull your skirt up and take it." "That was before I knew we were going to travel through the state of Po Dunk South Carolina." Shaune didn't expect Marcus to understand his plight. All he knew was that he was going to see Tory again. Lou came rushing to the front entrance to meet Shaune. "Mr. Guadau, My name is Louis Carrapellie. It is such a privilege to have royalty in my establishment. What can I do for you Sir?" "I'm looking to book a fund raiser in about two days. Is that possible?" "I usually let my Manager handle all my scheduling. Would you like to meet her? Maybe she could set something up." Shaune lifter his left eyebrow and said, "I would love to meet her."

Fernardo put the CD in the radio. The entire staff had dedicated the time to their down time so they could see Fernardo and Tory dance to their favorite song. The song was called "I beg u" by Basement Jaxx. They were a well know house music group that would cater to the underground house music community. And they happen to be fans of their music. They had rehearsed the dance a thousand times before and they studied it from off of Youtube.com. The dance was a fusion of Salsa, Tango, Meringue and house dance. They would always have fun using their down time to practice the dance and the moment of chance had come. Fernardo held Tory as the music started to play. It was about that time that Shaune and Lou had walked in. Marcus hung at the bar because he didn't care to watch Shaune conduct business. He'd much rather be having fun. As they started to dance, Lou attempted to stop them but then Shaune was intrigued at watching Tory so he stopped Lou and said, "Wait, let's see how this plays out." They started spinning and turning and with all the action, Tory's' hair started to unravel from her bow. She shook her hair completely free. Shaune was mesmerized by her body as well as her movements. Even Lou was fascinated with the song so he started bop to it. After some time had passed, the dance was coming to an end. When the music ended the staff started to clap and Shaune was expecting Fernardo to let Tory go, but instead he held her closer and went in for a kiss. And not only was he going in for the kiss but he started to grinding on her. Shaune, looking like he had seen enough of what he was seeing and shot Lou a look. Lou was caught off guard by the look and ran over to the radio and turned it off. Tory, Fernardo and the entire staff was totally caught off guard. Fernardo looked at Tory and said, "I must be forgetting my quiche." and sped off. Tory didn't realize yet that Shaune was in the room. Not realizing that they already knew each other, Louis introduced them. "Mr. Que'Shuane Guadau this is my Manager, Ms. Torianey Heckstall. She would be happy to help you with your scheduling needs." Tory stretched out her hand to shake his hand and said, "It's nice to meet you Mr. Guadau." As Shaune took her hand, he kissed it and said, "Trust me the pleasure is all mine Ms. Heckstall." He was anticipating a reaction from her, but just like at the airport, she was unfazed. Then Lou said, "Uh, Torianey, I have some business to conduct. But I will leave Mr. Guadau in your capable hands," "Sure Lou. I can handle everything from here. Mr. Guadau, would you like to have a seat so we could get started?" They sat down at the table and Shaune was waiting for her to give him some sign that it was okay to reminisce. "Mr. Guadau, when are you planning your fund raiser?" Feeling caught off guard by her demeanor he replied, "I was looking to book in two days is that possible?" "Actually, Thursday is open for you. Thank God you didn't ask for the weekend, I'm all booked those days. Now how many people are we expecting?" "About two hundred plus." "Okay. I happen to have a VIP room for that many. Is there any type of food you may have in mind?" "I'm not sure. What would you suggest?" He really didn't come prepared with anything in mind. In fact, he didn't think it through at all. All he knew was if he plotted a fundraiser he could reunite with her and then he could wing the rest of the way. But things weren't working to his anticipation or satisfaction. "What types of people are going to be dining at this function?" "Mostly rich and well to do financiers, there will be a couple of people from other countries as well as other states." "For two hundred people I would suggest two meats with two mixtures of vegetable. I'm thinking beef Wellington for one meat and how about pheasant con fiet. As for vegetables I would suggest various carrots and potatoes and specifically with the beef Wellington I would have string beans. Do you disagree?" "No not at all. Can I ask you a question?" "You can ask me anything Mr. Guadau." "What's your favorite meal?" Tory laughed and said, "Is this really relevant Mr. Guadau?" "First of all, call me Shaune and yes it is relevant." "I love duck braised with honey." "Sounds delicious. What is your favorite desert?" "Lemon meringue pie." "When was the last time you had it?" "Mr. Guadau we need to discuss your hors d'oeuvres…" "Why? Because you and your little dancer friend want to finish what you started?" "Excuse me? What are you talking about?" "After the song was over you looked like the two of you wanted to make out. Did I interrupt something?" "I beg your pardon? What does this have to do with you?" "I'm curious about the nature of your relationship with that guy?" "That guy is Fernardo and he's going to be your Chef. I'm sorry… Wait, are you jealous Mr. Guadau?" Shaune paused for a second then feeling confident in his answer, he said, "Yes I am." "Then maybe I should get Mr. Carrapellie to take care of you since you're feeling conflicted and all." As she got up to leave, Shaune grabbed her by her arm and said, "That won't be necessary. I'll try to keep my conflictions under control. For my hors d'oeuvres I would like a combination of escargot and I'm not sure if you are familiar with sea urchin tapas. I could get my assistant to get you the recipe. For desert, I'll play it safe with tiramisu." As Tory sat back in her seat, she said, "Fine. Do you have a selection of wine in mind?" "Do you have a specific selection I could see?" "Yes, if you would follow me I can take you to the wine cellar and show you our selections." Shaune started to think that maybe if he kept it professional with her until it was over he could change up the situation after it was all over. That way, she wouldn't be able to talk business anymore. Like a pro, Shaune picked out all of his wines; from his hors d'oeuvres wines to his main coarse wines and desert wines. Now came time to sign the contract. "Before you sign the contract, let me be clear that you are required to give half now and the remainder after the function is completed. Am I clear on that sir?" As he pulled out his check book, he said, "Crystal." Then he signed the contract and handed her the check. Tory extended her hand and said "It is a pleasure to do business with you Mr. Guadau." Shaune shook her hand but when she tried to withdraw it, he pulled her in closer to him. "Is there a problem Mr. Guadau?" "Cut the shit Tory, you don't have to pretend we don't know each other. Business is over. Plus, I have a pair of your underwear that says we know each other way better then this." Tory gasped and jerked away from him. "I'm not pretending. And as long as I am on my job, I have to keep it business. Since you say business is over then we have nothing else to discuss." "You can probably fool the last guy you played this game with but I'm not buying it. I understand we made a deal on that plane; that we would never see each other, but I would like to go back to the table on this." Tory paused for a few seconds and with a seriously stern look on her face she started; "You want to do this Que'Shuane? Do you really want to do this?" "Yes I do." "Okay, let's do this then. We made a deal in which you agreed that we would not see each other after that night. YOU AGREED! I didn't twist your arm. I didn't pay you any money to agree with me. Did you at least think to give it some thought? No. You didn't. I laid it out and you agreed. You could have easily said "no Torianey, I disagree" and maybe we could have worked it out…" Then Shaune cut in and threw the same line he threw at his Father. "First of all, let's be clear. It was you who suggested that we make that deal. All deals are negotiable. It's what you bring back to the table. That's business 101. Now I'm bringing it back to the table, how are we going to renegotiate this?" He was feeling all too proud of himself. Tory shook her head to agree with what he had said. Then she said, "There's no doubt about that, that's business 101. You see this contract? This is a true business agreement. If in the event you said right now that you were dissatisfied with the terms listed upon your contract, we just might be able to renegotiate the terms. Last night there were no contracts signed. You gave me your word that we would never see each other again. You accepted what I was asking. Do you know why there was no contract?" "No, why?" "Because it wasn't business. See, business is business; but when it comes to affairs of the heart, you can't renegotiate those things. Business 101." Suddenly he started to wonder if she had been speaking with his father. And deep in his mind he could hear his father saying those words that he said that she repeated "Les affaires sont des affaires," He tried to salvage his dignity by pulling out another one of his business cards and said, "If anything should happen to change please feel free to call me." After he picked up his face off the floor, he jogged up the stairs to leave. Tory watched him leave and that old guilt hit her again. "Damn! Here we go again." As Shaune and Mark jumped into the limo, Mark asked him, "So what happened? Did you turn Ms. Mile High into Ms. Wine Cellar?" Shaune was in no mood to deal with him especially under humorous circumstances. All he wanted to do now was see his father to find out exactly what is it that his father and Tory knew about business 101 that his school didn't teach him.

It was Wednesday night, the night before the fund raiser. Shaune, Marcus, Gregory, Lucas and Jacob were in the cabin. The cabin was a place where they would meet up and smoke their fancy cigars and hire a stripper/dancer or two and kick back and relax away from their wives and girlfriends. It was a spot where they could talk about anything and keep their secrets all to themselves. They had made a pact that if anyone were to take anything outside of the cabin that they would be dismissed from the "Brotherhood." Lucas and Jacob used to work for Que`Shuane; and while they worked for him Lucas went back to school to become a lawyer while Jacob went back to school for culinary arts. Shaune promised them that if they were to complete what they started, he would be more then happy to give them the seed money needed to get their businesses started. Since then the two of them have been successful in starting their own business and they agreed to make Shaune their co-owner of their establishments. Ever since then, the five of them have been the best of friends and when life would slow down, Shaune would get them all to come to the cabin to assess where their lives are to date. As they passed the bottle around of single malt scotch, Lucas made a toast; "To four successful souls. Oh and the fifth wheel." He was referring to Gregory because he still worked for Shaune. "I got your fifth wheel in the trunk of my car punk." Greg Joked back. Then Shaune cut in and said, "Like these guys Greg, your time is coming everyone has to start somewhere." "I agree Shaune, just like these two losers." Then Jacob said, "Not you though Shaune. You had it easy your entire life. You and Marcus inherited your lives. The rest of us had to scratch our way into this life." Feeling offended, Marcus cut in and said, "So it's our fault you were born poor? Perhaps, your parent should have made better choices in their lives and it wouldn't be up to someone else to fulfill your dreams for you." "Excuse me? First of all Mark, I don't see a damn thing that YOU have done for anyone other then yourself..." Marcus cutting Jacob off said, "That doesn't mean that I have to be responsible for you're impoverished life..." "I never held you responsible for anything..." Getting tired of the arguing, Shaune got frustrated and yelled, "ALRIGHT, DROP IT GUYS! I didn't come here to talk about who's responsible for who. Frankly we're responsible for our own lives. The truth is I need to talk about something." Then Lucas joke, "Ah Shaune, you're not going to tell us you're dieing?" "Luc, could you just be serious for one second please." "Sorry man, this must be really serious. What's up?" "I want to ask you guys; have you ever met someone you couldn't stop thinking about?" Greg Said, "I told you I married her." Jacob said, "Jenna and I are planning on getting married in the next two years. But when I met her, I couldn't stop thinking about her. I couldn't wait to see her when we would go out on dates. When we'd talk on the phone; I was as happy as a six year old. Now that we are together, I can't wait to marry her. I just knew that she was the one you know?" Lucas said, "I'm still dating so I haven't found the one yet but it sure is fun searching for her." Marcus looked at Shaune and said, "Oh don't tell me this has to do with that chic you met on the plane?" Then Greg said, "Wait, Ms. Mile High? No." Lucas and Jacob looked at each other then they looked at Shaune and said, "Who is Ms. Mile High and what happened on a plane?" "Shaune met this low rent chic who blew him then blew him off afterward. And now he's all caught up into her." "First of all Mark she didn't blow me and how could you say something like that you don't even know her." "So then what exactly happened Shaune?" Jacob asked. "We had sex on the plane. But it wasn't just sex it was different. I had never looked into a woman's eyes like I did this one." "What did it feel like when you did?" "It felt like I could stay trapped in her eyes for ever. I really can't explain it." Jacob said, "I understand how you feel Shaune. That feeling of her hands on your body. Touching you like no other woman has. It's almost like she knows how to get your attention with her hands." "Exactly, and she whispered in my ear and called me "Daddy" it blew my mind. I really would like to hear it again." "So what's stopping you?" Then Greg cut in and said, "Oh let me answer this for you Shaune. She made a deal with him that they would never see each other again after the sex was over. See, Shaune made the deal prior to the sex so it was after he felt all this nostalgia that he realized he had made the deal in error. Did I miss anything?" "No Gregory you didn't." "Okay, so did you try to reach out to her and try to explain that you made this deal in error?" "Yes, I went to Carrapellies to try to "renegotiate" the terms but she wasn't having it." Then Lucas said, "You're not talking about the Manager of Carrapellies?" "Yes I am." "Man I was trying to bang that chic. She got legs that won't quit and an ass that…" Everyone looked at Lucas like he was crazy. Then he had to change his story up "Uh an ass that's attached to her body and in great shape might I add." Then he took a gulp of his scotch. "Look according to my father, I don't have any other option but to leave her alone and let her make a decision to come to me when ever that will be. And frankly, I don't think that will be any time too soon." Shaune's heart started to break all over again. "Jacob said, "Gee Shaune it sounds like you've been bitten by the love bug." "What! No your wrong I'm not in love with her." "Seriously dude, when was the last time you ever chased down a woman before." They all looked around the room at each other and chanted "Yeah, when was the last time." "I'm not in love with her. I like her a lot but love is a huge stretch to say." Then Greg said, "Admit it man, all the things that she was doing to you no other woman has done to you; you said it yourself. You enjoyed her and you just want more. Not to mention, she's the one person on this green earth that doesn't know who you are. It's not a bad thing to admit when you're in love. Hey let's not forget there's the fund raiser tomorrow. Anything can happen before, during or after that day." Sounding like he had lost all hope in his heart, Shaune said, "There's that." Then he gulped down the rest of his scotch.

Chapter 4

Back to the Drawing Board to Lick My Wounds

Thursday, was the day of the fund raiser. Shaune met with his Father at Sr.'s home so they could make an entrance at the fund raiser together. The function was for Pediatric Cancer. The cost of the dinner was $1000 per plate and the entire proceed would go to the Pediatric Cancer Foundation. Sr. and Jr. wore matching suits. They were black Armani suits with metallic color shirts and the ties were black with metallic stripes that matched the shirt. They looked really handsome matching as they did. They had been moving early and that meant that Shaune could talk to his father since his plan failed and everything his father had told him made total sense. "Pare, apparently you were right about the deal that I made with the young lady. She didn't want to budge." "But you had to give it on more try huh?" At this point Jr. was ready to learn so he wanted to ask all the right questions. "Yes, and she said exactly what you said. That whole "affairs of the heart" thing; she said it exactly how you said it too. I've studied everything there was to learn about business. How come no one told me about these "affairs of the heart" stuff? Am I missing something?" Sr.

laughed and said "Qui mon fils, le Coeur." While his father laughed on, Shaune became discouraged and said, "Never mind. This is pointless." Then Sr. put his hand on his shoulder and said "When I mean the heart, I mean that you son have never fell so far in love that once you fell out of it you would make a deal to never allow yourself to experience that much pain again. Your young lady has experienced such failure of love. She loved someone who didn't reciprocate hers. And you made yourself an easy target once you agreed on her terms." Although he understood exactly what his father was saying; Shaune was still confused. "So how should I have done things?" "You should have never done it in the first place. People who experience pain while in love never wish to repeat it. How do you feel now that she turned you down? Now times it by 10, or 20, or maybe even 100. Now compare yourself to her. What makes this girl so much more interesting then any other woman you have met?" "While talking to her I saw a sense of vulnerability. It just felt good to talk to an actual human being instead of some mindless "Yes sir, no sir" drone. She didn't care what she said and she didn't have an agenda. She had these eyes that were attentive and honest. Her eyes looked innocent. Pare, my main question is how do I get back what I lost?" Sr. could only provide his son with the knowledge he himself had. He only wanted to see his son happy and something this woman did to his son made him happy. "At this point you are both like two forces caught in a rubber band. The more pressure you apply, the more resistant she becomes to you." Now He was getting the point. It was exactly how she was acting towards him. "So now what?" "Mon Fils, the easy part would be your acceptability of her." "Si que le partie dure serait?" "As I said before son, you have to wait for her to walk through the door. Until then, you have to sit back and wait. If she believes you have an agenda, prove her wrong. You make her believe that you're genuine with your love for her." Then Shaune started to stutter his words. "Uh Dad, I'm not... I'm not in love with her." "Pardon, no?" "No Dad, I like her a lot. I'm not in love with her." Shaune Sr. was now the confused one. He had never seen his son chase after a woman the way he has, but yet he wasn't in love with her? Then Sr. said "Why waste your time with someone you just like? May I ask a question?" "Sure Dad. You can ask anything." "Your wife Lisa, did you just like her when you met her? I don't remember you being this concerned about her when you met her or asked her to marry you." Shaune started to go back to the days that he and Lisa started dating. It was her that was pursuing him in fact. And like last night at the cabin, his Father was chiming in on what they were saying. Shaune tried to answer his father but then, his father cut in and said, "Don't answer that. Maybe it might be something you might want to think about." Greg came into the den to inform them that the limo was waiting outside to take them to the fund raiser. Sr. Greeted Gregory "Como tali vouz Greg?" Greg answered, "Oh thanks Mr. Guadau, tre beyond, tre beyond." Sr. turned to his son and said, "Oh qui, tre bien o tre beyond. Way beyond?" Both father and son laughed as they left.

7:40pm, the limo pulled up to Carrapellies. As everyone exited the limousine, the paparazzo was in full swing. Carrapellies parking lot was filled with limos of invites from in state as well as out of state and the country. Tory made sure that there was plenty of armed security visible and invisible. There was way too much money in the building to take any chances on some random happening. She and Louis would stay coordinated so that there were no confusions or mistakes. In Tory's' mind, error was not an option. This whole operation had to go off with out a hitch. She had checked the food to make sure it was cooked to its full capacity. The shipment of wine that Shaune ordered came in on time so that she didn't have to make any unwanted changes. There was plenty of Carrapellie staff around just in case anyone needed their drinks to be recapped; or when it was time to serve dinner and desert. As the venue went off, the Guadau's spoke in English and in French. There were interpreters for the Russian and German visitors just so that they could understand where their money was going to. As they wrapped up their speeches, they gave a special thanks to Torianey, Louis and the Carrapellie staff for making everything possible. After the speeches, everyone continued to loiter for the next 3 ½ hours. Louis was to get his commission as well as $100 off each plate sold. He seems to come off pretty good that night. Greg approached Tory to give her the check for the remainder of the balance for their services. When Tory looked at the check she noticed that the check was three times what it was supposed to be. "I'm sorry but do you realize that this is way more then his balance?" Greg not sounding concerned said, "He filled it out and signed it, and he told me to deliver it." "And who are you now?" Sounding confused Greg answered, "I'm Gregory Duvain, Mr. Guadau's Assistant and Publicist." He stretched out his hand to shake hers but she was reluctant. Then she said, "What does a business man need with a publicist?" Then he said "But he's Que'Shuane Guadau." Like he expected her to catch on. "But what does he need with a publicist?" He laughed and said, "Damn! You really are the one woman under a rock." "I beg your pardon?" Before she could begin to tell him off, Shaune called Greg over. Then Tory flagged Lou to tell him about the check. As Louis looked at the check, he said, "You better make sure that this is legit. The last thing I need is the Guadau's suing me for check fraud." As she went off to straighten out the check, she managed to get Shaune's attention. When he walked up to her she asked him, "Could you meet me in my office for a second." "Sure just give me a few minutes to say good bye to a few of my guest and I'll see you there."

Tory was sitting at her desk and a knock came at her door. "Come in." It was Shaune. He had looked a little tired from all that was going on. "You wanted to see me?" "Do you realize that this check is way more then what was agreed upon on your contract?" "Yes I signed it." "Why?" "That's my gratitude for your help and the help of the Carrapellie staff. Plus, I know your commission would be larger as well." "And this has nothing to do with what happened on the plane?" "What plane? And what happened on it?" Tory started to see what was going on then she said, "Never mind. So you're okay with the balance of this check?" "I'm very satisfied with the check and the services of Mr. Louis Carrapellie and his staff. Now if you don't mind, I have guest I have to attend to. It was really nice doing business with you Ms. Heckstall." Then he shook her hand and pat her on the shoulder. Just before he left her office he turned and gave her his business card and said, "We might end up doing business again; so here's my card." Then he left the office. Tory couldn't help but laugh that she got served her own shtick.

1am and the Guadau's and their guest had left the Carrapellie establishment. Louis and his staff were exhausted by now. He had given a toast to the night going well and he decided to give the staff the night off. As usual Tory stayed behind to count out the nights recipes and close up shop while Lou would make the bank run before he went home. Before he kissed her goodbye, Lou said "Goodnight my child. Enjoy your day off." "Enjoy my day off. I'll only be doing school work." "Good. At least I'll know where to find you." By now it was going on 2am. Tory's eyes were starting to burn and she was deliriously tired. When she got back to her office she saw a note on her desk from Fernardo that read "I know you must be hungry. You were working all day; so I manage to save you dinner before Guadau and friends eat it all. Check freezer. Love you, Fernardo." Sure enough, when she checked the freezer there was a large Tupperware bowl full of food from the fund raiser and a bottle of the wine Shaune had ordered. Then she said to herself, "God, I'm going to marry that man." She grabbed the food and wine and headed out. She shut off the lights and she set the alarm and shut down the restaurant. As she got into her car, she said to herself, "Lot's of school work tomorrow." As she put the key in the ignition, she heard her car stall. "Oh come on!" she yelled. She kept at it for at least a half hour only to realize that her car would never start again. Now was the task of getting a ride home. Her car was no longer an option. She pulled out her cell phone and called Lou. It went straight to voice mail. "Great! He sleeps like a log." Then she tried to call Fernardo and his phone went straight to voice mail. "Really Fernardo, Really?" She yelled in the phone. As late as it was, no one would answer their cell phones or they would only go to voice mail. She started to feel hopeless. She sat back in her car and started to cry. She tried to call a cab, but either the cabs wouldn't go that far, or they were closed for the morning.

When she looked at her watch, it was after 3am. Then she started to cry even harder. But then she looked down on the floor of her car and saw a business card. As she picked up the card, she realized it was the Redliner Oil Rig card. Although it was her only hope, she made the call. "This is probably useless to call. He's not going to pick up." She listened and waited for the phone to ring.

Shaune was in his favorite den callasped on his leather chase. He was in a deep sleep when he was startled by the sound of his personnel cell. It scared him so bad, it nearly angered him. He ran over to the phone and in his French accent screamed "Ello!" Tory was on the other end sounding scattered. "Thank God. Hello... Hello may I speak with Mr. Guadau?" While feeling for his seat at his desk he breathed "Speaking." "It's me sir, Torianey. Torianey Heckstall." He lost his balance from his chair and fell backward straight on to the floor. "Are you there? Hello?" Gathering himself, he said, "Sorry, I dropped my phone. What's up?" He said as he tried to recover himself. "I'm sorry to bother you and I know it's late. But I really need your help." "Sure, what can I do for you?" "Well, my car died on for good. And I need a ride home and you were the only person I could get. I really hate to bother you." Shaune's face lit up brighter then a Christmas tree and said, "No problem. Where are you?" "I'm still at Carrapellies. I usually close up the shop at night. And at this hour I discovered my cars dead body. Can you help me?" As he looked at his watch, he said, "Sure I can. Do me a favor, stay in the car and lock the doors." He picked up his jacket and headed for the garage. On initial reaction, he jumped in his usual car, the Aston Martin. Then he looked at the passenger side and said, "She's not going to be comfortable in this car." He got out and looked around to see just which of the forty cars would be accommodating for her. As he looked around, he realized that most of his cars were sports cars suited for smaller frames. Then he saw his burgundy Escalade. "Perfectioner!" he yelled as he grabbed the keys out of the box and jumped in and he sped off.

Shaune had arrived in less then ten minutes. He had driven between seventy and eighty miles just to get there. "Are you okay?" "I'm fine. At least for now thank you." "Did you call your insurance company to get a tow?" Tory, feeling embarrassed said, "Uh, about that, I had kind of let it lapse." Without showing any concern, he pulled out his cell phone and called Greg. "Hey Greg, I'm sorry to bother you at this hour. Can you call a tow truck from the shop to come to Carrapellies to pick up a car for me? No, I'm fine. Great, thanks man." Then he hung up his phone. As he turned to look at Tory, she said "I'm so sorry to bother you with this. I know you must be tired after the day you've had." "Don't worry about it. I'm glad I can help after all I did say that if you should need anything to give me a call." Tory huffed and started to say "About that…" Then Shaune put his finger in her lip to stop her and said "You can thank me later."

The tow truck finally showed up and pulled her car away. "Where is my car going? I didn't get a card from him." "Don't worry its going to my shop. I'll let you know in the morning what the problem is and how you could get it back. Just let me get you home at least." As they pulled up to her driveway, Tory said feeling relieved, "Oh what a night." "How will you get to and from work from now on in?" "Thank God I'm off for the rest of the day so I have a whole day to figure out who could give me a ride. I guess I could ask anyone of my coworkers; Lou or Fernardo or someone." Then Shaune remembered just who Fernardo was. "Oh Fernardo, the dancing, grinding chef; I'm sure he would love to give you a ride." Then he whispered to himself, "a ride or two." "Look, I want to thank you so much. You could have not answered your phone and I would still be there at Carrapellies parking lot. Is there any way I can repay you?" With out even a blink he quickly replied, "Have dinner with me." "Are you sure you don't want to think about this?" "I've been thinking about it for a while." Although she was feeling hesitant, she knew that payback was coming eventually. After all, from the beginning he was being nothing if not nice to her. "Why are you so nice to me?" "I like you; and lately since I met you this has been my nature." "And this has nothing to do with what happened on the plane?" "I don't know anything about this plane you keep speaking of or what happened on it. Perhaps, maybe one day you would like to fill me in on exactly what happened. But for now, I just want to feed you and get to know you. Can I do that?" Then she gave in "Fine, when and where?" Yet again without a blink he blurted "Today 7pm at my home. I'll pick you up at 6:45pm." "Well, I guess I'll be seeing you at 6:45 tonight then." Just as she got ready to leave his car, she turns back and leans in to give him a kiss on the cheek. He turned to face her and whispered, "Thank you." Then she leaned in farther to kiss him on the lips. Shaune paused to look at Tory to see if she was serious. Tory then leaned in to kiss him deeper and Shaune grabbed the back of her neck to kiss her even deeper. He was feeling like he could devour her he wanted her so bad. Both of their hearts were beating heavy. Tory started to move down to his neck. Shaune though to himself, "She must really love my neck." Suddenly, a voice came to him. "The easy part is your willingness to open the door." Then he realized that if he would continue on like this, it might prove to be a disaster. And as good as her kisses felt, it wasn't worth loosing her again. This time he had to play it right. Shaune grabbed her face and looked her in the eyes and said, "I am going to pick you up tonight at 6:45. So get some rest and be pretty for me." "I will, and thank you again." Then she left the truck and walked slowly to her house. Shaune watched every slow step she took savoring the moments. She reached her door and finally, she put the key in the door and opened it. Just before she disappeared behind it, she blew Shaune a kiss and closed the door. Shaune took a deep breath and exhaled as he started up his truck and headed back home feeling victorious.

Chapter 5

Blood, Sweat, Tears. Oh! And Hard Work

Tory was up at 6pm that evening. She was actually kind of nervous. It had been a while since she had been on an actual date. She had been all through her closet trying to figure out what would be appropriate to wear. The fear wasn't because it was Que'Shuane Guadau; it was because she was taking her steps backwards. She kept it in her mind that he wasn't an option but yet she forfeited her own deal. Now she had to be in another intimate setting and she had no idea what was going to transpire. "What am I sweating for? Worse case scenario, if I can't handle it, I can just tell him I'm sick and I need to go home. Yeah that's sounds about right. I can play the sick card. I can eat then say "I'm not feeling well. I think I need to go home. Kind of like the dining and dashing move." Then she started to realize that unsettled feeling of how he was nothing but nice to her and she wanted to dump him. As she looked in her full length mirror, she said to herself, "You know what? We're just going to have fun with it. That's all. I'm entitled to have some fun in my life. So what I broke the rules. Just play it safe and stay responsible. Keep your heart out of it." She was doing the best she could to convince herself that it was okay to go on this date. But no matter what she did, she couldn't shake her nerves.

Shaune had been on the phone most of the evening rescheduling meetings. He made a deal with Gregory that if he went to that 2 day meeting in Greece for him, he would let him stay for the entire week plus, he could bring his wife, and Shaune would pay for everything. After he got off the phone, he realized that he was moving late. He took his 10min shower and walked up to his mirror to put on his favorite cologne Armani Code. "I hope she likes this as much as I do." He thought to himself as he pat it all over his wet glistening body. As he looked at the time, he noticed that he was winding down to really being late leaving. He started to feel butterflies in his stomach knowing that he was about to be reunited with the one woman who captured his heart in one day. "Who are you Tory Heckstall?" He asked himself as he stared in his mirror. Shaune himself knew that he had never been this open about any women including his wife. He went into his walk-in closet to figure out what to wear. He didn't want to look too flashy cause he knew that Tory wasn't the flashy type; so he'd rather keep it simple. He went with his distressed jeans and a yellow polo shirt. Greg said it made him look younger. He gave himself the once over in his mirror and headed out the door.

Tory got out of her shower and rushed to get dressed. She had only 10mins to be ready. She had decided to wear her semi-flare mini skirt which showed enough leg. Plus, it was form fitting around her pear shaped figure. She put on a nice light camis for her top. She figured that she would put on a matching color sweater to cover up. She didn't want to show off too much skin. She was happy with what she looked like. As she applied her make up, her phone rang. "Hello?" Of course it was Shaune pulling up in her driveway on time. When he left his house, he kicked his truck up to 80mph just so he could be on time. "Hello Ms. Heckstall. Your ride is here to usher you off on your date." "Can you give me one minute more and I'll be right out?" "Take two if you need. I'll be right here." She hung up her phone and gave herself the once over and spritzed herself with her favorite perfume "Lovely" by Sara Jessica Parker. Then she headed out the door.

As Tory exited her house, she saw Shaune standing on the passenger side of his truck waiting with the door open for her. While she was walking towards him, she wandered what had happened to the rugged look he was sporting lately; then she said to him, "Good evening Mr. Guadau. You look nice." "Good evening Ms. Heckstall, you look beautiful tonight yourself. And I would appreciate it if you would please call me Shaune." "Then if that's the case, I wish you would call me Tory." Then she reached out her hand to shake his, but he kissed hers instead. As she was getting into his truck, Shaune couldn't help but steal a glance at her from behind. When she sat in her seat, he fastened her seatbelt for her. "Is this too tight for you?" While he was talking to her, he couldn't help himself so he gripped her thigh then rubbed his hand down her leg. Tory pretended to not notice him fondling her leg so she said, "No it feels just fine thank you." When he closed the door, he chuckled to himself as he walked to the driver side. While on the road to his house there was this awkward silence in the car. So Shaune felt he needed to break the ice. "Did you get enough rest?" "Yeah, I got up at 2pm to do some homework online." "So what are you studying"? "Psychology." "Do you enjoy it?" "I really do." "So tell me about it" "What do you want to know?" "Well, tell me why did you choose psychology?" "I've loved how the mind works; the fact that there is a thin line between sanity and insanity. Plus, I bet you didn't know that everyone has a little insanity in them. But the safest part is a mild insanity. And they can get out of hand." "What would be a mild case of insanity?" "Uh, well let's say a fetish of sorts. Like shoes, or hats, or cars; porn. However, these things can get out of control." "So how could they get out of control?" "Most men like porn right?" As he shrugged his shoulders, Shaune answered, "I guess." "A bad case would be like a man buys so much porn that it's starting to ruin his relationships; or he needs to masturbate to it so much that it's causing him to injure himself." "Wow that sounds deep. So do you think I may have a little insanity?" "I know you do." "Would you like to know what it is?" He asked her. "I would guess its money since your traveling a lot." Feeling offended by her comment, he shot back "No it's not money and that wasn't fair of you to assume that about me." Feeling the mood change, she tried to salvage the moment. "I'm sorry; what is it then?" Que`Shuane felt himself getting upset so he remained quiet. As they turned into his front gate, she noticed his vanity style QG logo. When they approached his mansion, Tory couldn't believe her eyes. His home was half the size of a baseball stadium. His house was immaculate and beautiful. It looked like a contemporary style mansion with all the fixings. The outside was red brick while the front entrance had a hand made stone pillar style canopy so if there were any inclement weather, it would protect anyone getting out of their cars. The doorman helped her out of the car and up the steps. When she got into the house, she couldn't believe her eyes. The house was just as gigantic inside as it was outside. The front door was huge; it had brass handles on them that only a doorman could handle them. While she was looking around, she mumbled to herself, "I hope he's not a drug dealing businessman." She hated thinking that way about him but after all, he had never revealed too much about himself. As she walked through the big doors she looked down the hallway. It was endless and there were chandeliers from one end to the next. All along the hallway were fresh flowers that resonated throughout the house. The floors and stairs were black and white marble. The place was breath taking. Finally, she regained her senses and turned to look for Que`Shuane. She ended up turning to see Greg standing in front of her. "I remember you; you're the one woman under a rock." "I beg your pardon?" Tory was extremely offended by the fact that Greg kept referring to her that way. "Why do you keep on calling me that?" "Because Gregory is a bonehead, and he is obviously leaving." Shaune walked up to Tory to take her by the hand and lead her into the den; but then Greg stopped him. "Shaune, we need to discuss your itinerary for next week." When they got to the den, Shaune said, "I won't be long. Have yourself a drink if you would like." After she made her drink, she looked around the den. It would have made two of her bedroom. There were books on shelves everywhere. They looked like law books and school reference guides. Then she walked over to the fire place in front of the room. There were three photos on the mantle. Before she could get a good look at them, Shaune entered the room. She was determined to get to the bottom of just who he was. She turned to him and said, "Who are you and why does your assistant/publicist keep calling me this "One woman under a rock?" "I would be happy to explain what ever you want to know. Have a seat please." He walked over to the mantle where the three photos were and picked them up. Then he handed them to Tory. She looked the photos over and saw that there was one of him at age three, one with his father and one with all three of them they took when he was just eight years old. Although she was fascinated with the photos, it didn't quite explain who he was. Then he started. "Have you ever heard of Redliner Oil Rigs?" "Yes, I watch the news sometimes; plus, I have a dozen of your cards." He pointed at his fathers' photo and said, "My father is the owner. Five years ago he gave me controlling interest of the family business." "That's got to be taxing. How do you feel about it?" "Redliner is a $300 billion dollar industry; Top of the line all on its own. And for the past five years it's been that way." Then he went on to explain the photo of the three of them. "I keep this picture here with me because my Mother died in a boating accident." "I'm sorry to hear that. Do you often think about her?" Shaune started to answer her but he pauses and actually realized that he never really did think of his Mother. In fact, he couldn't think of one memorable moment. Shaune cleared his throat and said, "Excuse me, I'll be right back." She watched him run out of the room and couldn't help but feel responsible for his discomfort. Shaune walked into the kitchen and leaned up against the island. He was searching his mind hard so that he could go into the den to have a story to tell about his mom. Marta walked in and saw the distress on his face. "What's wrong?" "Marta, how come I can't remember a single memory of my Mother? I remember her in my life but I don't have a single story to tell about her. With you, I have tons of stories to tell; fun memories, bad memories just none of her." She took him by his hand and led him to the dinner table. Then she made him sit down. "You were only 9yrs old when your mom passed. Even though you understood the experience, you weren't able to process it well. Your Father was so devastated he wasn't strong enough to explain it to you the way you needed to hear it. So, we both agreed that when the time came, I would be able to tell you." Whenever Shaune and Marta would have a heart to heart, he would reduce to that child she had always remembered him as. The truth was that she was more like his Mother then his natural Mother was. The story was that whenever Shaunes' Father would go away on business, his Mother would sneak away to her lover and wouldn't be seen for days. Marta knew that she was responsible for Shaune being the man that he was to this day. She taught him how to respect women whether he liked her or not; to open doors for women and secure their seatbelts when in the car. She even taught him how to cook. She also knew that if she didn't step in, he might have grown up to be a bitter, uncontrollable man. Although he was a handful to raise, she was proud of the man that stood before her. Marta made it her duty to teach him to be a responsible man that would learn to take responsibility for any situation that he would incur. Then there came that time in his life when she knew that there were some things that she could not teach him that he would have to learn for himself. Since he had met Tory, Marta had realized that the son she had raised started to change. She knew that Tory was special, because Shaune would never deviate from his mechanical state of mind. As he started to ask another question, Marta stopped him by putting her finger on his lips and said, "There is a time and place for everything. Now is the time for you to introduce me to your new girlfriend." They went into the den so that Shaune could introduce Marta to Tory and Shaune was still feeling a little embarrassed about not being able to tell Tory about his mom. As they walked into the den, Shaune said, "Torianey Heckstall, this is Marta Canto my caretaker." "Hello Ms. Canto nice to meet you." "Nice to meet you too Torianey; Shaune has told me so many great things about you." Tory started to feel awkward all of a sudden. "What could he have been telling her about me?" Then she turned to Shaune and whispered," look, let me apologize for upsetting you. It's none of my business for me to ask about your mom. In fact, I won't ask anymore questions." "Its fine Tory, you didn't do anything wrong. I just had a memory block that's all." Marta felt the giant elephant in the room; therefore she needed to clear the air with a distraction. "Did Que`Shuane tell you he cooked dinner to night?" "No he didn't. What did he cook?" As Marta took Shaune by the hand, she said, "He'll be right back to show you." When they got into the kitchen, he said to her, "Thank you so much for that distraction. I felt a little uncomfortable." "Shaune I want you to listen to me if you never heard anything I have said to you in your life. I want you to go out there tonight and have fun with her. Let her see that side of you that is open to having fun and be free with it. Also, I want you to stop beating yourself up for the things that you had no control over. God gave you this life to have as your own and you should make no apologize for it. Do you hear me?" "Yes ma'am." "I will always be here for you me Corazon."

Shaune returned with a couple of covered platters on a rolling table. Tory was excited to see what he had cooked. "Wow, a rich man that can cook? First we have to see if it tastes good." She thought to herself. As he sat down at the table he asked her, "Are you ready to see the first course?" "Yes!" She answered with excitement. Then he uncovered the first platter. It was her favorite meal; roasted duck braised in honey surrounded by assorted vegetable. She became so overwhelmingly emotional, she started to cry. Shaune thought that he had done something wrong. "Are you okay? Did I offend you? I'm sorry, I can get something else." As he started to cover up the food, Tory stopped him and said, "No, please don't I'm just so happy and shocked that you remembered. I guess I didn't expect you to make what I liked. No one has ever though of me that way before." Deep down inside Shaune was relieved. He thought that he had screwed up again. Unsure of her next reaction, he asked her, "Would you like for me to uncover the next platter?" "Sure." Then he uncovered the next platter and it was another favorite of hers, lemon meringue pie. The fact that he was so nice to her, she was feeling guilty. "I need to tell you something." "Baby you can tell me anything." "I feel terrible about the way I have been treating you. It's just when I make a rule, I try not to go back on it. The fact that you remembered my favorite meal says a lot about who you really are; and I'm so sorry for the way I treated you. You've been so nice to me and all I've done was throw dirt at you this whole time." He pulled out his handkerchief and started to wipe away her tears. Then he said, "Don't worry about all that. The point is I'm glad you're here now. You deserve the best and I want to give you that for now. Would you let me do that for you?" "Yes." "Good, so stop crying and let's eat." He started to fix the plates while Tory served the wine. Shaune gave a toast to the two of them. "To second chances." And they clicked their glasses and drank to his toast. Then they started to eat their meal. She noticed that he was looking at her oddly. "Why are you looking at me like that?" "Do you really eat with a spoon or are you 6yrs old?" "I guess it's obvious I need help. I never learned how to eat in a proper setting. Can you help me?" As he came over behind her he said, "Take your fork in your left hand and your steak knife in your right hand." Then he leaned in and held on to her hands to guide her. "Now as you take your fork and turn it backwards this way, you take the steak knife and cut diagonally to get a choice cut of your food." While he was talking, Tory started to deviate from the conversation. She could smell his cologne; plus, the way he was kneeling over her, his neck was completely with in kissing distance. She felt like she could just bite into him at that very moment. Her heart started to pound but then she was awakened from her train of thought when he moved to eye contact with her. "You got it?" "Yeah, I got it now." Then she thought to herself, "I got it. You're going to get it and I'm going to give it to you."

They finished off their dinner and polished off two bottles of wine. Now it was time for desert. Tory looked at the balcony, then she asked, "Can we take our desert out on the balcony?" "That sounds like a great idea; why not?" Then he picked up the pie, a knife and they headed to the balcony. He cut her a piece and asked, "Although I'm sensitive about my cooking, I would like for you to tell me how you liked it." She took her fork and cut into her slice. As she tasted it, she replied, "UMMM! This is so delicious. Here taste it." Then she dug into another piece and fed it to him. As he tasted it he couldn't believe it tasted as good as it did. "I thought it was going to be too bitter. But I have to admit this is pretty good." "I think sex would be the one thing better then this." He started to blush after hearing her comment. He cleared his throat and said, "How about some music?" "That sounds great. I'd love that." He went to go turn on some music and oddly enough to Torys' perception he turned on R&B music. When he came back she said to him, "I didn't think you would like R&B music." "What kind of music did you think I would like?" She squinted her eye as she looked at him and said, "Elevator maybe." Then they both laughed. "Would you care to dance or did you have me pegged as a left footed dancer." "That all depends on how good you are with your left foot." He took her by the hand and they started to groove to the music. "So how am I doing?" "You're aight. I'll give you an A for effort." Then she laid her head against his chest. She could hear his heart beating. She thought to herself, "And here I was thinking this was going to be a total bust." Shaune wrapped his arms completely around her while Tory held on to his back. The way he held on to her gave her a sense of security. Tory reached in to kiss him on his chest. Then he look at her and went in to kiss her deeper. Suddenly, she withdrew with a grimace on her face. Shaune didn't know what to think of it. "What's wrong?" He asked. "Shaune I don't know whether to kiss you or feed you carrots." "What?" "I thought the last time we kissed that you were just being anxious. Plus, I figured that since we weren't going to see each other again, I wouldn't have to be subjected to your kisses again." Shaunes' pride started to kick up. Then he said, "So how do I kiss?" Tory took a deep breath and said, "You kiss like as if a horse was kissing a cow." Feeling highly offended, he said, "Oh yeah, well if I'm the horse then who's the cow?" "I guess I deserve that. I'm just being honest." "Your honesty is not necessary. Hey I haven't had any complaint from any of the ladies before today." "I guess if I wanted to be surrounded by $300 billion, I would be willing to put up with anything. Let's face it; a hungry dog would eat cat food." Now he started to turn red with anger. "What is that supposed to mean?" "It means that when people want what they want, they'll tolerate anything." "Really? And what makes you so different?" "I don't want anything from you; and I'm willing to tell you that although you have really nice lips, your kisses suck. Look, I'm obviously elevating your anger. Plus, I'm getting a little riled up myself. Maybe I should just leave." "Yeah why not?" Shaune snapped. "Goodnight Que'Shaune." Then a though crossed his mind. "She is the one person who was honest enough to tell me about my flaws next to Marta." As he ran back into the den, he was lucky enough to catch her looking for her purse. "I can't find my purse. Do you remember where I put it?" "You left it in your jacket pocket." "Oh, yeah your right. Thanks." Then he stopped her "Tory wait. I'm sorry. Look, I didn't mean to carry on like that. No one has ever talked to me like that before. Well accept Marta; she doesn't count." "Thank you. Goodnight again." As she turned to leave, Shaune ran to block her from leaving. "I'm willing to admit I need some help on my kissing." "And they say admittance is the best way to get over a bad problem. Good luck with that." Then she tried to leave again but he grabbed her. "I'm saying I need… I would like… could you at least…" Having a hard time trying to get it out; Tory finished for him. "You want me to teach you how to kiss?" Feeling ashamed to answer, he looked away and shook his head yes. Then she said, "I'm sorry, I don't hear you. And I would appreciate some eye contact when you answer." Although it took him awhile, he looked her in the eyes and clinched his teeth and said, "Yes, I would like your help." Tory wanted to dig the knife in just a little deeper so she said, "With what Que'Shuane? Your plumbing, fixing your car, the dishes'?" He started to turn red again. But he sucked it up and said, "Torianey, could you please teach me the proper way to kiss a lady?" In her sarcastic voice she replied, "Why I would love to help you learn." Then she turned to go back to the balcony. They sat on the patio love seat and she sat across his lap. "Just follow my lead." She whispered to him. As she sucked on his bottom lip, he sucked on her top lip. This made him realize that his prior kisses were too loose where as him kissing her now was much tighter. After thirty seconds of kissing her he asked, "Is this the way I'm supposed to kiss?" Tory became dazed at how he learned so fast because it felt so good. "That's exactly how you do it. Now let's try it with the tongue." Then she took her tongue and went deeper into the kiss. Now they both used their tongues. It tasted like electricity on her tongue. This time it was much better. So much better she started to get swept up into his kisses. With a grin on his face he asked, "Was that better?" "Wait, I'm not sure. Let's try that one more time." Then he went in for one more kiss. He knew that he was doing better because she was moaning and he wasn't having sex with her yet. "Damn Daddy, that was excellent. You really learn fast." "I guess I have a good teacher." Just as she was going in for another kiss, he stopped her and said, "Torianey, we need to talk." "This better be good. My female wood is on." "I hate to bring this up but, we made a deal on the plane and I want to make sure we're clear on some things." Tory sucked her teeth and said, "Oh not this again. How is it you get to bring this back up; but when I do, there was no plane." "Just hear me out please." She sat herself up on the couch to hear what he had to say. "I want to continue to see you again. I don't want meaningless sex either. I want you as my girlfriend. I would like to be able to pick up my phone and see how your day is going; to take you out on dates and maybe see a movie or two. To be honest, I feel like I cheated you when I agreed on that deal. Something in me caught a feeling when we were together that day. It felt like I had a connection with you that I wanted to feel again. You made me come alive the moment we started to talk. You made me laugh with your stories. I really wasn't a happy person before I met you." Tory was taken aback. She honestly didn't know what to say. A billionaire was trying to win her heart. "Technically, you had me at dinner and desert. I accept." He was pleased to hear that he was now in a relationship with Tory. "And to solidify our relationship, let's make a toast." He poured two glasses of wine for the two of them and said, "To a meaningful relationship." Then they both took down their wine. Just as they were about to go in for yet another kiss, they heard a commotion in the hallway. He put his glass down to go and see what the disturbance was all about. As he got to the door of the den, he noticed it was his wife Lisa causing that entire disturbance. She managed to break free from his security. She ran up the hall to Shaune and started to yell. "We need to talk! Now!" "Only if you would stop yelling." "So what are you on a date? Is this what you do when you kick your wife out of our home?" "If you would have come to the divorce hearing, you have known exactly what I'm doing." Shaune turned and saw Tory witnessing what looked like a lovers quarrel. Then he walked over to her and said, "I know what this looks like but if you give me a minute with my wife, I'll be happy to explain everything to you." For a second, Tory was concerned about the woman in Shaunes' den. She knew exactly who she was. However, Lisa wasn't concerned about who she was. Then she said, "Take all the time you need." When they disappeared in the hallway, Tory asked the valet for a ride home in Shaunes' limousine. After she had gotten her jacket, she jumped in his limousine and was driven home. She thought to herself, "I feel like a really big, dump, third wheel." Shaune wanted to hurry up and get rid of his ex-wife so that he could get back to Tory. "What are you doing here any way Lisa?" "I want to talk about the divorce. I don't think we should." "Wow let me think about that. Uh, no. Now leave my house please." "Does your new girlfriend know that you are still married?" "No but I'm going have to do some explaining now thanks to you showing up." "Good. No matter how bad you want this to be over, its not." "It soon will be; now if you don't mind, I have some explaining to do. I'm sure you can see your way out." As he walked out to the hallway, he realized that Tory was nowhere to be found. He turned to the doorman and asked, "Where did my guest go?" "Sir, your driver drove her home." "What! And how did that happen?" "She asked the driver to take her home sir." Shaune started to get angry and said, "Does anybody even listen to me anymore. You let my wife in and my girlfriend out when clearly I wanted it the other way around. Do I need to hire new staff?" Then Lisa walked up to him; and as she put her arms around his waist she said, "See baby, this is a sign. I'm here and she's not. We were meant to be together." Shaune leaned in so close that she thought he was going to kiss her but instead he stopped short and whispered, "You are clearly delusional; and you should have though about all this when you decided to step out on our marriage. Now I'm going to tell you one last time, get the fuck out of my house or get thrown out. Make a choice." Then he looked up at the doorman and said, "Get my car please." Then he pulled out his cell phone to see if he could convince Torianey to come back, but it went straight to voice mail.

Chapter 6
Just When I Thought We Were Making Progress

The limo had pulled up to Torys' driveway. She was so angry she didn't even wait for the driver to open the door for her. As she stormed out of the car, she sped walked up to her door entered her house. She paced back and forth through her living room arguing to herself. "The fucking nerve of him; he put all that pressure on me to be his girlfriend knowing full well that he was still married." She even started to mimic his phrases. "I care for you more then I care to admit… Oh Tory I feel like I cheated you out of so much more… Yeah you felt like you cheated something you piece of work." She became furious with herself. So furious that she felt that she wanted to punch Shaune in the face if he were standing in front of her at that very moment. She ran upstairs to get out of her clothes and jump into her shower. She thought to herself, "Maybe a good shower to wash that dick heads lies off of me would help." Ten minutes later, she got out of the shower and she wasn't feeling any better. As she threw on her black robe and she figured that maybe a good hard drink would help calm her down. She went into the kitchen and pulled out a bottle of vodka from the freezer and mixed it with cranberry juice. She took a swig and said to herself, "Oh yeah, this will kill him from my system." As she took another swig, her doorbell rang. She walked to her door; and guess who it was? As she looked out the window, she said, "Shouldn't you be with your wife?" "She's not my wife. At least on paper she is. We're going through a divorce." "Then come back when it's no longer on paper. You know what? Don't even come back." "Please, let me in and I'll explain everything." "You don't have to explain anything, because I can't believe anything that comes out of you're lying fucking mouth. What did think, if you didn't tell me you were married at least you wouldn't have to lie?" "No Torianey, I thought that I didn't want to spoil a good night with having to explain the fact that I was a married man going through a divorce. The truth was I was having such a good time that I already had forgotten that I was even married." As she swung open the door, she yelled, "That's bullshit and you know it. Didn't it occur to you to tell me all this oh maybe back on the plane? How about during dinner? Oh and let's not get started on all that shit you was kicking about "I have these feelings for you Tory, I cheated you, I want more then just sex." Be honest with yourself, that was just a load of shit and you knew it. To think I was going back on my own deal because you convinced me with a stupid dinner. You're a real piece of fucking work." "Torianey, I meant every word of it…" She cut in and said "You meant for me not to find out this way, that's what you meant." Shaunes' mind became weary and he backed up and sat on the porch deck. Then he said, "I'll be honest, I don't know how this whole thing works." Tory, with her anger still visibly present said, "What whole thing?" He threw his hands in the air and said, "This life, love, marriage all of it. Some times I feel as though I'm blind folded and I'm just feeling in the dark. I put my hand on marriage; I try that and come to find out my wife is stepping out on me; and to make matters worse she never loved me. I was just an opportunity for her. I mean I knew that coming into the marriage but, I thought that maybe after sometime she might come around and start to love me. What was I thinking? I thought that I was doing everything right; but no one would tell me just what I did wrong." He looked like he was about to cry. Finally, she calmed herself and looked at her drink and looked at Shaune. Then she handed it to him. "You look like you need this more then I do." He took a gulp of the drink and said, "Nice and strong. Thank you." Feeling bad for him, she opened the door to let him in. He looked up at her to see if she was serious about him coming in. "I'm not holding it open for the bugs to fly in."

He took a seat at her dining room table, and Tory went to make herself another drink. While she was mixing her drink, she joked, "Gee, couldn't this night have ended any better? So let me get this straight, you're this billionaire married to this woman who only wanted you for your money? She cheats on you now you're in the midst of a divorce and you can't seem to understand why all this is happening to you. You didn't think the woman that you would marry just might be interested in your money?" "Of course I did. I just thought that maybe things might change after a while." As he got up to talk to her, he said, "You might be my first experience to what a real relationship is." "How do you figure?" "From the minute I met you, you gave it to me the way it was supposed to be. My wife never did that nor has any other woman. It was you who said that even a hungry dog would eat cat food. Just to get what they all needed, they tolerated me; my bad kisses, my bad attitude. But not you, you told me how it was and you were ready to leave when you couldn't stand anymore of me." "I was just doing what came natural to me. Being with you was never about what you have. It was how I felt about you." "So then, how do you feel about me?" She took a sip of her drink, looked him up and down and said, "You're aight." She said as she laughed. He shook his head at her response and figured maybe if he took it a little deeper she just might take him seriously. "How do you feel about me owning $300 billion in the bank?" "Okay Shaune, let me bottom line it for you. I'm not opposed to dating a hard working billionaire like you. It shows that you know that you deserve better. I always felt the same way. Not that I'm a millionaire or a billionaire but I deserve what I want in life and I would want to meet someone who feels the same way; with that having been said, the

fact remains that your life is your headache; and better you then me."
"Torianey, that's not what I asked you in the first place. I…" Then she
cut in and said, "I know you want to know how I feel about you? The
truth is I like you, I want to like you, and I want to trust you. But how
could I when you can't even manage to tell me you're still married."
Shaune followed her as she went to go take a seat at her table. Then he
asked her, "So can we explore this with the possibility of finding out if
you could?" Then she blasted, "Oh hell no, so the other shoe could drop
on my ass like it did tonight? I think not. I had that problem before
many times over including tonight and it always kept me picking up
the pieces, not us." She was so angry, she sat down too abruptly and
ended up spilling her drink on to her thighs and it ran down her legs.
As she reached for a napkin, Shaune stopped her and he reached for the
napkins and attempted to clean up the mess. He couldn't resist the urge
to lick across her thighs. All of a sudden he began to nibble into her
thigh and this time it didn't startle her it turned her on. Shaune looked
up and said, "I'm sorry Torianey, I couldn't…" And before he could
finish, she had grabbed him and threw her tongue down his throat. At
that point, Tory had forgotten everything she wanted to say. She even
forgot what the whole dispute was about. Shaune felt that this would
be the time to redeem himself so he had to do everything right. And
of course with his new skills with kissing, he had to try to win her over
again. Tory was getting swept all up in the moment, and she knew she
wanted him this night. There were no "Seatbelt on" signs, no ex-wives,
nothing stopping them from enjoying each other. Tory slid herself off of
her seat and onto the floor. Now they were both on the dinning room
floor and Tory was pulling off Shaunes polo and tee shirt so she could
devour him. Then she unbuckled his belt and jeans so she could get
at the rest of him. He opened up her robe and started to suck on her
nipples. It felt so good to her she didn't want him to stop. She whispered
in his ear, "I want to feel you inside me." Although her words blew
his mind, he tried to keep his composure and said, "Your wish is my
command." Shaune pulled off his jeans and boxer briefs. Tory sat in his
lap and slid his penis inside her. This time there was no tension; he went

right in and she started to ride him. They were breathing heavy and their hearts were pounding hard as they were grinding extremely fast. Tory took her legs and wrapped them around Shaunes' waist. Being the undercover freak that he was, he whispered, "Tighter." Then she tightened her grip around his waist and started moaning. "Yes, just like that." He moaned. As she was grinding, she started to suck on his neck. Her mind was moving a thousand miles a minuet. She felt she couldn't get enough of him. Then there was that moment in time when he they looked in each others eyes again. Shaune felt that connection he felt just like back on the plane. "I want you to take control." She whispered. Shaune didn't waist any time. He grabbed her by the back of her neck and threw her back on to the floor. As he lifted up her leg, he thrust deep inside her and she screamed, "Yes Daddy, just like that!" Now he really started to get worked up. While he was controlling her with his moves, she was controlling him with her words. With all the alcohol that they had consumed, they started to work up a sweat; and they both were delirious out of their minds. "Cum for your Daddy." And to help her along, he was grinding harder. He started breathing heavier. The sound of his breathing was turning her on more and more. So much that she took her legs and squeezed his waist so hard. Shaune moaned in pain, but he loved the feel of her thighs around his body. She felt her climax coming on and said, "Daddy, I'm ready to cum for you." As she started to cum, her legs got tighter around Shaunes' waist. He could feel her muscles contracting on his and she started to scream. Feeling like he was ready to explode, he held her tighter and whispered in her ear, "It's my turn now." While he was still grinding, he grabbed her by her hair and started to suck on her neck to hide his screams while he let loose. While they were breathing heavy from all that action, Shaune looked over at her and said, "Fountain pens." Feeling confused, Tory said, "What?" "It's my insanity; fountain pens."

The two of them lay on the dinning room floor both naked and dripping with sweat. Shaune had an idea that he had wanted to ask Tory since back at his house. Now was the perfect time. "I would like for you to come away with me." "Were too? Oh the state fair is this week. We can go there." Shaune giggled and said, "No not there. Some place better." Tory thought to herself, "What could be finer then the State fair?" Then she asked, "Where then?" "Jamaica." Tory, feeling too tired tried to fight back her laughter, but she couldn't help herself. She looked over at Shaune and noticed that he wasn't laughing. "Oh you were serious?" "Yes. What made you think I was joking?" Then she rolled over holding her stomach in laughter. Shaune started to get offended. "What's so funny?" She stopped laughing and got serious. "I can't afford a trip like Jamaica." "What makes you think I would let my lady pay her own way if I asked her to come with me?" "Which brings me to my next question? Aren't you still married?" "Yes I am, but by next week I'll be a free man." "Shaune, I don't get it. How is it you could be married and think its okay to take another woman to a place like Jamaica? And no, I am not your lady. In fact, this night shouldn't have happened in the first place. You shouldn't be here. I thought that after this was over, you would leave." "Do you want me to leave?" "I think it might be best if you did." "Why?" Tory was starting to get frustrated with him. "Because you asked and I answered." "Why that answer?" Then she yelled as she got off the floor, "Because I think it's best for the both of us." She put on her robe and left to go to her bedroom. Shaune put on his boxer briefs and followed her to her room. As she sat on her bed, she saw that he wasn't leaving. "Did I not explain to you that you shouldn't be here?" "Oh I get it now, when I leave you would probably delete my number and not answer my calls hoping that I would disappear." "Something like that." "Despite the fact that I gave you my seat when you could have been thrown off the plane and possibly put on a no fly passenger list; or when I rescued you from being stuck at Carrapellies parking lot. Now all I want to do is take you to Jamaica with me so that I can show you a good time and you make it seem like I'm trying to whisk you off to the electric chair." "I'm sorry Shaune, although I appreciate you for doing those things, I can't go with you." "You can't or you won't? Torianey, I like you. I like being around you. My Wife has been cheating in our marriage since we've been married. I have the photos to prove it. I would love to show you someday." "That's not my business to know about your marriage." "Wow, that's rich coming from the woman who keeps bringing it up and throwing it in my face. For the record, she stopped by tonight to contest the divorce. See, she knows that once it's final, she's no longer relevant in any social setting. She'll have all the money she'll need, but the attention that she was getting while being married to me, she'll never have again." "Why would anyone want to be in someone else's spotlight?" "She was runner up to Ms. America back in 2000. That sought of kept her in the spotlight for a while. But now she's not in that circle anymore so she meets me. At first when we met I thought she was genuinely interested in me. She knew almost everything about me. But who doesn't? I'm Que'Shuane Guadau; you can google me and find out just about anything. She did and she played me right into her hands. Next thing I know, I'm married to her. Since then, her social status has been on the elite list." "How did that make you feel?" "I didn't care. As long as she was happy, I was happy; at least before the whole cheating scandal came out." Shaune realized that he was deviating from the plan. He tried to salvage himself and said, "So how can I convince you to come with me?" "Maybe we could figure this out tomorrow." "Fine then." They sat there looking at each other for a second. Tory was expecting him to go get his clothes on and leave. Then he asked, "Is it possible for me to spend the night?" "Why?" "I've been drinking and I don't want to drive home." "Don't you have drivers that can take you home?" "Their all done for the night. So can I stay here until I sober up?" "Fine but you're going to have to sleep on the couch downstairs." "Actually, I would like to sleep on this big king size bed with you?" "You can't." "I can and I will." Shaune laid himself across Torys' bed and he made himself comfortable. "Man this bed is more comfortable then my own." He said as he stretched out. "Shaune, you have to go down stairs." He leaned over to kiss her on the cheek and said, "Goodnight Tory. See you in the morning?" Then he rolled over on his side and turned the lamp off. Tory stood in total shock. "Que'Shaune! Damn it Que'Shuane!" She really didn't know what else to do but let him sleep. Ultimately, she turned out her lamp and went to sleep.

Torys' alarm went off that morning at 10:55am. She opened her eyes to see that Shaune was no longer in her bed. She also saw that his clothes were gone. "Maybe he got the hint and took off." She said as she got up to sit on the side of the bed. She noticed that her slippers were gone. "Did he take my slippers with him?" Then she heard voices downstairs. She put on her pajamas and her robe and headed downstairs to see what was going on. When she got down stairs she was met by Greg and another guy who was dressed in a business suit carrying a clipboard. They were eating waffles and bacon as a sandwich and dripping what looked like her organic honey all over her rug. Greg said, "Good morning Ms. Heckstall." "Oh I'm no longer "the one woman under a rock?" "No you're not and I apologize if I offended you." Then the guy in the suit reached his hand out and said, "Hello Ms Heckstall. My name is Anthony Wright and you're going to love your brand new…" Greg cut in and said, "We have to get going. Tone, I'll give you a ride back to the spot." As they were leaving, Tory asked, "Where's Shaune?" "I'm right here. Did you think I would leave yet?" Shaune answered. She turned and saw him with her apron on with a spatula in one hand and a cup of coffee in the other. "Something like that." She replied. He walked over to her and kissed her on the lips and said, "Good morning to you too." "Why were Greg and that guy here and what am I getting that's so brand new?" "You'll see later but for now, let me feed you." "What did you make?" She asked. He grabbed her hand and led her into the dinning room. The dinning room table was set with two plates and two glasses of orange juice. In the center of the table were a plate filled with waffles and a plate filled with bacon. He pulled her chair for her to sit in. "You made all this by yourself?" "Yes. I hope you didn't mind but I used your waffle maker to make these waffles." "Not at all, I got it as a gift two years ago and never thought to use it." While he fixed her plate, he asked her, "So, have you made a decision yet?" "A decision about what?" "Our trip to Jamaica. I know you haven't forgotten already." "You can take any woman that you would like, why me?" "I don't like every woman that I meet. I like you and I think you're sexy and funny. Plus we make a great pair you and me. You make me happy. I don't remember the last time I can say that I was happy." Tory felt sympathetic to his comment; but none the less he was still married. "I'm sorry but I have to decline. But this breakfast is delicious." Shaune gave Tory a pitiful look then she said, "Maybe we could go to the State fair if you would like." "Gee let's weight that. Beautiful blue seas or trees and leaves; penthouse and Persian rugs or big, ugly, black palmetto bugs; I don't see anything good about spending a vacation in South Carolina as oppose to Jamaica." Tory didn't care to discuss the conversation any further. "Why aren't you eating?" "I'm not hungry yet. Plus, I tasted as I was cooking." The truth was, Shaune was so excited to show Tory her surprise, he couldn't eat. While he poured her cup of coffee, he said, "I have a surprise for you." "Oh, sounds kinky, I like kinky surprises." "Not that kind of surprise." Shaune knew that this would get her to want to go to Jamaica with him because he knew that Tory was always concerned about pay back and there was no way she could accept his gift without some form of payback.

After she had finished her breakfast, she started to feel sluggish. As she rubbed her eyes, she said, "Man, I got the "Itis". This breakfast was heavy." Now it was time to show her the surprise he had gotten her. "So are you ready for your surprise?" "Yes, what is this surprise you are speaking of?" "Close your eyes." "Really Que'Shuane? That is so cheesy." "Well then I am a cheesy dude then. Now close your eyes." She closed her eyes and she asked, "Now what?" "Now think, what would be the one thing you would have if you could have it?" "Anything?" "Anything." "An A+ on my public speaking paper." "No a little better then that." Then she joked, "$300 billion in the bank. Am I going to open my eyes to see it on the table?" Shaune was getting frustrated with her because she wasn't taking him seriously. "Seriously Torianey! You know what? You're hopeless. Open your eyes." As she opened her eyes, she saw on the table a set of car keys. "You got my car back." She yelled. "Something like that." Then she said, "You did get MY car back?" "Let's go see then." They got up to go outside. As she opened the door she noticed a burgundy Cadillac Navigator sitting in her driveway. She was speechless. "Is that my car?" "Yes and no." "What do you mean?" "I mean yes it's your car but no it's not the old one. See I got a call this morning from my mechanic and he said that your engine was shot and the motor was corroding. Needless to say, it was unable to repair. So, I had an idea that you might need a new car anyway. Well here it is. Do you like it?" Tory yelled, "Yes, yes, yes!" "Let's get in and look inside." As they got in the car, she noticed that her new car had all the bells and whistles. Updated GPS, heated leather seats, everything was automatic, digital dashboard. She became so overwhelmed, her eyes started to tear up. He reached over to wipe her tears away. "You didn't have to do this. I do thank you so much but I can't accept this car." "Yes you can and you will." "Then how can I repay you…" Then just as quick as she caught on to the whole scam, she started to shut him down but was quickly shut down when he put his hand over her mouth and said, "If you come to Jamaica with me, I'll act like this car never existed." She slapped his hand away; she took the keys out of the ignition and threw them in his lap. Then she said, "Enjoy Jamaica by your self." She hopped out of the car and went back into her house. He followed behind her and asked, "Did I offend you?" Sarcastically she answered, "No Shaune you didn't offend me by trying to bribe me into going on a trip with you. Why would I feel offended by being bribed?" "Obviously, I have offended you. That wasn't my intentions. I just wanted to take care of my lady." "I am not your fucking lady Que'Shuane! Stop saying that. I'm not some mistress, whore you can take on trips with you when you want to play; then when you no longer have use for me, you hang me up on the side till your ready for me again like your favorite pair of underwear. I told you I don't want that for my life." "What makes you think that I was trying to create that kind of life for you?" "Really, me waking up to a brand new car is not you trying to bribe me into going on that trip with you? That's what you do for your mistresses.

Its called "hush money" I've been there before I know the signs all too well. Next it will be diamond necklaces and rings." Feeling frustrated and confused with her, he needed to set the record straight. "Just so I can be totally clear about this, what would be the catalyst that separates you being my lady from being my whore? Not that I'm calling you either at this point. I just need to know how I make you one and not the other." "What's my favorite flower?" "I don't know, you never told me." "Lilacs." She answered. "Then what's my favorite color?" She asked him. "Again, you never told me." Shaune wasn't getting the point so she figured she would take to a more simplistic approach. "What if we were dating and you didn't have $300 billion in the bank? What if you were just a regular 9 till 5 man and you didn't earn a half of a quarter of what you have. You couldn't afford a trip to Jamaica for both of us. That would require at least a years planning. Nor could you afford a new car. How could you possibly make me happy with barely anything?" "Please help me understand so that I can have a better idea of where you're coming from." "The little things Que`Shuane; flowers, dinner and a movie, cheesy text messages letting me know that you're thinking of me. The little things that don't even cost as much; those things that take forever to prepare, but lets one know that you actually gave it some thought to make it what it is; and that would make me your girlfriend. For you, it's so easy to throw money at a situation and expect me to think that it was heart felt; then my friend that would make me your whore. Again, I thank you for all that you have done, but I'm not for sale. Goodbye Shaune." He watched her go back upstairs and he looked at the car key and left it next to her house keys and left. While he was driving away from her house, he started to feel like his heart was breaking again.

Later, Tory was dressed and ready for work. As she reached for her keys, she noticed that the car keys to the Navigator were sitting next to hers'. She looked out the window and saw that the truck was still parked in her driveway. Since she was about to call for a ride anyway, she figured she'd take it. She arrived at Carrapellies in her new truck and she wasn't ready to explain how she got it. Lou had seen her pull up in her parking spot so he had to ask. As she walked into his office, Lou didn't waste anytime. "You rented a new car I see." "Actually Lou, I got that car as a gift." "Really, who gave you a brand new car?" Tory paused and took a deep breath before she answered. "Que'Shaune Guadau." She could see that Lou was starting to turn red and when he did, that meant that the roof was about to blow. Then Tory tried to squelch his anger by saying "But I'm going to give it back. I told him that I didn't want it. However, he didn't take no for an answer so he left the keys. I needed a ride to work so I took it." "And what exactly did you do to get this brand new car that you plan on giving back to him?" "What makes you think I did something to get a car?" Even Tory thought that sounded ridiculous. So then she said, "Would you at least give me the opportunity to start from the beginning?" "I'm all ears." "The night before last after his fund raiser, I was closing up shop. When I got into my car, the engine kept stalling as it did many times before. I was calling any and everyone, but no one would answer their phones. I called you but your phone went straight to voice mail. Then I called my only option; Que'Shuane. Strangely enough he answered and he came to pick me up. He asked me to have dinner with him as payback for picking me up and I accepted." "Do you realize he's still married?" "I found that out last night when I was at his house." "Okay. You had dinner at his house and you found out that he was still married. And what happened after that?" "I went home in his limousine while he handled things with his wife who by the way showed up in the middle of desert." "Then what happened next?" "What makes you think anything happened after that?" "You have a brand new car in your possession. What did you do to get it?" "I didn't do anything to get it." "Well then let me ask the questions and you just answer yes or no. Did he come to your house last night after having dealing with his wife?" "Yes." "Did you let him in your house?" "Yes." Then Lou started to turn red all over again. "Did you... have sex with this man?" As she looked on to the ground, she answered "Yes." "And that's how you got the car I suspect?" "Not exactly Lou. See he had wanted me to go to

Jamaica with him and he said that if I went with him he would let me keep the car." "And you said?" "You would be proud of me. I said no. And I plan on giving back the car I just needed it for today." At that point, Lou was at least six shades of purple. Then he said "I'm only telling you this for your own good. You need to give that car back and sever your ties to the Guadaus." "I will Lou. Don't worry." Tory left Lous' office and headed to hers'. As she sat at her desk, she started to feel slightly overwhelmed. Then she said to herself "Why does everything have to be so damn complicated?"

Shaune came home to his mansion to find Greg, his Lawyer, his wife and her Lawyer there. "Finally, you know how to show up to something." He said to her. As he took a seat at his desk, he looked around and said, "Well?" His wife walked up and gave him his divorce papers. She leaned in and signed them herself. Then he said, "Great. The settlement still stands. $9 million, the condo in Mexico, the condo in New York, and the vacation house here as well." "Que`Shaune how could you be so cruel. Can't we just work this out?" "Wow, I'm cruel. I give you two condos and a house along with $9 million for cheating on me when we were only married for 5yrs, and I'm the cruel one. Well I'll be damned." His now ex-wife stormed out of the den in tears, but Shaune was no more concerned about her. Both Lawyers came up to shake his hand and left. As quick as it started, it ended for Shaune and he was relieved. He was now a free man and the first thought on his mind was Tory. He had sat back in his seat and started to reminisce about last night. His mind wandered back to when they were on her dinning room floor making love. He remembered how her thighs felt around his waist squeezing him and how much he loved it; the sound of her voice calling him "Daddy." He wanted so much to have that moment again. While he was deep in thought, Greg walked in abruptly catching Shaune off guard. "I have your copy of the divorce papers and I'm going to file them away shortly. Hey is everything okay with you?" "No I'm fine. I need to take a shower and then I have to take a short trip somewhere." "Are you sure you wanted to divorce Lisa? Are you having second guesses?" "No not at all. I'm extremely happy that she's out of my hair and my life. My mind is on something else." "Let me guess, Tory? Did she like the car? What happened after we left?" "She didn't want the car. In fact, she broke it off with me." "What! What did you do to her?" "Apparently, she thought that I was trying to buy her love. Well, not love but make her my "Whore" while I was still married." "So what's next?" "I'm divorced now so I'm going to give it one last college try to prove to her that I'm not in it for what she thinks I am." Greg came up and pat Shaune on the back and said "If you need me to do anything, I'm here for you." As he was leaving to go to his bedroom, he stopped and said, "There is one thing I will need you to do for me. I need you to order me 6 black roses in an arrangement with lilacs and have them sent here." "I'm on it right now."

3pm and Tory was at her desk when the front desk called to announce that she had a guest at the front. "Could you show them in please?" Now sooner did a tap come at her door and it was the least person she had expected. It was Lisa Mills-Guadau; Shaunes' ex-wife. "What can I do for you?" Tory asked. As Lisa took a seat at her desk, she said, "I have a proposal to make." "I hope this has something to do with booking a VIP room, because anything else I'm not interested in." Lisa picked up the suit case she was carrying with her and said, "Open it." "I don't want to." Then Lisa got up to open it herself. She had revealed a suit case full of money. "What is this? Why are you...?" Then Lisa said, "There is $100,000 in here for you. If you leave my husband alone, you could have it all; tax free, no contracts, no paper trails." Tory was stunned and offended at the same time. "I'm not holding your husband back from you." "But with you out of the way we just might have a chance." "Are we talking about the same chance that you cheated on with my man?" "That was for a different reason." "I never did understand that reason and by the way that robe you wore, I have the exact same one. I bet you were wearing the matching teddy that came with it too." "Are you going to take the money or not?" Tory leaned back in her seat; she crossed her legs and folded her arms and said, "I'm curious to know one thing Lisa. Did you ever once wander about me while you were screwing my man behind your husbands back? While you were cheating on your now so lovable husband with my once future husband, did you even bother to ask who I was or why would I be there that nigh? No, I don't think you did. See, you're so damn selfish that it didn't occur to you whose lives you would destroy in the process. Now you're on the verge of that same damaged life. How does it feel?" Lisa slammed the case close and said, "Take the fucking money and get out of our lives." As she turned to leave the office, Tory yelled, "How do you know I won't double cross you? How do you know I won't take your man and your money? I am capable of being just that cruel. After all, you said it yourself there is not paper trails, no contracts, not even a hand shake." Lisa didn't even look back; she just left the office with the money still on Torys' desk.

6pm dinner time for Carrapellies, Tory tended the guest list at the front this evening. While she was checking the guest in Que`Shuane walked up with flowers in his hands. "Mr. Guadau, what can I do for you?" "Please don't start that formal bullshit again Tory." "What can I do for you Shaune?" "I need to talk to you in private please." "Que`Shuane…" He stopped her and said, "Please Tory?" Tory called the desk clerk over to take over for her. "Follow me to my office please." When they got to her office, Shaune didn't waste any time. He pulled out the divorce papers with the flowers and said, "It's final. You can keep the car, go to Jamaica with me and you can show me what it means to be Torianeys' boyfriend." Tory was shocked. "When did she sign these?" "Just before 3pm today." Shaune saw the look on her face. He was expecting her to look a little happier then what he was seeing. "What's wrong?" She picked up the case and opened it for him. "A case full of money; what's this all about?" "Your ex-wife, that's what this is all about. She came here and tried to bribe me into not seeing you anymore. I have to admit, she must really love you to come here with this much money and ask me not to see you anymore." She doesn't love me; she's concerned about her little empire she's trying to build." "I was seriously considering keeping this money. I could pay off my mortgage, pay up my college tuition all the way till the end, get a new car and still live somewhat comfortable with my job of coarse." "And what about us?" "What about us? She wants you not me." "I want you not her. I'm a free man. There's nothing stopping us now. You can keep the money. It's mine anyways." He pushed the case towards her then she thought about it for a while and said "I can't do this."

Que'Shaune showed up at Lisa's house without calling her. He knocked on the door. She was surprised to see that it was him. "Que'Shuane, come in." "No, I don't want to come in. I'll make this short and sweet." Then he took the case and dropped it in front of her. Then he finished. "I'm sure you won't mind that I skimmed $30,000 off the top for Torys' troubles. The next time you go near my girlfriend with the intentions to bribe her with money or any other motive you have, not only will you loose everything, I'll make you so sorry that you even considered going near her. There's no reason you should have to put her in the middle of our mess." Just as he turned to leave, she called him back and said, "Que'Shuane, one day you will realize she was always in the middle somewhere." "What are you talking about?" "It's going to come out and then you'll know." Then she closed her door. He wasn't sure what she was talking about, but none the less she was out of his life definitely. He jumped in his car and called his new girlfriend and left her a voice message. "Torianey, you don't have to worry about her anymore I dealt with the situation. Are we still on for next week? Call me when you're done." Then he headed to his Fathers house. Tory was looking at vacation papers wandering how she was going to present to Louis that she had considered going on the trip with Shaune. Tory figured there was no other way to do it but to do it. She got up and walked into Lous' office. He was sitting at his desk reading through some receipts. "Lou, can I talk to you about something?" "Sure, what's on your mind?" "Remember when I said that I wasn't going to go on that trip with Que'Shaune Guadau?" "You mean the conversation we had this afternoon?" "Yeah, that one; well, there were some developments and it turns out that I think I want to go." Lou tried not to get upset with her this time. He'd thought that he would try to take a more patient approach. "What developments are you talking about?" "Developments like he's not married anymore. That he showed me the divorce papers developments." "Before I tell you this, do you think you can see yourself in a relationship with him?" "I guess I can. Maybe, I'm not sure Lou we just met." "Torianey, I look at you as the child I never had and I'll always be concerned about you. My honest opinion is that maybe you shouldn't see him anymore." "Why because he was married? Look he just got a divorce and to be honest, he's been jumping through hoops to get back with me ever since we met." "The Guadau's have some serious skeletons in their closet." "So what does that have to do with me?" "Did he ever tell you about his parents'?" "Yes he told me his mom died when he was a child. She died in a boating accident." "That boating accident met with foul play according to the authorities. For 20yrs her death has been an unsolved case." "I still don't understand what this has to do with me or dating Que'Shaune." "The word on the street is Que'Shaune Guadau Sr. had his wife killed. She was cheating on her husband and he found out." "How sure are you of this?" "Margarite Guadaus' lover was a business man like Que'Shaune Sr. Now there's no place he can go to earn a dollar. After the whole thing with him messing with Margarite got out in the public, his stocks started to plummet. The next thing you would hear was his business was going bankrupt. If you're still confused, then let me clear it up for you. This guy was Que'Shaune Sr. best friend. They hung out together and pretty much did everything together. They were inseparable; they would play golf on Saturdays and play poker. The only time they wouldn't hang out was when Sr. had to go away on business. Then that would be the time for him to creep to see Sr. wife. One day, his friend decides to move from France to right here in South Carolina. Sr. was none the wiser; he thought that he was doing it for their friendship but he was only doing it for himself and Margarite." Tory felt like she was trapped between a rock and a hard place. Ultimately, she made her decision. "I hope you won't be terribly angry with me if I say that despite your concerns, I'm still going. Lou, if it's any conciliation, I don't plan on marrying the guy, it's just a trip. If anything gets too hectic, I'll end it." "I'm sure if Margarite Gaudua had that option, she would be alive today." "The difference between her and me is I don't plan on marrying him. I mean look at it Lou, a free trip to Jamaica; I've never been there before. He's great in bed and he likes me. I'm all win, win here. There are no rings on our fingers so he can't have me blown up or killed. I haven't felt this good in a long time. I haven't been laid in a long time. The last time a man came to my house he was painting it or doing some form of maintenance. There's something about him, I don't know I can't put my finger on it, but I feel as though I can trust him. He's the one man who isn't scared to tell me what's on his mind. When I'm trying to find out what this man wants and he tells me without me having to ask. I'm starting to get into a stage in my life where I just want to have fun. No worries about school, bills, work, love, just hard core fun. So don't worry about me and just wish me well." Louis realized that it was time to back off from Torys' love life. He knew that at her age, she had to figure it out for herself about the game of love and pain. "I'm sorry; I didn't mean to put pressure on you. You do know that I love you enough that I have your best interest at heart?" "I do and you have to trust that I'm capable of making a formative decision." He smiled, took her vacation papers and signed them; and then he placed them in his desk and said, "Make sure you take pictures."

Chapter 7
Out With the Old In With the New

Que`Shaune decided not to go straight home; he wanted to pay his father a visit and fill him in on his progress with his new lady. As soon as he got into the house, he saw his fathers' care-taker getting ready to take him his lunch and meds. He told her he would do the honors himself. As he got to the bedroom door, he knocked to announce himself. "Entrée." His father said in his native French tongue. Normally, his dad would be in his den watching the stock exchange channel or CNN or possibly on his way out somewhere. Instead, he was in his house wearing his pajamas and it was only 12 noon. "Pare, why aren't you dressed? Its early afternoon." "Is there someone special coming to visit me?" "No but you…" Then his father interrupted him and said, "So I don't need to get dressed everyday in my own home." Now Shaune felt bad, then he said, "Sorry." "I'm curious to know why you are here." "My divorce is final and I'm going away to Jamaica to meet with those investors." Que`Shuane Sr. knew there was more to his sons showing up then just divorce and investment meetings. So he asked "And?" "And what?" "I know mon files, if that was all you had to say, you would have called me on the phone like you always do." Shaune couldn't hide anything from his father; most of all the truth. "The truth is I'm taking my new girlfriend with me." "This new girlfriend wouldn't happen to be the same girlfriend that you met on the plane?" "Qui pare, she is." "And how did you achieve this feat. Last I heard she was not that into you." "We had dinner and we talked; then the next morning, I made her breakfast and she told me that when my divorce was final, she would consider. And when it was, she did." Now Sr. wanted to ask the hard question. "Do you think you're moving too fast?" "Dad I know how this must look…" His father cut in and said, "This looks like you're not giving yourself time to heal. You just got out of a marriage and your head over heals for someone else. Might I suggest that you take some time?" "What is so awkwardly funny? The fact that for 5yrs I was married to a woman who only wanted me for money and fame; and no one even bothered to say a word. And what's even hilarious about the whole thing is that for 3 of those 5yrs, we lived in two separate countries; yet still no one managed to say a damn thing. Now I can admit that I was at fault for not being completely present in my marriage because I was so busy taking care of the family business; and it wasn't like she was complaining. I figured as long as everyone was happy, I had no reason to change things. Then I receive photos of my wife being bent over a penthouse balcony by a man that was not me. I thought to myself that maybe I should let her have her cake and eat it too. Do I change things? Then I found myself being belittled and humiliated all over the world. I even realized my wife was getting everything she wanted; the milk, the cow, the farm. So I asked myself, where is my pleasure? Where is my happiness?" Shaune never shared his pain with his father in reference to his marriage. Then he finished. "Now I meet someone who actually makes me feel happy; someone who only wants the little things in life and only now is everyone concerned. So concerned that she doesn't meet the financial requirements. Or that I might be moving too fast. Where were these opinions when I was marrying a gold digging, media whore? Where was the concern when the world was watching my marriage deteriorate from the inside out?" As he tried to calm himself, his father came over and put his hand on his shoulder to reassure him that his pain was heart felt. "I'm sorry

Que`Shuane; I didn't realize you were in so much pain." For out of fear and embarrassment, he tried desperately to shake his demeanor off. He laughed and then he said, "No, I'm not hurting dad. I was just making a statement." Even Shaune Jr. himself didn't believe those words that came out of his mouth. It was Sr. who was concerned in his own mind if his son was trying to convince his father or himself that he was okay. Then Sr. said "I just want you to be happy. Clearly you are and I didn't mean to question that." "I have to go now. I have other plans to make." Shaune Jr. was so uncomfortable that he had left without hugging his father goodbye.

Tory looked up at the clock to see that she had 30mins to clear up her next week schedule if she was going to Jamaica with Shaune. She said to herself, "First things first." She needed to create the menus for the next two weeks to get caught up, and then get caught up with all the VIP room reservations. It was going on 9pm; and Torianey was almost done with her projects. All she needed to do was email Lou with her plans and be on her way. All was going well when her office phone rang. She thought it was Que`Shuane calling but it wasn't; it was the one person she didn't anticipate. As she picked up the phone, she said "Hello?" "It really has been a long time since we had a heart to heart Torianey. Is there a possibility for reconciliation?" As Tory heard the voice, she realized that it wasn't Shaune. Her smile dropped off of her face. She knew exactly who it was. "How did you get this number; and why are you calling me? In fact, that's not important. Scratch all that, don't call me anymore; and hell no to your reconciliations." She hung up the phone and then her cell phone rang seconds later. "Surely he couldn't have my cell phone number." She thought to herself as she picked it up. She looked around like as if someone would pop out. Then she picked up the cell phone; this time she didn't say anything. The voice spoke. "That's not nice of you to treat people that way. You don't have to talk to me now, but it felt good to see you again and I look forward to doing so shortly." The phone hung up and she put her phone down. Tory had a disturbing feeling in the pit of her stomach.

There was a knock at the door that scared her. She didn't answer, but the door knob turned and she just looked. As it continued to open she took a deep breath and braced herself for what was next. It was Louis Carrapellie coming through the door. "I was coming to see you one last time before you go off to Jamaica." He noticed that she had a disturbed look on her face; so he asked "Hey is everything okay?" As she composed herself, she said "Yeah, I'm fine. What's up?" "Lou you don't have to worry about me like that. Que`Shuane is not a lunatic. Please trust me." "You know, that little girl in Portugal's parents were just as skeptical as I am before she came up missing." Lou said, but Tory was not in the mood. "Would you please just trust me?" "It's not you don't trust. Can't you understand that this guy just came off of a divorce? He's clearly rebounding with you. Torianey, rebound equals relapse. You don't deserve that Bella. I'm sure that he would get over it if you told him not this time; maybe some other time." "I told him that I was going and I am. Despite his reasons, I'm going to have fun. I want to go." "Okay then, I'm going to do what all fathers do and say call me any time. When you land, call me. When you go to dinner, call me. When he raises his voice to you, you call me. Even when you're having fun, call me. I want to make sure that you're okay. I love you me` Corazon." He kissed her on her cheek and left. It was now time for Tory to leave and lock up the restaurant for the night. As she got into her truck, another one of those knots hit the pit of her stomach. When she pulled out of the parking lot she would normally go left to go home; but this time she had a feeling and turned right. She found herself driving to Shaunes' house. Tory had been battling her mind the whole ride. She had no real reason to show up; but she didn't want to go home. She had made a deal with herself, "If it takes too long to get in, he's probably not interested. Or maybe he's resting." Her car pulled up to the guard shack. As the guard walked up to her truck, she thought to herself, "It's almost 10pm; he's going to tell me to leave. I know it." Then the guard asked her, "Can I help you Ma'am?" "Hello, is Mr. Guadau in?" "Is he expecting you?" "No. I should have called. You know what? Forget it, I'll go home and call him Sorry to bother."

Then the guard stopped her and said, "Hang on one second. He might still be up." The guard went to call Shaune as Tory listen on. "Hello Mr. Guadau, I know it's late but I have a young lady here asking to see you. One second Sir; Ma'am what is your name?" The Shaune heard Torys' voice as she announced herself. "Torianey Heckstall." While Shaune sat in his den he heard Solomon his guard announced that it was Tory but he couldn't believe that she was actually at the gate. He turned his 50" flat screen on to the front gate to see that if in fact it was her. Sure enough, it was her truck outside the gate. With a burst of energy Shaune jumped up and said, "Let her through." Then Solomon said, "Sir, I think she's changing her mind." "Stop her please." As he hung up the phone he watched in suspense to see if she was going to go back home. Somehow, his guard convinced her into coming back. After he hung up the phone he left to go meet her at the front door. "Solomon, you are employed yet another day." He whispered to himself. As Tory pulled up to the doorway, Shaune jumped in and said, "You can park in the garage. I'll show you where it is." "I know it's late; and I remember the last conversation we had…" "You mean the conversation where you were still considering blowing me off?" "I can understand how this must feel to see me show up unannounced after what happened. This won't happen again." "Tory I don't mind you coming by my home. You're the one with the hang ups. You can park in here." As she pulled in to his garage, she saw all of his expensive vintage toys parked in their place. "Wow, I've never seen an Aston Martin in real life before." "One I bought for myself and the other two were gifts." Tory started to feel a little out of sought by the fact that Que'Shaune had such expensive taste and she was merely a basic woman. As he got out of the car, Tory stayed in. "Tory what's wrong, you can get out now." "My fear with you is you will see me like one of these cars. I'll be nice for the time being. Ultimately, you'll park me in the garage just when you find another vintage care you like." "That sounds crazy. First of all, I would never consider you or any other human life in comparison to a car. You of all I can't compare to anything because you are so unique and that's what attract me to you. These cars, they all do the same thing.

Go fast, go slow, stop and go. You on the other hand I consider you to be the driver and myself the car." As he opened the driver side door she asked "Why is that?" He said "Because you drive me crazy." He reached in to unbuckle her seat belt. He managed to cop another feel on her thigh and down her leg. But she didn't notice this time. "Have you had dinner yet?" He asked Tory. "No. Have you?" "No, but I'm sure we can find something in the kitchen to eat." As he helped her out of her car, she stopped again and said, "Shaune I like you a lot. When I'm with you I feel the best I've ever felt in a long time. The problem is I'm scared of those feelings. I don't want to loose control again. I'm scared." Then Shaune grabbed her hands and said, "And you don't think I am?" "Are you?" "Hell yes I'm scared. Hello, I'm the one who just got out of a marriage that lasted only 5 years; 2 if you count the length of time we spent together. So when I'm not kicking myself trying to find out what went wrong, I'm scratching my head trying to avoid the past. So I meet you and I try to keep it real. Some people tell me I'm being too real. Others are saying I'm not being real enough. I'm totally into you to the point I can't see straight." "I'm sorry if I'm questioning you too much. I just wanted to be sure." "You have every right to question your feelings. Relationships are tricky. Shouldn't the psychology major be telling me that?" "I'm still learning. I should have it together by the time I get my degree."

The two of them were in the kitchen looking for something to eat. Tory suggested cereal. They had discussed their plans for Jamaica. "For those two days I will be in and out of meetings. And what ever you need, the hotel will be instructed to attend to you. Are you okay with everything?" "I have to be." Tory huffed as she took her last spoonful of cereal. Then she sat back in her seat and yawned. "Oh my, someone is sleepy." "Yeah I am but I'm still not ready to go home." Tory was still freaked out by her caller; however to Que'Shaune, that meant that she was in fact into him. "Not that I'm forcing you to but you could spend the night that is if you're not going to get into trouble." He said sarcastically. "Well, Lou did blow a gasket when I told him I was seeing you." "Why would he?" "He's like a father to me and he's seen when I was in a relationship. And when it ended painfully, he was always there to help me pick up the pieces. So he was just showing his concern. You know like a father." He got up and took the dishes to the sink and started to walk away. Tory stopped him, "Uh, aren't you going to wash these?" "No. That's what I pay my staff for." Tory got up to go to the sink to wash the dishes. "Tory, why are you doing that?" "Its jus two bowls and two spoons; plus, dishes mean rodents and bugs." Shaune felt bad that he made himself look lazy. He walked over and helped her with the two bowls and spoons. After they finished, they walked up stairs to his room. Shaune figured he'd be a total gentleman this night. As she walked into the huge bedroom that would have made at least two of her bedroom and it was dressed in bachelor black lacquer. Shaune was happy that she didn't get the chance to witness that ugly floral bedroom that he had when he was married to Lisa. This time his bedroom had a sexier, manlier look. She thought his bedroom looked like something straight out of MTV cribs. He had a huge California King sized bed. "How does someone sleep in all this bed?" Tory asked. "I manage sometimes. But it does get pretty lonely most times." At the end of the bed was a storage stool. She started to take a seat on it until she became distracted by the sight of his walk-in closet. It looked like it could be another room it was so big. Tory walked in and looked around and saw all the suits in its color coded place. And his shoes were shined and all pairs were put together neatly. His tennis shoes looked like they were never even worn. In fact, the entire shoe rack looked like something out of a shoe store. Then she walked over to his collection of colognes and started to smell them. There was one in particular that she had come across. She liked it so much that she spritzed herself with it. Shaune watched her fool around in his closet like she was a 6yr old playing in her parents closets. Then he realized he had nothing for her to sleep comfortably in. "I don't have anything particular for you to sleep in. I have a robe that you could sleep in but that might not be comfortable." "No worries, I'll sleep in my underwear." The more he thought about it, he realized that he was not going to be able to sleep in the same bed with her while she slept in her underwear. No matter how big the bed was. "I guess I'll be sleeping down stairs tonight." Tory laughed and said, "Why?" As she started to undress, Shaune stood frozen in his tracks watching her undress. She started to slide out of her jeans to reveal her green multicolored boy short. Also what were making a special appearance were her luscious thighs. He had wiped away a bead of sweat that had formed on his forehead. Although he heard Tory speaking, he didn't hear a word she said. Then she started to take off her top to reveal a matching camisole to her underwear. At that point his upper lip started to sweat. He woke up and said "I'll be downstairs if you need me." As she stopped him, she asked, "Why?" He was so busy looking at her body that he couldn't answer her with eye contact. Then he started to stutter his answer to her. "I… I… can't… I can't see you like that and not want you. It doesn't work that way." "But we've had sex before; twice to be exact." "That's not the point. I'm going to always want to have sex with you. I'm trying desperately to be a gentleman. God Torianey, I'm trying to refrain from throwing you on the bed and…" She took a couple of steps towards Shaune but before she could reach him, he turned, grabbed his pajamas off the bed and sped out of the room. Then headed to the den where he could recuperate.

The next morning, Marta walked into the den to see Que'Shaune sleeping uncomfortably on his chase. She woke him up and asked, "Why are you sleeping down here?" "Tory's sleeping in my bed." He answered with sleep still in his voice. Marta was perplexed. "Why aren't you in your bed with her?" Sitting up in the chase, he answered "I'm trying to show her that I'm not trying to be with her for just sex. I really do like her for more then that." Marta looked at him with a surprised look and said, "Good for you son. I'm proud of you." As he smiled with his pride before him, he realized that he needed to go and wake her up to prepare her for breakfast. When he got to the top of the steps he prayed that she was at least awake and dressed. He didn't think that he could stand the site of her sleeping in her underwear in his bed. As he walked to the door, the thought had already aroused him. He even started to get a slight rise in his pants. He knocked on the door, but there was no answer. Then he opened the door and he saw her sleeping in his bed on her back and she was undressed. "Torianey?" He whispered trying to wake her gently as he walked towards her side of the bed. He felt his rise in his pants get a little higher. He sat down on the bed next to her. "Torianey?" He whispered again. But she was unresponsive. He kissed her on the lips and continued his whisper of her name. "Tory?" Then he moved down to her chest and lightly kissed her there. He moved his lips down to her stomach that was peaking out of her camisole. "Torianey?" He whispered one last time before he moved down to his favorite part of her. At this point Shaune had a full blown hard on and it was only getting harder. He looked down at her thighs and his mouth started to water. He lost control of his mind and gravitated to her thighs immediately. He started kissing on her thighs. He started with the right one then he went to the left one. He was going in hard on her; so hard that his penis was throbbing like it wanted to bust out of his sweats. He started moaning and loosing control of his impulses to the point that he bit into her; again. And of course it startled her scaring her up out of her sound sleep. She screamed and yelled, "Why did you bite me?" In a confused and stuttered voice, he answered "What! Huh? Uh, because I'm a sick man and I can't help myself." "I see that." She said as she rose up to sit up. "I was calling you but you wouldn't wake up so I figured I'd take advantage of you while you were sleeping." Tory laughed and said, "You're the one who took off running last night. Now you want to sneak attack. I can't figure you out Guadau." "Are you staying for breakfast?" "No, I have to get ready for our trip next week. I have only three days to prepare." She said as she started to get dress. He wanted to convince her to stay but he knew that he had to peel his emotions back a bit. Tory saw that Shaune was not happy with her answer or her leaving. She came over and sat next to him to explain how she really felt. "Please try and understand that I am not trying to control this relationship. I just don't want us to fall too hard too fast and by the time we come up for air, we wouldn't have had enough time to have fun. I'm asking for us to not see each other so much. To give us some room to breathe; room to miss each other." Shaune didn't want to hear that; in fact, it upset him to the point where he didn't want to talk anymore. Then Marta knocked on the door. "Que Shaune, your company is down stair in the den waiting for you." Then he left the room without saying anything. Tory felt bad, but she knew it was all for the best. When she was done, she decided to leave without saying goodbye to him. She figured she would call him and deal with him later.

Chapter 8
Can't Get You Out of My System

Shaune and Mark were sitting in the den that morning. Marcus decided to pour himself a glass of single malt scotch. "Isn't it a little early to be drinking?" Shaune asked. "It's 5pm somewhere. So tell me what happen with your new Philly and what has she been up to lately?" "I can't figure her out. Most women I meet know who I am and I don't have this hard of a time trying to spend with them. Hell, I can't even get rid of them most of the time. But Tory, she's different. I can't figure her out. She suggested that we don't see each other again till the trip to Jamaica in two days." Mark gave Shaune a nonchalant look and asked, "And this bothers you because?" "Because I like her; she makes me happy and I can't remember the last time I felt this way." "Really Shaune? This girl is no match for you. She is clearly beneath your standards. Why on Gods green earth would you care how she feels about you? You can have any woman; rich, poor, beggar, thief. What does this girl have that makes you so crazy for her?" Shaune sat and pondered Marcus' words. He realized what the problem was. "That's it, I can't have her. She won't let me have her. The less she gives me, the more I'm drawn to want her." "Let her go man. We need to hit Cancun and party it up biblical style. We need to find some women who actually appreciate us and get laid with fewer headaches. What do you say brother?" "Sorry Mark, I'm going away to Jamaica and I'm taking Tory with me." "But I can still link up with you there though. I know that you won't be conducting business the whole week?" "I mean, we could link up, just that Tory will be there as well." "You know I was trying to bypass the fact that although there are plenty of gorgeous women ready to drop their drawl at your command, but you're still willing to bring your charity work along. Tell her to stay home and let grown folks party." Mark didn't understand that the trip was originally designed for Que`Shaune and Tory; that it was Mark that was the inconvenience to the crowd. But Shaune just wanted to please both sides as he normally did. Shaune was never a person to tell anyone that they were crowding his space. He was always a people pleaser. "Look, I would be more then happy for you to join us as long as my new "Philly" comes along." "Fine at your leisure. But just in case you decide to come back to reality, I'll bring along a few of our usuals." "That won't be necessary. I'll have all I require."

When Tory got home, her guilt was bothering her. She had wanted to call Shaune and talk with him to apologize for how she made him feel. "Maybe the conversation should have gone differently." She thought to herself. The problem was that she had found herself getting too close too soon. He would say all the right things and do all the right things that would make her want him more but, she couldn't afford to sink herself to the point where he knew he would have her and then he would drop her like what had happened in the past. As she sat on her couch, she reminisced about last night. How he was a perfect gentleman to not try to sleep with her as much as he wanted to; even though she wanted him just as bad. While she sat there, she had realized that she started to miss him. She missed his presence, his reassuring smile. Then she shook her head and said, "Where am I going with this. He's probably not emotionally available for someone like me. No man is ever emotionally available for a woman; only themselves." She also knew that he had a business to run and when it came down to the business, she was no match. "$300 billion, of course he would never commit himself to me." The more she thought about it, the more she knew she was doing the right thing. Tory had one last class she needed to hit before she would leave for her vacation. So she headed for her shower to prepare herself. When she got out of the shower, she figured she had wanted to have Ms. Sexy make an appearance for the day. She pulled out her beige pencil skirt and matched it with her red silk blouse. She figured since she was in a sexy mood, she would wear her red matching underwear and camisole. And for her shoes, she wanted to wear her red suede, open back, 3inch mules. Although they were high, they were comfortable and sexy. After she was done applying her makeup, she gave herself the once over and said to herself in the mirror "Damn you sexy!!!" And she was out the door.

Marta walked into the den to see Shaune sitting all by himself. She noticed that he looked unusually lonely. She figured she would give him some company. "Are you okay son?" He woke up out of his daze and said, "I'm fine." He tried to recover himself by picking up his pen to write but he couldn't remember where he left off. Then Marta sat in front of him and said, "Let me guess, Ms. Torianey is the reason." "The reason for what?" "The reason you can't focus; the reason you can't remember what you were doing." "Is it that obvious?" "Extremely; what is it about her that makes you so distracted?" "I can't understand her, the less she gives me the more I want of her. Why can't I just stop myself? Does that make me a sick person?" Marta giggled and said, "It's simple; It's the old cat and mouse game you two are playing. Women love to be chased and men love to chase. See, you have never had the experience of chasing a woman before. All your life you have had it so easy that no one has dared to challenge you. Now you meet Ms. Torianey, and she had become quite the challenge for you; and it frustrates you." "Yes it does. So how do I beat her at her own game?" "You have to ware her down. Play until she has no more game to play." "What if it takes forever?" "It won't; she's a smart woman and she knows a good man. The two of you are new to each other so this might take some time. Just be patient with her. She'll come around. Every woman has their breaking point." Marta wanted to dig deeper with Shaune because she felt there was more to the game then just the chase. "What are your intentions for her?" She asked. "What do you mean what are my intentions?" "What do you plan to do when the chase is over?" "I haven't thought that far Marta. I just wanted to make her my girlfriend. Is there something else I need to know?" "I don't know Shaune when you talk about her you start to look like a man in love." Feeling an embarrassingly laughter came on he said, "What... No... Wait, I'm not in love with anybody. I just like the woman that's all. I never spoke of love... Why does everyone think I'm in love?" Marta grabbed his face and said, "Don't fear love when it strikes your heart. You embrace it, show it and keep it. I'm not saying that this is where you are now, I'm saying that you are getting close to it." After having that conversation with her he knew he had wanted to see Tory that night. While he was in the shower, he had gone back and forth with his thoughts of whether or not he was going to see her because he knew that she just might protest. Ultimately, he came upon a thought that he just wouldn't care if she would or not.

While Tory was in her English class, she kept checking her cell phone to see if Shaune would have left a message. She was trying to keep her notes and focus on her phone at the same time. She realized that she would have to focus more on her class work if she was going to pass her test. She put her cell phone back in her purse and continued to listen in on to her studies. Finally, the bell rang for class to be over. Tory was relieved and the first thing she did was grab her cell phone to see if Que`Shaune had left a message for her. In frustration, Tory murmured "Umhhh! He won't call me." Then she calmed herself and said, "So what he won't call, he's just mad that I didn't have breakfast with him. Just calm down and go home." She took a deep breath and headed out the building to her car.

Que`Shaune got out of the shower and went into his closet. He figured he just put on something simple. Today was the day they would take their conversation to a deeper lever. He thought that if he was going to play the cat and mouse game, then he was going to chase her until she had no place to run but in his arms. He pulled out another one of his polo shirts; this time he wore a light blue one with a pair of straight leg jeans. For his footwear, he wore his Air force ones. As he looked himself in the mirror, he looked over at his collection of colognes. He had remembered the one that she had sprayed on herself when she was playing around in his closet. So, he figured that since she liked that one that it would make for a nice touch to the night. Shaune knew that when it came down to deep conversations with Tory, it was anything but easy. He had anticipated some kind of fight from her; he just hoped that it didn't become physical. After he gave himself the once over, he headed for the door.

When Tory got home, she looked at the mirror in her living room and said to herself "Time to put Ms. Sexy away. No one appreciates a sexy woman but if I had worn sweats and a tee shirt, I would probably catch Sundays finest." She dropped her books and ran upstairs to the shower. When she jumped out of the shower she turned the radio on to her favorite radio station. She walked over to her computer to turn it on. Then she put on her pajama sweats with her tee shirt. She threw her granny silk cap on her head and danced down the stairs to get something to eat. As she walked towards the kitchen, the door bell rang. She walked to the window to see who it was and she saw Que`Shaune standing at her door. She screeched in horror and hid behind the door. She knew she looked like hell but he didn't need to see that. Then she yelled, "What are you doing here?" "I wanted to talk to you. Can you open the door?" "You know you could have came at least 10mins ago and you would have seen "Ms. Sexy" but no; you show up now." "Ms. Who?" He yelled in confusion. "Never mind let me go upstairs and get dressed." "That won't be necessary Tory. I just want to talk that's all." Then she opened the door. She was so embarrassed at how she must have looked that she started to turn red. She had opened the door wide enough for him to walk through, but he didn't want to walk in. "Is everything alright? You don't want to come in?" "Actually, I wanted to know if you would join me on a night out?" "Let me go upstairs and get dressed." Shaune grabbed Torys' hand and said, "You look fine. You don't have to change at all." Tory looked at Shaune with a suspicious look and asked, "You didn't come here to kill me did you?" He laughed and said "I would like to take you for a ride and maybe we could talk a bit." "Can I at least get a pair of shoes and my robe?" "Sure, I don't want you to get sick." Tory ran upstairs to throw on her robe and put on her cozy clogs. Then she grabbed her keys and left. He drove them to the nearby pond. Tory asked, "Why are we here?" "This is where I come to reflect. Sometimes when I'm having a bad day, I come here and try to relax; maybe even sought some things out." "So what did you want to talk about?" Shaune got out of the car and got in the back seat. Then he said "Join me please." She got out joining him at the back seat. "Wait I get, we've moved from planes to cars now." "No Ma'am I didn't have any intentions on sleeping with you; at least not this night." "So if you didn't plan on killing me or sexing me, then why am I here at the pond?" "I wanted us to be alone so that I can clear up some things about us. I want to understand why do you feel the need to distance our relationship?" "It's like I said I don't want us grow bored with each other." "What makes you think that would happen?" "I'm not sure that it would happen; look why are you asking me these questions?" She asked feeling uncomfortable. "Tory, I want to see more of you not less. I want to get to know you and I can't get to know you if I see less of you." "What do you want to know Shaune?" she asked in an aggravated tone. "I want to know who scared you so bad that you need to run from me?" "I just met you and I didn't intend on getting this far with you." "So now we're here. Now what?" "Wait a minute; didn't you just get out of a marriage?" "Yes I did." "So what makes you so ready for any kind of relationship with anyone let alone me?" "You're right; how could I want to be in a relationship after just coming out of one. The question is, was I ever really in one? My ex-wife and I were married for 5yrs and for 3 of them we stopped being intimate. My ex-wife never loved me and I never really loved her. We were opportunities for each other. I for her was an opportunity to branch into the high-life of society. She for me was an opportunity at marriage. Yes it sounds stupid that we played these games with each others lives. I assumed that she would become the closest thing to love that I would find. But then I meet you; and you were this woman that challenged me from all facets of my life; from my terrible kissing to my poor attitude. Most women, because of who I am, would always give in to me; including my ex-wife. Before I met you, I didn't think I could feel as happy as I do now. I enjoy hearing you laugh; even when you get pissed off with me I still enjoy your energy." Tory saw that Shaune was getting emotional about what he was saying; she reach out her hand to grab his. Then he finished. "I guess this is me feeling in the dark again huh. I like what I found this time. What I want to know is how do I get into you? How do I tap into that loving side of you? I promise if you let me in, I won't let you down." Shaune was literally laying himself bare for her to see. She didn't know that she had that much power to make a pretty much, jaded man come alive. Not to mention that some of the stuff she was feeling about him he was feeling about her. As she grabbed both his hands she said, "Hello, my name is Torianey Heckstall. I moved to South Carolina 5yrs ago. I was originally born in NYC, Harlem to be exact. I have no children, never been married; in fact, my last relationship was painful and unforgiving. So you ask what makes me so scared to open up to you. There's nothing worse then being in love alone; or at least finding out that you were all alone in the first place. I was totally in love with a man that decided to stop loving me because he wanted to be with another mans wife. Do you have any idea how humiliating it is to hear from the man you love that he never intended on marrying you? So every time I meet a man who tries to form a relationship with me, I try to deflect him from getting too close. I'm a plan B type of person. I plan around everything I do just so I don't get caught off guard. And that day when he told me he never wanted to marry me, my heart was so broken. I just wanted to die. I couldn't plan B anyway to recover my heart. I couldn't shake the misery that I felt everyday trying to get out of bed to go to work, to go to school. I had to deal with it." Torys' eyes started to well up as her emotions got the best of her. As she wiped her tears from her eyes, she finished. "So, you say you see something of a loving side in me. Well my friend I think this relationship just started out as a lie; because quite frankly, I don't have anymore love left in me to give." Shaune drew closer to hold her. Surely he knew she had some damages to work out; he didn't realize she was that far gone. Tory tried to recover herself by wiping her tears away. "I know I must look pretty foolish crying like I am." As he helped her wipe her tears away, he replied, "You don't look foolish at all. You look like a woman who had a chunk of her life taken away from her and you didn't deserve that at all." "Thank you." She said choking back more tears. Then Shaune came up with an idea. "Seeing that I have this problem of feeling in the dark to find love and you on the other hand have a hard time sharing. So what I propose is why we don't combine our efforts to feel in the dark together and embrace each others loving side." Tory didn't know what to think of his proposal, but it sure did sound interesting coming from Shaune. "I guess it's a deal." "Can we kiss on it?" As she shook her head yes, she went in to give him a deep, passionate kiss. The time was 10pm when Shaune pulled up to Torys' driveway. He just turned to her and looked at her. "What are you looking at?" "You in that multicolored set you were sleeping in my bed on." "Why?" He drew in close to her face and whispered, "Because I'm a sick man and I can't help myself." As they both giggled, he leaned in closer to kiss her. Then he said, "I'll be calling you to set up the time for the limo to pick you up. Goodnight." Tory took one last gaze into his eyes and replied, "Goodnight." She jumped out of his truck to head for her door. As Shaune watched her leave, he had that sinking feeling of missing her again. Tory turned to look back at Shaune and had the same sinking feeling when it all came to a screeching halt. She had noticed a note taped to her door. She pulled it off and read it.

"I came by to talk. I've missed you so much and if you would just give me a chance to explain, you

might understand. I wish you wouldn't avoid me like you do. You know how I get when you play the silent treatment with me. You can't forever.

See you soon.
Your one and only

After reading the letter, Torys' feelings of missing Shaune changed to feelings of fear. She put her hand over her mouth in disbelief at the fact that he found out where she lived. Shaune saw the discomfort in her face and honked his horn to get her attention. She looked up and realized that he was still parked there. She quickly waved at him and ran in her house. Perhaps this was some sick mind game he was playing with her. If he knew where she was, why did he wait so long to contact her? She put both locks and the chain as well as activated the home alarm system.

Chapter 9
A Much Needed Vacation?

Tory was packing for her week long vacation in Jamaica with Que`Shaune. It was a much needed vacation. She had never been to Jamaica before so she'd thought the best time to go would be with a lover. "They say Jamaica is for lovers." She giggled to herself. Shaune had told her to pack light because he had a couple of surprises for her and she loved surprises; at least the good ones. She made sure she had called Louis to inform him that she had all appointments booked and confirmed. That even if something went wrong, she had a backup plan in tow. Tory had wanted so badly for this trip to go off without a hitch. She knew an opportunity like this doesn't come alone this easy. The limo driver had pulled up and called her on her cell to inform her that he was there to pick her up. She excitedly ran down the stairs and out the door to the limousine. When she got there she was expecting to see Que`Shaune, but he was not in the car. "Where's Que`Shaune?" She asked in disappointment. "Mr. Guadau is at the airstrip waiting on you Ma'am." The driver said as he opened the door for her. After he secured her in the limo, he put her bags in the trunk.

The limo pulled up to the airstrip in front of the Guadau family jet. The jet was all black with his last name in big red letters. As Tory got out of the car, she said out loud, "If you want to make an impression, just go and get a big, black jet with your name in big, bold letters." Then she heard a voice behind her, "So are you impressed?" She turned around and saw Que`Shaune walking towards her. He was dressed casual but he looked sexy. He was wearing a pair of light blue, faded jeans and a vintage Ed Hardy shirt with a pair of sun shades on. As he walked up to her, she put her arms around his neck and said, "Largely impressed." "I know how you like things done small but I'm sorry to say G5's don't come that small." "I'll make an exception." As they boarded the plane, they were met by Gregory, Shaunes assistant. Greg passed Shaune the phone and said, "Shaune, you might want to take this." Shaune took the phone from Greg and asked, "Greg can you take Tory to the rear of the plane so she could get comfortable. And tell the pilot we'll be ready to leave in 5." "Is everything alright?" Shaune turned and gave her a quick kiss on the lips and replied, "Everything is fine; I'll join you after this call." Tory followed Greg to the rear of the plane. As she walked in, she couldn't help but feel like she was a kid in a candy store. The jet was hooked. It had a fully stocked bar with lounge style white leather love seats that faced each other. Across from there was two executive style leather white swivel chairs with tables made of granite marble that sat in front of them. The entire interior of the plane was a soft color of beige that was pleasing to the eye. Tory sat at one of the booths so she could just take it all in. Greg sat across from her and saw how in awe she was. "Shaune said this kind of stuff didn't impress you." He told her. "When it's largely exploited and over done, yes I feel less impressed. However, I'm equally not opposed to it. Sometimes we deserve the finer things in life to reward ourselves. That's why we all work hard. The little things in life let us know that there is a much bigger purpose in our lives." "You know I can see how Shaune could be into you. Most women don't say the things you do. Plus, what ever it is you're doing is making him happy." "What does his happiness do for you?" Tory Asked. Greg got out of his seat and sat closer to Tory. Then he whispered to her, "See, usually when I'm taking these trips with Shaune I'm alone with him. However, he suggested I bring my wife along. Do you know how many times he suggested that I bring my wife along?" He paused to ponder again and then he finished, "Never. Usually I fly to France, Germany, England, etc, etc. Never in the 6yrs have I had the privilege to breathe without having to chase Shaune. I love my job; please understand that. But when he's not happy; when Que'Shaune Guadau is not in good spirits, he can be worst then the Kremlin. So between you and me, you're my new BFF. As far as Shaune is concerned as long as you're happy he's happy and that means I can stay married and happy." Shaune walked up and sat across from the two of them. He tossed the phone back to Greg and said, "I took care of the problem." "Great, if you don't mind I have to go to my wife now. I can feel her calling me. Are we all set to leave?" "Yeah, we've been ready since Tory got here." Greg looked at Tory to confirm what he had been saying all along. Then he left. Shaune looked back at Tory and asked, "What was that all about?" "I'm not sure but my guess is once he gets to his wife, he'll be just fine." "Would you like a drink?" "I would love one. What would you suggest?" Shaune started to think about what drink would be best suited for her; then he remembered the drink that his mixologist asked him to try last time. "Can I surprise you with something?" "You know I love surprises." He ran to the bar to chat with his bartender. "Hey Reuben, remember that drink you asked me to try last time?" "The Forever Passion; yeah why?" "Do you think you could whip some of that up again for me and my lady?" As he reached into the fridge, Reuben replied, "Actually, I have some already made." He pulled out two glasses and poured the neon purple liquored drink for him. Then he said, "Now you have to be careful. This drink is strong and it tends to have a lasting affect on people. I remember last Saturday I made this at a private pool party. Man, everybody was hooking up with everybody. By the time that party was over, I think I saw the family dog leaving with someone." As he took the drinks, Shaune replied, "Thanks for the warning." He came back over to Tory with the glowing drinks in tow. "This is called "The Forever Passion.""

He gave her one and started to make a toast but Tory stopped him. "Do you mind if I make a toast?" "Not at all; go ahead." Then she started. "I toast this drink to two people who are finding each other and may they have fun for as long as it lasts. Cheers!" As they joined glasses to the toast, Shaune joked, "And may their relationship shine as bright as these drinks. I often wonder what he puts in this to make it glow like it does." Tory took a sip of her drink. She thought it tasted really good. It had a hint of cherry flavor with a hint of lemon. In fact, it didn't even taste like it had liquor in it at all. "You might want to be careful. This drink is pretty strong." "You don't think it tastes really good." "Yeah I do but Reuben said that it can sneak up on you." "Do you think I can have another one?" "Sure let me go get it." Shaune had to admit that the drinks were good and even he wanted some more. As he went back over to the bar, he asked, "We both loved that drink. Is it possible I could get the pitcher?" "Oh, okay somebody's getting lucky tonight." As he gave him the pitcher, he finished. "Remember, it's strong now." 15min later, they were stoned out of their minds. Not to mention the pitcher was half empty. "OMG! We drank most of this stuff." Tory said. "No worries. At least we're not driving the plane." Tory busted into laughter and said, "That would be tragic." Then they both laughed. "Do you think we could listen to some music?" Shaune looked at his wait staff and asked, "Do you think you could turn on some music for us?" "Is there anything in particular you would like?" "How about something slow and hip." Then he asked Tory to dance. Tory laughed at Shaune and said "You sound like Humphrey Bogart." "Do you want to dance or not?" "I would love to… Bogart." She snickered out. As they started to dance, they started to kiss. Then things got progressively worse. The kissing moved to touching; then eventually, promiscuous touching. The Bartender and the wait staff all looked on at the two of them acting out. One of the waiters coughed to see if he could get their attention. But it didn't work. It was the Bartender who thought that he should get Greg to squelch the situation. When he got over to the side where Greg and his wife were, he said "Mr. Duvain, Mr. Guadau needs your help." "What's the matter?" "Well for the record sir, I told him to be careful. That my drinks tend to be strong…" "And he didn't listen." Greg said. "Let's just say the two of them are about to get into something." Greg excused himself from his wife and went to check on Shaune and Tory. When he got there, he was glad he did. They were pretty much undressing each other. Greg yelled "Hey! Hey! Hey!" He grabbed Shaune and whispered "Don't you know you got grown folks up in here watching this mess." Shaune, drunk and embarrassed as he was managed to wave his hands and yelled, "SORRY!" Greg grabbed him and made him sit away from Tory then he said to the Bartender, "If you give anything to these two for the rest of the night, it better be water. Speaking of water; I want both of them to have glasses now. Shaune did you eat anything yet?" "No we didn't eat at all." "Wait staff; get them something light like a salad or biscotti and cheese. Water only no more liquor. You do realize you have a meeting in the morning?" "I guess I had forgotten. I just wanted us to have a good time." "After these two days, you can have all the fun you'd like. For now, you need to stay focused. I'll keep this quiet as kept because it was just the two of you and it was on the jet. In the mean time, just focus on recovering and drink as much water as you need to. I'll check on you later." "Thanks Gregory. I preciate it."

A couple of hours later, the jet had landed. Tory and Shaune were passed out like they had been partying at the club all night; and it was the 5am hour. Greg came to wake the two of them up to run some interference. "Here's how it's going to go down, when the limo pulls up to the hotel, you and I are going to go in through the front entrance while Tory and my wife goes in through the back. That way no one will know about who you came to Jamaica with." The plan went off without a hitch. Greg had booked the last two penthouse suites for the four of them. Although the day was still early, Shaune had to look over his facts and figures for the meeting the next day. Tory was in the bedroom scrolling through the channels on the television. She could hear on the patio that it had started to rain outside. She got up to go onto the terrace to see if she could see the beach, but the night's sky had darkened. The rain was heavy so she went back inside. Then she had an idea. She went into the room where Shaune was and grabbed him by the hand and led him into the bedroom. "I can't play right now but if you give me another hour I'll be happy to give you my full attention." Without words, she continued pulling his hand. She led him onto the balcony. Although he stopped at the door, she continued on. "Tory, baby, it's raining out." "Come out with me. I have a surprise for you now." "What kind of surprise?" "Come out and see." As Shaune stepped outside, he could feel the rain beating hard. But he continued on. When he reached her, she started to kiss his lips. Then she went to his neck. Then she stopped and looked at Shaune and said, "I know you're busy but I just want to give you something to make you remember me while you're HARD at work tomorrow." Then she got on her knees and proceeded to open his pants. Suddenly the rain pelting down on him didn't feel so bad anymore. When she got his pants open she pulled them down to his ankles. Then she pulled his underwear down. Tory could see that he was ready for whatever she had in mind. She took his hard member into her hand and gently started to stroke it. She watched his every emotion. Shaune started to breathe heavily with each stroke. She licked the tip of his head with her tongue. Then she licked from the bottom of his penis to the tip and engulfed the entire thing in her mouth. "Oh Tory!" He breathed as she proceeded to go faster and faster. Every time he looked down he could see the rain running down from his penis and into Torys' mouth, and he could feel her slurping it up; it made him more and more aroused. She then took his member back into her hands and started to lick his sac. He felt his stomach jump he could feel her sucking all over his testicles. "Oh my love, I'm ready to cum for you." He said as he struggled to get the words out of his mouth. She went faster and faster until he shot his entire load in her mouth. Although Tory hated the taste, she found the sounds of his moans and the throb of his penis letting off equally intoxicating. She let go of him when she felt him getting soft. He took two steps back and fell to his knees; then collapsed in her arms and whispered in her ear, "Torianey what am I supposed to do with you? That was fucking amazing."

It was 8am the next day when Tory woke up and realized that Shaune was gone. She thought he might be in the shower until she looked over on the pillow and saw a black rose with a letter attached. She opened it and it read:

> **"Good morning Mi Cheri Amour. I so enjoyed your surprise last night. I'm sorry I had to leave you so soon. I'll be in these forsaken meetings all day thinking about everything you did last night as well as that sexy body of yours. I hope I can get through it all. I'll give you a call when I can come up for air. However, tonight when I'm done, I want you to look sexy for me for dinner. If you would take a look over in the dresser on my side, there is a pouch..."** there's money in it. I hope this is enough for you to find something in the area..."

Tory had yelled "Is he serious? There has to be at least five grand here. I can find a wardrobe for two years here." Then she finished reading the letter.

> **"If not, then we'll figure something out. After dinner, we're going to meet with my friend at this exclusive club. I can't wait to see you tonight.**
>
> **Yours always,**
> **Que`Shaune**

Tory looked at the pouch of money and screamed, "DAMN FIVE GRAND TO SPEND!!! How do I spend it?" She knew today was going to be a good day.

Tory went from shop to shop trying to find something that was appropriate for tonight. She had been having a hard time trying to something that was sexy without over doing it. She ended up finding a spot that may have been on the level. She tried on a several different outfits. Finally, she came up with a pair of Tru Religion jeans that fit her perfect. Then she found a halter blouse that would cater to her unusually smaller upper frame. The out fit looked nice in her eyes; but did it pass the test for, Que`Shaunes standards. "We'll just have to see." She thought to herself.

It was 8pm and Tory was at the bar in her new outfit. She liked it and apparently someone else did too. The Bartender gave her a drink and said, "This is complements of the gentleman over there." As he pointed across the bar, she saw a handsome dark-skinned brother with dread locks and a perfect set of teeth that made his smile even more handsome. She smiled and waved at him while mimicking the words, "Thank you." to him. When she started to pick up her drink and toast it to him, a hand picked up the drink instead. Tory looked up and saw it was Que`Shaune. After he drank it, he yelled to the brother "UMM! Lemon drop; I love these." Shaune waved over to the brother while mimicking the words "THANK YOU!" to him but he was not by any means amused with Shaune. Then he re-ordered the drink back to the gentleman. "Shaune that was so rude of you." "He should know better then to try and pick up my lady. I play for keeps." Then he tongue kissed her deep and looked over to the brother who was ice grilling him. Throughout the night she waited for him to give a comment on how she looked but he never did. They seem to talk about everything else but her outfit was never one of them. Then she thought to herself, "At least he didn't tell me I looked terrible." When they were finished with dinner, it was time to go to the club. All was going well until he asked her, "Would you like to go back to the hotel to change?" She looked at her clothes and started to feel self-conscious. "What's wrong with what I'm wearing? I thought…" Shaune cut in and said, "Nothing I thought…" Then she cut in and said, "Do I look terrible?" "No, you look great. I just thought you had something else to wear." He had tried to clean it up but Tory was convinced that she was not fit for his standards. "I don't want to go now. I should have brought something else. I'm so sorry Shaune, I…" Then he had to cut her off again and stop her from imploding. "Tory, stop it. You look great. I was asking you just in case you had something else you wanted to wear. Most women tend to buy an extra outfit for other functions. For the life of me I don't understand why they do but, I was just checking. In my eyes, you're perfect. Now step away from the ledge." He laughed as he grabbed her hands. Tory smiled and said, "Sorry Shaune, I was feeling a bit self-conscious. I need to be honest sometimes when I'm with you I don't know if I can live up to your standards." "What standards are those?" "High." Then he asked her, "What makes you think I have high standards. I mean I don't settle for less but what gave you the impression that you had to live up to anything by me?" "You know what, never mind I was just in a moment." Shaune responded with anger in his voice. "Well now you have me in the moment so explain what you meant." "Look if you want an answer, then all I was saying is that you have so much more then I do and I don't know if I can live up to that." "Are we in some sought of competition? I'm not getting what you're saying." Feeling frustrated, she said, "Sometimes I feel like the charity case around you." Tory calmed herself because people started to look on. "I feel like I'm this "Make a wish" kid and you are the person that makes wishes comes true. You have this expensive taste for all the lavish things. For God sake, you were married to the runner up to Ms. America; now you have… me." Tory felt a ting of embarrassment come over her as her truth managed to slip itself out in a heated debate over her clothing. "Before I try to change your mind, let me just request one thing from you; don't judge me. It's hard enough being me and living with myself without the woman I care for passing judgment on me. The last thing I would want is this. With that having been said, I admit I do enjoy the finer things in life at times. A harsh lesson in life taught me that the finer things aren't always monetary. Sometimes the finer things can come in a human form and doesn't have half as much, but tends enjoys the life that God gave them. Did it ever occur to you that I don't think I can live up to your standards? You are the woman who doesn't mind the little things and until this moment I thought wasn't intimidated by anything. I'm not going to apologize for having money; and there isn't one person who would in this world. And no, I'm not going to give up my love for fancy cars and suits. My motto is work hard, play harder; that's what I do. I'm not going to make any excuses for wanting to enjoy my life. I would like you to share in it but if you want to avoid it then that's your prerogative. Look, it's getting late and we need to get to the club where my friend is. If you're still feeling a certain way, then we can talk about it later agree?" "Agreed." Tory whispered.

They had arrived at the exclusive club where Shaune was meeting Marcus. They made their way to the VIP section where their party would be. Shaune had announced himself and his plus one for Marcus Swain. The matron went to get Marcus but came back and yelled, "Mr. Que`Shaune Guadau plus one for Mr. Marcus Swain step this way please." As they approached the door, Tory said to herself, "Who did he say?" Shaune led Tory by the hand through the crowd of people. He turned to her and said, "I want you to meet my best friend. We've been friends for a long time. He's a little arrogant for your taste, but he's an okay guy." Shaune started to look around. As he turned around he saw Mark walking towards them. "Here he is. Tory I want to introduce to you my good friend Marcus Swain. Marcus, this is my girlfriend Torianey Heckstall." When Tory turned, she couldn't believe her eyes as well as her ears. She looked at him and tightened her grip on Shaunes' hand. She almost looked like a 6yro trying to avoid a stranger. Shaune was oblivious to her avoidance of Marcus. As he gave Marcus dap, he said, "Sorry we're late. We had dinner and drinks." Marcus took Torys' hand and kissed it then he said, "Its okay. I'm charmed to meet your lady. However, you seem familiar." Tory shook her head and pleaded inside. "He wouldn't." Then he said, "Oh, I know." Then she exhibited a look of fear. "Carrapellies!" Shaune said, "She's actually the Assistant Manager." Tory sighed in relief that he didn't say anything of how they knew each other. "Either way I feel as though we met before. Shaune speaks of you constantly; so much I felt I had to meet you. Trust me; his words do you no justice. You're far more striking in person." "Thank you." She responded without eye contact. As they sat at the booths,

Tory sat so close to Shaune she almost sat in his lap. Marcus brought along a one of his escorts who was half dressed and Tory noticed that every time she got up, Shaune would sneak a peak at her. In fact, she realized that Shaune didn't pay her any attention when she stepped on the scene. "This is Candy, my date." "I'm going to get me a drink. Would you like one?" She asked Shaune. "I'll go get us some drinks." When he got up to go to the bar, Marcus whispered in his date's ear. Candy went over to the bar and stood next to Shaune. Tory could see that she was starting up a conversation with Shaune but who she didn't see was Marcus sliding next to her in Shaunes' seat. Then he said, "You see that woman standing next to your man? See, that's what he's looking for. That's the caliber of woman he wants. Not you. Do you honestly believe that what you two have is something special?" As he started to laugh he finished. "I think not. I know the kind of woman you are and he's not looking for cookie cutter, Holly Hobby to play house with. Your best bet is to quit while you're ahead or he will hurt your feelings." Then he moved closer to her ear and whispered. "Worse then I did." Tory felt like she wanted to kill Marcus. If she had a knife, she would bury it in his skull. Deep down inside she actually sided with the devils advocate. She thought to herself, "Why else would a billionaire want to be around someone as common me?" When Candy and Shaune came back, Marcus asked Candy to dance with him. "I brought you a lemon drop. That's the least I could do for drinking yours earlier." Shaune said while laughing. But he noticed that she wasn't responsive to his joke. "Tory?" She blinked and realized that he was talking to her. Although she was looking at him, she couldn't bring herself to keep eye contact. As she looked over at Marcus dancing with his date, he was looking back at her with his evil eyes driving the knife deeper into her heart. Shaune managed to get her attention. "Tory? Where did you go?" As she woke up, she said "Huh? No where. I'm here with you. I'm sorry, I got distracted." "Would you like to dance?" "I would love to." The music was nice and slow and Tory was glad, because she wanted to bury her face in Shaunes' chest to hide her emotions.

It was 1am when they got back to the penthouse. As Shaune closed the door behind her, he asked "Is everything alright?" "I'm fine." "Don't lie to me Tory. I may not know you one hundred percent but I know you well enough to know when something is bothering you. If you didn't like the club you could have said something and we could have gone somewhere else..." She cut him off and yelled, "It wasn't the fucking club Shaune. Please drop it!" "So what was it? Talk to me please." She took a seat on the couch while Shaune sat on the ottoman in front of her. "Do you think I dress sexy enough?" Shaune looked at her for a second and then he busted into a hard, hard laugh. So hard it insulted Tory to tears. She jumped up and left him in the front room by himself. She went into the bathroom, locked the door and cried her eyes out. All he could do was let her cry it out. Finally, she emerged from the bathroom with her robe on. Shaune stood at the end of the bed waiting for her to come out. Although he was tired, he was mostly concerned and felt terrible for making her cry that badly. "Talk to me baby, what's got you crying for hours. If I offended you, I'm sorry. I thought you were kidding." She didn't say a word; in fact, she shut down completely and went to bed. She turned off the lamp on her side. After Shaune turned off his lamp, he slid under the covers and slowly put his arms around her; and she didn't bother to put up a fight.

6am Shaune had to make his second and last meeting. Although he was happy about the last days meeting, he was still concerned about Tory. "Good morning, I wanted to make sure you weren't still upset with me" She shook her head, "No" "you want to talk about it?" He asked but she shook her head, "No" again. He looked at his watch and noticed that he was moving late. "Are we still having dinner tonight?" "If you want to." She replied. He looked at her for a second because he didn't know what mood she was in. Then he kissed her. "I have to go." Although he had gotten a few hours sleep, the only thing he was more concerned about was her being upset with him. He picked up his brief case and headed for the door. Before he left, he said "I'll call you later." Tory shrugged her shoulders at him without looking at him.

Torys' cell phone had been ringing all morning threw the afternoon; she left it at the hotel. She didn't want to be interrupted by anyone as she decided to do things differently. Today, she was going to let Ms Sexy out of the box. Only for short moments would she have done this, but since she felt her moment of weakness yesterday; she felt that it was time to show everybody that she was not playing. She could do it up just like that rest of them. "I'll show his ass whose cookie cutter." She said to herself. Tory went to the tailor made shop where she could get anything in the store she wanted custom made to her measurements. She had seen the store yesterday but she didn't think that it was fitting for that day. Today was a new day. She knew that this place was made for her and this is why she passed it twice. As she looked around, she saw a dress that was just what she wanted. "How much would it cost to have this dress made with my measurements?" The woman with the thick heavy Jamaican accent responded "To fit you like a glove, $2000." Tory gave the dress one more look to make sure in her mind that she wanted that dress. Then she said, "Can I have it by this evening?" "Yes Ma'am." "Fine." She pulled out the money that Shaune gave her and paid the woman. She took her measurements and Tory gave her the hotel suit to deliver it to.

8:33pm, Shaune and Marcus were at the restaurant waiting for Tory to arrive. She was late; and Shaune was getting worried because of what happened last night. Plus, she never did pick up her cell phone when he would call. Then Shaune told Marcus, "Last night we had a bit of a blow out and I think she's still angry with me." "Maybe she realized that she couldn't cut it and went back home." Marcus said snidely. "I hope not. I've been calling her cell and she's not answering me. Maybe I'll give it one last try." He picked up his cell phone and dialed Torys' cell. This time she picked up, and she sounded in better spirits. "Hey you." She answered. "Hey baby, I've been trying to call you all day where have you been?" "I was a little busy taking care of some business." "Where are you now?" The waiter came up to refresh Shaunes' drink.

He realized that the waiter was distracted, because he almost spilled his drink in his lap. "I'm right here." Tory replied. "Here where?" Shaune asked. Marcus gave Shaune his focus. He pointed and said, "Shaune, there." When he did get his focus he saw his girlfriend walking towards him in a white halter, goddess dress. The dress was flawless; it was long all the way down to the floor and had a split on the left leg that went all the way up just three quarters before her hip. Here hair was pinned up in a tamed style and her make up was just as flawless as the dress. Apparently, Tory spent the day trying to make this moment possible. She had wanted to let Ms. Sexy out of the box, and she did. While she was walking to the table, Shaune couldn't take his eyes off of her. He almost couldn't recognize her. As she came over to the table, Shaune stood up to help her in her chair. Then he leaned in and kissed her. He couldn't help but pause and look at her because he felt something was a foot with her. The waiter came over immediately to take her order on drinks. "Ma'am, is there any drinks I can start you on?" Tory positioned herself in her chair. Then she crossed her leg; the leg that had the open split revealing her entire leg up to her thigh. At first sight, Shaune was intrigued. But then he looked around the restaurant and saw that most of the men as well as the waiter could see what he saw. He leaned over to talk to her. "Tory, please put your leg down." "Why?" "Because I'm asking you to." "Since you're asking then no, I don't want to." "Well then, I have to insist that you do." "Why does it bother you so much?" "Your show is supposed to be exclusively for me not everyone in the restaurant." She ignored him and decided to order. "I'll have the braised duck with the garlic mash potatoes and carrots. For my drink, hummm; I'm undecided between the lemon drop and the pomtini. What do you all think?" She looked at Shaune first who was not happy with her at all. Then she looked at Marcus and his date Candy. Marcus said, "Well if you can't decide then have them both." He gave her an evil look that would make the devil cry. Then Tory said, "You're right Marcus, I'll have them both. It's more satisfying that way." She said as she raised her eyebrow at him. There was obviously rough tension at the dinner table. The oblivious one was Candy and she was safe that way.

Dinner was finally over for the unusually awkward table. Before they left, Marcus asked Shaune, "Would you and your lovely girlfriend be joining us tonight? I still have VIP open for us." Tory stepped in and said, "We would love to…" Then Shaune grabbed her and told Marcus, "We'll sit this one out tonight. But thanks for thinking of us." He literally dragged Tory towards the elevator. Shaune stood looking at her. Then he stormed over to her and grabbed her. "You're hurting me Shaune." She said as she tried to pull away from him. He managed to swing her around and push her up against the elevator wall face first with her arm pinned behind her back. Then he moved in closer and whispered, "You think this was so funny. That little stunt you pulled wearing this dress." "What are you talking about? I wanted to feel Pretty something you couldn't make me feel like." Then he turned her back over to face him and said, "Pretty? Is that what you thought you were doing? You know what I think? I think you became so insecure with yourself that you were trying to be slutty and you were trying to put on a show for every man in the restaurant just so you can feel sexy. That's what I think." She broke herself free from his grip and yelled, "Maybe that's what I was going for and frankly Shaune; I don't give a fuck what you think." After hearing her smart remark, a fuse blew in his mind. He then grabbed her by the throat and re-slammed her against the elevator wall. He started to choke her. She struggled to get free, but his grip was too strong for her. He eased his grip a bit and came in closer to her ear. "Well since you were so interested in every other man then let me give you what they wanted to give you." As he reached under her dress, the elevator door opened at penthouse one. It was Greg who was actually on his way to see Shaune. "HEY, glad you're here man…" Shaune cut him off and in a soft spoken tone said, "Not now Gregory." "But I need to ask you…" Shaune cut in again. This time he clenched his teeth and look at Greg with an evil look. "I said not now Gregory." As Greg backed out of the elevator, he said, "You know what, it's not that important. Good night all." When they got to their penthouse, Shaune grabbed Tory off the elevator and proceeded to drag her down the hall. His grip was hurting her arm. He opened the door and swung her in to the penthouse. She fell up against the couch and managed to get her balance but was thrown off again by Shaune grabbing her from behind. He then started to push her into the bedroom. He threw her on to the bed. She tried to get up and run across the bed, but he was too quick. He grabbed her leg and pulled her back to him where he laid on top of her from behind. "Now, where was I before Greg interrupted us? Oh, I know." Then he went back to reaching under her dress again. He had her pinned faced down holding her head down pulling her hair. He was literally crushing the air out of her. She managed to whisper, "Shaune, please don't do this." "Isn't this what you wanted? Isn't this why you wore this dress?" Tory, now in fear for her life screamed and begged him, "Please don't do this! Please, PLEASE!" Shaune put his hand over her mouth and said, "Why not? This is why you wore this dress. Now I'm going to show you what women get when they ask for too much attention. Try not to scream." She freed her mouth from his hand and said, "I thought this was what you liked." Then he stopped and looked at her. "Why would I like this? Did you even bother to ask me?" "When I asked you last night if I dressed sexy enough you laughed at me." "So why didn't you talk to me when I asked you about it?" Tory didn't respond. "Talk to me now!" He screamed. She just turned her head away from him. "You better talk to me or I swear…" Then she yelled to stop him, "Marcus said that his girlfriend was your type of woman. I guess I wanted to live up to that." "Marcus! Why would you let a no-account, self-conscious piece of Euro-trash like him in your head? I thought you were stronger then that. Wouldn't it have occurred to you that if she was my type I would have her type here instead of you? DAMN! Maybe I am with the wrong woman." He climbed from over her and grabbed his pajamas and went into the front room where he would spend the night. As she lay on the bed, she tried to silence her cry. A few minutes later, she staggered into the shower to wash the aura of the day off of her. While she was in the shower she figured she should cry it out some more.

The next morning, Tory heard the front door open. Then someone knocked on the bedroom door. She didn't bother to answer, but the door opened anyway. It was the room service that Shaune had given permission to enter. Apparently, he had taken the liberty of ordering breakfast for the two of them. She didn't want to eat her stomach was still in knots. She remained catatonic to the waiter as he left the table in front of her. Tory hardly slept the nigh being in fear that Shaune might bust through the door to choke her out some more. As Shaune knocked at the door, she was still protestant to speak. Even though she didn't answer, he let himself in. Shaune hadn't slept most of the night either because he felt bad that he was moved to snap that badly. No one has ever moved him to that level of anger before. He came around to the lounge chair and sat down. "You're not going to eat breakfast?" He said as he tried to give small talk. Tory didn't respond. "Are you hungry?" Again he tried to but she shook her head this time "No." He started to feel a little better that he had managed to get some response out of her. Then he took the cart out of the room and when he came back, she had gone into the bathroom. A few seconds later, she had emerged fully dressed. "Where are you going?" He asked. She grabbed her suit case and it was clear that she was leaving. "Can we talk about this?" Tory would never respond. "Baby, I'm sorry and if you would let me explain my actions." Tory never bothered to listen to anything he had to say. In her mind, Que`Shaune Guadau was a mean, calculated, rapist that was no longer the man for her. He reached in to stop her from packing; then she started to fight and slap him. "Don't touch me. Don't you ever touch me again! You will never put your hands on me again. You will never have me again. EVER!!!" Then she ran out of the penthouse.

Tory found herself at the beach. She wasn't dressed for it because she left everything she had back at the penthouse. That included her clothes, money, and cell phone. That meant she couldn't call Lou to see if she could get a plane ticket back home. Not that she would. She knew that he had warned her about the Guadaus and she didn't listen. Now it blew up in her face and the only thing she could do was try and devise a plan to extract her property from his penthouse so that she could get back to South Carolina. Her mind was weary because she hadn't had any sleep the entire night. She sat down on the sand at the beach. The sun was bright and hot but there was a breeze blowing to cool her down. She was so tired that she laid herself down on the hot sand which didn't bother her at all. A few hours later, she opened her eyes to see a golf cart in front of her. It was a staff member from the hotel trying to wake her. "Ma'am, please come with me." The gentleman said as he was trying to help her up from the sand. Tory felt disoriented from the heat and she didn't bother to put up a fight with the staff member who was worried about her well being; not to mention she was hungry. When they got back to the hotel he escorted her to the managers office where Que'Shaune was waiting for her. He didn't say much to her, he was just glad to see her safe. They got onto the elevator together again. This time Shaune kept his distance. Tory was so hungry, her stomach wouldn't stop growling. "Would you like for me to order dinner for you? Or is there something you would like for dinner?" She never responded to him. As the doors opened, Shaune said, "After you Ma'am." Then she walked off the elevator and headed straight for their penthouse. When they got into the room, she sat on the couch. "Tory, I know you're angry at me, but I know you're hungry. They found you sleeping on the beach? I'm sure you haven't had anything to eat since this morning. Please let me feed you." "Yes I'm hungry. Can I please eat something?" "Would you like to shower before dinner?" Tory got up to go into the shower, before she went into the bathroom she said, "I want to go home. I don't wish to sleep around a violent man." Then she left.

It was time to eat dinner. Tory had put on her pajamas; she had wanted to get a little more comfortable. As she walked to the table, she could smell the food that was waiting for her. It was roasted lamb with wild rice, gravy and vegetables. The smell was intoxicating and the fact that Tory hadn't eaten all day made her into a ravenous animal. She took a seat at the dinner table and proceeded to make herself a plate. The servant poured her some wine and she drank it. "Thank you so much." She sighed in relief. Que`Shaune finally came to the table. "You couldn't wait for me so we could eat together?" At first, she didn't want to answer him but then she realized that this was all on his dime and the room was in his name. "Sorry. I was really hungry." "This is because you were sleeping on the beach I was told. Can you explain that to me?" "I don't care to; I just want to enjoy my meal." "Can we talk about what happened last night?" "What happened last night was you tried to hurt me all because I wanted to look sexy for you. Now I realize that that was a huge mistake. A mistake I will never repeat again." "I take it it's too late to apologize?" "I don't know have you tried?" "I'm sorry Tory for hurting you." "Too late; now can we finish our meal please?" "So what can I do to change this around?" "Nothing; just let me eat my meal in peace thank you." Shaune then got up from the table to leave her alone.

The next morning Tory was packing her clothes to go back to South Carolina. There was a knock at the door. "Come in." She responded. It was Que`Shaune. "I just wanted to see you off. Is it possible that I could have a word or two with you before you leave?" With her back turned to him she said, "What do you want Que`Shaune?" "Would you please have a seat? I would like to talk to you face to face." As she went to sit on the bed, Shaune knelt in front of her. He spent the night trying to rationalize his behavior that night. He felt it was time to take a page out of Marta's` book. If she was going to walk out of his life, she should know how he really felt about her. "Last night you wore that dress and oh God you looked like such a Goddess in it. But the problem was that I felt like every other man could see what I saw." Tory asked him, "What do you see?" "I see a beautiful, sexy woman that can light up a room without saying a word. I was up the whole night trying to figure out why was I so angry when you looked so beautiful. Then I realized that all those men could see all those qualities that I saw and that made me feel insecure. See, when I was married it didn't even faze me half as much that my wife cheated. However, the way I feel about you is far deeper then my ex-wife." "Am I supposed to feel better that you would rather shake me up for wearing a dress that made you feel insecure as opposed to your ex-wife cheating on you and you not reacting?" "I guess it does sound a little crazy when you put it that way. But in any case, you didn't deserve what I did to you." "So why should I stay and accept your apology? What's to stop you from doing this again? If not something I wore you wouldn't like, it might be something I might say you wouldn't agree with and fly off the handle again…" "Tory, I need you. In this short time that we've been together, I've experienced so much more with you then I have ever had my entire life. Usually every woman I meet has an agenda and they try to conform to me. With you it's the other way around. I have experienced feelings and emotions that I never knew I had. And I guess jealousy is one of them. And as a jealous man would it be selfish of me to want you all to myself? It probably is; but you didn't deserve what I did to you, and I promise that I will never hurt you again or try to strike fear in you." As he got up on his feet, he reached his hand out and finished. "Torianey if you walked out that door, I wouldn't blame you. But I would be so very broken hearted if I never saw you again. I'm asking you… I'm begging you to please give me one more chance. Stay with me." Tory looked at him with his hand out to receive hers. As she rose to her feet, she took his hand. As they embraced each other, he whispered in her ear, "Baby, I'm so sorry I scared you."

Chapter 10
The Wrath of Swain

T ory awoke in that afternoon next to Que`Shaune who was still sleeping. He looked just as peaceful sleeping as he did awake. She felt she should take the time to observe his body. She took her finger and ran it across his thick black, eyebrows. They even had a shine to them. She then took her hand to feel his rugged and defined face. She took her fingers and felt how soft his lips were. Then she moved down to his neck. Tory especially loved Shaunes' neck; the way she could feel his pulse when she kissed it. She moved to his chest; it was hard, firm and muscular. She could feel the ripples of his six packs as she glided her hands on them. Tory started to get turned on by touching him. Before she knew it she was nibbling on his stomach. Shaune woke up and said, "So you like to molest men in their sleep do you?" "I'm a sick woman and I can't help myself." Then they both laughed. "Let's hangout together; just the two of us? This could be our day." Tory loved the way that sounded. No Marcus Swain and his escort girlfriend, no VIP clubs. Just then and that was all she wanted.

They were walking along the shopping centers. Tory pointed out the store where she had gotten the dress from. They proceeded to walk in and she showed Shaune the dress she had made for herself. As he looked around the store, he was trying to find something that was less revealing as the dress; but he could see that most of the wears in the store was pretty much on the revealing side. His next thought was to grab Tory by the hand and leave as fast as he could. But then Tory called him. "Since you didn't like the dress, maybe you would like this." It was an a-symmetrical blouse with spaghetti straps. He didn't particularly like it. "Wouldn't it show too much of your arms, shoulders and cleavage?" Tory looked at the blouse and said, "Come on Shaune, would you rather I wear a burqa?" "As opposed to exposing yourself to the hungry dogs, then yeah I'm all in on that concept." "What you fail to realize it that as a woman other men are going to look at me. I don't mean to sound shallow but wouldn't you want a woman that looks pleasing to the eye? It would be much better then all men frowning and wondering what is that guy doing with that dog? Also, you need to understand that when other men see me looking sexy, I'm doing it for you. I'm going to always be your lady. I don't want everyman that wants me. When I'm in a relationship I'm committed. So all you have to think about is they all want what you already have." "So are you admitting that we are in a relationship?" "Is that what it seems like to you?" "I don't know. I almost lost you today. So you tell me." Tory walked in close to give him total eye contact. "If I'm going to be your lady and if I'm going to be in a relationship with you then you need to put that big bad wolf away. I want to be able to look sexy for you. Not just the plane Jane sexy. And not like Marcus Swain escort sexy either but my kind of sexy." Then she held up the blouse and said, "This kind of sexy." Shaune thought to himself; "Could I handle her wearing these clothes around other men and having to deal with the looks? Perhaps it is a small price to pay as opposed to not having her in my life." Then he said to her "Fine, the wolf goes into the cage. But know this, at times I won't always be able to tame myself as I will be tested by some other guy trying to come on to you. Just like the other night with the guy who brought you the lemon drop." "And you handled it well. You brought it back for him and no one got hurt." "I guess we can give this a try."

For dinner that evening, they went to an Asian fusion restaurant. Tory was wearing her a-symmetrical blouse that she brought from the clothing store. The entire night Shaune had been trying to fight off the looks of all the guys that would look at her. They ordered their appetizers and meals when Shaune figured he'd pay her a compliment. "You do look very sexy tonight." "That was the look I was trying to achieve for my man. Are you satisfied?" "Mission accomplished." "What I'm slowly realizing about you is you're a regular guy." "What kind of guy did you think I was? Please be gentle, I'm sensitive to criticism." "Well, you're an oil conglomerate with $300 billion in the bank. I mean if I had that kind of cheese hanging around, I would be putting on some kind of airs. You have two mansions, three Aston Martins, two Rolls, two Maybachs and a whole host of cars I can't pronounce." Shaune couldn't help but laugh because her comment was the typical comments that he would always hear. "So what you're saying is I should be conceited?" "Hell yes! You're not Joe Blow from the town of anywhere, you're Que`Shaune Guadau from France; Single man, no children, bachelor of the century. Essence magazine dubbed you as the black super hero of our time. Due to all the charity foundations you and your father support. Man, the Guadaus' are some bad ass people." "When you bring it to my attention, I see what you're saying. However, I never felt like the man you're talking about." "Why, you live such an exciting life. What am I missing?" "That's the point, what you don't see is when I'm going through the motions. It always looks fun when you're the spectator; but as the spectacle, not so much. It can get pretty tedious and tiresome. Not to mention I would often get lonely sometimes. How do you know so much about me now?" "One day I had some down time and I googled you on a search engine. I got a lot of information about you. The only thing I didn't get was a nude photo." "I'm sure there's one out there somewhere. Maybe even photo shopped." They both chuckled. He then asked her "If I googled you, what would I find?" "Hopefully, not a damned thing. See, unlike you I'm nobody; one of the little people." At that point he had to let her in on a little known fact. "If you stick around with me long enough, you won't be for long. Unfortunately, the women I associate myself with tend to end up on the front pages of news papers, magazines and sometimes billboards; hence my marriage. But if it's little comfort to you, I'll try to shield you as best as possible." Tory shrugged it off and said, "Don't worry about it. But can you just clear up one thing for me?" "Sure what is it?" She took a deep breath in hesitance. "I understand you. At least now I do, what I don't get is Marcus Swain. You two are so different. Why do you hang around him?" "The truth is he hangs around me. It was my fault that he came to Jamaica. I let it slip that I was coming her for business and he opt to come along. I told him that I was bringing you along but he still showed up. The truth is, sometimes I feel sorry for him. He treats women like dirt to make himself feel superior. I really can't understand why he does these things. I try to straighten him out; he just doesn't seem to get it." "So how do you feel about him personally?" "I never gave it any thought." Then he took Torys' hand and said, "Since I met my new best friend, I haven't been too concerned." She started to smile and looked away as she started to blush.

The night was coming to an end and Tory wanted to casually put in her request for Shaunes' attention that night. After he paid the bill, she leaned in to nibble on his ear. He turned to her and said, "Dinner, desert and a treat. I still have room for more." "So let's go back to the hotel and see what's on the menu." As he slammed the tip on the table, he yelled, "Bet!" When they got back to the hotel, Tory said, "Let's play a game." "Really, what do you have in mind?" "Hide and seek." "Sounds kinky; what do I get if I find you." "How about you get it where you find it." Without hesitation, he said, "I'm all in." As he covered his eyes, he started to count to ten. Tory ran off down the lobby hall. Little did she know Shaune never really covered his eyes fully. When got to ten, he started to look for her. When he got to the end of the hall, he saw a series of doors that she could be in any one of. "Come out; come out where ever you are Torianey." She hid herself in one of the janitors' closets. She could hear him calling her but of course, the name of the game was "hide and seek." Little did Tory know that he was a known cheater. Since he was a child, he was notorious for his cheating methods. He was always quick on his feet when it came down to games like this. He knew exactly how to find her without touching any of the doors. "Marco? I'm going to make this real easy for both of us." He joked. Then he pulled out his cell phone and dialed her cell. Tory was in the closet trying to silence her phone but it was too late. He had found her. "That wasn't hard at all." "You cheated. I want a do over." She yelled. Shaune walked into the semi-small closet. "What was the prize again? I get it where I find it. Found it." "You clearly cheated. Cheaters never win." "I beg to differ; it looks like I just came up big on this one." As he closed the door on the closet, he moved in on her and started to kiss her. With in seconds, they were clawing at each others clothes. They were kissing and breathing heavy. The fact that they were about to get it on in such a concealed but public spot turned them on to a higher level. Tory was already wet from the excitement of the game. Shaune was getting harder and harder by the second. She reached down and felt his hard penis. He whispered, "He's ready for her, is she ready for him?" "She is so ready for him." Then he lifted her blouse and started to suck on her nipples. The feeling of his soft tongue on her hardening nipples made her want to climax. "I want it now Daddy. Please let me have it now." Tory pleaded as she felt she couldn't stand much more. "You want it now baby? Daddy's going to give it to you so good." Just as he started to unbuckle his pants, his cell phone rang. "Don't answer it." Tory demanded. He let it go to voice mail but it rang again. He pulled it out of his pocket to answer it and Tory tried to stop him. "Don't answer that thing Shaune!" But it was too late. He picked it up and it was Greg searching for him. "What do you want Greg?" "I have a call you need to answer." "Can it wait?" The party went on for Tory as she continued to molest Shaune while he tried to conduct business. "I'm sorry Shaune but this is really important. It's from France. Why are breathing so hard?" Then he realized he had to snap out of his erotic trance. "Look, where are you?" Shaune asked Greg. "I'm in the lobby." "Me too; I'm around the corner." Greg came around the corner and said, "Where around the corner?" "Hang on a second. Tory, we have to stop. I have a call I need to take and it's important." As she backed away from Shaune she whispered, "Fine." "I really am sorry baby." Shaune opened the door to go see Greg. His shirt was half buttoned and his belt was unbuckled; which was an indication that he was obviously in the middle of something. Torys' hair was a little out of place which gave the same indication as well. "This kind of explains a whole lot now. I guess it's safe to say I interrupted something. How come I keep catching you too in the most awkward situations?" "What ever funny guy, what's the problem?" "You need to take this call and from what it sounds like, your plans might have to change." Shaune turned to Tory and said, "Can we continue this up in the penthouse? I shouldn't be long." With frustration in her face, she said, "Take all the time you need." Shaune leaned in to kiss her, but she had turned and left them alone. He felt terrible that they were having such a great time and in one phone call it had to end. He feared he might be in the dog house again.

As she stood waiting for the elevator, someone came up from behind and grabbed her and rushed her into an empty conference room. The lights were off and everything was covered. When she turned to see who it was, she saw Marcus Swain. "I really don't have time for you Marcus." When she tried to walk away, Marcus grabbed her arm and demanded, "I suggest you make time." Trying to keep her distance from him, Tory asked, "Why did you bring me here?" She remembered Marcus as a man with a short fuse and extremely unpredictable. "Ever since I found you, I can't get to be alone with you. You're always with him." "He's my boyfriend, and we don't have anything to say to each other. Last I remember, after you broke it off with me, you said you never had any intentions on marrying me." "That didn't mean I didn't want to be with you anymore. Nor did it mean that I didn't care for you." "I can't believe anything that comes out of your fucking mouth. You're a spoiled man with selfish tendencies and I can't see you ever caring for anyone human or animal." Marcus tried to come in closer to hold her, but she slapped his hands away. He grabbed her by her harms.

She tried struggled to get away from him but his grip was too strong. Then she screamed, "GET OFF ME!!!" with his tight grip, he forced her to sit in the chair that was behind her. "Please Marcus let me leave." Marcus was notorious for being lose cannon. Not to mention, when threatened he could even become dangerous. "Torianey, he doesn't know you like I do. He doesn't have the skill to push your sexual buttons like I can." "Don't flatter yourself. But if you must know; if I had the choice to pick between the two of you it would be him. He knows how to satisfy a woman in more ways then one." As he tried to laugh off her comment, he said, "Okay then, and is it money that you require? I can take care of you, you know I can." "This has nothing to do with your money Mark! I really do like Que`Shaune. I've never asked him for anything and frankly, he's not a monster like…" Before she could finish her statement, Marcus started to choke. As his grip became stronger, Tory felt scared that he last moments would be spent in Marcus' hands. Literally. "No matter what man you find your way to, we will always find our way back to each other because we are soul mates. And I won't be second best. Don't you know that Torianey?" As Tory tried hard to remove his fingers from her neck, her air supply was getting shorter and shorter. Then her cell phone rang startling both of them. She was able to push him away from her as she staggered to get out of her seat. Then she collapsed to the floor pushing herself farther away from Marcus while she was struggling to fill her lungs with air. Marcus started to walk towards her, but then she pulled out her cell phone to answer it. "Hello!" She screamed. It was Que`Shaune trying to find her. "Baby where are you?" She stuttered to get her words out. "I… I'm… on my way…" "Are you okay?" "I… I'm fine." Marcus decided to leave abruptly. He wasn't sure where Shaune was so left her where she was. "Where are you, I can come to you…" Then she yelled "NO!" and hung up her phone. She sat up against a wall to regain her composure. Tory managed to get on to her feet to make her way back to the penthouse. When she got there, Shaune was in the bedroom on the phone. "Where have you been?" He asked then his concerns grew even more when he had seen the condition she was in. "What the hell happened to you?" She nervously laughed and said, "Nothing. What are you talking about?" Shaune walked over from around the bed to look closer at her, then he turned her towards the mirror and said "What is all this on your arms?" She tried to play it off "Oh this is nothing. I think I may have bump into something while on the elevator." "So did what ever you bumped into mess your hair up? When I left you, you were supposed to be coming back here; but when I got here, you weren't. So did something happen between the times you left me and now?" Tory couldn't lie her way out of this one. It was too evident that someone had tried to harm her. "Someone grabbed me from behind in the elevator and I couldn't see them." "What! Do you know who it was?" "No I told you I was grabbed from behind." Feeling angry and frustrated, Shaune started to pace back and forth in the room. He almost felt powerless that someone put their hands on his girlfriend and he couldn't protect her. Then he picked up the phone. "Who are you calling?" "I'm calling security. Maybe they can see on their cameras who may have grabbed you." Tory ran to the phone to cut off the call. Then she snatched the receiver from him. "What the hell are you doing Tory?" "Forget about it. I'm sure that who ever it was is long gone. They didn't get anything. I didn't have any money on me; so they probably took off and kept going. Let's just forget about the whole thing." Shaune grabbed the receiver back from Torys' hands. Then he yelled, "I will not forget about it; first I want to know who put their hands on my lady and just before I press charges I would like to return the favor and put my hands on him." "How do you know it was a man Shaune?" "Seriously Tory? Do I look that dense? And speaking of dense, why are you so resistant to finding out who did this to you?" Then he paused for a second and said, "Or do you already know?" He became dead locked in her eyes to see what her response would be. She looked on the floor as she responded. "I don't know what you're talking about." He shook his head and put the receiver back to his ear. Then she stopped him and said, "Alright, I saw an ex-boyfriend. We had a conversation, it turned into an argument, and then it turned into a physical altercation; hence the marks." "Who is he? Have I seen him before?" Although she told him the truth, she knew she couldn't tell the entire truth. "He's no one you would know. We dated years and years ago. It ended badly and this was the first time we had seen each other. But trust me; I won't be seeing him again." "Can I see him?" Shaune started to turn six shades of red as he heard the story of her ex-boyfriend putting his hands on her. Her effort to squelch the situation was barley working for him. "Look I knew him, you didn't. He was my ex and I handled it. He's in the past. Let's just let it go." He took a deep breath and said, "I can't. Who am I if I can't protect my lady?" As he picked up the phone, she ran to him and said, "This was my fight." "Tory, your fight is my fight. You're my lady; if some guy feels he needs to harm you I have to take it personal and even out the odds." "Please, settle it another time. Let's just continue to enjoy this vacation." Then he went to sit on the bed. Although he wanted to really find out who and what happened to her, he felt he had a much more pressing issue. "I'm going to put this conversation on hold because we need to talk about something that can't wait." She took a seat next to him on the bed. As he looked at her bruised arms in disgust, he had to gather his thought to say what he needed to tell her. "I have to go away to France for another business trip." "Okay, when?" He paused to figure out how he was going to say it, but he said it the only way he could. "Tomorrow morning." "Okay, for how long?" He was slightly hesitant to answer because he could see the expression on her face change. "At least three and a half months." "So when you say at least, does this mean that you could be there longer?" "Possibly; but I'll move as fast as I can." A slight feeling of devastation came over her. She felt that things were finally going well for them. "What am I supposed to do without you for three plus months?" "I was thinking the same thing about you." Although he knew the answer to his question, he had to give it one college try. "Do you think you could come along with me?" "I can't, I have school, work, and I have other obligations. I can't just pick up and leave. Do you really have to go? Can't you just send Greg?" "Unfortunately there is a really big problem with one of my oil rigs, and I need to settle the problem personally. This problem Greg can't solve." As he held her in his arms, she asked him, "How are we going to spend the last few hours?" He knew it would be selfish of him to ask for sex after the bad news he had given her. "I just want to hold you until the 11th hour if that is okay with you." They undressed each other and lay across the bed holding each other. Tory cried and cried the rest of the night. Shaune felt a little emotional but he felt he needed to be strong for his lady. Ultimately, she stopped crying and they both drifted off to sleep. The next morning she awoke to see Shaune fully dressed to leave. Then the painful memory of him having to leave came back. "I didn't want to wake you I went ahead and slipped into the shower." As she felt her heart breaking, she felt she didn't want to talk. Noticing that she didn't respond to him, he walked over to the bed and asked, "Are you angry with me?" She wasn't as angry with Shaune as much as she was with the situation. "Please baby, talk to me. Is this how we're going to leave things?" Shaune asked. Tory turned away from him, grabbed her pillow and buried her face as she started to cry. He came around and sat on the bed next to her. "I'll be back in three months I promise. I'll try and call you everyday when I can. Please don't run away from me now." While she was crying her heart out, she had a thought in her mind. She then turned back to him and hugged him tight. "I'm so sorry. I know this must be equally hard for you as it is for me. Even though you're not gone yet, I miss you already. My heart is breaking and I can't stand this feeling." Just as he started to speak, a knock came at the door. It was the bearer of bad news himself, Gregory. "Shaune the limo is ready to take us to the airport." "I'll be there shortly." He said as he wiped her tears away. "Can I call you when I get on the plane?" "Call me anytime; call me every time." Minutes later, another knock came at the door. "Shaune, we need to leave now if we're going..." "I remembered that I have a flight to catch Gregory!" Shaune yelled. Tory raised herself from under the covers and hugged him tight. Then she whispered in his ear, "You better go now. As much as I would love to keep you all to myself, your business needs you." Then she kissed him deeply. At that point, Shaune had the strongest urge to tell her he loved her but instead he stuttered, "I... I... I'll call you when I can while I'm away." She watched him leave the room; and when she heard the front door close, she began to cry in her pillow again.

Later on that day, Shaunes' limo dropped Tory off at her home. She walked into her house and had a depressed and lonely feeling. She sat on her couch and didn't move for hours. All she could think about was for the next three months or more she was going to have to keep busy. Not that keeping busy was a problem. It was trying to stay focused and not miss Shaune.

Chapter 11
She Loves Me? She Loves Me Not?

Thanksgiving day, Carrapellies was closed to for the holiday just so they could celebrate with each other. Most of them didn't have family including Torianey. She and Fernardo cooked the thanksgiving banquet that took most of the morning to prepare. Lou gave his usual yearly toast to his staff. "I would like to give thanks to all of you for making Carrapellies yet another phenomenal success. If we keep it up, we might see some Holiday bonuses. Fernardo, I would like to thank you and Torianey for preparing this beautiful feast for all of us. I thank you two for not killing me yet another year. To be honest, all of you at times have been challenging but you were always managed to make this establishment feel like we were family. And I want you all to know that there is nothing I wouldn't do for any of you. Del La Famiglia!!!" He yelled as they all raised their glasses to toast.

Tory had so much to drink that night even she felt she was too tipsy; and even though she tried to play it off. "Are you okay to get home?" Lou asked her. "Sure I can get home. I always make it. You know that." Lou looked at her side ways and as he walked away, he said, "Thank God she has help." "What?" she yelled in her drunk and confused voice. As she opened her door, she stumbled into her office and saw someone sitting in her office chair. At first glance she didn't recognize him. "Who are you...?" Then she got her focus. "Que`Shaune!!!" she yelled as she ran over to him. She wrapped her arms around him and kissed him. The beard that he had grown stung her face. She withdrew with a screech and said, "How come you look like the black grizzly Adams?" "I haven't had time to clean up since I've been back. I wanted to see you as soon as I got home to the States." Then a knock came at the door. It was Lou. "Are you going to make sure she gets home safe? She's pretty drunk." "Of course I will." Tory stood up and said, "No I'm not. I've drank whole bottles of your sangria and I still been able to get home." Lou looked at Shaune and said, "Right. Shaune?" "Lou don't worry I got this. Goodnight." As she stumbled backwards, she said, "Really, I can handle myself." Shaune caught her and said, "I know that. That's how you got this far in life." "Exactly. Hey are you trying to politic me?" Then he grabbed her keys and said, "I would never do that to you. You're way too smart for that." "Exactly, and don't you forget it Guadau."

Que`Shaune drove Tory home and she was passed out in the passenger seat. He got out and opened her door for her but she didn't wake up. He kissed her on the lips to wake her; then she woke up; but she was no more sober then she was back at Carrapellies. "Where are we?" Then she managed to get her focus and said, "Oh Shaune, I'm sorry. I'm just so sleepy." "I know baby. Come let me take you home so you can get some sleep." She held on to him so tight as they walked towards the house. He though it to be quite comical to see her so unstable. They walked through the door of her house, she said, "I love you so much Shaune." "Why do you love me so much?" "I love you because you're attentive, you're caring. I never had too much of that in my life." "Really? What else?" As he sat her on the couch, she continued. "Don't tell anybody but, I hate those rich pricks who think that the world is at their feet. I personally try to avoid them. I want a man that can appreciate me. A man that can bring me flowers, remember my birthday, our anniversary of our first meeting, when we got married, the little things that money can't buy. I… Sometimes envision us getting married." "Really, when?" As he sat next to her on the couch, he waited with great eagerness for her response. "I always envisioned a December wedding." "Why December?" As her eyes got more and more heavy she struggled to answer his question. "Because it's untraditional, and I don't want to wear a white dress either." Then she laid across the couch and put her head in his lap. Shaune wasn't expecting her to sleep in his lap, he wanted to move her up to her bedroom but if it could keep her answering, this was where it was going to go down. "Why not a white dress?" "We're not virgins. It would be a slap in Gods face to disrespect him and I would never have another good day in my life or my marriage if I did that. I don't know about your wedding day, but me and Shaunes it's going to be hot and heavy but it's going to be done right." It Then she drifted off to sleep.

Tory awoke on her bed completely naked with her throw over her. She had no recollection of how she got home and how or why her clothes came off. As she sat up abruptly, a wave of nausea hit her. She ran to the bathroom to let it out. While she was throwing up, a voice came from behind her, "Here, take this. It might make you feel better." As she looked up, she saw that it was Shaune holding two aspirin and a glass of water. She didn't remember that he was the one who brought her home. "Damn Lou and his sangria. He does it to me every year." He kneeled down on his knees to hold her hair for her. "No worries. I didn't take advantage of you no matter how much I wanted too." "Thank you." She said as she hurled some more. After she was done, he helped her back to the bedroom. "Oh my God, you're back from France." "Yes." As he laughed. She was happy to see him but a thought came across her mind. "What did I do last night? What did I say? I woke up with no clothes on. Did I dance naked for you? Oh Lord not another year." Shaune started to laugh and asked, "Who did you dance naked for?" Before she could catch herself, she managed to slip out, "Fernard…" Now Shaunes mood changed from funny to serious. "Wait, you danced naked for that guy?" "Scratch that, that's not the important part. Did I act a fool last night?" "You were fine. You fell asleep in the car and I brought you home where you slept on the couch then by earlier this morning I brought you up here to the bedroom and took off your clothes; then I ravaged your body." "This is important Shaune. What did I say last night?" Although he had totally remembered what went down last night, he didn't want to exploit her feelings. "You were tired. I barely noticed you had been drinking. In fact, it was Lou who had told me. And that's why I had to take you home. Unfortunately, I didn't get a butt naked dance like the Chef did. Maybe one day though." Tory looked at him with a skeptical look and said, "And I didn't do anything surprising? Not one thing?" "Nope. You fell asleep. Nothing happened." Although it was killing him inside to tell her what she had said last night, he knew that there were a time and a place for everything and now was not the time. So he switched up the conversation. "So what's on the agenda for you and me today?" "What do you mean?" "I mean what are we going to do today? It's the day after Thanksgiving and I'm thinking we should do something. You have me all to yourself." "Oh yeah just like I had you all to myself back in Jamaica. And let's talk about how three months turned into six." "I did explain that it might take a little longer." "Let's talk about how after the three month mark I couldn't get in touch with you anymore. You weren't picking up your cell phone, you wouldn't return my calls. You stop calling me. I actually thought you weren't coming back and you just rid me off altogether." "Why would I write you off?" "You tell me, you're the one who stopped communicating. And let's be realistic, one phone call and its Jamaica all over again. Who are we kidding? We can't possibly try and maintain a functioning relationship like this." "What are you saying?" "I'm saying that maybe we should just be friends." "You can't be serious!" "I'm very serious Shaune. I thank you for all that you have done. The trip to Jamaica, the car, getting me home safe; but the fact remains that your business is your highest commitment and I can't compete. I knew it before but I know even better having experienced it first hand. I can't go through that again." Then Shaune was enraged, because a single thought crossed his mind. "Are you seeing that Chef?" "Maybe." "Don't mess with me Tory, are you fucking him?" "Yes." His first impression was to grab her and shake her. Then he realized she had a point. "Okay. You do raise a good argument so I'll give you a pass on this one." "What do you mean by a pass?" "I'll let that go. You were right, I wasn't around and I didn't communicate like I should have so I'm willing to look the other way with the whole fling you had with that Chef." "It's not a fling Shaune. And his name is Fernardo. He's here; he's been here and he will always be here; which is not what I can say for you." If she was going to walk out of his life, he wasn't going to make it easy for her. "Remember the day at the pond? You were talking about being in love alone. How it hurt so bad to find out that you were in love all by yourself while in a relationship. I want to ask you this one question and if you say yes, then I'll walk out of your life and I won't bother you ever again. Just answer this one question for me." Then he drew closer to her. "Am I in love alone? See I know that I haven't been at my best when it comes to communicating. I need you to know that all that time spent in France I couldn't get you out of my mind. You're stuck in my system. The smell of you is embedded in my brain. See, I knew I loved you the day I left you and I was too chicken to say so. I didn't but I should have. So am I in love alone?" "Why are you toying with my emotions?" "I'm not I swear. Torianey I love you so much." He then reached out his arms to hold her, but then she stopped him by pushing him away from her. Then she said, "Don't... Don't you dare do that...? Get out." "You didn't answer my question." "I don't have to do a damn thing. You decide to blow back into town and assume that we can pick up where we left off without any real explanation, and now you want to challenge my feelings for you? Get out of my house." As she walked over to the window to look away from him, Shaune said, "My father always said drunk men tell no tales. It's usually the sober ones that do." Looking over her shoulder at him she said, "What the hell are you talking about?" "Last night you confessed that you loved me. YOU said that you envision us getting married. YOU said that you wanted a December wedding. It was YOU who said that YOU didn't want to wear a white dress and when I asked why on December without a white dress…" Then she cut in and said, "Because it's nontraditional and we're not virgins. I know what I said. I've always said that to myself." "Which I thought was quite noble of you to say. With that having been said, I ask you once again; am I in love alone?" Tory had a sinking sad feeling in the pit of her gut. They both knew the answer to his question; it was him who wanted to hear her say the words. But instead she said, "Shaune please just go. I can't do this with you. Just leave please." Shaune turned to leave but before he left the room, he looked over his shoulder and said, "I love you Torianey; and at your request I will not bother you anymore. Good luck with Fernardo." As he headed towards his car, he looked up at her bedroom window to see her still standing there. He looked at her for one last time and then he got in to his car and drove off. Tory collapsed on her knees and began to cry.

Shaune went to see his father to brief him on the situation in France. As he pulled up in his fathers' driveway, he sat in his car trying to gather himself. Although his father was good at prying through his moods, he still wanted to try and cover it up. After he pulled himself together, he walked into his fathers' house. He made his way to the den where his father was. "Pare, how are you feeling today?" "Like I'm getting old. How was your trip?" "As you know there was an explosion on the oil rig. We lost a couple of employee." "We must do something for their families." "Redliner picked up the tab for their funerals. I made sure that I was in attendance for the services. I also compensated the injured employees as well as the families of those who were lost." "Very good mon files. You have done your father proud. Now what else is new?" "Nothing else to report except for there is plans to rebuild the oil rig that was damaged. I went to assess the damages. I think we can salvage it." "Very good. Now you want to tell me what's going on with you?" "What do you mean?" "Why do you look so sad?" "Take a good guess." "Your lady friend again I take it." "She's not my lady anymore. She broke up with me. The time and distance was too great for her. She feared that we couldn't sustain a meaningful relationship due to my constant need to be summoned away. Why does everything have to be so complicated?" "Not everything my son, just women. They make the worlds go round and they can make our worlds crash. Either way, we can't exist without them." Shaune really wasn't in the mood for his fathers' speech. "Dad I hope you don't mind if I head home. I have a lot of things to do since I'm home now." As his father got up to hug him, he told him, "Don't stay down for long. If she's worth fighting for, you'll find a way to get her back."

He got into his car and sat for a few minutes. He really didn't have much to do at home accept sit and think about how he was going to deal with this whole situation. Then suddenly, his cell phone rang. It was Gregory. "Yeah Greg." "Hey Shaune, were you expecting company?" "No not that I know of. Why?" "Your girlfriend Torianey is here." Suddenly, he lit up like a Christmas tree. "Really. Did she explain why she's there?" "No but she looks pretty distraught." Then Greg started to whisper. "She actually looks like she's been crying. I tried to get her to talk to me but she won't." "Ask her if she's hungry or thirsty. If she's tired, let her go upstairs to my bedroom to lie down; but don't let her leave." "What if she decides to leave?" "If she leaves, then you might want to consider unemployment." "Okay, keeping her here, I can do that." "Smart man. I'm on my way." Shaune kicked up his car into gear. He made it home in less then tem minutes. When he arrived to his house, he ran to the den where Greg was but Tory wasn't in there. "Did she leave?" "No. I asked her if she wanted to lie down, and she said yes. So I escorted her to your bedroom." "Thanks man." Then he sprinted up the stairs and as he got to the door, he put his ear to the door to hear what she might be doing. Then he opened it. She was lying on his bed waiting for him to come in. He crawled across the bed and they lay parallel facing each other. "If I answer your question, would you promise me one thing?" "Of course." "Promise me that you won't hurt me like he did." "I could never hurt you. I promise I won't hurt you." "No you're not in love alone." Then he held here so tight in his arms and started to kiss her. Then she withdrew with a cringe.

"Oh yeah, my beard; it's pretty coarse huh?" "A little." "Kinda make me look like the, what was the words you used? "The Black Grizzly Adams." Tory started to giggle and said, "I said that?" "Yes Ma'am you did." "Honestly, I thought I said that in my head. I'm so sorry Shaune." Shaune started to grow insulted as he saw she couldn't stop laughing at him. "Alright laughing girl, can we please go to the barber so you can stop laughing at me?" As tears ran down her eyes, she managed to squeeze out, "Please let's go."

It was early afternoon; Shaune had finally emerged from the back room where his personal barber was. He had looked like a new man. As he approached Tory, he asked her, "Is this better?" Then she looked him up and down and said, "Who are you and where is my boyfriend?" "Yuck, yuck, yuck. You're such a comedian Tory; where do you get your material?" "From my un-kept boyfriend." Now he started to get insulted again. "I'm sorry lover. Did I hurt your feelings?" "Ah, yeah you did." Then she grabbed his face and kissed him softly on his lips. "What can I do to make you feel better?" "You can tell me where we're going next." As she looked outside the door, she saw her favorite store; Ashley Stewarts. "Do you want to know my true insanity?" "Due tell." He asked. Then she pointed at the store. "Tory, that's typical. Every woman loves to shop for clothes." "Naw, my insanity is specific. Follow me please." As they walked into the store, Shaune walked over to the first thing he saw that looked good to him; while Tory walked straight over to the underwear. Shaune was eyeing a really sexy blouse that he thought would be perfect for her. He turned to show her because he thought she was still behind him. Then he became intrigued. He walked over to where she was and with a voice of shock he said "Wow, is this your insanity?" "Yes, I'm bordering on extreme. Every time I see this store, I have to buy underwear from here." Shaune was turned on by the fact that Tory had a fetish for sexy underwear. So turned on that he started to look through the selections to see just what might be sexy enough for her to wear for him. "Do you like these?" He asked her as he rummage through the endless selections. From pink argyle boy shorts to yellow silk and lace booty shorts. Shaune was fascinated with them all as he picked them up one by one. "These are cute. I don't have a pair." "We're getting them then." He said as he tucked them all one by one under his arm pit. You would think he was buying them for himself he was so fascinated. Then he saw his favorite color red. They were glowing like they were angels leading him to heaven. As he grabbed them, he turned to Tory and said, "Baby, you gotta get these." Tory looked at them and said, "Shaune, their cute, but I…" Then he cut in and said, "We're getting these too." He yelled in an excited voice. Tory managed to turn away from him and whispered, "We are?"

When they finally left the store, Tory was holding an impressive twenty five pairs of underwear that he paid for; not to mention the hard on that could drill a hole in the wall he was sporting. "Seriously Shaune, is all this necessary?" "I'm sorry baby; all I could do was visualize you in every pair. It drove me nuts." "I think a peek into my world was a look too long for you." "Your world is exciting to me." "The point is, it's my world and you invaded it. I'll be honest with you, some of these I might never wear. They're simply not my style." Shaune started to feel bad. Then he said, "You're right. I shouldn't have invaded your space." He paused and then he finished, "Baby, you have to understand that when you tell a man certain things like that, that's how he reacts." Although he was extremely aroused, he managed to huff out a puff of breath and said, "Baby, I'm not making any promises, but I will try not to invade your space anymore. However, you can best believe that I will be hitting that store up from time to time." All Tory could do was shake her head and promise to herself that she would never let Shaune in on a private moment ever again. "So where are we off to next?" He asked trying to change her anger. Tory looked around and saw a Game Stop shop. "Hey I have an Xbox 360, why don't we get some games from there?" Shaune smiled and said, "Why not? I haven't played video games in a couple of months." Then they were off. When they came from the Game Stop Shop, they came back to Torys' house. They had decided to play the Gears of War game that they were playing. While they were playing Shaune made Tory wear those red silk booty shorts that he liked so much. "Okay Daddy this is how this part works, you have to have my back so that I can run to the machine gun and clear the path for us all. So do you have my back?" "Yeah I always have your back. Let's do this." Needless to say, he didn't have her back because he was too embarrassed to tell her that he had no knowledge of the game and she ended up getting shot in the head from behind. "I thought you had my back. You said that you always have my back." "And I do. I just didn't quite understand the game that well." "You're useless Que'Shaune Guaudau." Then Shaune heard his personal cell phone go off. "Can I get that?" "Can I say no?" "It's my personal cell, so it might not be from you know who." "It's your phone so go and answer it." Event though she was okay with him answering his phone, she was equally concerned that it just might be one of the two. Then he kissed her and ran down the stairs to answer his phone. As he managed to catch the phone on its last ring, he realized it was his cousin Celia from his mothers' side. He hadn't spoken to her in 2yrs and at that point she had just met her then boyfriend now fiancée. They had finally decided to tie the knot and picked a wedding day and wanted to invite Shaune and his new girlfriend. It had appeared that she had heard that the New Que'Shaune Guadau had changed from miserable mogul to man in love. When he got off the phone, he was so happy to hear from his cousin and that she was getting married that he turned to run upstairs, he knocked over Torys' planner on to the floor. When he picked it up, he noticed there was a book mark on Friday, December 3. It read, "My Big Man Brandon's' B-day. Cooking class at 6pm @ the Gala Grill." And along with the appointment date was two movie tickets. Shaune had realized that Tory had a date with another man. His first reaction was to go upstairs and confront her about the situation. Then he had another idea. He pulled out his cell phone and called Greg.

Chapter 12
December 3rd... DAMN!!!

December 3rd that evening, Tory was standing in front of the Gala Grill with Mr. Richman. Mr. Brandon T. Richman was a white male in his 40's. He had been married for 8yrs to his wife Sandra, an African American female in her 40's as well. The two had known each other for five years and decided to marry after Sandra had given birth to their only son Brandon T. Richman Jr. who was now turning thirteen. "Tory, I really appreciate the changes you have made with my son. After his bout with cancer, and going through chemotherapy it left him pretty sickly. Now that he's recovering, he's starting to get his energy back and I wanted to get him strong for his birthday. This is the day for him not to be in bed. Since he's been hanging with you, he talks about all the fun things you two do all the time. His face lights up every time I mention your name." "Oh the pleasure is all mines. I am truly blessed to be in the midst of such a great kid. Brandon is a very strong, child. I have a feeling he's going to live a long time. My heart broke when I was informed about his having to go through chemotherapy. I want to be here for him as long as I can. He deserves all the life that God has to give him." "Thank you Torianey." Brand said just as they both embraced in a hug. Then a limo pulled up. And guess who pulled up in it? Que`Shaune Guadau and his side kick Gregory Duvain. Tory hadn't noticed that Shaune was on the scene until she un-embraced Mr. Richman and turned. Shaune walked up with a calm look on his face but in his mind, he had murder on the brain. "Hey baby. What's going on?" He asked sarcastically. Tory was stunned; taken aback even. "Hey, what are you…" Shaune cut in before she could finish and said, "What am I doing here? I've decided to take a cooking class. You know I love to cook; at least when I can." Then Mr. Richman introduced himself. "Hello Mr. Guadau. I'm Brandon T. Richman. Wow, I've only seen you on TV and the news papers. Never would I have ever imagined standing this close to you." Shaune replied sarcastically, "Really Brandon, really, it's not that serious." Then Tory drew close and whispered, "What was that all about?" "What are you two doing here?" Tory replied, "It's my big boy Brandon's' birthday." "Oh, and he needed you to celebrate it with him?" Suddenly, Tory caught on. So then she played along just to see the look on his face when he found out the truth. "Yeah Shaune he did need me to celebrate it with him." "Really? He couldn't get his own date?" He yelled as he stared Mr. Richman in the face. "Actually I kind of insisted that I celebrate it with him. You didn't mind sharing did you?" "With him…" Shaune was about to go off until a woman with a young male walked up and kissed Mr. Richman on the lips. Then Tory looked at Shaune while his facial expression changed from angry to confuse; and possibly embarrassed. Now Tory knew it was time to go in for the kill. "Que`Shaune Guadau II, allow me to introduce you to the Family Richman. We have Mr. Brandon T. Richman Sr. along with his wife Mrs. Sandra Richman and their son, my Big Homie Brandon T. Richman II. Oh wait you would know about Sr. and Jr. Aren't you a Jr.? I know Brandon Jr. is a little young for me but I like to call him my Big Homie but that's something he and I decided to change in the program; right Brandon?" Brandon slapped Torys' hand and replied, "Right." Then Tory continued. "See, Brandon Jr. is really my little Homie from the Big Homies, Little Homies program if you've never heard. And Brandon here has just conquered a bout with serious cancer.

Also, today is his birthday." As she drew closer to him, she pats him on the shoulder and finished her annihilation on his self esteem. "So yes Shaune, he does need me to celebrate it with him." Yet again; Shaune had managed to drop his face on the floor. He thought he was going to have to cut into a man, only to realize that he was in competition with a child. Then to make matters worse, the paparazzi showed up. The six of them were caught totally off guard and now exposed; all because Shaune was a jealous man. Quickly, Tory turned to the Richman's and said, "We should go inside now." As the cameras started to flash, the line of questioning started. While they were rushing up the stairs, Tory turned to Shaune and said, "This is your entire fault Guadau." Then they disappeared into the Gala Grill. As the doors closed behind them, Mr. Richman turned to Tory and asked, "Torianey is everything alright? Is there something wrong?" "You know what? I think the class is about to start. Why don't you guys go ahead inside and I'll join you shortly." As she watched the family leave to go into the kitchen, Tory turned to face Shaune and Greg. They both looked like two high school kids sent to detention. Then she scowled at Shaune and said, "Spill it Guadau." "Well, remember last week when I was on the phone with my cousin? Well, what had happen was I was so overjoyed when I made a mistake of knocking over your planner, and I made a mistake of seeing the two movie tickets. When I needed to see the date that they fell out of so I could place them back; I made a mistake and saw "My Big Man Brandon's' b-day." Cooking class @ 6pm at the Gala Grill. Then I called Greg and had him schedule the same class so I could catch you with Mr. Richman. Sr." Then she crossed her arms and asked, "And what would you have done if I were with him?" "Possibly kill him." Greg and Tory both looked at Shaune and yelled, "SERIOUSLY!" Then Shaune cleared it up and said, "Maybe not kill him, but I would have been moved to some kind of premeditated violent action at least." "And why is the paparazzo here? Who told them?" Shaune and Greg looked at each other, and then Shaune said, "I didn't say anything. I didn't tell Greg to say anything. Did you say anything to the paparazzi?" Jumping on the defensive, Greg shot back, "I swear, I didn't say a word Tory.

Shaune you know I would never set you up like that unless you said to call them." Shaking her head in disbelief, Tory walked up to both of them with her fingers pointed. "Here's how it's going to go down; we are going to avoid all contact from each other. No touching, no talking, none such as a glance. Do you copy me?" Shaune and Greg both shook their heads in agreement. Then she continued, "After this is over, we're going to wait till the cameras leave. GOT IT!" Then Greg raised his hand like a he was trying to answer a multiple choice question in class. "Speak!" "Uh, yeah about that, their not going to leave. Since you, Shaune and the family were spotted together, their going to pursue you to no end." "So how do we make this disappear?" "You have to come out with your relationship to Que`Shaune Guadau." Then Tory turned and yelled, "Not going to happen." While she was trying to walk away, Greg grabbed her and said, "The more you hold out, the uglier it can get. Trust me it will." As she shrugged away from him she spat back, "My life will not be a public spectacle; not even for the Great Que`Shaune Guadau." Then she left the hall. "Shaune we've been her before; this is Mia Alexandra all over again. You need to talk to your girlfriend if you wish to keep her."

The cooking class session had finally ended. As Tory and the Richman family came into the hall, they started to converse. "I had wanted to call Chef Winston to make the meals accamodable for Brandon because he needed to learn about some healthier choices of food. Plus, he needed to know that he doesn't have to conform to just eating trees and leaves all the time." As they all laughed Mr. Richman said, "My wife and I were al little concerned about the selections of food that's why we came along. But you had it all together, thanks." Tory, sounding arrogant said, "Brandon, I'm your girl. I got this." And then they left the building and the flashes started all over again. Not only was the paparazzi there, the crowd had expanded to news networks. Now the endless stream of questioning commenced. "Ms Heckstall, are you the new love interest of Mr. Guadau?" "Ms. Heckstall, is this your family?" Referring to Mr. Richman, one of the newsmen asked,

"Is this your husband? Are you having an affair Ms. Heckstall?" After hearing that, Mr. Richman became enraged and yelled, "HELL NO!!!" He then turned to Tory and said, "Look, I don't know what's going on but, I'm going to take my son home. He doesn't need this right now. I'll call you." Tory watched them run off and jump into their car, but not just before she saw little Brandon turn around and wave goodbye to her. Then she heard the doors behind her open. Yet again, caught together by the cameras and the news; it was Shaune and Tory on the steps of the Gala Grill. And the line of questioning poured out. The never ending speculative questioning came in like rapid fire. Greg looked at Tory and shrugged his shoulders to confirm what he had been trying to tell her. Tory decided to try and brave the crowd to get to her car. Now it was just Shaune and Greg on the steps of the Gala Grill when Chef Winston emerged to come and personally greet Shaune. "Mr. Guadau, I want to thank you for attending my session and if I can encourage you to come to another one of my functions...." Shaune cut in and said shaking his hand, "Thanks, great! I'll call you when I'm ready." Now it was evident who orchestrated this whole thing. Shaune and Greg headed to the limo to leave.

8:45am, the next day Tory awoke to a mass of chaos. It all started with her phone ringing. It was the Rickman's on separate phones tag teaming her about their exposure to the press; and how they couldn't take their son to school because of the press. "I'll take care of it. I promise I'll take car of it." She said as she stuttered over their yelling voices. After she hung up with them, the phone rang again. When she picked it up it was a news reporter. And she had a thick English accent. "Hello, may I speak with Ms. Torianey Heckstall please?" "Speaking." "Hello, my name is Cheryl Blake. And I'm a reporter from BBC World news. I was wondering if you would like to give a statement in reference to your relationship with Mr. Que'Shaune Guadau II?" "How did you know my name and how did you get my number?" Dodging her question, the reporter then went on to ask, "Can you confirm or deny any relation to Mr. Guadau II?" Tory hung up on the reporter. Then the phone rang again. "Look I have nothing to say to you; so you can stop calling." "Hey Tory, its Lou." "Hey Lou. Oh I'm so sorry about that. I've been getting disturbing calls all morning." "Quick question, are you sitting down?" "Should I be?" "I'll be honest; you won't be able to stand for this one." "What's up?" "I happen to have a hand full of reporters with cameras at my parking lot requesting to speak to you. Is it safe to say that you're not coming in today?" Tory took a deep breath to calm her and said, "No, I'm not coming into day. I need to pay someone a visit. If it's any comfort, I'm sorry for all this trouble." Lou laughed and said, "It's not a problem for me; along with your exposure my business does as well. So I'm really not concerned about me. It's you I'm more concerned about." "Thanks Lou. I'll probably see you tomorrow." As she hung up the phone, it rang again. This time she let the answering machine get it. Tory ran upstairs to get herself dressed. Tory jumped into her car and opened the automatic garage door. In her rear view mirror, she could see a barrage of paparazzi and news reporter behind her. She almost backed into a truck that tried to obstruct her driveway so that they could get more shots of her, and possibly get her to react. But she didn't. She managed to drive onto the grass to drive down her neighbors' driveway. Then she made her escape.

Tory arrived at Shaunes gate. Solomon didn't even bother to come out of the booth. He just opened the gate like he was instructed because Shaune had suspected that she would eventually show up. She thrusted into the den to see Shaune and Greg playing video games. As Shaune got up to give her a hug to console her, she took the news paper and slammed it into his chest. Then she walked over to Greg and asked, "How do I make this go away? How do I stop them from harassing the Richman's?" "I explained this to you yesterday. You have to come out with your relationship with Shaune." Feeling choked up like she wanted to cry, she wined, "But I don't want to." Then Shaune approached her and said, "It's only going to get worse baby." "Who called them anyways? They knew my entire name, where I lived, where I work. How did they find me?" "It was Chef Winston. After you left, he came out to shake my hand and exploit his business. This is another tactic that people do to boost their businesses." Tory knew she was experiencing what she could only classify as a "Quagmire." Yet again it was time to turn her anger and frustration towards the person who caused this whole thing; Que`Shaune. "This is your entire fault. The Big Homies, Little Homies program dismissed me from the program because the Richman's expressed their discontent with everything that went down last night. Not to mention the cameras showing up at their home. Brand is a 13yr old cancer survivor. He just got off chemotherapy last month and for the first time since his bout with cancer I got to see him. And now I will never see him again." Now tears started to trail down her eyes profusely. Then she continued, "All because you had some crazy notion in your head and you ran with it. You could have simply asked me. The minute you "Made the mistake" of seeing the appointment, you should have talked to me. Now did you not think your antics just might cause a problem like this? Did you not care that there were lives in the balance?" Shaune tried to give her some solace and said, "Tory, baby I'm sorry I…" "No Shaune, you didn't think. Because this is what you do. Que`Shaune Guadau gets what he wants. He gets a thought in his head and he goes after it. Not ever considering what the consequences are. Just like a spoiled 4yr old, you have to keep that tantrum going until ultimately, you get what you want. Seriously Shaune, are you proud of your results?" Shaune was now speechless. He felt as though he got his ass handed to him by Tory. After all, he knew she was right. He could have confronted her; the thought did cross his mind on first sight of the appointment. Now he was beginning to realize just how dumb his plan was looking hearing it from Torys' perspective. At that point, all he could do was throw up his hands and sit back down. Tory then turned her focus back to Greg. "What do I have to do?" Greg stood up and asked "Before I help you with this, just answer this one question. Do you still love him?" Tory looked over at Shaune who easily gave her a pitiful look and said, "Unbelievably, I still do." He thought she was at least three words from telling him it was over. Greg grabbed her shoulders and said, "Great, then I can get you through this."

Chapter 13
Felling in the Dark

I t was 8pm on the dot that night. Tory and Que`Shaune had agreed to meet with the press at Carrapellies just as Greg set it up. He had made separate statements for both of them. He had spent the better part of the day calling all his contacts to get the word out that Que`Shaune and Torianey were going to give their statements at the restaurant. While they waited in her office, Shaune and Tory sat in total silence. For the first time in his life, Que`Shaune knew what it felt like to be in the dog house. Fed up with the uncomfortable silence, Tory slammed her pen down on the table. "Look Shaune, we need to settle this." "I agree." Then she started, "Not to apologize for what I said because I meant it. However, how I said it was not necessary. Although your actions were childish, you're still a grown man." When she got up to approach him, he asked her, "Freedom to speak." "Speak at will." "I'm so very sorry about this whole thing. I had no idea that Chef Winston would have done this. And after hearing you spell it out to me; I realized just how dumb I looked. I promise I'll never do anything like this again." Then she pulled him up out of his seat and hugged him. "If you ever feel curious, just talk to me. Isn't that what you're always telling me? "Talk to me Torianey please!" It goes both

ways. If you want me to reach out to you, you have to reach out to me."
As they embraced each other in a deep passionate hug, Shaune said,
"Fair enough. From now on in, I'll always talk to you before I react
selfishly." As he kissed her to make up with her, she broke away and
said, "Oh don't think you can kiss me and this is going to go away.
You have weeks to make this up to me." "That's fine with me. And I'm
going to have all the fun in the world trying to do so. Besides, I can live
with that as opposed to losing you." Just as they were making up, Greg
popped in. "Great, you two finally decided to make up. This would
be very helpful for the interview. Besides, that silence in the limo was
choking me; now on to more important things. Shaune, you're going to
speak first. Then you're going to pass the floor over to Tory where she
will read her statement. Once she's finished with her statement, Shaune
is going to answer any and all questions thrown at the both of you."
Tory started to interject but then Greg said, "Tory trust me. I know he
might not seem capable of handling it; but the boy can hold his own.
Any unpredictable interference, I got it. Trust me on this."

Tory, Shaune and Gregory walked into the huge VIP room where
all the news networks and their reporters waited. Having never been in
an actual news conference, Tory was extremely nervous. The lights in
the room were so bright she could barely see who was there. All they
could see was the table that had three chairs behind them along with
two microphones. To her it almost looked like a sporting event. As
Shaune helped her to her seat he could see the distress in her face. When
he sat next to her, he reached under the table to get her attention. "Are
you okay baby?" "I'm fine; just a little nervous." "This will be over
before you know it." "Honestly Shaune, I want it over now." Then he
put his arm around her shoulder to try and console her. As Greg took
his seat, he started, "Hello all, my name is Gregory Duvain. As you
know I am Que`Shaune Guadaus' Assistant/Publicist. And with him
is his very close and personal friend Ms. Torianey Heckstall. At this
time Mr. Guadau would like to issue a public statement addressing the
rumors regarding his and Ms. Heckstalls' relationship. After his

statement, Ms. Heckstall will issue hers' and ultimately, any and all questions will be handled by Mr. Guadau or myself. Now that we have all the rules, I'll gladly hand the podium over to Mr. Guadau." Then Shaune took to his microphone. "Hello, as you all know I'm Que`Shaune Guadau. There has been a buzz of speculation in reference to my relationship with Ms. Heckstall. The truth is yes we are intimately involved. We have been for the past 7 plus months. However, I wish not to divulge too much more information about our relationship only that which was stated. Unlike my life, Ms. Heckstall is a very private person and under her wishes I can only ask that you respect the intimacy of our relationship. With that having been said; without further a due, I will pass the microphone over to Ms. Heckstall." As Tory drew her statement and the microphone to her, she glanced at the paper. Then she cleared her throat and spoke. "Hello, my name is Torianey Heckstall. My statement is as it stands. First of all, I would like to ask that you please respect the privacy of the family Richman. They do not share in the goings and comings of Mr. Guadau or myself. Their son is a 13yr old who's just recovered from a serious illness. During his healing process, neither he nor his parents need the aggravation of the media or its public. Now going forward, I do not wish to discuss the dept of my relationship only on the basis that Mr. Guadau and myself are just two normal people like any other feeling in the dark to see where we are in each others lives. We're just trying to see where things might take us. My involvement with him is not motivated by any other angle a love craved women would hold. And yes, I admit to the whole world I am in love with this man. But how it all unfolds is contingent upon how much space we have. That's all I have to say. Thank you." Greg covered his microphone and leaned over to Tory and whispered, "Damn, that sounded better then what I wrote. Good job Tory." Greg then took back to his microphone and said, "Now at this time any Q&A will be addressed by me or Mr. Guadau." One by one they all screamed Que`Shaunes' name. The first question came in. "Mr. Guadau, as busy of a man as you are; how did you meet Ms. Heckstall and where did you meet her?" "We met on the plane on our way back to South

Carolina. Her seat was badly soiled and most times when I'm traveling, I need an extra seat for my paperwork so I can stay organized. I saw that Ms. Heckstall was in terrible distress and she needed to get home that night or other wise they would have made her take a later flight. So, I gave her my extra seat." Then another question came in. "Mr. Guadau, Ms. Heckstall admits that she's in love with you. You never did explain to us what your feelings towards her are and what makes her the perfect woman for you?" Shaune and Tory looked at each other. Then he answered, "That is a really good question and I'm glad you asked. I knew she was the perfect woman after the plane ride. First of all, she didn't even know who I was. When we got off the plane, I tried to get to know her a little bit. But she wasn't buying it. I, being Que'Shaune Guadau thought I could go in for kiss; but nope, she wasn't having it. Ms. Heckstall was one tough nut to crack. I literally had to chase her down to let her know just how serious I was about her. And here I was thinking I was invincible. I meet her and realize just how human I really am." The crowd started to laugh along with him and then he finished, "The fact that she was no easy catch is what made me appreciate her more. As far as my feelings for her, I've fallen head over heels for her." As things were going well with the questions, of course there was one who managed to defy the rules. "Ms. Heckstall, although I was blown away by your speech, I'm sure that everyone else would conquer that I was left wanting more. Please explain to me exactly what is this "Feeling in the dark" you speak of?" Tory had remembered her voice from this morning. She was that nosey reporter who called her on the phone. Then Shaune cut in and said, "I'm sorry Ms. Heckstall isn't taking any questions at this time." "Mr. Guadau, we've all had this conversation with you before in some way or another at some point or another. Frankly, I would like to get to know the woman who makes a man who once used to scowl in front of the camera to a man who can crack a joke in front of us. Even if I weren't a reporter, I would still want to know who she is." Feeling like he was caught between a rock and a hard place, Shaune looked at Tory with nothing to say. Then Greg leaned over and said, "Tory, you need to give the people what they want. I had a feeling it would come to this point. I tried to create the rules but there's always one. Trust me, just from the way she set that question up, you can best believe that there would be more coming your way." Tory looked over at Shaune watching him nod in agreement with Greg. "Don't be so quick to throw me under the bus Guadau." Tory spat. Then she pulled the microphone over to herself. "Feeling in the dark is a metaphoric phrase for well, in our case two people who are in love trying to put their relationship in perspective; two people trying to put their hands on something their not sure of as of yet. Who knows, this might work out; it might not." "So what are you not sure of? Does this mean you're having reservations about your relationship with Mr. Guadau?" "What gave you the indication I had reservations?" "You say you're "Feeling in the dark" one just might get the impression…" "I'm sorry Ma'am, what is your name?" "I'm Cheryl Blake from BBC World News." "Oh Ms. Blake, I remember you now. Let me ask you one question. Have you ever been love before?" Cheryl started to answer her question but then Tory cut her off. "Don't answer that. However, when you did realize that you were in love didn't you kind of second guess yourself a couple of times? Maybe you felt somewhat inadequate; or maybe even he might be inadequate. Remember, sometimes as women we tend to over think things. So back to you being in love if you ever were. Do you remember when you were together wondering if you should kiss him or not? Or remember when you had your first disagreement? Then you asked yourself, is this man for me? Based on the conversation that ensued, is this what I signed on for? That was you feeling in the dark. If you already had the answers you wouldn't have to ask yourself in the first place. But because you're in love with that man, you continue feel around and see where this is going. You make sure that if you're going to stay or go, you know for sure. See, some women make the wrong decisions based on someone else's information or just bad speculation. A good woman, a real woman would stick around and feel it out just to see if in the event she had to leave, she knew for sure. Sometimes you end up finding so much more to be had as a result of. In other words, feeling in the dark is finding your fait. Fait gives us light." Another reporter asked Tory, "Do you think this fait might give way to marriage?" Then everyone started to laugh. As she looked at Shaune, she smiled and said, "I can't answer that right now. This is all so very new to us." Finally, Greg took a hold of the microphone and said, "Uh, this concludes the interview. Thank you all for coming out and enjoy the rest of your night." The three of them got up and went to another room where they could let off some steam. As Tory sat down, Greg walked up to her and said, "Congratulations, you did a pretty good job out there. I'm proud of you; you really held your own." Shaune sat next to her and asked her, "Did you really mean all that?" "Actually, I did. I took a page out of your book. Feeling in the dark was your phrase. I just elaborated on it a bit." "I said that?" "Yes, you don't remember the night you came to my house after our first date. I was so pissed with you after your then wife showed up and ruined our date." "You're right. I remember now." "So are you happy with what you found Mr. Guadau?" "Extremely Ms. Heckstall." Then they heard a familiar voice say, "Then lets explore that with an exclusive; how about tomorrow night?" It was the annoying reporter Cheryl Blake. "Shaune, this woman is worse then herpes. I can't get rid of her." Then Shaune said, "Cheryl Torys' not interested in an exclusive. I explained that her life is private. However, if you want me to give you one, then I'll be glad to on her behalf." "Sorry Shaune, that's way too easy. Plus, we have exhausted that option to bed a thousand times. No pun intended." Then she winked at Shaune and finished, "In more ways then one." Tory, catching on leaned over to Shaune and whispered, "I could just punch you in the throat right now." Shaune, feeling embarrassed and scared looked away from Tory and shrunk into his seat. "Look, the buzz right now is Torianey Heckstall is a media mystery begging to be solved. All I'm asking is 30min." "Thanks but no thanks Ms. Blank. Not interested." "It's Blake without the n and an e on the end. Frankly, this could benefit all of us." "I fail to see that. Seriously, you are just one piece of a puzzle that doesn't fit in my life. Again, thank you but no thank you." Cheryl walked up to Tory and said, "I could spin this in a bad way or I could spin this in a good way. You can decide for yourself." "Are you threatening me?" "Ms. Heckstall, I'm trying to reason with you." "Then call me unreasonable. Now please go away." As Tory left the room, Cheryl tried to follow her, but not just before Greg stopped her. "Cheryl, Tory actually happens to be one of the good girls. Give her a pass on this one." "You know I can't do that Greg. Because she is a good girl and she's with Que'Shaune is why I need this exclusive. You know Shaunes' track record with women. His ex-wife Lisa Mill, Mia Alexandra..." Then Greg cut in and said, "YOU! Yeah let's not forget about you and how you did him dirty. Sleeping with him just to expose him; but of course you sleep pretty well at night, I wonder how Cheryl? Oh yeah, because you're one of those women on Shaunes' list that can be evil and live with themselves." Then Shaune asked, "What's in it for you anyway?" "What makes you think there's something in it for me?" Then Shaune and Greg looked at her with straight faces. Then she laughed and said, "Okay, I would be guaranteed the lead Anchor at BBC World. Come on guys, you know that if this were you, you would do the same thing. Then Greg said, "In that case then the lady said no and I have to go with that." Cheryl squinted; her eyes at Shaune and said, "Be leery of me. If I find so much as a jay-walking ticket on her, I will annihilate her reputation. TRUST!" As Cheryl stormed away, Greg turned to Shaune and said, "I hope she doesn't have any jay-walking tickets."

Shaune knocked on Torys' office door to see how she was doing after all that had gone down. As he walked in he saw her working to keep herself busy. "Is everything alright?" "Everything is fine. I'm just clearing up a few loose ends before next week. Is that specimen of a reporter gone yet?" "She's gone. I'm sorry about all this. I know you must want to lay into me again. That's why I came back." "Shaune the only thing I want to know is how did you end up getting involved with a woman like that?" "The relationship between Cheryl and I is not so complicated. She, like my ex-wife dug up information on me. She, like my ex-wife had motives." "Let me guess, you were a career move for her. And if she got the digs on you, she would get the job." "Something like that. We did fall for each other for a short stint, but her career was more important to her." "Ouch Shaune! You have had some hard luck with women. I'm just curious to know why we are together if you continue to have your streak with women is this way." "What do you mean?" "I mean, I feel lucky to have met you, but to some degree I can't help but wonder what made you want to pursue me? I feel like I should have some superficial motive or something." "Were you not listening at the conference? You weren't like the other women. Even when you knew who I was and what I was capable of, you didn't care. That was the type of woman that I have never encountered. I remember hearing my dad tell me about women who make you hold out; that those are the women who are worth it. See, I always took the easy way when it came to women. When they gave it up easily, so did I. Needless to say, it would prove to be useless to deal with such a woman. Now I meet you and I see exactly what my dad was talking about all this time. Tory I haven't regretted one moment with you and that includes my childish moments." "Shaune, I gave it up quickly. Actually, that night you met me on the plane. Remember?" "That's not my point Tory. It was more then just sex with you and I. I felt a certain connection with you and it felt much different, much better then what I felt before. " Tory grabbed her keys, turned off her computer. "Daddy, I'm so sorry that you've been through all that. Damn and I was complaining about how bad I had it. I guess we can both swap notes from each others books." Then they left to go home.

The next week, Shaune and Tory were in their hotel room getting themselves ready for his Cousin Celia's wedding. She had wanted to have her wedding in Hawaii on the beach. Shaune was more then happy to help pay for the wedding. Although Richard was not a rich man, but he had his pride; so secretly Shaune had contacted him and collaborated a way for Richard to put up his portion of the money and Shaune would match the rest. Shaune was so excited for the wedding to start that he kept pushing Tory to hurry up out of the bathroom.

As he knocked on the door, he started to yell, "Baby, come on. I don't want to be late for the wedding." "Would you please stop rushing me? Beauty takes time; I'm sure your cousin is not ready yet either." "We need to be in place before she gets there." Then Tory finally came out of the bathroom. When she stepped out, Shaune hushed his rant and couldn't stop staring at her. In his eyes she was a stunning beauty in a beige one piece strapless halter gown that was long and flared out with a split. It was perfect for the beach. "Daddy, could you please help me with my shoe straps?" He was more then happy to help her. As he knelt down on his knees, he helped her put her feet in her shoes then one by one he strapped them in. After he was done in his normal perverted fashion, he couldn't resist the urge to caress her thigh. Tory bent down and whispered, "Don't start something you can't finish." Then she grabbed his hand and said, "Besides, you don't want us to be late for the wedding, remember?" As they were leaving the room, he said, "Whatever. When we get back, I'm going to start something alright."

Everyone was at the beach waiting for the famous couple to arrive. They were on the beaches of Coconut Island on Hilo Bay where the wedding was going to happen. The day was perfect. The sun was shinning and the wind was a warm breeze that swept off of the ocean. It was a small wedding with the attendance of fifteen which consisted of family, friends and co-workers. The wedding was somewhat non-traditional. There were no bridesmaids or groomsmen; only Tory and Shaune, their maid of honor and best man. As the wedding started Richard, Shaune and Tory took their places and waited for Celia to arrive. The music started to play and everyone clenched in anticipation. Then Celia finally came down the isle. Her dress was a beautiful off white strapless bodice dress that flared out just a little below her knees. Her dress was custom made by Caroline Herrera; and her shoes were by Christian Louboutin. As the ceremony started, everyone watched in anticipation as Celia walked down the makeshift wedding isle tent. In Richards mind, she wasn't moving fast enough to get to him. He couldn't wait to kiss his bride and make her his wife. When she got to him, the priest started the ceremony. When it was time the bride and groom gave their vows in French. Unlike Que'Shaune, Tory didn't understand what was being said; seeing that she only spoke and understood English. But none the less, she felt that it was their moment so she should just smile and enjoy the moment with them. Shaune found their vows to be touching and inspiring. As he looked at his girlfriend, he felt a ting of nostalgia. Now it came time for the ring to exchange. They separately recited their promises as the priest told them to say it before they placed their rings on each others finger. The ceremony ended when they kissed and everyone clapped.

The night was coming to a close and while everyone had gathered at the banquet for the luau-style reception, the servers were preparing the food to be served. The menu consisted of a huge roasted sucking pig, as well as sword fish, and roasted duck. For the sides and noshes, there was assorted veggies, rice pilaf, assorted salads, gourmet meat balls, assorted flavor mini wings; along with plenty of wine and hard liquor to go around. Everyone was eating and socializing when Celia decided to give a thank you toast. "Will everyone please allow me to say something right now?" Everyone started to clap as she started her speech. "First of all, I would like to thank everyone for coming out. I want to thank all of you for being so very patient with me, I do realize that I've been a total nightmare all the way up till today. The truth is I've allowed my nerves to get the best of me time and time again. I mostly want to thank my cousin Que'Shaune. I know all about how much you helped out to make this whole thing happen. If it were not for you, things would not have gone as smooth as they it did. And to your lovely partner, Tory I would like to extend my arm and bring you in as family. I hope that you would consider me more and more as your family as time goes by while we continue to get to know each other. When the two of you get married, I'll be the first one you call." Tory choked on her own spit. Shaune just rubbed her back to help her clear her throat. Finally, Celia finished her speech and everyone clapped, drank and ate merry for the rest of the night as it went on. Shaune and

Tory danced the night away. Then when they got tired, they went to sit by the bonfire that was going. Following them were his cousin Celia and her now husband Richard to join them. They sat and chatted for the best of the night. Then Celia asked the burning question in her drunken mind, "So, when are you two getting married?" While sipping her wine, Tory started to choke. "Are you okay?" Celia asked. "I'm fine. It just went down the wrong pike."

On the way back to the hotel room feeling drunk and horney, Tory tried to get frisky with Shaune. But he wasn't very interested in sex at the moment. He had other burning questions on his mind. While on the elevator, she started to nibble on his neck. However, Shaune managed to bring everything to a screeching halt and asked, "Would you consider marrying me?" "Can we talk about this later?" "Sure we can, just answer the question." "That's really not a question; it's more of a conversation." "So let's explore that conversation." "That would be fine; just later." As the elevator opened, Shaune lightly shoved Tory aside while he was exiting. When they got into the room, he proceeded to take off his jacket and tie. Tory walked up behind him and tried to wrap her arms around him but he managed to free himself from her hold. She could clearly see that he had an attitude. "Que'Shaune, we're in paradise. Why can't we just enjoy ourselves?" He didn't bother to answer her. "Are you going to act like this for the rest of the vacation?" Then he took off his shoes and reclined on the bed and turned the television on. Tory, feeling tired of his childish antics took the remote from him and shut off the television. "Okay Guadau, you want to take it to that place, so then let's take it there. Are you sure you want to have this conversation?" "I wouldn't have asked if I didn't." "Okay then the answer to your question is no." "You wouldn't consider marrying me?" "NOPE!" "Why not?" Then Tory asked "Give me three reasons why I should?" He looked at her like she was crazy and replied, "Hello Tory, remember me? I'm Que'Shaune Guadau. I don't need three reasons. That speaks for itself." "Gee, I must obviously have it all wrong then. That one reason trumps everything." "Damn right it does." "So what was I thinking? But just in case I might not be too sure, indulge me and give me two more reasons." Feeling all too proud of himself, he cleared his throat and started, "Alright fine then. Two, I run an extremely lucrative business; which brings me to my third reason, I can take care of you far more better then any man can. How about that? Tory I have a thousand reasons why you should marry me." Tory folded her arms and looked down at Shaune while he gloated in his own pride. She wanted to see that look on his face just before she went in for the kill. "So tell me is the same reason why you got married in the first place?" Shaune paused for a minute. Then he took a deep breath and said, "That wasn't fair. You didn't have to say that." "So then help me understand one thing, how is it that while you're busy running around being Que'Shaune Guadau, running an extremely lucrative business, how are you supposed to take care of me? Oh wait, the same way you took care of your last wife right?" "You know you're being really disrespectful right now." "No I'm not. I'm just trying to be the voice of reason to your arrogant, selfish and extremely ignorant ass. You screwed up your first marriage and now you want to marry me and do the exact same thing. How many lessons do you want to learn? Or do you even learn from your mistakes?" At that point Shaune jumped up off the bed and stood directly in Torys face. Tory felt scared that he might have a Jamaica moment and proceed to choke her out again. But ultimately, she stood her ground. "Look I'm trying to answer your questions. Play by your rules; all the while keeping it 100% with you. When I do that, you blow a fuse. What? Do you want me to lie to you?" He stood in Torys face looking delirious like he wanted to do something. Then he sat back on the bed and put his shoes back on his feet. "Where are you going? I thought you wanted to finish this conversation." He didn't respond to her because he was so enraged at her and her ability to challenge him the way she did. As a man he knew that in order for him to say what he wanted to say and do, it only took another man to be in the room, and there wasn't; so he knew he needed to leave. "Que'Shaune where are you going?" She asked again this time in fear that he would leave her in Hawaii. But he just left without even answering her.

Shaune found himself walking along the beach. He couldn't fathom why Tory wouldn't marry him. "We would make a perfect couple." He thought to himself as he scratched his head while looking around the beautiful Hawaiian beach. While his back was turned, a hand patted him on his back. It was Celia. "Hey what are you doing out here and where is Richard?" "He's coming. We're having a light picnic on the beach the night before we leave. I told him I didn't want to lose anytime here in paradise. I called your suit to see if you and Torianey could join us but she said that you ran out. Mona Me, she sounded a bit upset. And now I find you here looking like a lost puppy." "We kind of had gotten into an argument." "It wouldn't happen to have anything to do with my nosey question of marriage would it?" "It had everything to do with it. She told me she wouldn't consider marrying me. ME QUE`SHAUNE GUADAU!" "Mon cousin, make a note to yourself that although you may have it all together, there are a few rare handful of woman who don't see you the way the masses do. Tory is that one rare woman. She happens to manifest a genuine heart for you." "And I want that in my life for ever. How do I prove to her that I'm capable of being the man for her?" Then Richard came on to the beach to join them. "You know what Celia, forget about it. She and I will figure it out. Go and enjoy your picnic." "Que`Shaune, we have plenty of cheese and fruit and wine. I insist that you join us." Although he didn't want to ruin their night with his dry spell, he did want to hear what she had to say. After all who better to tell about the game of love then two people who found it? They found a nice spot to sit and eat all the while enjoying the beach. "Now cousin, I have to ask you did she at least explain why she wouldn't want to marry you?" "She asked me to give her three reasons why she should." "And they were?" "At first, I said I didn't need three reasons; the fact that I'm Que`Shaune Guadau was reason enough." Both Celia and Richard both cleared their throats. "What was that supposed to mean?" Shaune asked. "May I?" Richard interjected. "Qui, se vous plait." Celia laughed out in her native French tongue. Then he started, "Your cousin like you was very arrogant and

some might have even called her a stuck up prude." Celia slapped
Richard on the thigh as they all laughed. However, hard as it was for
me to get into her life, I found a way." "How did you do that?" "I used
those everyday cheesy style tactics." He knew what he meant, Shaune
needed some more ideas. "What do you mean by that?" "This might
not apply to you but as you can see I'm not a rich man like you or your
family. I work everyday and I come home to my now wife in the same
fashion. However, before I got the chance to be in her life I would do
little things for her. I cook a romantic dinner for her, I send her flowers
to work, and I read little corny poems. Ultimately, I wore her down. I
let her know that I was the one man in the world who was thinking of
her night and day. And I always will." When he turned to look at his
bride, she leaned in and kissed him on the lips. Shaunes mind started
to revert back to when he had brought her the car. How she didn't car
for the car as much as she did the breakfast he made for her as well
as her favorite meal he cooked for her. He had even remembered the
conversation he had with her about how much she loved the little things
in life as opposed to the much bigger things. Upon his reminiscence,
Shaune had a revelation. He finally got the point. "Thank you so much
for telling me this. And if you don't mind I have some making up to
do." He quickly kissed Celia on the forehead and he shook Richards
hand and fled back to the suit.

Tory was sitting on the patio taking in the fresh air while enjoying
her glass of wine when she heard Shaune walk in. He walked up to her
and asked, "May I sit next to you?" "Sure you can." As he sat next to
her at the patio table, he took the glass of wine out of her hand and took
a sip of it. "Where have you been all this time?" "While I was walking
on the beach, I saw my cousin and her husband." "I bet they must be
having a great time." "Yeah, they were going for a light picnic on the
beach for one last night before they leave in the morning." "Wow! That
sounds fun unlike us huh?" "Torianey can we talk please?" Tory knew
that when he wanted to talk that meant that a potential argument was
amidst. As she got up to leave, she said "I don't want to argue about

this anymore…" Shaune jumped up to stop her from leaving and it startled her because she thought that he was still angry with her. Shaune composed himself and said, "Baby please let me say what I need to say. I promise I won't argue with you." He gave her back her glass of wine and they both sat back down while he started. "You were right. All this time, everything you said was right." Torianey was shocked. Before he left her he thought that he didn't have to explain anything. But somehow he managed to come to his senses. Then he finished, "I hated the fact that your decision to challenge me was about marriage. We both know I suck at it." "I never said you sucked at marriage. I thought that if you had a better plan on how to keep your next marriage better then what you've been through prior, then maybe that would be something worth working towards." "Anyway you put it, you're right. I allowed my money and my pride to get the best of me. Now I need to know from you what can I do to make myself worthy of being your husband someday?" Yet again he managed to daunt her with his words. Last time in Jamaica he told her she was the "Rock Star" and he was her "Biggest Fan" and now this. She quickly gathered her thoughts and said, "Well I mean, look the truth is you can take care of me far better then any man could. Better then I could take care of myself. But that's not what I'm in it for." "So that's what I'm asking you. What are you looking for? Are you in love with me?" "Of course I'm in love with you. With everything I have in me. But what is the point of being in love and being married if you're not around to be in love with. If you're away all the time, how can we enjoy each other? Sometimes, love is just not enough." "Baby I'm going to do what ever it takes to prove to you that I'm the man for you." Tory smiled and they both leaned in to kiss; but just then his private cell phone rang. Then they stopped just short of their kiss and looked at each other. Tory leaned away from him and took the glass of wine and placed it back in his hand. As she got up to leave, Shaune could see her eyes well up in tears. While he was watching her leave the last ring woke him from his thought. "This better be important." "It's me Greg Shaune. I have your father on three way." "Okay so what has the two of you calling me in the middle of the night?" "Germany!" His father yelled. "This wouldn't happen to do with the stock market again?" Both Greg and his father yelled, "YES!" Shaune paused for a second. Then he said, "Greg you go to Germany and handle it for me." His father yelled, "What are you crazy? We can't afford to lose shareholders like Germany." "Dad I'm busy right now and I know that Greg can handle it. He's done it before. Germany is no different." "And what are you busy doing?" "Something else right now." Shaune paused again for a second and had an epiphany. "Gregory, remember we talked about that VP position?" "Yeah, what about it?" "If you handle this Germany thing for me, it's yours." Greg started to laugh with joy in his voice because this was what he was looking to hear for a while. "Shaune man don't say it if you don't mean it." "I'm saying that if you come out victorious, it's all yours. Pay increase, your own company car, stock options, you name it." "Game on!!!" "Great. Call me tomorrow and we'll run interference tactics." Greg hung up. Just as he was about to hang up the phone, he heard "Jr. am I left to assume that this has everything to do with your little girlfriend?" "This has everything to do with my future." "Your future is to be the head of Redliner." "I have to go Dad." Before he hung up the phone, his father quickly said, "Mon Files, when ever you're ready to relinquish your position at Redliner, please let me know." "I'll call you tomorrow Dad." Then he hung up. This time he turned his phone off. He stepped off the patio and saw Tory lying in the bed under the covers. As he sat on the lounger he asked, "Are you sleep?" "Um hum." She replied faintly. "I'm about to take a shower, would you like to join me?" "Nope! But you enjoy yourself." "Okay, but I'm going to be pretty lonely in that warm shower all by myself." "You have your hands to keep you all the company you need." Feeling rejected and offended, he got up and left to take his shower. After he got out of the shower, he had an idea. As he dried his body off with his towel, he grabbed his cologne and started to rub some all over his body. He had remembered that Tory loved the way he smelt after he showered. Plus, he also knew she loved the smell of the cologne he wore. As he looked in the mirror he couldn't help but laugh at himself and say, "Just keeping it cheesy." He came into the room and removed his towel from around his waist. Then he slid under the covers. Her back was turned so she couldn't see what he was doing. He started to fan the scent of his cologne across to her. He even started flailing the covers around to get the smell up in the air. When that wasn't getting her to respond, he started clearing his throat loudly. Tory thought it was comical how much he would go through just to get her attention. Ultimately, she gave in. "You smell nice." As he moved in to get closer to her, he said, "I'm sorry I didn't hear what you said." "I was saying you smell... Are you naked under the covers?" "Huh? What? Uh yes. But I can explain. See, what happened was I was fully dressed when I came out of the bathroom. Then as I was walking towards the bed, my clothes fell off." "Wow! Is that true?" "Yeah and then I realized something; my clothes really don't like being in the bed with you." "That is one startling revelation for the books." "Yeah and what's even better then that is my body loves being in the bed with you." Tory busted into laughter. "Was that too cheesy for you?" "Actually, that was more creative then cheesy. But I like." As they started to embrace, Shaune moved in to kiss her. After he kissed her, he said, "Was I not supposed to do that?" "Alright buddy, the joke is over. This is exactly what you planned." "What are you talking about? What is this plan you're speaking of?" Then he kissed her again. Now he started to position himself on top of her. Tory took her legs and wrapped them around him. "You know how much I love that." He whispered in her ear. Then she whispered, "If you let me ride, I promise I'll give you as much as you want." "Oh Memoiselle, your wish is my command." He quickly got up and reversed positions with her. Now she was in the drivers' seat. She sat in his lap Indian style. Shaune proceeded to remove her gown so he could feel her body on his. She started to ease his hard penis inside her. He was definitely ready for her. Tory started to ride and they both inhaled and moaned at the same time. While she was slowly grinding on him, she started to bite and suck all over his neck. She started to tighten her legs around Shaunes body. "Oh my love, please, tighter." He whispered seductively. "Uhh, yes daddy, anything you say." Then she tightened her grip even more. Feeling every inch of him inside her made her feel like she was going to go crazy. He held her body so tight that she felt like she could burst. Nonetheless, she didn't seem to mind because she kept going in on him like it was her last day on earth. They could feel each others heart beating heavier and heavier. Tory started to grind harder. Shaune could feel her body trembling. So he flipped her on her back changing positions. They started to kiss all over each other when Tory whispered, "Que'Shaune, please make it hurt." He grabbed her legs and thrust deeply inside her one time. She cried out so loudly. "Oh, yes just like that." "You want it like that Baby?" "Yes Daddy, please make it hurt." And he gave her more as she requested. He drew himself in closer and gave her all of him. The more he gave her the more she cried out to him. Shaune felt her body trembling harder. He knew that she was at her climactic moment, but he wanted to be where she was. So he sped his groove up even faster. So much faster that Tory started to groove with him. "Shaune, I want cum now." "I want to cum with you baby." He whispered. As Tory started to cum Shaune could feel her muscles contracting. He felt like he was getting sucked inside her it felt so strong. Now he felt his time to cum and when he did, he grabbed Tory so tight and buried his face in her body to hide his yells. Shaune was cumming so hard that he started to drool on Torys neck. When they came off from their high, they laid in each others arms. Then Tory said, "Can I tell you something?" "You can tell me anything." "The reason why I told you that I wouldn't marry you was because I was really scared of the idea of marriage." "I can understand. Having been married once, it is a scary experience." "No. Not because of the experience itself; because that I wouldn't be able to have this moment again. I've imagined us being married. But then when I do, I imagine you gone all the time. I guess what I'm trying to say is since I've fallen in love with you, I find myself needing you. I don't like feeling needy." Tory tried to pull away from him. He grabbed her and said, "I want you to need me. It's my job as a man to rescue you when you need me. Like I said before, I'm going to do all I can to prove to you that I am the man for you. Can you at least give me that chance?" "As many chances as I can stand."

The next morning, the two of them were sharing their last breakfast on the patio. It was their last few minutes in paradise but of course, the moment of spoil didn't waist it's time. Just as Tory was about to ask her question, Que`Shaunes' cell phone rang. "I promise I'll be right back." He quickly jumped up and went back into the hotel room to answer his call. Tory sat and listen to him conduct his call. She could tell it was Greg of course. She couldn't make out what it was they were talking about. The only thing she didn't want to hear was him having to leave her. Then she thought to herself, "There goes that needy streak in me again. I have to be prepared for the fact that he's going to have to leave sometime." Shaune came back to the patio; and as he sat down, he saw the look on his girlfriends face. "That was Greg you know." "I know." "He's going to Germany for me." "Really?" "Yes. See, last night when you left, he called to see if I would go to handle some important business. But I suggested that he go because I was here and I didn't want to leave you like I did in Jamaica." Strangely enough, his words were meant to sound well but Tory begged to differ. "I guess I should be grateful then huh? I'm going to check the closets to see if I left anything." As she got up to leave the patio, Shaune stopped her. "What's wrong now? I thought you would be happy that I'm not going." "And I am; but I have to check the closets to make sure I didn't leave anything." As quick as she left the patio, Shaune followed suit. When she opened the closet door, he slammed it close and said, "Let's talk about this now; because as soon as we get on the plane, I'm going to get all sorts of ugly eyes, crying and sighing, along with attitude. So spill it." "What makes you think I would cry over you?" "Look, I don't want the back and forth business with you. What's with the attitude? I thought you would be impressed that I made a sacrifice for you." "You made a sacrifice for me Shaune. You managed to make me feel worse. You know what you said? You said that you sent Greg to handle some important business for you just so you could stay with me here. Do you know how that makes me feel? Like I'm inconveniencing your plans; like you had to stay here for me." Shaune laughed in confusion.

"What are talking about? Woman why must you put words in my mouth? You know for a fact that is not what I said." "It is what you meant." "No it's not. I was saying that from an important meeting in Germany that I needed to attend, I found you more important. You know what, why don't you look in your closet and see if you left your common sense in there. I'm done with this conversation. I'll be in the car when you're ready." Shaune stormed off and left her by herself. Now it was Tory feeling like the heel this time. "Maybe he did give up his meeting for me, but did he have to tell me that? But of coarse he did. I'm such a fucking idiot." Then she grabbed her jacket to and left to go to the car. When she got to the car, he was on the phone doing his usual dictating to Greg. When he was done, he said to the driver, "We're ready to go when you are." Then he looked at Tory and said, "Or are we?" Then she pulled out an African Lilac and handed it to him. "Truce?" He took the flower from her and smiled at her. "I was never at war with you. And although I appreciate the gesture, this is your favorite flower." "And what is yours again?" "Haven't you been paying attention? I've been giving it to you a thousand times." Tory paused to think again what his favorite flower was. Then she said, "Oh it's the black rose right?" "Exactly!!! And here I was thinking the only thing that you could remember was me making you feel bad." "I guess I had that coming. I understand that you're upset with me right now. But to squelch the situation, I want to say that I realized that I was being a little irrational." "NO, not you Tory? Why would I think that?" He said sarcastically as he scrolled through his cell phone. Tory was trying to level with him because she knew that she was wrong for pushing his buttons. "Shaune I want to apologize because I was out of line to think that you were putting it all off on me. It all goes back to last night when I was saying that I have a tendency to act needy. That was my way of trying to avoid that. I know it sounds crazy…" Shaune cut her off and said, "Tory I really don't care. Your issues are for you to deal with." Shaune was fed up with dealing with Tory and her insecurities which was another thing he had never had experience dealing with women about. As the car entered the tarmac where the plane was, he continued to mess with his cell phone. Tory felt like she had burned her bridges with him at that point. Although she tried to restore it, her efforts proved to be useless. She just got on the plane and figured the less she would say, the better the ride home might be. After he got off his phone, Shaune realized that the two of them sat at separate ends of the plane. He felt like he may have stepped in a deep puddle by blowing Tory off as he did. He saw her sitting away from him on the opposite side of the plane. He quietly picked up his cell phone and called his cousin. When she picked up her phone he started to whisper. "Celia, it's me Shaune. I was wondering if you could help me." "What's the problem? You and Tory aren't still going at it about the whole marriage thing? I thought you were running off to make up with her." "We did. And it was great. Last night after we made love she told me about how she had her needy moments. Well, my phone rang and I answered it during breakfast. Needless to say, we got into an argument about it. When she got in the car she tried to apologize to me and I was so upset with how things went and I kind of blew her off." "Wait, you blew her off while she was apologizing to you?" "Yeah. I feel like that was the wrong thing to do. Was it?" "You're damn right it was. Not very often does a woman ever apologize to a man. I tell you one thing; if she ever apologizes to you again it will probably be because she made a mistake of shooting you in the face." Richard just happened to be listening along with the call and he gave his opinion. "Hey Shaune I have an idea. You give her a piece offering." "Like what?" Richard though for a second; then he said, "What is something the two of you share in common?" Then he remembered. "Pie!" "Okay. I'm not exactly sure what it is you're talking about but if you can get her a pie and if it makes her happy, then get her a pie." "We share a fancy for these little pies that I used to eat when I was a kid. I have them on the plane. Thanks for your help. Got to go." He hung up the phone and ran to the pantry. He picked up one of the cherry pies, opened it and put in on a plate. Then he got himself a knife and cut it in half. As he approached her, he sat down and said, "Truce?" "I...I..." Tory didn't know what to say because she had been trying to end the whole thing in the first place. "Baby, I want to squash this whole thing between us. I was acting like a jackass when I just wanted to not argue in the first place. But understand one thing; if I'm not away on business, I'll have to conduct it some kind of way. But it doesn't mean that I want you to feel bad because I can't go. I have to keep the order of things." Tory just shook her head and said, "I understand." Shaune exhaled in relief. Then he asked, "Can we kiss on it." Tory smiled and kissed him. As the plane started to leave the tarmac, they shared their pie. And it was the end of their battle.

Chapter 14

Waiting for the Dust to Settle. Or Will It?

I t had been one year since the exposure of Que`Shaune and Torys relationship. Tory had hoped that the world would have moved on so that she could maintain her normalcy. Since their coming out, they started spending more time together; mostly at his house. They had become the new catch of the public. Wherever either of them was spotted whether apart or together, it was reported. However, Tory never fed into it. Plus, she had more pressing issues to worry about. It was Shaunes birthday and she wanted the night to go off without any hitches and most of all, no news media. She had been corresponding back and forth with Greg and a party planner behind Shaunes back. And she asked Lou if she could throw the party at one of his VIP rooms. She got Greg to do the guest list of at least fifty of his closest friends and family members. Tory knew that Shaune didn't like large parties unless he had thrown one of his fundraisers. Only then would he want two hundred or more because he was trying to raise money for a specific cause. Since it was a surprise, she didn't want to inundate him with a lot of people. As she took the list from Greg she asked, "Did you confirm everyone on the list?" "List is confirmed. However, there were a few plus ones." "I just don't want it too big. Shaune likes intimate settings. And since it's a surprise, I don't want to overwhelm him." "Okay and what is the plan on getting him here?" Greg asked. "He already thinks that we're going to another exclusive restaurant in downtown Columbia. So he's going to meet me here. I'll have to concoct a way to be in distressed and then he'll get lured into the VIP room and from there, everyone will catch him off guard."

Que'Shaune arrived at Carrapellis on time at 7:45p. Tory gave him the impression that they had reservations somewhere else at 8p. As he was getting out of his car, he dialed her cell. "Baby, I'm here. Where are you?" "I'm in my office finishing up something. Come on in." As he shut his phone off, he sucked his teeth and said, "This is my damn birthday, you shouldn't even be working." Shaune had been looking forward to spending his birthday with Tory, so he made sure that he would work hard the whole week and get all the stats and marketing business out of the way. But now, they were going to be late for dinner reservations. Or at least so he thought. When he got inside the foyer, he saw no one was there to greet him. Then he stepped inside the mostly empty restaurant and yelled, "Torianey! We're going to be late for dinner." I'm in here." She yelled back. He walked to her office and saw her struggling with a box. "What are you doing? Can't this wait till tomorrow?" Watching her struggle with the box, he picked it up and said, "Where do you want this?" With a look of fake relief, she said, "I need it to go in that room." She was pointing to the VIP room. Just before he turned to go to the VIP room he said, "You look very sexy tonight." "Thank you." When he got to the VIP room, it was dark. "Alright, where do you want me to put this?" "Wait one second; I'll turn on the lights." As she turned on the lights, Que'Shaune was greeted with a flood of "HAPPY BIRHTDAY!!!" voices. He was indeed shocked. He saw all the people that he was closest to. Some he hadn't seen in years. His cousin Celia and her husband Richard was in attendance. Marta came to the party. His father was even there. There were fifty plus of the people Que'Shaune had associated himself with at some point or another. As the crowd calmed down to hear his response, he said, "You all scared the shit out of me. Thank you very much for that." As they all laughed, he cut in and finished. "It's so great to see all of you. Most of you I haven't seen since I was a child. Oh my God, Aunt Claire you look great." Then he turned to his girlfriend. "Torianey, you are going to get it when this is over." Then he turned back to the crowd and said, "Well let's get the party started. Oh and uh try not to get dysfunctional tonight. You got that Earle?" As the music started to play, Shaune looked at Tory and said, "How did you do this?" "I had help from your trusty Vice President and your father." "I wasn't expecting this. I guess it's safe to say that our reservations are a bust?" "I'm sorry Daddy. I didn't know any other way to steal you from work to pull this off. Besides, I have your special gift back at your house." He pulled her in close and asked her, "Does it entail me unwrapping you from this dress?" Tory laughed and said, "You're a dirty ole man. But that's after you get the original gift. But now, I think you have some mingling to do." Tory backed away and watched Shaune do his thing. After sometime had passed, it was time for Tory to take the mic so that dinner would be served. Plus, she had a list of people who had wanted to speak on his behalf of saying happy birthday. "Hello, I would like everyone's attention please. We are about to serve dinner now and if everyone would take a seat. That includes you birthday boy. And now, I'm going to hand the mic over to Gregory Duvain, Shaunes VP." Greg took the mic and started his speech. "My speech goes out to both Guadaus', Jr. and Sr. although it has been extremely challenging these past five years between the two of you, I can honestly say there has been no shortage on adventure. However, I can't certainly say that I didn't enjoy most of it. As for the birthday man Mr. Guadau, this past year I have seen you change from a straight edge, always on the job, twenty four seven, mechanical minded man to a man that has learned to loosen his collar; a man that has learned to laugh and love. And believe it or not everyone, he now has patience." Everyone including Shaune busted into laughter. As Greg finished, he said, "And now I have to pass the mic back to the one person responsible for that change, Ms. Torianey Heckstall." As Tory came back to claim the mic, she started to give her speech. "I really want to thank everyone for their compliance in making this whole thing happen. You were a huge help to pull this off. To the love of my life, Que`Shaune Guadau; it has been a blast dating you. Like Greg, it has been adventurous, challenging but most of all fun. I could remember when we first met; I had no idea who you were. Greg was right; I was the one woman under a rock who didn't have any idea who you were. When I got to know you, I realized that you were way different then the average business man. You didn't have that air about you. You're a man of true depth. You speak from the heart and you identify with everything I say. You managed to put a common, everyday woman like me on a pedestal that high. I don't know what I did to deserve such a high standard, but if I ever deviate from the standard, you let me know. To you birthday boy." As they raised their glasses to Torys' toast, they clapped afterwards. One by one the roster went on with congrads of happy birthday. Shaunes father came on then Marta was next. After she was finished, it was his cousin and her husband. But to Torys' dismay, there was one person she didn't anticipate coming to the mic. Marcus Swain. As he took the mic to speak, Tory leaned in to Greg and asked, "How come he wasn't on the roster?" "He didn't want anyone to know he had some special surprise for Shaune." "And you couldn't tell me this?" "He made me promise not to tell." Tory became concerned. She knew that Marcus' surprises were anything but subtle. All she could do at that point was brace for impact. "Shaune, we've been best friends for years. And so many of these years we spent getting into so much trouble. At least I remember myself more then you. However, I don't want to stay too long because aside from my original gift that I brought you, I have a very special gift. I was in England last week vacationing with my father and I ran into an old friend of yours. And the thought of reuniting you two would prove to be; well let's just say it might just cause a mixed bag of emotions if you will." Marcus stared straight at Tory as he said that last part. Then he finished. "Without further a due, please take the microphone, Ms. Mia Alexander." While everyone clapped in happiness, Shaune choked on his drink. She leaned back over to Greg who looked just as daunted and asked, "Whose Mia Alexander?" Without even looking back at her, he replied, "Trouble." Then Mia came to the stage and started her speech. "Hello Que`Shaune. It's been a long time. I heard that you were a changed man. Plus, I saw your television interview introducing your new girlfriend. Then I bumped into Marcus and heard you were celebrating your birthday. I asked if I could attend. I do hope that we could catch up on old times. Happy birthday and many more." As everyone clapped accept Shaune and Greg, Tory jumped up and ran to the mic and with nervousness in her voice and said, "I guess that concludes the birthday wishes. Everyone please have dinner and enjoy yourself. Again thank you for coming out." As she stepped off the stage, she saw Shaune and Mia talking. Torys' insecurities started to kick up into high gear. As she looked at Mia, she saw a very beautiful woman. The type of woman she would expect him to fall for. She had flawless brown skin, her makeup was flawless. She even had long flowing, flawless black hair that fit her thin physic. Tory thought her to be the superheroes of sexy women. "Pocahontas looking bitch." She thought to herself. Tory started to see her relationship fail right before her eyes. She saw it in Shaunes face. He didn't even try to look for her. He was truly taken in by Mia on sight. As she started to walk towards them, Marcus emerged. "You like my little surprise?" "I don't have time for you." Tory snapped. When she tried to pass him, he hugged her and said, "I think you will after tonight. Just look at them. See, they used to be in love. She left him heart broken and for two year he searched for her until eventually, he was forced to give up." Then Marcus let her go and left. She made her way to Shaune and Mia, but Shaune didn't even realize Tory was standing in his sight. So she touched him. "Hey Daddy, are you going to introduce me to your friend?" Then Greg walked up while Shaune started to introduce Tory. "Ah, Torianey Heckstall, this is Mia Alexander." Mia held her hand out to shake hers' and she accepted. Nonetheless, Shaune continued on like Tory was no one special. Greg notice how crushed Tory felt after that sub par introduction. As she headed to her office, her eyes started to well up. She figured she'd cry it out in there instead of in the public. Back at the party, Greg felt he needed to pry Shaune out of Mia's grip. "Shaune, can I talk to you?" He became upset that Greg would cut in on his reunion. "Not right now Greg. Give me a minute." While Tory was in her office crying her eyes out, a knock came at the door. Surely she thought it was Que`Shaune coming to mend things back up with her. As she opened the door, she saw it was the devil himself again. "You brought that woman here specifically to sabotage my relationship. How dare you?" "I'm just trying to show you your place in life. This was the woman that Shaune wanted to marry. Before you, before Lisa; when he could no longer find her, he settled for the two of you. But Mia, she was his main woman." While Tory was in her office being tortured by Marcus and Shaune was deep in Mia's eyes, Greg had to do something to alter the change of events; and he knew exactly what to do. Just as Sr. was about to check out of the scene, Greg stopped him. "Mr. Guadau, I need your help big time."

Back at Torys' office, Marcus was trying to put the finishing touches on killing her self-esteem. "Que`Shaune loves me. You played that nonsense back in Jamaica, but he proved you wrong. And he'll do it again." "Oh come on you foolish girl. If he loved you that much, then where is he now? Oh, wait, he's with the real woman of his dreams and not you. If it's any comfort, I'll take you back and we can make it like it used to be." "Was this actually happening?" she thought to herself. And why didn't Que`Shaune follow her to her office? "You should leave." She told him. As he tried to come in to hug her, she stopped him and said again, "You need to leave. See, even if Shaune leaves me for and ex-bimbo like her, that's fine. I'll live with it. What I can't live with is a trouble instigating, miserable monster like you. I'm going to make this very clear and take with it what you will. I will never in my lowest points in life ever on a night like tonight ever conform back to you again. You had your chance and you blew it. You have no place in my heart." As she opened the door to let him leave, he said, "You'll be sorry you said that." When he left, she whispered, "I don't think so."

Shaune Sr. and Greg had walked up to his son and his ex-girlfriend deeply engaged in their conversation. "Pardon mi. You don't mind terribly if I steal my son away?" see, Shaune Jr. would tell Greg no but not his father. As Sr. pulled Jr. aside he asked, "Where is your lovely girlfriend?" "Tory?" As Shaune scouted the room to see if he could find her, he realized that he couldn't. "She might be in her office." It was time for his father to get real with him in order to bring him back to his senses. "Who brought that woman here? Just think to yourself, you're about to lose the one woman in your life that meant so much to you. You said that yourself. I remember that woman; your ex-girlfriend. I also remember the pain you felt when she left you; the look on your face daily. Now son, I am not one to get involved with your relationships or your decisions; but think just as quickly as she blew herself away breaking your heart, and now she's back just as you found what you confessed to be the love of your life? How soon will this woman decide to blow away again once she's gotten all that she was aiming for? Torianey has exposed her life on your behalf when she didn't have to. And this is how you repay her?" Suddenly Shaunes cloud lifted and he started to come back to reality. Shaune started to feel really terrible and said, "I need to find Tory." Then his father said, "I would suggest you do it sooner then later." Now he sped off to find his girlfriend leaving Mia behind. He went to her office and realized that she wasn't there. Fernardo saw Shaune knocking on her office and said, "Mr. Guadau, Torianey left the restaurant." Assuming that she might have gone to her house, he made his way.

Tory was on her way to Shaunes house. She needed to pick up her things before he had totally forgotten about her and threw her property in Monday's trash pick up. She entered the gate and Solomon had opened it. She drove through waving at him. Then Solomon had called Shaune to notify him that Tory was in fact at his house; which was a good thing because he was not too far behind. Solomon was a smart and loyal employee for five years to Shaune. He had purposely left the gate open until Shaunes' truck would screech through. And predictably, he pulled through the gate pushing sixty mph. He didn't stop until he got to the garage. He used his truck to block hers'. He knew he had some explaining to do. How he could get it across, he could only pray. He sprinted up the stairs to only see what he had anticipated. She was packing. "Torianey..." Tory stopped him by throwing up her hands. She didn't say a word. "Can I say something?" He asked. But Tory was too hurt and distraught to voice her anger. "Okay, then I'll just speak if it's okay with you." She still remained silent as she worked to get her stuff together. "I totally understand how you feel. You put that awesome party together and I show my appreciation by cohorting with my ex-girlfriend. There are no words to explain my actions." While he was talking she went into his drawer and pulled out his birthday gift. As she passed it to him, she grabbed her rolling case and proceeded to leave. He grabbed her, and just before she could walk out the door, he said, "Aren't you going to watch me open it?" She still didn't answer. Between watching her relationship go up in flames and Marcus the devil confirming it, she was feeling pretty devastated. Shaune stood in front of the door so she couldn't leave. Then he opened the card. He read it out loud:

Que`Shaune,
I know that this gift isn't as expensive as the other gifts you had received but what do you get the man who can afford any and everything? Well, here's a hint? It's not as expensive as your insanity, but its close.
Yours for as long as it takes,
Torianey.

He unwrapped the wrapping to reveal a velvet box. In the velvet box were two fountain pens. Tory had remembered that Shaune had an insanity for fountain pens. So much that he had purchased a $30,000 fountain pen. As he looked at the pens, he noticed that one was red with his initials in black; while the other one was black with his initials in red. He couldn't help but become emotional. As his eyes began to well up, he looked at her. She herself became emotional, but then she started to yell. "No, no, no. I will not fall for the okidoke. That may have worked before, but not now." She started to leave again. Then Shaune stopped her again. Now her anger had gotten the best of her. She started to punch and slap him uncontrollably. Then she started to cuss him. He took her hits because he knew he was wrong and she was hurting as a result of. As she became out of breath, she tried to talk. "You mother fucker. I hate you. I wanted you to have a good time on your birthday. Marcus brings that boney bitch here and you totally forgot about me. I'm such a fucking idiot. What was I thinking? And yes, I let Marcus get the best of me because you proved it. Did you realize how you introduced me? "Mia Alexander, this is Tory." Like as if I was nothing to you. I was supposed to be your god dam girlfriend. I'm such a fool. My plan was to give you your pens tonight and have an intimate night after all the festivities. But I really don't care anymore. I refuse to take a second seat to that bitch. And don't you dare say she didn't mean anything to you. I saw how the two of you looked at each other. Tell me one thing, if she's so fucking special, why did she run out on you?" He was speechless. He said the only thing he could say, "I never got a chance to ask her." Tory laughed like she was hysterical. "You mean to tell me, all that time you spent drawling in her face; you never bothered to ask her? That would have been my first question had it been my ex. You are at least deserving of an explanation. But here's what I don't get. She broke your heart and took off on you. Why I don't know. But despite every fucking thing I've been through with you and for you, I was still here. I was still mother fucking here. Did she remember that you liked fountain pens? Did she even bring you a gift other then her skinny pretty ass? I need to leave now; I'm done playing the puppet role." As she left the room, she ran down to the garage to get into her truck. But Shaunes' truck was blocking hers'. "Damn!" she whispered. Shaune appeared behind her. "Can you please move your car?" "It's late Torianey and I'm not moving my car until we can talk rationally. Maybe tomorrow is a better day." As she turned to go back upstairs, she spat, "Go to hell." Although he understood her anger, he didn't know how many of those "Go to hells" he could take. When she got upstairs, he saw she got into bed fully dressed. "Aren't you going to take off your clothes?" She didn't bother to respond. After he changed his clothes, he laid her robe next to her and said, "Just in case you get too uncomfortable." Then he turned off his lamp and jumped under the covers and waited like a tiger waiting for his prey. As stubborn as she was, she felt like she had wanted to take off her clothes and put that robe on. The more tired she got, the more uncomfortable she became. Finally, she had made a decision to take off her clothes and put on the robe. When she turned off the lamp, Shaune played his hand; literally. While she was getting more comfortable under the covers, he didn't waste any time. He quickly slid himself over to her side and said, "See how comfortable that feels. And you know what else will feel comfortable? Me holding you." As he laughed, he tried to put his arms around her; she demanded, "Take your hands off me. The only reason why I'm here is because I can't get out and it is late." "Come on Tory, you can't expect me to lie next to you and not want you. I can't live with you being this angry with me." "Then go kill yourself." She said as she tried to push his hands from off of her. But he didn't give up; because he knew his girlfriend. All he had to do was keep it up and ultimately, she would ware down. As he kissed her neck and back, she began to feel weaker and weaker for him. When she turned herself to push him away, he took his opportunity to slide between her legs. Between his strong arms holding on to her and his kisses, all bets were off. Eventually, she gave up her struggle and gave in. At that point, all her no's turned into moans. Now Shaune was about to go for broke when Tory regained herself and said, "So what is it about her that made you forget about me?" "What? Are you serious?" "Yes, she left you in the dust, but yet you were looking at her like none of that mattered tonight. If I had done that you would of never have looked back." "You don't know that." "Yes I do, because I saw it tonight. When I left the room, you didn't even bother to come after me." "Baby please let's not get into this now. Let's just make the best of it and talk about it tomorrow." Shaune tried to continue what he started but his last comment managed to put him in it a little bit deeper. "Let's make the best of it? Is that what you said? I guess if I were Mia Alexander I would be the best. So who is Torianey Heckstall? Sub par to the best?" "Torianey, you're turning my words again." "So what did you mean by the best of it?" He was literally trying to find the right words to say to squelch the situation, but he couldn't. And the long pause in him trying to find the answer was only confirmation of his real feeling. Then he tried to salvage things as best as he could. He sat up and while trying to console her he said, "Baby, I don't know what to say. I just know I don't want to loose you." "Why is that Shaune? Is it because she's more capable of running out on you then I am?" She broke away from his hold and proceeded to leave the bedroom. "Where are you going?" Just before she left the room, she turned to Shaune and said, "In the morning, please move your truck out of the way of mine or I will run over your Mabach to get out. And if you think I'm joking, please fuck around and try me." Then she slammed the door and left.

Chapter 15
Kicking and Screaming!

The next morning, Shaune had been searching all around his mansion for his girlfriend. He knew she was still on the premises; after all her clothes, purse, and cell phone were still in his bedroom. Most of all, her truck was still blocked by his. Since he got tired of looking, he went on the intercom and called her. "Torianey, come out so we can talk. I know you're still here." Shaunes' yelling over his intercom startled Tory and woke her up. Although she heard him calling her, she wasn't coming out. "Let his wack ass find me." Then she went back to sleep.

Later on, Shaune was in his den having breakfast. Tory awoke to seeing him through the surveillance monitor. She could see he was on the phone with his father getting chewed out. "She's around here somewhere... I know dad, I'm stupid... I was going to ask her last night, but she brought up Mia... No, I didn't. I had more pressing interests to focus on like asking her..." While he was being chastised by his father, Marta walked in to announce that Mia was requesting to see him. "Dad, let me call you back." When he hung up the phone he told Marta to show her in. Mia walked in to the den looking fabulous and radiant as she did the night before. As Tory positioned herself closer to the monitor, she said to herself, "This can't be happening again." "May I sit down?" Mia asked. "Of course you can." Tory can see that same captivated look he had last night when they were together. "You went running off last night. We didn't get a chance to finish up on old times." "No we didn't." "So where did you run to?" "Oh, I had some old pressing issues to take care of. More importantly, what brings you here?" Shaune was positioned in front of his desk; while Mia wanted to get closer. "Que' Shaune, I'm going to bottom line it, I want you back." "Really?" He asked sounding shocked. Then she put her arms around Shaunes' neck and said "Yes; and I know you do too." Tory was again watching the man she loved walk out of her life. "You know what? I hope the both of them roast in hell." She said to herself out loud. "Mia, can I ask you a question?" "Sure you can. What is it?" "Why did you leave me in the first place?" Mia, trying to laugh it off said, "Do we really need to go into that thing again? Can't we just start over?" "Sure, we could start over. After I get an answer." In confusion, Tory said, "What kind of shit is this?" "I thought I told you before, I didn't want to be apart of the whole paparazzi spiel." "If that's the case then nothings changed. I'm still Que' Shaune Guadau, my bank roll is still in the billions, and I'm still most of all in the eye of the paparazzi. The only thing is now I have Tory to help me through it all. What brought you back?" "I saw your interview with you and your playmate Tory. I saw how happy you looked. Frankly, I can't remember when you looked so handsomely happy. Then I thought why can't we have that?" Then she started to kiss him; but he stopped her. "We were happy; at least I was. But then you left me. Then I wasn't so happy; and now here you are just as I claim to love another. So you'd much rather steal a page out of some other woman's book then to be honest? God Mia!" "Yes I would. Just so I could be with the man I love. Come on Shaune, I know you can't be serious about this… this…" He cut in and said, "That woman, my girlfriend? Yes, I'm very serious. In fact, if it wasn't for you showing up uninvited and unannounced to the party that she set up for me, I would have asked her to marry me last night. But you changed all that by causing confusion between the two of us." Tory yelled, "NO!" Then Mia said, "Baby, she's nothing. She has nothing and she will be of nothing to you. But you and I, we have so much more." Shaune pushed Mia away from him and said, "Had." "What?" "We HAD something. And since I've moved on, I have so much more with Tory. Maybe about 4 or 5 years ago you could have come back and ran that story. And like a lost child I would have ran back into your arms. But now, I don't think so. Plus, in the past few years, I don't know what you may have had or have, but it's not me. I'm not in love with you anymore Mia. And after what I've just witness, I don't think I quite like you as much. If you don't mind I'm playing hide and seek with my girlfriend. I would appreciate it if you left my home. Be well Mia." As he kissed her on the cheek, he escorted her to the door. Tory stood looking at the monitor in shock. Not only did he stand up for her, he was going to ask her to marry him. Now she felt like crap. She had dragged him all through the mud last night. Just as she began to beat herself up mentally, Shaune walked back into his den. He sat at his desk looking weary. Then he yelled, "Did you get all that?" She didn't understand if he was talking to her or himself. Then he continued. "And I meant it; every last word of it." She still didn't catch on. But then, he pulled a small box out of his pocket and opened it. Then he said, "Torianey Heckstall, would you do me the honors of being Mrs. Que'Shaune Guadau II?" Now the bell started to ring in her head. He knew she was in that room; and he needed her to see that Mia was in fact no match for her. Tory really began to feel like shit at that point. Not to mention her breath smelt like death warmed over and her hair was ratty. Plus, she was still wearing yesterday's underwear. "But so what?" She thought she would face the music now and clean up later. As she walked towards the door to open it, she saw Shaune on his knees waiting to put the ring on her finger. "How did you know I was in there?" "My staff went through every room accept this one. So will you marry me?" "Yes." She nervously responded. Then he put the ring on her finger and it was a perfect fit. It was an eternity style ring with at least eight diamonds going around the band itself at 5carats each. The top two stones were rubies that were ranged at 8carats each and the top stone was a huge 10carat diamond that you could see a mile away. "This is so beautiful Shaune." "Not as beautiful as you are." Then a really real thought came to Torys' mind. "What is it baby? Is it the ring? I could get another one." "There would be no way we could get married without the public knowing?" "I was just wondering if we could make love on this bed for the next two days and worry about the public and the paparazzi later." Then Tory said, "I guess that's a no huh?" "Tory I thought this was a happy moment for the both of us." "Don't get me wrong I love you. Just the thing is that this is how our lives are going to be? Every big thing we do they have to be there?" Shaune had wished that he could fast forward through the conversation, but again it was inevitable. "Yes they will. We talked about this before. Once it gets out, the less the media knows the worst they could spin it." "How could they spin us getting married? That's usually a good thing right?" "And Mia showing up to my party had nothing to do with it? Oh and don't think the party didn't get leaked; and her enter and leaving my home. You know she had to be seen. So now let's just keep it under wraps. Now you get spotted leaving the supermarket wearing that beautiful engagement ring on your finger. One might put two and two together. Mia Alexander shows up to Que`Shaune Guadaus' birthday party and now Torianey Heckstall is now engaged to be married to him. Perhaps, she got scared and asked him to marry her in desperation?" Tory sucked her teeth and said, "That's not true. Plus, how does anybody know that? Didn't everybody get to know from the first time?" "If we don't give them what they want, it will ultimately put a strain on our marriage. I don't want that for us. Do you?" Feeling frustrated and backed into yet another corner, she sighed and said, "What would you suggest?" "I suggest that we scream it to anybody who would listen." As he sat down on the bed next to her, he put his arm around her to try and console her. Tory had thrown in the towel; she knew he was right. "So what's next?" Then Shaune picked up his cell and called Greg. He knew exactly who to call to give the exclusive to.

Mia was in her hotel room making a phone call. Since it was Marcus who put her up to the whole scam to separate Shaune and Tory in the first place, she had to report her failure in the mission to him anyways. "Mia? I take it you were successful?" "No Marcus, I wasn't." "What happened? You two were inseparable last night." "His father interrupted our conversation and shortly after, he went running after her. Today I went to his house to try for another time but as quick as I came, he threw me out." Marcus' efforts were yet again thwarted. Feeling frustrated he yelled over the phone, "Useless wench." "Excuse me? This was your dumb ass plan in the first place. Didn't it occur to you that he just might be in love with her?" Then a thought crossed Mia's mind. "Wait a minute. This isn't about Shaune. This is about Tory. You're still in love with her aren't you?" "Since you're such a professional at relationships I guess it should have been easy for you to get your man back. Oh wait, you failed at that didn't you. So I guess this no longer concerns you. Goodbye Mia." Then he hung up the phone on her. As he sat in his recliner, he started to clench his teeth in total frustration. "Torianey, you're really starting to piss me off."

Tory and Shaune were in his den waiting for the reporter to show up. "So who's the famous reporter that's coming?" Tory asked Greg. Feeling leery of answering her, he looked at Shaune and Shaune said, "Cheryl Blake." "You're kidding me?" She yelled as she jumped out of her seat. Shaune jumped up and held her. "Look, just let me handle it. Trust me she is the perfect person at this point." "Oh is that right? After she threatened to expose me because she wanted better ratings; that perfect person Que`Shaune?" "Look I don't like this anymore then you do…" She cut him off and said, "Yes you do. You love this plan. You said it yourself; you want to yell it to anybody who would listen. So don't lie to me and tell me how much you don't like this." Then he came closer to her and said, "Do you trust me?" "Yes." She whispered. "Good, because if I had one person I could pick to do this it would be Cheryl. Like it or love it, she is the one to get the job done." Then a voice from the door yelled, "How touching. May I get a photo of that moment?" Greg walked up to Cheryl and said, "This is only an exclusive in reference to the two of them getting engaged. Not about his business. Got it?" "What ever, I just care about my ratings and my career plans. What Que`Shaune Guadau does with his business and/or his piece… is his own business." She said as she looked Tory up and down. "Can we please just get this over with so we could get this specimen out of our lives?" Tory spat back at Cheryl. "Fine then here's how it's going to go, I'll ask the two of you several questions and ultimately, it will lead to the coming out of your engagement. How does that sound?" The both said "Fine."

As the camera started to roll, Cheryl started. "Hello, I'm Cheryl Blake and this is a BBC World exclusive. I am at the beautiful and intimate home of Que`Shaune Guadau. And accompanying him is his lovely girlfriend Torianey Heckstall." They both echoed, "Hello." "So Que`Shaune, it's been almost two years since the two of you came out that you were dating. How goes it?" "It's been a blast." "Really? I'm sure your fans and the rest of the public would agree if I asked you to elaborate just a bit." "My pleasure. Ever since the first time Torianey had come out about our relationship, we have had time to explore where we wanted to take it." "And that is where?" "We found ourselves more in love with each other then ever." Shaune kissed Torys' hand. Then Cheryl said, "So much more that I hear congratulations are in order." "Yes Cheryl, I asked Torianey to marry me and she accepted." "Tell me, how did that come about?" "Yesterday was my birthday and she surprised me with a birthday party. All my friends and family was there. She was quite detailed on who was there…." Cheryl cut in and said, "How nice Que`Shaune. But Torianey I can't help but ask you; was Mia Alexander a detail in the party plans?" Then suddenly the elephant was in the room. Tory felt that uncomfortable feeling. Then she answered, "Actually, she was someone's plus one on the list." "I'm sure you've heard the story of just as he confessed his undying love for her, she took off and left him to pick up the pieces of his broken heart. And now she pops back up just as the two of you are engaged to be married. I can't help but feel that someone's arm is being twisted here." At that point Tory felt like if Cheryl Blake would have punched her in the stomach any harder it wouldn't have felt half as bad as the question she just imposed on her. "Ms. Blake, have you ever been in love?" "Although this isn't about me, but…" Then Tory cut in and said, "Oh yeah wait, it was back in 2004 and your fans and the public would agree it was with our very own Que`Shaune Guadau. But that's not why I asked you. My point is since you know him like I do; we can agree that his arm is not easily twisted." "I can certainly agree with you on that, but how did it make you feel seeing him standing there with his ex girlfriend? I mean this was the one woman he thought he was destined to marry." Tory started to feel annoyed and now her answers became real. "How did I feel? Like any other woman would; insecure." Shaun gripped Tory's hand because he felt that she was stepping into a potentially more questionable zone with Cheryl. Then Tory continued. "I didn't invite her but I allowed her to stay because I figured they needed to get reacquainted. See, I believe that if they got themselves reacquainted, then maybe they could figure out what it was they wanted to do. In my opinion, I felt it was better this way then for us to be in a marriage and find out it was a lie all along." "That was pretty risky of you. It could have ended the other way." "Well, now that we have exhausted that option to bed, we can move on with our lives." "With that having been said; when he asked you to marry him, was yes your first answer or were you hesitant?" "For about thirty seconds, I was a little hesitant. But when I thought about what happened last night, I knew I wanted to marry him." "And why the thirty second hesitation?" Tory started to think about why she hesitated and she really didn't realize why she did until Cheryl asked. As she cleared her throat, she said, "About four and a half years ago, I was engaged to be married with another man that I was madly in love with. He made all these promises and I soaked it up. Then one day, another woman steps in to the picture and just that quick I was all alone. Fast forward to today, and all over again, I find myself in love and the rug gets pulled from under me again." "So what's changed? You obviously accepted." Trying to wipe her tears away, she responded, "He set her straight. I didn't have to say anything or do anything. And I believe that if he wanted to be with her, he wouldn't have asked me to marry him." "There you have it; in the words of their own the engagement of Mr. Que`Shaune Guadau and Ms. Torianey Heckstall." Then Cheryl signaled for the camera to stop taping. Tory got up to leave. Shaune tried to follow but Greg intercepted him and said, "Give her some time. She just poured her heart out on national television to make you look good. I don't quite think she's feeling the same way." Shaune sat back down on the couch. Deep down inside, it was killing him see her hurting and not be able to console her.

Tory had pulled up in her driveway tears still fresh from her eyes. She poured herself out of her truck and dragged into her house. She couldn't help but feel guilty for not telling Shaune she was leaving but she knew that she would have to face him and talk about how fearful she was about marrying him. She lay across her couch and continued to cry until she fell asleep from mental exhaustion. A couple of hours later, she awoke to her doorbell ringing. Surely she thought it was Que`Shaune coming to talk about what happened in the earlier part of the day. "At least I got some sleep to help me deal with this." She thought to herself as she went to open the door. When she opened the door, it wasn't Shaune. It was the least person she had suspected to show up at her door. "May I come inside? I really need to talk to you if you don't mind?" "Mia Shaune's not here and I thought he told you what you needed to hear." "This isn't about Shaune anymore." "Then why the fuck would I want to talk to you?" "It's about Marcus." "Why are you screwing him too?" "No but I know about your relationship with him." Tory looked at Mia like she wanted to jump on her. Then she calmed herself and said, "So you know about us. Who cares?" As she attempted to close her door, Mia stopped her and yelled, "Que`Shaune doesn't know; does he?" Then Tory opened the door back. And Mia said, "He doesn't have to know. I just want talk to you." Tory opened her door to let her in. "Don't bother sitting. You're not staying long." "Fine then. I needed to tell you that Marcus is coming after you." "I can see that and I really don't care. Marcus Swain is a bitter man with no good intentions and he's destined to be alone for the rest of his miserable life." "Of course you know he's never going to stop. And if you knew he was coming after you why won't you tell Shaune?" "Shaune and Marcus are friends. If I tell him about Marcus, it's no telling what kind of rift would come between them. I'd much rather let Marcus blow off his steam and eventually, he'll go away." "Tory I know you can't be as foolish to believe that he's going to just vanish away. He sabotages all of Shaunes' relationships. He did it with his ex-wife, he did it with me and he'll do it to you. It's only a matter of time. You need to tell Que`Shaune." Then Tory yelled, "I'll tell Shaune when the time is right. And now it just isn't." "The longer you drag this out, the worst it's going to get. Shaune loves you and you have nothing to lose by telling him." "Like I said Mia, I'll tell him when the time is right. He just proposed to me and how am I supposed to bring up Marcus at a time like now?" "Its better you bring it out now then for something tragic to happen to make you have to tell him. It's only going to piss him off." "And why do you care so much? I wonder did Marcus set you up to do this. You weren't successful the first time so you come here and give it one more college try?" Mia, feeling like she was loosing Tory in the conversation walked towards the door and said, "I have a plane to catch." "So you're running away again?" "No Torianey, I'm ducking for cover in your case. Although my efforts were useless, I tried. You take care." As she sat back on her couch, Tory couldn't help but feel Mia was right. Marcus was coming for her and it could only get worse each failing turn.

Later on that day, Shaune was in the neighborhood and he called Tory to come out of the house. "Where are we going?" She asked. We're going to my favorite spot; the pond. As they drove up and parked along the pond, Shaune didn't waist anytime on the twenty questions. "You took off and didn't even say goodbye. What made that happen?" "I just needed some time alone." "You could have stayed we could have talked about it then. Or after the interview you couldn't stand to be around me anymore?" "Don't jump to conclusions please. This had nothing to do with you so much as it did me. I just needed to come back to a place of normalcy and that felt like my house. I wanted to be alone to figure things out." "Figure things out like why would it take you a thirty second pause to figure out if you wanted to marry me? And why were you so insecure about Mia?" Of course, Shaune couldn't let the night go without bringing up the interview. Bad enough she had to deal with Mia and her bull. "Shaune, again it had nothing to do with you…" "I know it had everything to do with your last relationship and how he left you in the dust." "That's not fair Shaune. That really hurt." "Well let's talk about unfairness. How unfair is it when every time I try to make a happy moment happen in our relationship, you manage to make a dent in that? How unfair is it that you keep comparing me to the last relationship in your life? How unfair is it that you keep twisting my words to sound like something you concocted in that pretty little head of yours only to make it seem like something it's not?" Abruptly, she screamed, "Stop it! I don't know what this is you're trying to do by bringing me out here and literally trying to pick a fight with me, but you need to stop." "Or else what? What are you going to do Torianey?" "I don't have to take this from you." as she struggled to get out of the car, Shaune got out of the car and ran over to hold her. "So what are you angry now? Are you good and angry?" "I don't understand why you're being so cruel to me?" "I'm trying to burst that bubble in your soul that's holding you from me. You need to scream, kick, and yell as much as you need to get it out of our lives. Because when we get married, I don't want this in our marriage. Don't think I don't notice it. The lack of trust you have in me. The constant disconnect after making love to you; did I leave out twisting my words around? This has to end." Torys' first impression was to punch Shaune in the face. But she knew he had a point. "You're right." "What?" "You're right Shaune. I was thinking the same thing on the way home today. I know I can't continue to put you through all that. You have been doing everything to make me feel accepted when I was trying to find ways to not feel accepted. I had no right to treat you that way. You didn't deserve that kind of treatment; you're a good man." Shaune was baffled. He had expected her to start kicking and screaming at him with all the jabs he shot at her. Was it too good to be true? Was she telling him what he wanted to hear? Or was she actually ready to make a change? "Tory that was too easy to believe. Any other day you would have tried to tear my head off." She walked in to hold him to reassure him. "I mean it Shaune; I want to be the wife you deserve to have in your life. I don't want the pain and dissention in our marriage." Then she put her arms around his neck and hugged him tight. Shaune was in utter shock that he didn't have to put on the boxing gloves to fight her. Deep down inside, he was still not convinced but he looked at her serenity as a step in the right direction.

They had pulled up to Torys driveway. Before she got out of the car, he asked her, "So do we have a date set?" "A date for what?" "For the wedding. Cheryl asked after the interview was over; I told her I would talk it over with you." "It's funny that you would ask; I was thinking about next year in December." Then Tory saw the look on his face and said, "Okay, spit it out Guadau. Is December too soon for you?" "No, not at all." He said still with the sad face. "So why do you look like you're ready to cry? If next December is too soon for you, we can wait till the following year." "No Tory it's not too soon." "So what's the god dam problem?" She spat feeling fed up. "It's not soon enough." "So what month were you thinking of?" "I was hoping that you would consider three months from now; hell, maybe even two months from now. Aren't you ready to get married?" "Perhaps not as ready as you are." She laughed. But Shaune wasn't laughing. "So I guess next December it is then." He jumped out of the car to go and open her door for her. As he opened the door, she got out and said, "Why don't you stay for tonight and we can mull it over? Come to an easy medium maybe." "Sure why not." Shaune thought spending the night would be a great way to get her to change her mind.

Tory came out of the shower later and saw Que'Shaune sitting up in bed. He was reading the days paper exhibiting that same puppy dog face. Even though they didn't say a word to each other, the silence spoke volumes. "I thought you would be sleep by now." He only shrugged his shoulders without looking at her. She realized that she needed to settle this whole thing. She crawled over on to his lap and said, "I guess you're never going to let this go until December?" "I don't know what you're talking about." He said while rifling through the news paper. Then Tory took the papers from him and placed them on the nightstand. "Okay Shaune, we need to do this in two months. If nothings ready by then, then it would have to happen by December." Finally, his mood went back to happy. "I agree. What made you change your mind?" "Like you don't know; I got tired of seeing that sad face. Also, I'm a little excited to get married to you." "Really?" "Yeah really. Plus, I was hoping I could get lucky tonight." As they kissed, he said, "I feel so used. You'd accept my proposal just for sex? How dare you?" They both laughed.

A month before the wedding, Shaune had called all his boys to the cabin. He wanted to have somewhat of a last hoorah just before he jumped the broom. He invited his brothers; Gregory, Lucas, Jacob and of course, Marcus. As usual they sipped on their expensive cognac and smoked their expensive hand wrapped Cubans cigars. This night was all about Shaune. And the night wasn't complete without Marcus hiring his hookers. Marcus had hired one of them specifically for Shaune, but Shaune wasn't interested; and as a distraction, Greg gave his toast. "I would like to give a toast to my boss and best friend, Shaune. Man, I can't believe you're doing it." Then Jacob yelled, "AGAIN!" And they all laughed. Gregory said, "But this time you got it right." "Or so we think." Marcus said in his drunken stupor. The four of them stopped and looked at Marcus. Then he continued with his rant. "Seriously Shaune, how much of this girl do you really know other then how her womb feels?" Then Jacob spat, "Don't you think you're being way out of line here?" "Says the man with no spine." Marcus said as he laughed. "What are you talking about Marcus?" Shaune asked. "Go ahead Jacob, or do you want me to tell him?" "Jacob what is he talking about?" Jacob looked around like if he could hide somewhere, he would. Then Marcus said, "He dumped his Fiancée. He couldn't handle the pressure. Isn't that right Jacob?" In shadow of his embarrassment and shame, Jacob jumped up to try and beat Marcus to a pulp, but it was Shaune who stopped him. "I'm sorry Shaune; I thought I wanted to marry Jenna; but things started to go south. She started acting possessive. The closer we got to the wedding date, the worst she became. And I just couldn't take it anymore. So one day I went out for a drive and I found myself driving back to North Carolina to my parents. I explained to them that I couldn't do it anymore. She was driving me nuts. The next day I invited her to my parents' home and we talked. Ultimately, I ended it with her. She wasn't happy." Although Shaune was feeling disappointed in Jacob, he also felt sorry for him. He could see in his eyes that he was broken as a result of his life having to change drastically. But that didn't stop Marcus from going digging the knife deeper in him. "Will someone please bring out the violins and trumpets? This is starting to feel more like a funeral." Deep down inside, Jacob was burning to kill Marcus. Shaune took him outside to talk to him. "I hope I didn't ruin your last days with my nonsense. I wasn't meaning for this to come out; least of all now." "No you didn't. I'm more concerned about you. How has this been since the breakup?" "I miss her. She won't answer my calls, I tried calling her mother to see if I could get her to talk to me; nothing. I tried to show up at her job, she just calls security. Now I'm not so sure if I wanted to break off the wedding so much anymore. Maybe we could have just talked it over." "Maybe she just needs some time to process it all. I'm sure you'll get your chance to make it right." "Yeah, or maybe not." As Jacob walked back into the cabin, Shaune had a memory of Tory being hesitant. Perhaps, she could pull the same stunt. He was sure he wanted to marry her, but it was her who had the traumatic history and slight reservations. So he pulled out his cell phone and called her. When she picked up the phone, he was happy to hear her voice. "Hello Daddy. How's your boys night out?" Shaune was happy to hear those words. At least for the most part it didn't mean that she was feeling insecure or hesitant. "Everything is fine. I was calling to check in and see how everything with you was." "Everything is fine. I finally got the cake situation together. You're going to love it. I got my dress and it's beautiful." "I'm sure you could put on a burlap sack and you would still be beautiful to me." "That was sweet and corny of you to say, but we both know I'm not going to show up in a burlap sack." Then Tory fell silent for a few seconds. "Why did you get so quiet?" "I don't know; can I ask a question?" "You know you can ask me anything." Then there was that awkward pause that sent a nervous feeling in Shaunes' stomach. "Speak Baby, you're making me nervous." "Are you sure you're not having any reservations about marrying me?" "No. God not in the least bit. Why would you ask that?" "As I was picking up my dress today, I was kind of imagining myself being left at the alter in such a beautiful dress. We're a month away Shaune and if you're having the slighted bit of doubt, now would be the time to cast it." "Are you having doubts about getting married?" "No I'm not. I'm just concerned about you." "If there are any doubts, it wouldn't be by me. I know for damn sure that I want to marry you. I knew that when I asked you, and I know it all too well now." Then he paused and said, "Le votre pour pourvu qui`ill pond." "And what does that mean?" "I'll tell you on our wedding day during my vows." Then he heard her sniffling over the phone. "What's the matter?" "I don't know what you said, but it made me want to cry." They both laughed over the phone and he figured he need to end the call there. "I'm going back inside and I'll see you tomorrow for dinner." "That sounds like a plan." "Torianey... I love you." "I love you too Que`Shaune." As he hung up the phone, he heard clapping behind him. Of course, it was Marcus coming to stir things up with him. "How touching. You love her." "Marcus, why don't you go home and sleep that off." Shaune said as he tried to pass Marcus. But he stopped him and said, "Shaune, let me apologize for my display of inconsiderate behavior. You have a good woman in your life and I want to see you happy." Shaune wasn't feeling totally convinced of his comment; seeing how he managed to cut into Jacob as if he was butter. But he played it off anyway. "Thanks Marcus. I appreciate that." "Good, now I'm going home to sleep it off like you said." As he watched Marcus get into his car, Shaune started to think about his friendship with him and thought that since he was getting married, hanging around Marcus would prove to be an unhealthy relationship.

Chapter 16
Times for Changes

Torianey sat in her bedroom staring in the mirror. It was her wedding day and her nerves were shot. She had only one hour left on the clock to get to Carrapellies so she could get married to Shaune. As she fidgeted with her hands, she said to herself, "God I'm getting married today. Who'd ever thought I'd be getting married to anyone." Then a knock came at the door. When she ran down to open the door, she saw a woman holding a huge rolling suitcase. "Can I help you?" Tory asked in confusion. "Hello Mrs. Guadau. My name is Ingrid; may I come in?" "Who are you?" "Mr. Guadau hired me to assist you during your process to get ready for your wedding." As she opened the do to let the woman in, she tried to say, "I had told Shaune that I was going to do everything on my own." As Ingrid looked Tory up and down, she said, "Mrs. Guadau..." Tory cut in and said, "It's Ms. Heckstall. I'm not married yet." "Either way you have less then an hour to walk down the isle, and you are nowhere next to ready. I suggest that you come down to Carrapellies and I'll get you ready there." Tory heard her say, "Walk down the isle" and her nerve kicked up even more. "Alright, let me get the dress and get myself ready and we can leave." Ingrid stopped her and said, "No, you get ready, I'll get the dress."

Now Tory was at Carrapellies staring in the mirror looking at her wedding dress laid out on the sofa. It was a beautiful black dress with white design. Her shoes were by Christian Louboutin 4" pumps. And now she was an hour late for her wedding ceremony to start. She had come to the realization that she was suffering from cold feet. Then a knock came at the door. It was Louise Carrapelli coming to see what was holding her up. Tory just stood staring in the mirror as he walked in. "What am I doing here Lou?" "You're here because there's a man out there waiting to marry you. Is there any reason why you're not in your dress yet? Your makeup looks beautiful." "After tonight I'll be Mrs. Que'Shaune Guadau II. Where will I be? Where will Torianey Heckstall be? My legacy, my namesake." "Are you kidding me? Your legacy will be with the man you love building a whole new legacy together. Maybe even a much stronger one. Do you realize that in the past year you have changed that mans reputation tremendously? Not to mention his personality, his emotional state; and trust me, I know; I had a conversation with the man." "Really? What did you talk about?" Knowing this was going to take a while, Lou took a seat next to her. "He came to me a week before his birthday and he said that he wanted my blessing for your hand in marriage." In amazement, Tory said, "Seriously!" With the same amazement, Lou shot back, "Extremely! So as the father that I assume I am, I asked him, "What makes you the right man for Torianey?" Do you know what he said?" Sounding like she had a high school crush, she replied, "What did he say?" Then Lou continued. "He said, "I can't answer that question "SIR!" He called me sir. So I asked him, "Then why should she marry you?" He said in his own words, "After having her in my life for such a short period of time, I can't see myself without her. And THIS is how I know that I have to have her as my wife." Tory I was so blown away, that if he'd asked me to marry him I just might have said yes. My love, I know that I have had some reservations previously about the Guadaus' and their sorted past; and that was just me as an assumed parent being concerned about you. But looking at Que'Shaune, he's actually a really good man." Lou looked at his clock and realized time was wasting. Then he finished. "Time is winding down and you either need to get that dress on or the limousine is parked outback. You can have it run you to the airport where you can get the first thing running out of the country. But it would be a terrible shame to run out on one of the best moments of your life." Just before he left, he kissed her on her forehead. "I'll be waiting just outside this door to give you your final walk as a single woman." Then he left. Tory felt better after her talk with Lou. She put on her dress and refreshed her makeup. As the music started to play, everyone took their seats and the lights started to dim. While she was walking down the isle with Lou, she could see all their friends and family that they had invited. As Que'Shaune took his place at the end of the isle, he was amazed by his beauty in black and white. While Lou escorted her down the isle, Shaune looked like a deer caught in headlights. In his eyes, she was a stunning vision. He himself was wearing a black Armani tailor made suit with a white dress shirt and black tie. And he wore regular black paten leather Armani shoes. As she approached Shaune, Lou hugged Tory and whispered in her ear, "I guess this is goodbye." When she let him go, she could see tears streaming down his eyes. As he backed away, she continued down the isle. When she got to Shaune, he whispered, "You look amazing." "You do too." She whispered back, starting to feel emotional. As the Pastor started his sermon to wed, Shaune couldn't keep his eyes off his bride. Now came time for the moment that everyone was waiting for, the vows. As the Pastor gave Shaune the floor, he started:

"Torianey, we've been through so much to get to this point. From the day you accepted my proposal till today, I couldn't contain myself. As I look back and think of my life before I met you, I realize I was not a happy man. After I met you on the plane, I came home and did something I never did. I stopped at my staircase and I looked up at the moon and I thought of you. Normally, I think about stats and figures

when I come home. But that entire night into the next day, I couldn't get you out of my mind. Then I thought to myself, is she thinking of me the way I'm thinking of her? You asked me what makes you so different from the next woman? That question is always a no brainer. The next woman doesn't inspire me to make changes in my life like I did with you. Because of you, I am a much different man, a much happier man. I see the man I want to be as opposed to the man I used to be. So when the question of marriage came into play, I knew you were it for me. Love doesn't get any better then this, and the truth is I fell in love with you way back on the plane. I was just too chicken to admit it. Going forth, I want to make a promise to you that I will always be your protector. No one will ever hurt you; physically, spiritually, mentally. You will always be treated like my queen. I promise that you will always be at the top of my list; my first concern. I will love you forever. Le votre pour pourvu qui`ill pond. I told you last month that I would tell you what it meant. It means "I am yours for as long as it takes." You wrote that on my birthday card that you gave me when you gave me the fountain pens. Those words stuck with me. And I pray that it will be forever."

Shaune tried to widen his eyes so that his tears wouldn't run down. But it was too late; his emotions got the best of him. Tory tried to help him wipe them from his eyes. Then the Pastor gave Tory her turn to give her vows. And she started:

"Que`Shaune, you are an amazing man. I feel so privileged to have known you. You tell me that you were a different person prior to us meeting, but I only know you as the man that I know now. I never knew you had an unhappy side to you because you

make me happy to be with you everyday. I feel truly blessed to have found a love that I have never known before. Your love is so sincere and kind. You accept me as I am and you never tried to make me change. I know that I have been a handful during our dating process, but you have been so patient with me. Our miracle lies in the path we have chosen together. I enter this marriage with you knowing that the true magic of love is not to avoid changes, but to navigate them successfully. Let us commit to the miracles of making each day work... Together. To marry the person you have set your heart upon is a joy unparalleled in human life. I pray that you take my ring as a sign of my faith and my commitment to our love, and share this joy with me today."

They both were getting emotional as it was time for the Pastor to end the ceremony. "As we conclude this ceremony of matrimony, to start these two on their way to wedded bliss; is there anyone who objects to these two getting married let them speak now or forever hold your peace." For 15 seconds passed by, everyone sat in total silence. Needless to say, no one interjected. Then the Pastor finished. "And now to complete the two adjoining as one flesh, I will ask you Que'Shaune Guadau Jr., do you take Torianey Heckstall to be your lawfully wedded wife to have, to hold, through great fortune and great misfortune?" "I do." He said quickly. Then the Pastor turned to Tory and said, "Torianey Heckstall, do you take Que'Shaune Guadau II to be your lawfully wedded husband to have, to hold, through great fortune and great misfortune?" "I do." She answered. "What God had put together let no man put us under, I now pronounce you Mr. and Mrs. Que'Shaune Guadau II. Que'Shaune you may kiss your wife." Finally after they exchanged rings, the time came for Shaune to kiss Tory and he didn't waste anytime. He grabbed Tory so tight and kissed her as everyone clapped. There wasn't a dry eye in the house. Tory had a surreal feeling about the whole thing. She was now a married woman to the man she loved; and life as she knew it was changing. Que'Shaunes' father as usual was about to check out of the scene. But Tory had another idea in mind. She never got the opportunity to meet his father officially, so she figured she would take the initiative to do so. As Sr. was getting into his limousine, Tory knocked on the door. He opened the door and she leaned in to speak to him. "Mr. Guadau, we never officially met before and since it was our big day, I didn't want the night to pass without the two of us at least getting acquainted." "Qui Memoiselle. Please have a seat." "Thank you sir." "I know that it would be quite presumptuous of me to ask you to refer to me as Dad. So the least you can do is call me Shaune." "Fair enough. Shaune, I don't know how you feel about me. Your son never speaks of you to me so I figured that I should come to you and build my own reputation. First of all let me explain to you that I love your son like I love my life. I don't know what he has said to you about me but I want him in my life forever and I know that for sure…" His silence was starting to make her nervous and uncomfortable, so she started to blabber. Then he cut in and stopped her. "I understand your point. I can see you love my son. I can see he loves you too. I've known this for sometime. My son has spoken of you many times before. I can remember when he spoke of you the first time. I remember the hard time you gave him to get to you. He came to me and told me about you and I was shocked that he was so hell bent on one woman. That was when I knew he was in love." "How did you know?" "I knew because I did the same thing when I first met his mother. Unfortunately, she is no longer with us but the relationship that the two of you have will keep that memory alive for me." Despite of what she knew of Shaunes mother and fathers relationship, she managed to connect with the loving side of his father. Then she had another thought. "There is a point where the father and daughter are supposed to dance together. My original parents aren't alive. Would you consider taking the place of my father and having one dance with me? I mean I hope that I'm not taking you away from your important business. It's just one lousy dance. But it would mean the world to me if you accepted." Que`Shaune Sr. smiled and said, "There is nothing else I'd rather be doing at this time." Tory walked back into the building. This time she was holding on to Shaunes' fathers hand. She went to the DJ and requested that he play "Love Ballard." By LTD. As the music played, they embrace hands. Shaune was stunned that his father and now wife was engaged in a dance. He was actually quite happy to see the two people he loved getting along. Everyone stood around and watched the newly father and daughter dance. After the third song, Sr. was getting tired; not to mention it was past his hour. Sr. waved his son to come and dance in his place with his wife so he could make his escape. The song "You are everything." By the Stylistics came on. It was the song Shaune had requested when it came time for their dance. As the two embraced each other, they both waved goodbye to his father. Que`Shaune held on to Tory like she was about to vanish somewhere and he didn't want her to go. As they danced the night away, one by one friends and family joined in to dance with their dates. Although they were surrounded by a ballroom full of people, they felt like they were the only two in the room. Jacob was sitting on the side watching the two dance while Jenna, his ex-fiancée was sitting on an opposite side of the room nursing her drink. Even though he was enjoying the night dancing with his wife, Shaune couldn't help but feel he needed to somehow get them together. Plus, it was time for them to be getting on the plane headed to France. As he spun her around he whispered in her ear, "We need to try and make our way out of here." "How do you suppose we do that?" "I figure you head to the car, and I'll be right behind you. There's something I have to do right now anyways." "Please don't be too long." "I promise I won't." Then he kissed her just before she left the ballroom. He went over to Jenna and said, "Jenna, it's good to see you again." "It's good to see you too Shaune. Congratulations on your wedding day. It must feel really good to marry the one you love; which is something I can't say for myself." She said as she glanced over at Jacob. "Jenna, Jacob loves you and I'm not sure what happened that day. But that's not why I came over here. I was wondering if you would like to dance with me?" "Oh Shaune, I'm not really feeling like I want to dance. In fact, I was contemplating on leaving." "So then just one dance with me come on, you would tell the groom on his wedding day that he can't dance with you? That's a low blow." As she laughed, she said, "Okay. Because it's your wedding day I'll commit to one dance and then I'm out of here." As he took her by the hand he said, "Deal." While they were dancing, Shaune kept trying to cue Jacob in to come and dance with Jenna. Finally after some time had passed, Jacob made his move to take over the dance floor. "Thank you for the dance Jenna. However, I have to get going myself. My wife is waiting for me on the plane and I don't want to keep her waiting. I do have a replacement though." Then Jacob walked up to the two of them. "Jenna, can I interest you in a dance?" "No thanks Jacob." Jenna said. Shaune cut in and said, "Give him another chance." "Why so he could dump me like he did? I don't know what got into you that day or what dirt Marcus put into your head, but I can't go through that again." "Did Marcus have anything to do with your decision to break up with Jenna?" "Sought of." "Now you tell him the truth that Marcus was the exact reason why you didn't want to get married. You allowed him to get into your head... Like he always does. The more you hung around him the worse you became." Jenna was becoming emotional and Shaune didn't plan for that to happen. "Look, I understand that Jacob is a bonehead for listening to Marcus. However, this is a day of happiness and I would love to see the two of you enjoy the rest of the evening. Please for me." "Fine. For you." Jenna said. As Shaune started to make his way out of the ballroom, he turned to look at Jacob and Jenna deeply embraced in each others arms, he said to himself, "God, I hope this works."

Chapter 17
Newer Beginnings

Finally, they were on the jet waiting for take off. It was just the two of them making their way to what was going to be a new life; a new beginning. The plan was after the wedding they would take a 5 month honeymoon in France so that Tory could get acclimated to her new home when she got done with her studies in the States. When he sat next to her he took her hand and said, "We finally did it." "Yes we did." "Are you ready to see your new home Mrs. Guadau?" "Yes and no." Then he shot her a look of concern. "Okay Mrs. Guadau, spit it out. What's the hang up this time?" "I just don't understand why I have to totally relocate to France. I don't know one word of French nor do I understand it. I don't know anyone here accept you. Everything I know is here in the US. Why can't you just shuffle back and forth?" "Because I'll be spending more of my time in France and eventually I'll have to permanently relocate there. We talked about this and you were fine with it. I don't want to be so far from you for so long. When I come home, I want you to be there. I really do enjoy that feeling of knowing that when I come home, my wife will be there. I don't have to remind you of my last marriage do I? You know I could be going see my mistress." "Really then if that's the case, then I could be off seeing; wait what did you call him again? "The Dancing Chef." "You're a real comedian. And that's why you're moving to France with me. So I can keep my eyes on you." "Why you're not threatened by him are you?" "Maybe a little. He's a handsome guy, he cooks really well, and I see the way he looks at you." "You're all of those things; the difference is I married you and not him." "Yeah you did; didn't you? So guess that makes me the better man." "Yes it does." She said as she held his hand.

The jet had landed in France at the later part of the morning. Shaune awoke anxious to show his wife their new home. With excitement bursting inside him, he tried to wake her. "Tory are you awake." Tory, wiping the sleep out of her eyes said, "I am now." While she was trying to regain her thoughts, she realized that the jet had landed; and that meant that they were in fact now in France. "We're here?" "Yes we're home baby." They de-boarded the jet and they were met by a limo and Shaunes' driver. As they passed through parts of the country, Tory could see the beautiful houses in their neighborhoods. They even passed by a couple of farms and vineyards. Trying to take in the experience of being married and living in another country proved to be quite overwhelming, but she tried to contain her emotions as best as possible. Finally, the limo arrived at the QG vanity style gate; just like back in the States. The limo had driven down to Shaunes' Château style home. It was much bigger then the home he had back in the States. "Is this supposed to be our home?" She asked in amazement. "I know this seems a little bit bigger then the one back home…" Cutting in on his comment, she replied, "What do you need with this much house? This looks like a big ass hotel." Upon hearing her comment, the driver couldn't resist the urge to laugh. Then Shaune shot him a look that made him stop. Then she finished, "I'm not impressed by this. In fact, I'm more turned off then anything." Shaune realized what a diva he had on his hands; and he could only handle a diva the way she should. "I could care less if you decided to pitch a tent in the woods with the animals. The truth is, this is your new home; our home together. How acclimated you decide to associate yourself is contingent upon you. It is what it is so get used to it the best way you know how." Then he left her in the car by herself. And although she didn't want to accept what he had told her, deep down she knew he was right. They were married and there was no turning back from this. As she got out of the car, with her teeth clenched she whispered under her breath, "He better be glad we're married, I swear I would be on the first thing smoking back to South Crack!"

Tory followed the servant into the bedroom were she saw Shaune unpacking their clothes. As she looked around the room and despite the fact that the Château was huge, she did like the bedroom. It was big but it had a romantic feel to it. She particularly liked the two-way fireplace. It too had a romantic feel to it. On one side, you could cozy up and enjoy it from the bed; while on the other side you could enjoy the fireplace just by cozying up on the couch with a nightcap. Then there was the balcony; which was just as huge. It went from one end of the bedroom to the other end, with two entrances. And it had patio furniture nicely decorated around it. Shaune definitely lived in style. While she was casing the place, she heard him say, "Are you going to help me unpack or are you going to continue to complain about the house?" "I actually love this bedroom. It feels really romantic. Did you and your ex-wife ever stay here?" "Nope, she was never interested in coming to France. She felt that leaving the country would bury her dreams." "So what time is dinner?" "In a couple of hours; but if you're hungry, you can find something downstairs in the kitchen." "Like I know where that is. I don't know where I am right now. Is there a map that comes with this place? Maybe even a tourist guide for newcomers." Shaune then remembered about what was going to happen in the upcoming months. "Speaking of dinner, we were invited to have dinner with the French Consulates and their spouses." "Sounds fun, you do know I'm going to need a really spiffy dress to wear?" "And I'm already on top of that. I had scheduled an appointment for you for a fitting." "What kind of dress am I getting?" "When you look through the stylist book, you can make a decision of your own. Just nothing too raunchy; these are much older people." "What makes you think I would dress like that? Have you ever known me to dress raunchy?" Tory started to take offense with his comment. "Look baby, the truth is you're an American and these people have their opinions of whom and what Americans are." With an angry attitude, she grabbed her clothes and headed towards the closet. Then she turned and said, "Well if they already know about me, maybe I shouldn't disappoint and not go then." Shaune walked over to the closet to try and console his wife because he knew that he was stepping into a divided type of conversation; and needed Tory to be onboard with him as best as possible. "I'm sorry if I may have sounded a little too brash with my wording. The truth is, my last wife whom they've never met only found out about her through the public media. And what they found out about her they didn't like. And that mixed in with their impressions of America doesn't go over too well with them." "Oh so wait, you marry another American and now they think you may have made another mistake? So is it up to me to get you your redemption? First of all, I'm proud to be an American; and this was your idea to move to this racist, classis country; and it's your people who have a problem with me, and I have to be the one to set the record straight. Maybe I shouldn't go then. I will not conform myself to be somebody else for someone else. You married me. What you see is what they get." Tory was started to get pretty worked up and Shaune didn't know how to take her down. "Please just calm down. No one is asking you to conform to anyone's status…" "No Shaune, you're not? Please allow me to paint the picture. You started the conversation off about getting me fitted for a dress. "As long as it's not raunchy" you say. Not that that bothers me because that's not my style anyways. However, you go on to say that the French Consulates already have a low opinion of us filthy Americans." "There you go throwing words into my mouth again." "Well the filthy part was my word. But I wasn't too far off was I? You don't have to answer that. But then you go into how your ex-wife screwed it up for me and you so I have to become someone else just to redeem their faith in you. Forget about the filthy American whore he married, as long as Shaunes' a good boy." Although he wanted to prove

Victoria Rene'e Manley

her wrong, he realized that she was right. He wanted to mold her into the perfect wife just so that he would be able to get back into the good graces of the Consulates. There was nothing else he could say to her. She wasn't on board with his idea and there was nothing he could say to persuade her to do so. "That's classic. You can't even dispute what I'm saying because I'm right aren't I?" Feeling embarrassed, he still couldn't answer her. "If I can't be the woman that you married, what did you marry me for? Am I not worth standing up for despite what country I come from?" She started to leave, but then she turned back to him and said, "You know what? I'll go to that dinner, and I'll be someone else just because I love you that much. If this is what will make you a better man in their eyes, then I'm all in. Just you remember this; this will be the start of a marriage of deception. Something I'm sure you're privy to in your last marriage." The she left the bedroom.

Later on, Shaune managed to build up enough pride to come and apologize to his wife. He found her in the kitchen eating banana peppers out of the jar. "May I sit down?" "This is your house; I can't tell you where to sit." "This is your house too." "What do you want Que`Shaune? I really am enjoying this quiet moment." "I managed to find my back bone. It was buried in the trash can somewhere. I wanted to apologize for trying to make you someone you're not. You were right and when you put it the way that you did, it hurts too much to admit. I guess I was just trying to water down the idea of getting you to change. As your husband, I'm appalled at myself for even thinking that was okay. For the record, if you decide to go to the dinner, I want you to be you and no one else." As he held onto her hand, he finished, "I love who you are and it would be total deception for you to change who you are." "Thank you Que`Shaune, I appreciate you for saying that. I know how hard it must have been for you to come to that conclusion." Then he leaned over and kissed her. "Those peppers are pretty spicy. I didn't know you liked spicy food." "I didn't either, I was thinking of making a sandwich when I ate one and I just couldn't stop. So I eighty six the sandwich and went for these instead."

Today was the day the Guadaus' were going to meet with the French Consulates and their wives. Shaune and Tory spent the night discussing the who's who and also rehearsing some popular French words as well as phrases. Tory spent the most of her afternoon fighting back nausea from her nerves. Shaune walked into the bathroom and saw his wife sitting on the bathroom bench. "Baby, come on. We don't want to be late." He tried to tell her calmly, but deep down inside, he wanted to yell it to her. "I've been feeling really queasy the entire day. Maybe I shouldn't go." Shaune took a deep breath and said, "See, I knew this was going to happen. Torianey you cannot decide to not go; you're the soul reason why they invited us to dinner. These are the kinds of people whose folds you would want to get into. It could prove to be beneficial." "Beneficial to whom you or me? Didn't we have this conversation a couple of months ago?" "Yes that was because I was trying to get you to be someone else; but that's not the case this time. It's obvious you're trying to start an argument just so you can cancel out; but you can't." "Why not?" "Because we accepted two months ago and you were on board with going. What's going on with you now?" As Tory sat on the bed, she became emotional. Then Shaune became frustrated with her. Of all the times and moments to hesitate, she picked the 11th hour to do so.

Finally, Tory and Shaune managed to make it to the French Consulates home and although they were a few minutes late, no one noticed. It was an intimate dinner setting of the two Consulates and their spouses along with the Guadaus'. The plan was that since the hosts were more prone to speak in their native language of French, Shaune would interpret for Tory when necessary. The night was going really well but Tory was still experiencing her slight queasiness. She couldn't understand why she was still feeling this way when the worst was over. Or so she thought. But things got progressively worse when dinner finally arrived. It was salmon, a dish that the Consulate Pierre's wife had prepared. While Tory was holding Shaunes' hand, the salmon passed by her causing her to get a whiff of the smell taking her totally by surprise. Then she gripped Shaunes' hand even tighter. Seeing the look of distress on her face, he leaned in to ask her, "Are you okay?" Struggling to answer him she said, "I'm still feeling nauseous. I feel like I might want to throw up again." "Take a deep breath and let it out slowly." He told her. As she did as he said she took a deep breath but the room was so consumed with the smell of salmon, it became too much for her to handle. She caught a case of the dry heaves and now she made an obvious spectacle of herself. "I need to go to the ladies room. Please!!!" Shaune turned to Mrs. Pierre and asked, "Can my wife use your rest room?" "Sure I will show her where it is." Tory got up to follow Mrs. Pierre. Her next and final wave of nausea got the best of her. She saw a trash can by the door and she ran to it. She collapsed on the floor vomiting in the pale. The sound was so retched and disturbing. Que'Shaune was overly embarrassed but equally concerned about his wife. He walked over to her after she was done to help her on her feet. Consulate Pierre insisted that she rested in the den until the paramedics arrived.

The paramedics had soon arrived and while they were attending to Tory, Mrs. Pierre walked up to Shaune and asked him, "How far along is she?" "I apologize, but what are you talking about?" "Your wife is with child no? Did you know?" "My wife is just fighting back a bad case of nerves." "I don't think it's her nerves that are the case Monsieur Guadau." Without responding to her, he just jumped into the ambulance to accompany Tory.

After a couple of hours in the hospital, Tory was cleared to go home but not just before getting the news that her and Que'Shaune were twelve weeks pregnant expecting their first set of twins. While on the way home, Shaune was trying to thank the Pierre's and apologizing for ruining their dinner. Tory was trying to do the math trying to figure out when exactly did this happen. When he got off the phone, he noticed that there was the elephant in the car again. He looked over to her and noticed she had an aggravated daze on her face. "Torianey?" He whispered. Shaune knew that with her, the pendulum usually swung one way or another. There was never any middle ground with Tory. "What do we do now?" She asked. "What do you mean? We raise two children." "After we got engaged, we stop using protection." "I think you're right." "So if I would have insisted on using protection, this would have never of happened." Shaune was confused at what she said. For fear that she might say what he thought she was going to say, he'd rather that he himself remained silent. "What about my schooling? What about my career plans?" "You can finish school after you give birth." Then she began to yell. "When 18yrs after the babies are born." "No, I'm not saying that. We can take care of our children together; and in between, we can hire a caretaker." Then a fuse blew in Torys mind. "How easy it is for you to throw that out there. Says the man who was raised by his caretaker; not having one single memory of him own mother. Good times huh Shaune?" Shaune not wanting to stoop to her level of anger, he lowered his voice and said, "That wasn't fair of you to say that." As the car pulled up to the mansion, Tory leaned in to Shaune and said, "You know what is equally unfair? The fact that you don't fucking get it." Then she left the limousine slamming the door causing the window to break and the lock to jam. Before he knew it, Shaune was covered in glass. As he was trying to get out of the car, he injured his left hand in all the broken glass. And Tory left him and didn't even bother to look back.

Shaune was in his den making some calls to get the broken car door fixed. When he got off the phone all he could do was think of how a disaster his day was from the Pierre's dinner to the car door; breaking; and not to mention his entire left hand getting cut up requiring him to need 30 stitches. And although he was in a bit of shock about his wife's expectancy, he was equally happy. Then his wife walked into the den. After the day he had experienced, Shaune was in no mood for anymore of Tory's antics. Plus, he was in excruciating pain from his hand. "Can we talk?" She asked. He sat back in his chair and didn't say a word.

"Fine then, I'll just say this; I was wrong for yelling at you in the car. I heard you got hurt after I broke the glass. I can't help but feel terribly responsible for that. The fact that I didn't look back to check on you doesn't make me feel any better either." As she walked around the desk to kneel to him, he still remained silent. Then she continued. "Hey, I'm trying to master this whole getting married thing and just when I think I got it wrapped around my head, I end up pregnant. This is scary for me Shaune. Everything is happening so fast." "So what are you saying?" "I'm sorry." She whispered. Then he yelled back at her. "I'm sorry; I can't hear what you're saying." He actually managed to startle Tory yelling as he did. Then he continued. "Are you sorry about the $15000 car door you just broke? That's not even the concern right now because I spend that much on free lunch for my staff every month. Do you want to know what the lowest point was for me? Was when you went in on me about my relationship with my parents versus my caretaker. And you knew I had no control over that. God Tory, I would have never in all my life thought that you, my wife would go for my jugular the way that you did. You berated me in front of my staff. Then you have the nerve to come in here and try and softly apologize like that's going to make any damn difference. And why when there is a situation concerning us, you manage to make it about you? "Oh Shaune, I'M scared." "Shaune how am I supposed to handle this?" "This is so stressful for ME." Note to self Torianey, we are in this together. Being pregnant, being married, any form of stress; that's just as much my concern as it is yours. I'm not some deadbeat dad that's trying to make a run for it. I'm right here trying to figure it out with you. Don't you for once try and remove yourself from center stage and try and look at it from the other person's perspective? No you don't; which is why I'm paying $15000 for a car door and my stitched up hand." Out of frustration and anger, he left her in the den.

The time was close to 2am and Tory was sitting in front of the fireplace sipping on a cup of tea. She hadn't see hair nor hide of Shaune since his outburst in the den earlier. She couldn't sleep because she was concerned that he might still be angry with her. Finally, he walked in and saw that she was still awake. "What are you doing up at this hour?" He asked her. "I couldn't sleep. After you blew up on me, you kind of scared me a bit. Where did you go?" "I went to clear my head." He started to take off his clothes. Then he headed to the closet; when he came back out, he had on his sweats and tee shirt. As he lay across the bed, he asked her, "Aren't you coming to bed?" "Are you still angry with me?" While moving over on his side of the bed, he waved for her to come over to him. Tory came over to him and she laid herself across the bed next to him. "No I'm not angry with you anymore. However, I am concerned that the next time we have a disagreement, are we going to have a repeat performance? Or are we going to talk about it?" "I promise I will talk about it and try not to yell. But can I ask you something?" "You can ask me anything." "How do you feel about having twins?" While he was staring at the ceiling, he began to smile. Then he said, "While I was over by the pond, I had some time to process this whole thing. Despite everything else, I'm overly in joy. I'm equally scared; I mean twins for god sakes. I anticipated a child, but we're having two children. And I do agree with you when you say this is all happening so fast." He then positioned himself so that he could look her in her eyes and he finished. "Torianey, I need you to understand that you're not alone in all this. There's no time you can't grab my attention and tell me what you're feeling; especially now. Are we okay with that?" "Yes we are." He reached over and turned the lamp out. "Good. I love you and I'm tired. Maybe we can talk about it some more tomorrow." Then he held her in his arms and kissed her forehead.

Tory woke up the next morning and Shaune had already gone to work. Since he didn't bother to wake her, she had assumed that he was still upset with her. Usually, he would have wakened her to kiss her goodbye. Then she sat up in bed and saw the huge plush teddy bear on her left side of the bed with a black rose and a note attached:

My love,

I'm sure you're upset that I didn't wake you to say goodbye. I read online that pregnant moms need lots of rest. Also, they need lots of cushion. I read that either you would require a body pillow or two regular pillows. In this case, I give you "Que`Shaune the Teddy Bear." It is imperative that pregnant moms get the cushioning they need between their legs for the support that their back requires; and since I can't be around all the time to give you the support your back needs (And trust me, I love being between your legs Torianey.) I will allow my sidekick "Que`Shaune the Teddy bear" to help me. If you feel you need to call me, I'm always available to you. Remember you're never alone.

Le votre pour pourvu qui`ill pond,

Your loving husband,

Que`Shaune

As Tory giggled at his humor in his note she sighed, "Aww, how sweet."

Tory spent the entire day wandering through the huge mansion. She started to get board because everything started to look the same. After all, it had been a two months of wandering through the château style mansion with no place else to go, she had managed to figure out where mostly everything was. Finally, she had wandered her way back to the den and she started to scroll through the computer. She was reading through the news articles to catch up in the current affairs of what was going on back at home. As she started to feel board, she was ready to shut the computer down. Then she stumbled upon an article that mentioned a particular homeless hostel that was in dire need of donations in Massongy, France. From that, she had an idea. While she was googling all the information about the hostel, she was taking notes to make sure she had her facts straight. See, she figured that if her husband could be a man of philanthropy, then why couldn't she? Plus, she felt that if she had to spend another day in that mansion alone, she would rather chew her arms off. Then she picked up the phone to call the homeless hostel.

Que'Shaune was in his office and you would figure he would be working hard on his financial projects, but he wasn't. He had been online for hours searching through search engines about pregnant mothers. He purchased a whole bunch of books ranging from first time parents to baby names and their meanings. It was for certain, Que'Shaune was bitten by the baby bug. While he was sitting and daydreaming about watching his babies being born for the first time, he didn't take notice that his father had entered his office. "Mon Files?" His father whispered as he eased up to his desk. "Dad?" Shaune replied, shaking him out of his daze. "Qu'estes-vous alle?" "Wasn't it obvious when I called you to tell you my wife was expecting. I can't stop dreaming about the future." Since the news of Torys expecting broke, you would have thought it was Shaune who was pregnant because he couldn't stop glowing. "I bet you were dreaming about my grandioses bebes." "Qui pare`. And I can't stop." "And how is Torianey these days?" Sr. saw his sons expression changed from a huge grin on his face to a dull smile. "She wasn't too thrilled. When she first found out, she was a little disturbed. She's a little over three months; and we've talked about it last night, so you can say she's okay with it now. I just can't understand why can't she just sit back and enjoy the ride? She's always so concerned about her future. I try to tell her that her life is set in stone; that I can take care of her and the babies." It was Sr. to the rescue again, for he needed to help his son understand what was going on with his wife. "It took me a long time to understand that the things that make a man fall in love with a woman are the things that make him regret her sometimes. My son, did you honestly think that after she married you she would lie down and play dead for you? She is a strong willed woman with determination in her heart. Isn't that what attracted you to her? You have to remember, she had an entire game of her own before you stepped into play. She's not a switch you turn off when she's no longer required." "So what do I do?" "You listen and you deal with it. She's just a few months now; wait till she's between six and nine months. Then you can start jumping out of windows, cars and planes." As they both laughed, Sr. finished his speech. "I remember your mother when she was pregnant with you. When she wasn't threatening my life, she was cussing me. But when she finally gave birth, she turned back into the woman I married. Needless to say, your wife is going to become what looks like someone else. And you as a father are going to have to deal with it. You created this monster; the least you can do is deal with her." "You know what dad, you're right and I'm sure you can understand that it's almost overwhelming how complete it feels to be married, in love and expecting children." With all the stories that his father had mentioned about his mother, he realized that they were always before his time so he had to ask. "Hey dad, I remember my relationship with you and Marta; how come I can't remember my relationship with mom? Better yet, I can't remember the three of us together. What memories I do have are few and in between, and I see the pictures all over the house; how come I can't remember one straight good day with mom?" Sr. looked down at his watch and got up out of his seat and replied, "Take your wife to dinner tonight, hold her hand tell her everyday how much you love her." Then he left. Shaune couldn't understand why his father felt the need to rush out so abruptly. And since he couldn't get a clear concise answer from his dad, he brushed the moment off, followed his orders and picked up the phone to call his wife.

Tory was still on the computer when the caretaker walked in. "Mamoisell Guadau, your husband is requesting to speak with you." Then she handed her the phone. "Hey you!" She yelled in excitement. "What have you been doing with yourself all day?" "I've been bored all day but I got an idea in my mind and I went to research it and I've been at it ever since." "Does this involved schools here in France." "Not really, but I'll explain later." "Great then, maybe we can talk it over during dinner tonight." "What do you have in mind?" "I was thinking maybe we could go to a nice French restaurant just the two of us." "I'd love that." "Great, then be ready by six. I'll have the car take you to meet me there." "This sounds like fun. I can't wait to see you. I love you." "I can't wait to see you either and I love you too. Bye." Then he hung up the phone and went back to daydreaming.

6pm, Tory pulled up to the restaurant. As the doorman came to the limo to help her out, she looked up at the prestigious looking French restaurant; she whispered to herself, "This looks expensive." When she walked in, she saw Shaune at a corner table waving to her. While he was helping her into her seat, she said, "I have to admit, I was a little nervous about tonight. I kind of felt like it was our first date again." "Actually, I had those butterflies in my stomach that I had when I came to pick you up that night. I guess some things never change." Then they both giggled. "How was work today?" "I'm having a little trouble at work. The industry had been experiencing a slight drop in revenue." "How slight?" "Only a 5%; I know it's not a huge dip but usually, investors start to question these things just before they decide to jump ship." "Wow. That sounds scary." Shaune didn't want to burden her with his bad news. After all, this was supposed to be a good night for the two of them. "Forget about that; let's talk about your day?" "I already told you it was boring. Can I ask a question?" "Shoot." "How often do you give back to your customer or investors?" "What do you mean? I throw fundraisers for communities all the time." "I'm not necessarily talking about that. Lou used to tell me that if you take care of your customers and investors, then you'll never lose them. In fact, you might gain more because the word will get around." Hearing her say that he started to get more interested in what she had to say. "Sounds interesting; do you have any suggestions?" "I'm not sure how the oil industry works but, periodically Lou would give dinner on the house to a couple of his loyal customers as well as a complimentary bottle of his wine from his selection. I mean people who drive cars have to buy gas and a lot of people have to use oil to heat their homes. So, if you cut your rates for a few customers who buy your product periodically, they just might reconsider going to the next company. You don't have to cut it a huge amount; just by a small fraction that way they stay happy. You will lose some money but by the end of that fiscal year you might end up making it back up. Business rule number one; you have to lose money to make money." Shaune had forgotten that she was business savvy. After all, she was Louise Carrapellies Assistant Manager, and he was successful. Not to mention that what she was saying made total sense. "Everybody loves a sale." "Exactly; especially when they don't expect it." "Thank you baby; what would I do without you? I know what I have to do now." Finally, the waitress came to take their orders. Throughout the night they talked, ate and laughed. Then Shaune took the liberty of ordering the dessert. It was his favorite French dessert; Tart tatin, which was sautéed apples sprinkled with powered sugar. He ordered a scoop of vanilla ice cream with it. Then he fed her the first bite to see her reaction. "Oh this tastes delicious." "I know it's my favorite desert. I always order it when I come here." "It's mine now, I'm stealing it." "I wanted to take you out tonight because a birdie told me that in the next upcoming months your body is going to be experiencing a lot of changes. Also, you'll be having more hormonal moments as well. With that having been said, I look forward to more days of me hanging around the pond." "Thank you for being so understanding. I'll try not to blame you for all the worlds' problems." Then Shaune called the waitress for the bill to pay. He then helped Tory out of her seat and held her hand. Out of nowhere, Tory experienced a flash back moment. "Wow, I just had a dejavou moment." "You think you've been here before?" "I remember I was working at Lous' and there was always this older couple that came to the restaurant. They were usually my last customers to leave for the night. But when they did, he would help his wife out of her seat; she would kiss him and they would hold hands as they left the restaurant. I would always look at them and wish I had it like that. And now I do." As she turned to look at him, Shaune kissed her and held her hand to lead her out of the restaurant.

Chapter 18
The Beginning of a Totally New Problem

Shaune awoke the next morning and found that his wife was not next to him. He decided not to go to work that day. As he came down the stairs he asked the servant, "Have you seen my wife?" "Memoisell Guadau is in le den sir." He responded. When he got to his den, Tory was so engrossed in what she was doing. "Hey you. I didn't want to wake you so I came down here to finish my research." "Oh yeah, you were supposed to tell me about that last night. So exactly what was it you were researching?" Then she showed him the picture of the homeless hostel in Massongy, France. "Yeah, it's a soup kitchen in France. Why would you be researching this?" "I'm glad you asked. I was wondering if I could sponsor this place?" "That's noble of you. I would love to send a check in your name." "Shaune, I was actually thinking more along the lines of hosting a banquet for the homeless and the community there." He closed his eyes, took a deep breath and said, "Please tell me you're not for real?" "I'm very serious. I don't want to just throw money at people. I would like to be a part of the experience." "Wow! How can I answer that without being confrontational? Huh, I guess I could just say NO!" "Why?" "That place is dangerous and I am not risking you and my unborn children. I'll be more then happy to messenger a check in your name; but I would not suggest that you go there ever. I have a meeting I have to attend. When I get back, we could discuss the particulars of your check when I get home." As he left to get ready for his meeting, Tory turned her back and whispered, "No that won't be necessary."

In the later part of the afternoon, Que`Shaune had concluded his meeting. As he let the board members out for a brief break, Greg came over to him and said, "I think that was a great idea giving your customers more for less. I don't know how you thought that up, but you got the members eating it up." "Actually, it was Tory's idea. And speaking of, I was a little aggressive with her this morning and I probably need to apologize." As he picked up his phone he called the Chateau. "Hello, may I speak with my wife?" "Monsieur Guadau, Mamoisell Guadau has left the grounds sir." Shaune had feared that his wife had done the unthinkable and did what he had advised her not to do. "Who was her driver?" "Tony sir." "Please connect me to his phone." Shaune patiently waited for his servant to connect him to Tony, Tory's driver. Then the driver picked up. "Hello?" "Tony please explain to me where did you take my wife?" "She wanted me to take her to Massongy sir." Now Shaune was officially pissed off. Despite his interjection, Tory still went to the homeless hostel. When Greg stepped in to the office, Shaune said, "Greg I need you to wrap this meeting up for me." "Why Shaune, you have the investors eating out of your hand. Why would you want to leave things this way?" "I have to get my wife. She's in Massongy. Please handle this for me." Then he left in a hurry.

Shaune made it to the soup kitchen and his wife was in fact, still there. He had spotted his limousine still parked and waiting for her to come out. As he walked over to the window he knocked and said to Tony, "Go back to the mansion, I will deal with you later." Shaune's pressure was sky high at that point. He was at a meeting that was going so well but might take a turn for the worse because he had to extract his wife from potential harms way. As he walked in, he spotted Tory walking into the pantry area with another woman. While Tory had her back turned to the woman, Shaune walked in and the other woman tried to greet him. He shunned her to keep her silent. "How often do you get these types of can goods?" Tory asked; but then she realized the woman wasn't answering her back. As she turned, she saw her husband scowling at her. "Please let me explain…" Without as much as a blink Shaune said, "Torianey Guadau, please get into the car now." Then she headed to his car. As they drove back home, there was that tension filled silence. Tory could feel that he was enraged with her. When they got to the mansion, the doorman opened her door and Tory quickly made her escape upstairs to the bedroom. There was plenty of room to run from him there she thought to herself.

Tory was in the bedroom pacing back and forth. She was waiting for Shaune to bust in with guns blazing. Then there was a knock at the door. It was the maid. "Mrs. Guadau, Your husband is requesting to see you in the dinning room." Tory came downstairs, and she walked as slow as she could to the dinning room. She knocked on the door and opened it. Shaune was sitting in his seat waiting on her. "Please sit." He said calmly. "I know you want to discuss what happened this evening…" Shaune put up his hand to silence her. Then he said, "We're going to look at it like this, you went out to get some air; and there's nothing else to talk about because you will never go there again. Now let's have dinner." "Why would you say that?" "Because it's true. I forbade you to ever go back to that place again. This conversation is over." Feeling slighted by his statement she shot, "What… Did you just… What?" Then Shaune started to clench his teeth. "I said this conversation is over. Please let's eat." "I'm just curious to know exactly what would you do if I did go back there?" "Torianey, please tread lightly with me tonight. I'm in no mood for your antics. Your little stunt may have cost me big." "Please make no mistake Que'Shaune, I am a grown ass woman; and the day I let you decide where and when I can go anywhere, well that just has to cease." Tory realized that both their moods set the stage for more then just an argument. So she tried to calm the situation. "Look, I'm sorry I said that. However, I don't want to be the barefoot, pregnant wife of Que`Shaune Guadau. I want to do something positive with my time." "There are plenty of positive things to do here for you." "Really, like what?" "Shopping!" Then she got upset again. Now she was no longer concerned about the tone or her demeanor. As she picked up her glass of water and threw it in his face she yelled, "Fucking chauvinist!!! I can't believe you said that to me." Just as she was about to leave, she came back and said, "Note to self, your wife is going back; and you just try and stop her." Then she left slamming the door.

Tory was in the kitchen rummaging through the fridge. She had managed to find some vanilla ice cream and cranberry sauce; which in her mind didn't sound like a bad idea since she missed dinner. While she was eating her concoction, the maid walked in. "Memoisell Guadau, your husband has requested to see you again." "Tell my husband that I request that he go to hell." She spat as she left the kitchen. She went and found a nice spot at the back of the mansion where she could enjoy her ice cream and try to be at peace. However, Shaune didn't waste too much time spoiling that moment. As he walked up behind her he said, "I really do enjoy pushing your buttons sometimes. That was the best glass of water I had in a long time." "Shaune, what do you want. I was trying to enjoy peace of mind and here you come." "So you'd rather bust my balls all night then to make up? I'm trying to apologize if you would let me." "So say what you have to say then." "I'm sorry baby. I was way upset." "Please let's not forget degrading and inappropriate." "Yes it was." "Okay, I forgive you. You can go now." "Must you sass me all the time?" "If you want to be a dick, yeah. I'm going back to the Massongy shelter with or without your help." Shaune knew that his wife was equally stubborn as he was and it made no sense to go on with her that way. "Fine then, if we're going through with it we're going to do it my way." "Why do we have to do it your way?" "Look baby, I'm trying to meet you half way. Plus, I've been at this a little bit longer then you." "Fine, you win. We'll do it your way." "With you everything is a competition. I was never trying to compete with you. I have your every interest at heart. I'm doing this because this is what you want; and I want it to be done safely and right." Then he put out his hand for her to shake. "Truce?" As she took his hand, she said, "Truce." As he sat down next to her, he started to explain the ins and outs of philanthropic work. He had given her a multitude of tasks to fulfill just to keep her busy and out of Massongy as well as out of his hair.

Shaune was in his den on the phone when Tory walked in. As he hung up the phone, she handed him a folder of all the things he had set out for her to do. Initially, he gave her till the end of the month but she was bored and resourceful. "Wow, I didn't think you would finish this at all let alone in two weeks. Impressive." "So do I get to throw the banquet or what?" "Let me look through everything with my lawyers and I'll get back to you." Then he shoved the folder aside. Out of frustration, Tory grabbed the folder and yelled, "You lying son of a bitch! You had no intention on ever going through with it. This was just a wild goose chase." "That's not true. I didn't expect you to finish so soon. I wasn't prepared for this today." "So call your lawyers now. How hard is it to do?" She yelled. "Calm down Tory. I would like to be at the meeting to make sure all ducks are in a row. I really do admire your passion, but the truth is this a little more delicate then you think. It's all about politics being involved. Please trust me." Tory slammed the folder on the table and left the room. An hour later Shaune came upstairs to see his wife rummaging through a magazine. "Look Shaune, I'm shopping. This must make you more impressed then my finished project." "I came to give you what you wanted. Inside your folder is a signed affidavit funding your banquet." "How much can I contribute?" "As much as you need." Her face lit up brighter then a Christmas tree. Then she hugged him so tight. "Thank you so much. You don't know how much this means to me." "Oh yes I do. You've cursed me to no end until the end. And now I'll be able to get some sleep at least."

Chapter 19
That Which Does Not Kill Us
Sets Us Up for Greatness

It was the moment Tory had been waiting for. She finally got to throw her banquet in the shelter. Herself and Mrs. Gudice, the caretaker had been corresponding all week until the big day. Shaune and Greg had been calling different food companies for contributions to the function. They even hired private caterers to prepare the meals for the guest in the community. And like clockwork that evening, the people started to dwindle in. The meals consisted of whole chickens, hams, roast beef, and pork loin. For the sides mashed potatoes, whole potatoes, rice, and assorted pasta salads and for deserts apple pie, cherry pie and Tory's favorite, lemon meringue. The flyers had read in native French:

> **Attention community of Massongy. All are welcome to join tonight's banquet. Time: 6pm – 9pm. Food and drinks are free to all. Don't miss out on the festivities.**

It was 6pm; starting time, and the house inside the hostel started to fill up. Tory had hoped that she didn't have to turn away any hungry mouths due to occupancy restrictions. She had Mrs. Gudice speak on her behalf since she couldn't speak for herself that the banquet was from the entire Guadau family.

The time was winding down. A quarter of nine was her cut off point, and she was starting to feel exhausted. All the gift cards were raffled off and/or given away, and the food that was left was being packed away for another day. It was at the point she realized she needed to call her husband and tell him that she was coming home soon and that all was well with the function. As she called his phone, it went straight to voice mail. So she left a message. "Hey honey. I was calling to tell you I'm fine and I should be leaving in less then 15min. I will call…" Just then she heard a scream that startled her. Then she heard Mrs. Gudice speaking frantically in French. There were the voices of two men sounding just as frantic. Tory's first impression was to run out to her to help her. But then Ms. Gudice came running into the pantry. The short five foot, pale elderly woman tried desperately to shove Tory into the pantry closet. She quickly whispered, "You must hide; they have guns and they will kill us unless I give them what they want." "What do they want?" Tory tried to ask her as she'd stumble into the closet. Gudice locked the door behind her just so no one could get into the closet; and that way Tory was safe. She had watched through the grid on the door when she saw two men roughing up Mrs. Gudice. Tory couldn't understand what they were saying but it seemed as though they wanted something from her but she clearly didn't have it to give. She managed to get a clear view of the two men. There was a really tall man with black hair wearing a grey leather motor cycle jacket and black jeans. He was carrying a machine gun. While the other man who was much shorter, had blond hair and was wearing a three quarter length black leather jacket and black jeans. His weapon was an automatic handgun. Judging from the way they were smacking the woman around, Tory got the impression that they were going to kill her eventually. Tory closed her eyes and prayed to God that they would stop and leave the building. Just as she opened her eyes, she saw the tall man raised his gun and commenced to firing his weapon on the woman. The sight of seeing all the blood splatter all over the wall sent Tory into immediate shock. She didn't want to see anymore so she backed away from the door. Then she heard Mrs. Gudice speaking and she came back to the door. But her voice was silenced when the shorter guy shot her in the face killing her instantly. Tory grabbed her mouth trying to hold back her scream in horror. Now the men were searching around the area to see if they could find what ever it was they were looking for. The shorter man came over to the door to open it but it was locked. They started to leave the pantry room when they heard Tory's cell phone go off. She tried to silence it as fast as she could but at the point, the men had an idea that someone else was in the building.

Que'Shaune was in his limousine on the way home from his late evening. He was trying to call his wife to see if she was in fact on her way home. Her message to him gave him a bad feeling. He kept trying to assume that maybe he was overreacting; "but this was Massongy." He whispered to himself. He tried calling her again but this time her phone went to voice mail. Now a strange feeling came over him and the next call he made was to the driver. Tony picked up his phone and said, "Good evening Monsieur Guadau." "Are you and my wife on the way home yet?" "No sir, Memoisell Guadau and Memoisell Gudice are still inside." While Tony was talking to Shaune, he noticed that the lights in the facility had been off for a while and no one had come out for a while. Shaune looked at his watch and said, "It's a quarter till ten and I would appreciate it if you bring my wife home. I don't care if you have to drag her out. Thank you" As he hung up the phone, Tony started to have a bad feeling. He tried to call Tory only to get her voice mail. Before he got out of the car, he leaned over to his glove box and pulled out his revolver. He thought that if he didn't need it at least he would have it. He placed it on his side and commenced to walking into the building.

The men had shut the lights off so that no pedestrians or straggler would be tempted to come in and interrupt their search. While Tory was in the closet, she started to feel hopeless that her fate would be met by her dying at the hands of these cold hearted murderers. Her heart sank as she thought about where her husband was and how great it would be if she could be back in the safety of his comforting arms. She also realized that if she would have listened in the first place, she wouldn't be here. As she opened her eyes to see where the men were, she was met by a pair of eyes starring back at her through the other side of the door. It was the taller man; and with a sinister voice the he said, "I found you!" Then he shot the door open with his gun. Tony heard the shot and quickly withdrew his revolver. As he slowly crept up to the pantry entrance, he saw the taller man lift his gun to fire on Tory. But then, he started to fire heavy rounds at the men. They started firing back at Tony as they were trying to run out the back door. While all the action was going on, Tory was trying to back away from all the heavy firing. When she stepped on a large rock, she lost her balance and fell backwards hitting her head on a cabinet door. She fell down and was starting to loose consciousness. Tony ran to the closet and yelled, "Memoisell Guadau! Are you alright?" "I… I…I'm." Now Tory was totally unconscious. Tony immediately called for an ambulance; then he had to call her husband and explain what happened and why.

Que`Shaune was at home waiting for his wife to come home when he got a phone call from Tony. Tony had explained that Tory had fallen and hit her head. Tony didn't want to give too much detail over the phone. He'd rather explain everything to him when he got there. Shaune ran to his car and sped off to the hospital. When Shaune got to the hospital, he saw all the paparazzi at the entrance; but he didn't care. He had no idea as to the extent of her injuries; nor did he know what condition the babies were in. All he knew was he had to get to his wife. He walked up to the receptionist and said, "I'm Que`Shaune Guadau; I'm trying to find my wife Torianey Guadau." Mr. Guadau, your wife is having a series of test ran." Frantically he replied, "A series of tests? Is everything okay? Is she alright? The babies…" The nurse cut him off and said, "Sir, the unborn fetuses are fine. However, your wife stumbled and hit her head pretty hard. When she came in, she was unconscious. Right now she is having a cat scan performed on her head." "When can I see her?" "She shouldn't be very long. I promise I will keep you updated on everything that is happening. If you would sir, the waiting area is behind you." When he entered the waiting room, he was met by Tony; his wife's driver. "You want to tell me what happen?" Tony took a deep breath and explained what had taken place. "When I got off the phone with you, I had realized that the lights in the shelter had been turned off for a while. I was expecting to see your wife come out, but she never did. As per your request, I went in to see what could be holding her up. When I got there, there were two men with guns at the pantry closet where your wife was. I heard the gunshots go off and I took my gun out. Just as one of the gunmen were about to shoot her, I shot first; and they ran out the back door. When I got to her, she had already hit her head and was unresponsive." "Was it a robbery?" "I'm not sure sir. I wouldn't be surprised. But I gave my statement to the police." Finally, the nurse came in to take Shaune to his wife." When they reached the recovery room, the police were trying to take her statement. Shaune ran to Tory and hugged her so tight. Then he whispered, "Thank God! I'm so happy to see you." "I'm happy to see you too after the night I've had." The police officer cut in and said, "Memoiselle Guadau, can you tell us what happened to you this evening?" "Can she do this tomorrow officer? My wife has been through a lot tonight and I just want to take her home." Then Tory said, "Please let me do this. It's the least I can do for Mrs. Gudice." "Fine then; but if at any point you get too aggravated, you can stop." Tory took a deep breath; then she started, "Mrs. Gudice and I were closing up shop since the banquet was over. I stayed behind to help put the food away. There was a knock at the front door. She went to go answer it. Then I heard her screaming and arguing with who ever they were. Shortly, she ran back into the pantry. She was shoving me into the closet and she locked me in. Then two men came in and started pushing her around and hitting her. They kept demanding her to get something that she wouldn't give them. I couldn't understand what they were saying; everyone was speaking in French. I though they wanted money, food; gift cards maybe? There was a tall man who hit her in the head with his gun; and she fell to the floor; and that's when he shot her." Having recalled the memory of seeing Mrs. Gudice being killed in front of her, Tory stopped talking and went into a daze. "When he shot her, she was still alive. But then the shorter man shot her in her face and she stopped talking." Tory felt overwhelmed by watching her friend being killed. "It was a horrible site. She didn't deserve that. OH GOD, SHE DIDN'T DESERVE THAT!!!" Shaune, sensing her distress said, "That's enough for tonight officer. I'm taking my wife home; and tomorrow we can finish this." "Monsieur Guadau, just one last question. Memoiselle, your driver said that just before he fired upon the men to save you, one of them lifted his gun to kill you. Did either of them say anything as to why they wanted to harm you? Was there anything they said after they found you?" "No. Not that I could remember. Wait! Just before the taller man shot open the door, he said that he had found me." "Do know what he meant by that?" "My cell phone had gone off while I was in the closet, and they heard it." With a look of skepticism, the officers asked her, "But why kill a witness if there was no robbery?" Feeling confused, Shaune said, "Wait, there was no robbery?" "No Monsieur. All the money that the shelter received was still in the drawer." "Look, I don't know why those men were there. I don't know why they would kill an innocent woman in cold blood…" Then Shaune cut in and said, "Enough! We're going home. This will have to wait till tomorrow."

That night on the drive home, a million thoughts raced through her head in reference to how she could have prevented Mrs. Gudices' death. Perhaps, could she have done anything differently? Then maybe Gudice would still be alive. Then she thought that if she would have intervened, there just might have been two dead people instead of one. As they reached home, Tory felt so good to be back at that ever so huge estate they called home. When they got upstairs, Shaune wanted to help her get more comfortable. As he was helping her out of her clothes, she said, "Go ahead and say it." "Say what?" "I know what you want to say. You want to say I told you so." "Torianey, I would never try to throw anything back in your face; especially at a time like now. The last thing we need right now is an argument. You've been through enough. If it's conflict you're looking for, you're not going to get it from me." As she slipped into her robe, she asked him, "So what is it you want to tell me then?" Shaune got frustrated and wanted to walk away; but Tory stopped him. "I can feel that you have something on your mind that you want to get off; now spit it out." "Fine; want to know what I think? It's not so much I told you so as to I wish you would have listened to me. You are a beautiful, sexy, kind hearted, stubborn, pigheaded woman who fights tooth and nail for what she believes. This is one of the reasons why I fell in love with you. If something ever went wrong and I needed you, I know that you would be up for the challenge. However, when I tell you what I know about a potentially dangerous situation, I need you to listen to me." "You're right. You had explained on several occasions that Massongy was dangerous. Maybe if I didn't throw the banquet, Mrs. Gudice would still be alive." "We don't know that for sure. The main fact is that all are accounted for in this house." Now Tory started to feel even guiltier about Mrs. Gudices' death. "The writing on the wall was so clear and I ignored it. If I didn't push so hard to do that banquet she would have been alive today. This is all my fault." Shaune saw that she was becoming irrational and he needed to stop her. "Baby stop it! That's enough. Again, we don't know that for sure. So stop beating yourself up. If it was meant for her to live, something else would have intervened. She risked her life to save yours and now you have to make amends the best way with it. You owe it to her." "So what do I do?" "You live. You live with her happy memories." Shaune went into the bathroom to fill her glass with water and he came back and dug into his pocket to pull out the pills the doctor had prescribed. "What's that?" "It's a low dose of melatonin. The doctor had said that it's a more natural supplement for valium. This is to help you relax; and the way you have been going on, you can use them. Now open wide." As she took the pills into her mouth, then she drank the water. After he helped her into bed, he kissed her on the head and turned off her lamp. As he began to leave, Tory asked, "Are you leaving?" "Yes, I thought maybe you might want to be alone so you could get some rest." "The last thing I want is to be alone. I know you have a lot of work to do but I need you right now. Could you at least stay with me until I fall asleep? I promise I won't argue with you. In fact, I won't say a word." Shaune realized that his strong, stubborn wife was exhibiting signs of vulnerability. When he removed his jacket, he laid across the bed and put his arms around his wife. "You can say anything that comes to your pretty mind." Tory cracked a partial smile then she buried her head into his chest. "Just before the man found me in the closet, my most hopeless thought was I would never get the chance to hold you again. Never feel your warm body against mine, smell your cologne, hear your heart beat again." "You sure did beat those odds didn't you?" Minutes later, she went to sleep. "That melatonin works fast." He whispered. He waited a little while longer to make sure that she was well asleep. Then he went downstairs to his den.

While Shaune was in his den, he called for Tony to meet with him. Tony had twenty years as a member of the French Secret Service; and he always had a source or two to help him investigate things. "Sir, you called for me?" "I wanted to know if you got a look at those men? Have you seen them before?" "I'm not exactly sure and I don't want to make you worry just yet. So I will wait until tomorrow when your wife goes to the sketch artist." "So what are you not sure of?" "Sir, again, I'd much rather…" Shaune cut him off and shot back, "Look, I almost lost my wife tonight. I need to know what you know now and not tomorrow so I can figure this out." As Tony sat down on the couch, he removed his hat and started. "These men your wife described, I'm not sure if it's them, but they might be professionals." "Really? How do you know?" "Their style of assassination; they turned off the power to detour people from coming in; the fact that the money wasn't missing. I've been around the secret service long enough to know what a professional hit looks like. Then there's Gudice; they tortured her to find what they were looking for. Any common criminal would have robbed her and or raped her. But instead, they killed her in cold blood with no money or motive and they left with nothing." Shaune had a scary thought cross his mind. "Do you think my wife was the intended target?" Tony was hesitant to answer. He knew how sensitive Shaune was about his wife. "Again sir, I would much rather wait for tom…" Shaune slammed his hands on the desk and yelled "DAMN IT TONY!!! I'm asking your professional opinion. Did it look like my wife was the intended target of these men? Qui O NO!!!" "Qui Monsieur. It looks that way." "So who would want to do this?" "Perhaps, you may have made some enemies sir; I don't know as of yet. But if I may suggest something." "What is it?" "Until I can find out more, I suggest that you take Memoiselle Guadau back to the states. At least she might be safer that way." The honeymoon was over and Shaune knew Tony was right. His wife needed to be back in the States until this whole thing could be figured out.

Torys cell phone woke her up that morning. It was after 8am and it was the police Sergeant that had been calling her. He needed her to come down to the station so that they could do the sketch of the two men that she saw last night. After she hung up the phone she needed to look for her driver and husband so they could make their way to the station. Shaune was in the wine cellar with his assistant Julia. Julia was a 25yro college senior who was interning for Que`Shaune. He had hired her as a favor to the Consulate Pierre. She was also engaged to be married that summer to her boyfriend of 6yrs. She and Shaune were inventorying the wine cellar, when Julia asked, "How is your wife?" "She's resting. She could use a little rest right now." "Qui Monsieur. I'm sorry to hear about her and Memoiselle Gudice." "Memoiselle Gudices' pain is over. It's Tory who has to deal with it all." Then Julia had taken him by his hand. Although Julia was getting married to her boyfriend, she equally had a crush on Shaune that he didn't know about.

Tory came down stairs and she was met by her driver Tony. "Have you seen my husband? I have to go to the police station to give the sketches." "We can find him on the security cameras. Come please." When they got to the security office, Tony asked the security officer to pan around for Shaune. After sometime had passed they found Shaune in the wine cellar with his assistant. It was just at that very moment that everyone saw Julia and Shaune kissing each other. Although she kissed him, he wasn't resistant to her. Deep in his mind, he knew it was wrong, but who would know? Of course Tory would never find out about Julia kissing him; and Julia would never tell. So he would just enjoy the kiss for what it was. Tory stood at the monitor and watched; and for every second that she watched the flame grew bigger. Finally, Shaune stopped kissing her and said, "I appreciate your sympathy, but you must never do that again." "I am sorry Monsieur. I..." He cut in and said, "Let's take the wine upstairs." As she watched them leave the cellar, Tory turned to Tony and said, "I need to see my husband please." In her calm voice. When they got to the kitchen, she saw Shaune putting the wine in the chiller and his young assistant sitting on a stool at the island. Julia got up and walked towards Tory and asked "Memoiselle Guadau, how are you feeling this day?" Tory gave her such a right hook to her face; it sent her flying across the kitchen. Then she grabbed a large, sharp knife out of the holder, knelt down and put it to her chin. Then she said with her teeth clenched, "If I ever see you near my husband again, I will cut your fucking heart out. If I see you anywhere in France, I will cut your knee caps off and watch you walk home. Do you understand me? DO YOU FUCKING UNDERSTAND ME!!!?" Then Julia screamed, "QUI MEMOISELLE!" "GOOD! NOW GET THE FUCK OUT OF MY HOUSE!!!" As Julia ran weeping with her hand over her face, Shaune tried to play ignorant. "Tory baby, just calm down please. What's the problem?" Then she turned her fury on him. She grabbed him and took the knife to his throat. "Are you serious Shaune? Are we supposed to pretend that I didn't see you kissing that woman in the wine cellar? Oh wait; I was supposed to look the other way wasn't I? Can I kiss another man? How about Tony, he's really not that bad looking." Shaune glanced over at Tony who managed to disengage his eye contact. Then she finished. "As much as I love you, as much as I am committed to this marriage; if I see you near another woman and I draw the wrong conclusion, just before I divorce you, I'll cut your nuts off. Oh and if you think I'm playing, just fuck around and try me." Just before she left the room, she took the knife and dropped it on the floor. While she was leaving the kitchen, she said to Tony, "I need a ride to the poste de police. Maintenante!" Tony turned to Shaune and asked, "Monsieur Guadau, are you okay?" Shaune, holding his neck said, "I'll get my coat."

That afternoon, Shaune, Tory and Tony were making their way back home after an exhausting day. Tory spent the most of her morning throughout the afternoon trying to get her memory straight on what the hit men looked like. She felt like her brain was going to bust. She sat in the limo with her head perched in her hands. Que'Shaune hadn't said too much to her since he knew he was number one on her hit list. He felt he needed the perfect moment to break the ice. So he asked, "You must be hungry. Is there anything I can get you?" "No thank you; I'm fine." "Baby, you're four months pregnant and you…" "Que'Shaune I'm glad you can count; but your help is not necessary." She said as she cut him off. As the limo pulled up to the estate, Shaune wanted to give it one last shot. "Can we talk about what happened this morning?" Tory didn't bother to respond to him. She just got out of the car and headed inside. Shaune started to run after her, but Tony stopped him. "Monsieur Guadau, we need to talk." When they got to the den, Tony pulled out the copies of the sketches the police gave him of the hit men that Tory had identified. "These are the professionals that I was telling you about sir." "Tell me about them." "I made some phone calls and I found out that not only are they professionals, they have been implicated in a number of high profile murders." "So why my wife? She's not a high profile person." "Maybe their using your wife to make a point to you." Feeling confused and angry, Shaune said, "And what point would that be?" "Monsieur Guadau, I'll keep digging.

Please don't hold it against me if I cannot find it for you. These are very discreet killers. The majority of their kills have been unsolved." "Pleas keep digging. I need to get my wife out of France until then."

It was dinner time and Shaune couldn't find Tory. Somehow, she was on the lamb from him. He went to the security room to see if they would know. "Has anyone seen my wife?" Then one of the security guards replied "Second wing, in the den. She's been there for a while sir." Then he was off to find her. When he got to the den on the second wing, he knocked on the door but Tory never responded. He opened the door to see Tory starring out the patio window with her back to him. "Torianey, may I come in?" He whispered. "This is your house. I have no stake in any of this." As she walked in slowly, he jokingly said, "Says the woman who assaulted, fired and kicked my assistant out of MY house. I keep telling you this is your home too. Just like our home back at the States. When we got married, my home became your home." "What happened to us Shaune?" "I don't understand." "When was the last time you made love to me?" "I guess we can try tonight. If that's what you want." "When is the last time you kissed me goodbye before you went to work? Brought me flowers; sent me a text messages telling me you miss me. When was the last time you thought about me on a whim?" "We had dinner a couple of weeks ago. Baby, I think about you all the time." "Really? Or do you think of ways to get away from me. Is that the one time you think of me." "Never that baby, where is this coming from?" "So where have you been besides in the wine cellar kissing your assistant?" "Torianey, I told you she kissed me." "I am not as concerned about the kiss as I am the length of time it took you to disengage your lips from hers. You wanted to kiss her just as much as she wanted to kiss you." Shaune couldn't think of anything to say to in reference to that kiss. His wife was right. He did want that kiss just as bad as Julia did. He didn't think it would cost him this much. Then he tried to change the subject. "Why don't we go have dinner? I know you must be famished. You haven't had anything to eat all day and the babies must be hungry." Then Tory yelled, "Your parasites are fine. It's

the host that's suffering. Can't you tell?" Shaune became shocked at
the fact that she called their unborn children parasites. "Tory… Why
would you…" "You know I've been standing here the whole time trying
to process our relationship. I keep going back to that night on the plane.
And if I just would have done things differently, I wouldn't be here."
He was curious to know exactly what she meant so he asked, "What
would you have done differently?" "I knew when you offered me the
option to have sex with you, I wanted to do that; but now I'm thinking
that the next time I saw you I should have issued a restraining order
against you." Now feeling confused and shocked he asked, "Why?"
"Because I would have never have had dinner which lead to more sex,
which lead to feelings. I would not be married to you. I would not be
pregnant by you. I would not watch a friend die in cold blood. Most
of all, you screwing your assistant wouldn't be my concern right now.
I wouldn't be here feeling all this misery." Shaunes heart was breaking.
He couldn't believe what he was hearing. "Why would you say such
evil things Torianey?" "Why Mr. Guadau, you didn't know? I am evil.
Do you know why? Because my husband is the devil." Now with his
shock and confusion, came his heart breaking. Then Tory said, "Please
leave me alone. In fact, the next time we talk, I would like to be on a
plane back to the States. We can figure everything out later." Shaunes
eyes started to well up as he left the room. When she heard the door
close, she started to cry as well. "Perhaps she's ready for divorce." He
thought to himself. Shaune walked back to the first wing to his den.
When he got there, he started to feel hopeless. In fact, the way he felt
if she would have stabbed him in his gut, that wouldn't have felt half
as bad as her words. Feeling he needed to fix the situation, he picked
up the phone and called the two people who could help him do just
that. His cousin Celia, and her husband Richard. Shaune knew that if
he wanted to salvage his marriage, he needed their advice. He would
do what ever it took to fix it.

The next morning, Que'Shaune was on the plane waiting for his
wife to arrive. For the first time since they were married, they slept in

separate bedrooms and that bothered him so much that he barley got any sleep. Since Tory had taken the liberty of firing Julia, he called Greg the night before and asked him to fly to France and join him on the ride back to the States. Greg walked over to Shaune and said, "Your wife just arrived. You look like hell; is everything alright?" "No, she saw Julia kiss me; and along with the craziness of her friend getting killed, things just got way out of hand. I just need to fix this." Then Tory stepped on the plane and there was total silence between the three of them. Now Greg felt the awkward silence; and he felt he needed to break the tension. "Tory, you look radiant." "If you mean fat, yes I am." "No actually, pregnancy kind of suits you. And when I say that I mean you look really good. Not that you looked badly when you weren't pregnant you just..." Greg felt like he was embarrassing himself, so he tried to clean things up. "You know what? I am going to throw myself off the plane right now." "I think she gets it. Can you give me some time with my wife?" "I would love to do that." Then Greg immediately left. Now Shaune and Tory stood looking at each other. She had looked a mess. Her hair was barely brushed. Her eyes were tired looking from a mixture from lack of sleep and crying. Shaune gestured for her to have a seat next to him. Then he said, "I don't know about the host, but I myself could use a bit to eat." Shaune went into the break room and came back with a covered platter. He placed the platter on the table and uncovered it as he sat back down. In his hand he had two forks; one for her and one for himself. When he uncovered the platter, he revealed an extra large blueberry pancake that he made a smiley face with whipped cream out of. Tory cracked a smile when she saw the pancake. He gave her a fork and she commenced to cutting into the pancake. After he took a bite, he said, "MMM. I remember Marta used to make pancakes like these for me. They remind me so much of my childhood. I remember hearing someone say there are no small accidents. Things happen for a reason; and despite how you feel about me at the current time, I believe we were meant to be together. If not your seat wouldn't have been soiled that day on the plane. And how is it that I decide to purchase an extra seat that day of all days. Then there's the sex we shared; that connection

I felt with you. However, I wouldn't call that an accident, one might call that an incident." Tory started to chuckle at Shaune's joke. Then he continued. "Then there was your car breaking down in the middle of the night. No one answering you, but you managed to get me. To be honest Tory, that night I gave up pursuing you. I thought to myself, that maybe it wasn't meant to happen. I was so happy you called that when I got into my car, I must have kicked it up to eighty miles per hour trying to get to you. What you're missing is this was supposed to happen. We were supposed to happen. My heart told my brain that this was how it was supposed to go. So you could have issued as many restraining orders as you needed. I would have gotten right out of jail to come back to you. Tory I screwed up big time. In the midst of your crisis I dropped the ball. I started to take advantage of my marriage and neglected you. I never forgot about you; I just forgot to nurture you. You asked me what happened to us? I take full responsibility for my actions and for what happened to us. Julia kissed me and I did want that kiss. After it was over, I instructed that she never do that again. Now going forward, I'm willing to fix this as best as I can. If you can just tell me what I need to do to fix this. I don't want to loose my wife because I acted negligently." Shaune was getting emotional and choked up. Then Tory said, "Can I tell you something?" "You can tell me anything." "I think last night I was having some sought of nervous breakdown. It was like everything was moving so fast and I couldn't keep my feet on the ground. Oh God Shaune, I said those terrible things. I called you the devil; I called my unborn children parasites. I was loosing it. When I said those terrible things, I saw how it affected you but I couldn't stop myself. Look, I know that I haven't been the perfect wife these past few months. In fact, I've been acting like a mad woman. I don't want us to go on this way. I'm so sorry about all those things I said." "Does that include assaulting, firing and threatening the life of my assistant?" "Don't push it buddy." Then they both laughed.

Chapter 20

We Need to Have That Conversation

The plane landed back in the United States. Tory couldn't be anymore happier to be back in the comforts of everything she knew. The paparazzi was in full swing; snapping their photo shots of the two walking through the Metro-airport. Of course the word was out that Tory was expecting but it was never confirmed. They sped walked through the terminal with their security service trying to be as discreet as possible. Que`Shaune held on to his wife's hand tightly as they arrived to the limousine. He then slid her into the car and jumped in behind her while Greg got into the passenger side with the driver. Sounding out of breath, Tory looked at Shaune and said, "What the hell just happened?" With fear in his voice, Shaune said, "Who told them we were coming?" As Shaune and Tory looked at each other; Greg turned to them and said, "Someone must have tipped them off." Tory looked at Shaune and nodded her head towards Greg. Shaune whispered, "I'll talk to him when we get home."

When they got to the estate, Shaune kissed his wife and said, "I'll be up stairs shortly." Then he turned to Greg and demanded, "I need to see you alone." As they walked into the den, Shaune said, "Have a seat please." Greg sat down and Shaune didn't waste any time cutting into him. "Now I'm going to ask this one time. Did you tip off the media about Tory and me coming into the states?" Greg became hesitant; then he said, "Look Shaune, while in your absence, your rating fell. The public started to stir. They were saying that since you got married to Tory, you started to fall off. For months they kept going on about how the Great Que`Shaune Guadau finally called his celebrity status quits. I felt I had to do something." Then Shaune got upset and yelled, "Yeah! You call me. That's what you should have done." "Wait a minute, any other day; you wouldn't have a problem with the media. What's changed?" "I wouldn't have minded if two hit men weren't trying to murder my wife." "What? Wait! Hit men?" "Yes; three days ago two men walked into the Massongy Hostel while Tory and the Caretaker were throwing a feed the homeless banquet for the community. While they were wrapping thing up, the men came in and tortured then murdered the Caretaker while Tory hid in a closet looking on." "How do you know their hit men?" "Tony did some checking around based on her photo sketches of the men. He found that they are in fact professional hit men." Shaune realized that he was veering off of the subject. "I was trying to bring her home in a quiet manner; and your little stunt may have tipped them off." "Oh Shaune, I'm sorry. I had no idea. I wanted to reboot your rep a bit. You know, bring your swag back." "I don't care about my swag. I'm about to be a father. I could careless about my image. My business is my image." "So what now?" "We beef up security around my wife. She doesn't drive alone, and anywhere she goes I want an update." "You know your wife isn't going to stand for all that? "She doesn't have a choice." Shaune said as he left the den.

Shaune came upstairs to meet with his wife. He had remembered the conversation he needed to have with his wife in reference to her permanently moving into the mansion; and with all the mayhem going on, he felt that it was the perfect time to seal the deal. He picked up the suit case and placed it on the bed, and then he started. "Torianey do you remember the conversation we had before we got married?" Tory had her back turned to him and she didn't want him to see her reaction. She had hoped that the conversation would come later then sooner. But however, it had come. "Torianey..." Then she cut in said, "Yeah I remember." See, Shaune knew that whenever he drew a line with her, she would try to blur it so she could maneuver it to her discretion. Then he continued. "So can we re-explore the conversation?" As she took a deep breath, Tory said, "After the honeymoon, I was supposed to get moved in permanently." "And?" "And after the school semester was over here in the states, I would transfer over and conclude my studies in France. Did I miss anything?" "No I think you covered it all." "Look, I would like to have the opportunity to go back to my old home and pack up my things. There are some things I need to put in order." "That would be fine. You can do it in a couple of days." "Why not now?" "Do I need to remind you of that last few days?" "Oh come on Shaune; how do you know their here in the States?" "If you find out that their not, then you can let me know. Until then, you don't leave this house without me or proper security." "I'm not handicapped." "But you are pregnant. You will stay here for now until I schedule round the clock security for you." Are you serious about this?" "Yes my love, I am." "Don't you think you're being a little irrational here?" "No not at all. Look, I managed to get you out of France without incident; and after Greg's little paparazzi stunt this morning it might have tipped those guys off and let them know to come to the States to find you. Sorry if I seem paranoid, but at the expense of my wife and unborn kids, it's priceless." As Tory walked over to the armoire where she put her toiletries, she started experiencing intense abdominal pain. Shaune, who didn't notice her distress, kept on talking. "Look baby, can we at least agree to disagree?" When she didn't answer him, he turned to see her keeled over holding her stomach. As he ran over, he yelled, "Torianey! What's wrong?" Then he called his servant to call for an ambulance.

After some extensive testing, a series of sonograms, blood work, amniocentesis, and pain meds Tory laid in her hospital scared of the news she had been awaiting. The doctor finally walked into the room and sat on the bed next to her to tell her what she needed to know. "Mrs. Guadau, after talking with your husband, I am to understand that you were traveling by plane am I right?" "Yes, we flew back from France on my husbands' jet. We were coming from what was left of our honeymoon. Are the babies okay?" Watching the doctors' facial expressions; and the not knowing what to expect frustrated Tory. "Could you please tell me what wrong?" She yelled. "Relax Mrs. Guadau. Your unborn babies are fine. What you were experiencing was pressure in the amniotic sac where the babies are. Kind of like cabin pressure for the babies. The fluctuation of the plane caused your pressure to go up and down. When pregnant, these things can trickle down to the fetus; and when it comes to hormone levels and chemical imbalances, the babies can become affected by this. Needless to say, their fine. After the IV fluids run out, you can go home." As the doctor started to write out prescription, he finished. "Rule #1. No more flying or long term traveling until the babies are born. #2. You can walk as much as you can tolerate. Walking is good for the babies, but not for your pressure. #3. Get lots of rest and drink lots of fluids; mainly water. Oh and, #4. Sexual intercourse is okay, but not in excess or extensive. We don't want the sac to rupture right now." Tory started to feel ashamed and said, "I don't think that would be a problem. I can't remember the last time he made love to me." Sensing her sadness, the doctor put his hand on her shoulder to console her and said, "Usually, after the babies are born, things tend to return to normal." Then he turned to leave the room. When the doctor came outside, he saw Que'Shaune coming into the room. But then he stopped him and told him, "Everything is fine with your unborn fetuses. She needs to stay off her feet for the next few days, and a little TLC from you every now and then wouldn't hurt." Shaune looked at the doctor and started to feel his pride being challenged. Feeling insulted, Shaune said, "I got it; thanks." Then he went into the room. When he got to the bed, he hugged her so tight. "How are you feeling?" "Much better now thank God." "No more traveling for you." Then Tory started to feel like this was becoming another one of those

"Jumping the gun" moment from Shaune where he would become overly concerned and go overboard. "He didn't say I couldn't travel by car, he just said no more traveling by plane. I don't need to be trapped up in that house like an invalid." "The doctor said for you to stay off your feet, and this is a sign that you don't need to go to that house and do any strenuous working." "He said for a few days Shaune. In fact, he said that walking is good for the babies..." He cut her off and said, "That's debatable. And for now, you're not leaving the house." Tory felt like she wasn't getting anywhere with Shaune. He was obviously unreasonably upset and there was no getting threw to him. He heard what he heard and drew his own conclusions and his own rules; and she had to eat it.

On the way back home, Shaune was on the phone conducting business as usual. Tory had an overwhelming sense of emotion hit her. Then she started to cry. "What's wrong baby?" With a combination of everything that was going on in her life, she started to have another breakdown. Trying to choke back her tears, she said, "I get it now. I totally get it now." Shaune couldn't understand what was happening to his wife. Nor could he understand what she was talking about. "What did you get? Frankly, I'm not sure if I want it either." He chuckled. "I understand why you would want your assistant." "Tory I thought we were over this already. She's gone, we're here in the States, and you're the only woman in my life." "No Shaune, I get it now. I was a big girl when you met me, but now that I'm pregnant with twins I must be so unattractive to you right now. Of course she's more attractive and not pregnant and she doesn't have hormonal issues like I'm having right now. I could see how you would want her over me." "You can't be serious!" "Yes I am. Maybe I should give you a pass on this one; at least until the babies are born." Shaune couldn't believe what he was hearing. His wife was pushing him to cheat on their marriage. Out of respect and embarrassment, Solomon drew up the partition for their privacy. "Torianey, where is this coming from? Frankly, I think you're just being hormonal." "You haven't touched me since we found out

I was pregnant. So I'm sure you must be feeling a certain way that makes me unappealing to you." Then Shaune laughed out loud. Then he explained to her. "Baby, I've been dying to make love to you ever since we found out you were pregnant. But I thought it was customary to not have sex because of the fact. Look, I've never fathered children before. I don't understand how this works. I mean, can we make love?" "The doctor said that it's fine, just not excessively." Shaune grinned, shrugged his shoulders and asked, "When we get home, do you want to... You know?" As they looked at each other, they started to giggle like two teenage virgins.

As anxious as they were to make love, they tried to rush up stairs to their bedroom. Marta ran up to Tory and said, "Tory, you're home. I thought you were having contractions." "It was false labor pains. But everything is okay." "Glad to hear it. Que`Shaune, you have a guest in the den waiting for you." "Who is it?" He breathed out of frustration. "It's Marcus Swain." Then he turned to his wife and whispered, "DAMN! Baby can you wait upstairs for me? Just let me get rid of him." "Take all the time you need." She drew in closer to him and kissed him on his lips. As he licked his lips he said, "That tasted so good." "There's more where that came from." Then he watched her stroll upstairs. Shaune walked into the den and saw Marcus helping himself to his liquor. As Shaune sat down, Marcus said, "And when were you going to call me again?" "Marc, I'm sorry. I've been busy." "I can see that. Twins huh? Why are you back from your honeymoon so soon? Speaking of honeymoon, I don't recall being invited to the wedding. What happened?" "Well, with the honeymoon, I can't talk about it; but with the wedding, I did send an invite to you." Marcus could see that Shaune was lying to him. He had seen that same look on his face before when ever he was with a woman that he didn't want to hang with. "It must have gotten lost in the mail." Marcus said. "Yeah I guess so. I'm sorry about that." "Is there anything I can do to help with this trouble that you are experiencing?" "Uh... No, but thanks thought." Looking skeptical, Marc took a sip of his drink and asked, "And where's the newly wedded, newly pregnant Torianey?" "My wife is upstairs relaxing. Hey what's new with you? Found anybody yet?" Marcus took another gulp of his drink and shrugged off the question. "No, no one worthy yet." "You know marriage really isn't that bad. I really do feel happier. You might want to consider settling down. We're not getting any younger." "So this is you handing in your wingman pass?" "Yeah man I'm a family man now. No more wild away parties waking up in a hotel room next to a strange woman. Tory is my finale destination." Marc started to hear the final nail in the coffin of his friendship. "Please tell me you're kidding me? The world famous Que`Shaune Guadau just letting go?" "That's where you're wrong Marc; for the first time I feel like I'm living." Then Shaune got upset and said, "You know what, I don't expect you to understand. You're too busy being jaded and small minded to realize that there are women of depth in this world." Marcus tried to laugh it off and said, "Ouch! Touché! Went for the jugular did you?" Shaune was getting frustrated with Marcus' inability to take him seriously. Plus, he had plans with his wife. "Look Marc, I'm sorry if I seem too testy. I hope you don't mind if you let yourself out. Please feel free to enjoy your drink. I have to go and check on my wife. See you around." As Shaune left the den, Marcus looked on and whispered to himself, "Oh you will see me around again. This I can promise." Shaune sprinted upstairs to see what his wife was doing. He was more then anxious to make love to her. When he got to the bedroom, he knocked on the door. When he opened it, he saw his wife lying on the bed. He came over to the bed and lay next to her. As he put his arms around her, he realized that she was passed out sleep. Shaune was ready to make love to his wife but she was not up to the challenge. "DAMN!" Shaune whispered out of total frustration. All he could do was go to the shower and cool his frustrations there.

Chapter 21

Here We Go Again

The next morning Tory was awakened by Shaune who was dressed to go to his meeting. "Baby, where are you going today? I'm so sorry about last night. I was more tired then I thought." She said. "Don't worry about it. I have a meeting to attend. More importantly, what are your plans for today?" Feeling hesitant to answer, she said, "Well I did want to go to my old home and…" Shaune immediately cut in and said, "Not today." "Why?" "Not until I get proper protection for you." "Shaune please. You and I both know that you'll always have one of your "emergency meetings" and the whole protection thing will never happen. I can handle myself just fine." "You're not going to that house alone." He said as he clenched his. "We've been back home for two days and already you have to run off. My question… My concern is when can I stop living like a prisoner in this house?" "You're not a prisoner; just give me some time." "How much time? A week, two weeks, a month?" "I promise it won't be that long. I have to go; we can talk about this when I get back." As he leaned in to kiss her goodbye, she turned away from him in protest. But he kissed her on her cheek anyway. Then he whispered in her ear, "I'm sorry I have to do this to you; but you can't leave this house. I'll call you later." Just before he left the bedroom, he turned to his wife, who refused to look at him, and said, "I love you." When he closed the door behind him, he started to feel like a common criminal holding his wife hostage as he did.

Later on in the afternoon, Tory figured she'd defy Shaunes' rules once again. She was determined to get to her old house regardless of what he said. As she came down to the garage, she noticed that the box that held the keys to the cars was locked. "Damn it Shaune!" She yelled in anger. Then she ran to the security room. She figured that she would give it one good try to see if he hadn't tipped them off. "My keys are locked in the box at the garage. Is there anyway I could get them?" "Sorry Mrs. Guadau, your husband gave us strict orders to not let you or your car off of the mansion grounds." Feeling defeated, Tory went back upstairs to their bedroom. While she sat on the bed; she had an idea to call Lou. "God please tell me he hadn't spoken to him yet." She picked up her phone and dialed his number. "Hey Lou." "Torianey, you're back home so soon. I hear congratulations are in order." "Yeah, twins huh? Hey I have a favor to ask you. Could you give me a ride to my old house?" "Sure when do you need?" "As soon as you could get here. I'll meet you at the side entrance." "Okay, I just happen to be in the area anyway. I'll see you in about ten minutes?" "That'll be just fine. We can catch up on old times." "See you then." Minutes later, Lou pulled up at the side entrance, and Tory jumped in the passenger side of his car. Greg had walked into the security office and said, "Hey isn't that Mr. Guadaus' wife getting into that car?" Out of fear and shock, the guard said, "How did she get out of the house? I better call Mr. Guadau…" Then Greg stopped the guard and said, "No, I'll call him. It looks like she's with Carrapelli. At least she's not alone."

On the way to her house, Lou had a feeling Tory was up to no good so he asked her, "I'm just going to go out on a limb here and ask; and please feel free to answer anyway you feel fit. Where is your car? And why are you creeping through the side entrance? And are you supposed to be going back to that house?" Lou had all the right questions but too bad she wasn't going to give the right answers. "I can't find my keys to my car and I needed a ride so I called you. Is there something wrong with that?" "Yes, Shaune has private drivers. I would assume that you would too." "I guess I wanted to see an old friend. It has been a while." Finally, they pulled into the driveway of her old house. Tory felt happy to be back; it was the most freedom she had felt in months. When they got inside the house, Lou said, "So where do you want to start?" But just as he asked his cell phone went off. It was his newest manager. Apparently, there was a small fire in the kitchen and the fire department had to be called. After he got off his phone he said, "Torianey, I have to go back to the restaurant. There was an emergency, I hope you don't mind. As soon as it's over I'll be back." "Is everything alright?" "No only that my new manager is going to be the death of me." Just before he left he turned to Tory and said, "You know you might want to give some thought to coming back to Carrapellies. I could really use you." Although Tory laughed it off, deep down inside she did miss her old life. She managed to shake off the depressing though that she had and got started packing up the final chapter of her life.

Shaune was at his office finishing up some last minute details. He hadn't spoken to his wife all day since that morning. It was out of guilt that he hadn't called her. Ultimately, he had to face the music. He though maybe he should call her before he came home so he could get a fair read on how the mood was going to be when he got home. As he called her cell phone, it went straight to voice mail. Then he called the mansion. "This is Mr. Guadau; I would like to speak to my wife please." Feeling hesitant, the guard replied, "Mr. Guadau, your wife left the grounds." "How is that possible when she didn't have a car to leave in?" Then the guard started to stutter, "Uh, well, see, Mr. Carrapelli came and picked her up outside the side entrance. I never saw her leave until Mr. Duvain pointed her out. But he said it was okay to let her go; that he was going to call you." "Obviously he didn't or I wouldn't be looking for my wife at home." He yelled. Then he stopped himself and finished. "From now on when I give you orders, you follow it to the letter. Secondly, you don't take orders from Gregory Duvain; the both of you take orders from me. So when I tell you to call me if my wife leaves the grounds, seconds later you should have picked up the phone and called me because you work for me not Gregory Duvain! I hope I'm clear on everything I'm saying." "Crystal sir. I apologize sir." Then he hung up the phone and called Lou Carrapelli. Minutes later, Lou picked up his phone and said, "Shaune I'm glad you called, I was just about to call you." "Is Tory with you?" "No, that's what I wanted to call you about. The restaurant had a fire and I got called away from her. I told her that I would be back but this problem is going to take a little longer then I thought. Could you pick your wife up tonight? She's not driving her car." "She wasn't supposed to leave the house. But let me guess, she lied to you?" "She told me that she misplaced her keys and she wanted to catch up on old times." "She lied to you Lou; at least about the car keys. I told her not to leave the house until I got proper protection for her." "Well that explains why she was sneaking through the side entrance and not the front. If I may ask, is everything alright?" "Not really, she's in a bit of trouble and it eats at me how nonchalant she takes it." "Well, you know your wife; she lives by her own rules. You can't "Tell" her anything." "I keep learning that rule everyday." "What kind of trouble is she in?" "I can't talk about it right now but I'll call you later. Right now I have to get to her." After he hung up his phone, he raced off to get into his car.

Tory was putting the finishing touches on sealing her boxes. She put the sheets over all the furniture. She turned the power box off on the upstairs since she was done. Her boxes were neatly stacked and labeled for storage to pick up. She then found herself getting winded; so she sat on her couch and started to sip her cranberry juice. Then the doorbell rang. She thought it was Lou coming back to pick her up. "Man you must be psychic. I was just about..." As she opened the door, she realized it was not Lou. It was Marcus Swain. "My husband isn't here." "I wasn't looking for Que`Shaune, I was looking for you."

"I don't have anything to say to you nor am I interested in anything you have to say. You're not invited in my home. Please leave." Just as she tried to close the door, Marcus pushed it open really hard causing Tory to loose her balance. She fell up against the mirror that was on the wall and it came crashing down to the floor. Marcus threw open the door causing the glass to break. He walked over to Tory and grabbed her by her throat. "See, I don't think you get it. This isn't a fucking social call. I'm not here because I'm concerned about your well being. I'm here because I warned you and you just won't listen." "Marcus, I don't know if you've noticed but I'm pregnant and now is not the time for this. So please don't hurt me." She said sounding fearful. "So now you're not so smart with the words after all. And this pregnancy thing is another problem I'm facing. Shaune meets you, he marries you, and then he knocks you up. Now he's this changed man. But see, what I'm thinking is give or take a few month of him dealing with your death, he'll come around. A little encouragement from me, oh and maybe a few of those expensive whores he's used to banging; you'll be reduced to his homie he used to have feelings for." "No, see, we both know that's not how it's going to go. Allow me to paint a better scenario. See, once you kill me, you'll kill his unborn children as well. And that will set him into overdrive. And when the authorities can't find out who killed me, Que'Shaune; my husband who has the means, resources and the drive will find out it was you. You want to know what you will be reduced to? Puree." "Well let's find out then." Marcus started to tighten his grip around her throat. While Tory was struggling to get free from his grip, she kicked him in his groin causing him to keel over. Marcus regained himself and caught up with her. She tried to go for another kick, but this time he caught her leg and pushed her onto the floor. He jumped on top of her, grabbed her face and gave her two right hooks to her face rendering her defenseless. Then he continued to choke her again. Tory was feeling that hopeless feeling again. That feeling that she was going to die at the hands of Marcus Swain. Just as she lost hope, she glanced down and saw the canister of bug spray she had knocked down earlier. Trying to stay awake, she reached for it. She quickly raised it to his face and sprayed him. Marcus screamed in great pain. "AAAHHH! BITCH!" He quickly jumped up and staggered around the living room knocking over furniture and boxes. With one good eye, he managed to get to his car. Tory was heaving to get air. As she reached for her phone, she tried to dial 911, but then she was overcome with chest pain. Her heart started to give out. The operator came on and said, "This is the operator, what is your emergency?" Tory was struggling to talk. "I need an ambulance…" "Where are you located?" the operator asked her, but Tory was on her way out. It was at that moment, she had collapsed and died.

Shaune was driving up the road to get to his wife. He had been contemplating how he was going to tare into her. Then a car came swerving down the road causing him to loose control of his car. He stopped and regained his footing and proceeded on. He pulled up to the house and saw the door was opened and there was broken glass everywhere. A terrible feeling had come over him. "Torianey?" He called out to her. Then he looked to his left and saw his wife on the floor lifeless. He ran over to her to see if she was conscious. But she wasn't. In fact, she was dead. He picked up the phone with the operator still on. "Hello, This is Que'Shaune Guadau. I just got here and my wife was on the floor. She's not responsive." "Where are you located sir?" "1060 St. Vine. I'm going to put the phone down and try to revive my wife." Then he started to perform CPR. After a couple of rounds, she started to breath again. He wanted to make sure she was fully awake. "Tory baby, can you hear me? Please answer me." She managed to stutter out, "Yes, yes, I hear you." Then he hugged her so tight and said, "I'm going to burn this fucking house so you'll never come back here."

The ambulance had arrived at the hospital. Since Tory was awake and responsive, they took her straight to the OB floor to check on the babies. Shaune couldn't go in with her for procedural purposes. Just before he left her he said, "Baby, I'll be right out here. I'm not going anywhere." Then they rolled her past the doors. Greg, who was standing behind Shaune felt guilty and thought that he could salvage his credibility with him. As he walked up to Shaune, he said, "She's going to be fine…" Shaune slammed him up against the wall. He saw that people noticed his angry stint; and he tried to calm himself. Then he drew in closer to Greg and said, "The day you tell my staff to defy my orders. The day you think you know what's better for my wife then I do, we'll just have discuss your future at Redliner." Then he left Greg standing at the wall.

Chapter 22
The Truth Comes Out

Tory lay in the hospital bed; her face was badly battered by the beating Marcus had ensued on her. The police was questioning her as to who and why she was attacked. The police officer asked her, "When you opened the door, did you see your attacker?" She started to fidget with her hands and loose eye contact. "Uh, no sir. No I didn't." "Is there anyone that you might know of who might want to harm you?" "I really don't have a clue sir." As the officer put his pen and pad away, he handed her his card and said, "If you could remember anything, please feel free to call me at the office." After the officer left, Shaune came over and sat down on the bed next to her. Then she said, "I'm glad that's over. I just want to go home and relax." "You want to explain to me why you lied to the police?" "What are you talking about?" "Tory, you may have the police fooled, but I'm not buying that shit. You want to fill me in?" Although she was caught in her lie, she continued to play ignorant. "I don't know what you're talking about Que`Shaune." "And now you're lying to me. But just in case you're really in a coma about what really happened, allow me to demonstrate the truth. See, the police asked you if you had seen your attacker? You said you didn't. But your body seems to tell a slightly different story." Shaune then moved in closer so he could demonstrate to her the lie that she had concocted. "What I think happened is where these two red welts on both sides of your neck are, they kind of resemble two thumbs." Then he positioned his hands around her neck to imitate what looked like him choking her out. Then he finished. "And these five welts back here are indicative to where the rest of his eight fingers were wrapped around your throat. Am I right Tory?" He slightly gripped her throat startling her. "Shaune, please don't." "I think you saw... No I know you saw who did this to you. And for the life of me, I can't understand why you would want to protect someone who clearly wants to kill you." Tory still remained silent; and for ten uncomfortable seconds they stood staring in each others eyes. He then took his hands from around her neck and placed them on her face to kiss her on her lips. "If you keep protecting him, I can't protect you from him." She turned her head away for feeling ashamed of herself.

The next day, that evening Tory and the babies were given a clean bill of health to go home. Shaune helped her into the car and as he always did. As he secured her seat belt for her, he asked, "Does this feel okay for you?" "It feels...Fine." He just slammed the car door shut. He was obviously still upset with her. Then he got in the car and drove off. Suddenly, there was that elephant in the car. There was that awkward silence that had tension written all over it. Tory could look over and see that Shaune was visibly upset with her. After sometime had passed, he got so angry, he had swerved the car over to the medium, shut the car off, He unbuckled his seat belt and went into a fueled filled rant. With his teeth clenched. "I almost lost you in France. Yesterday, I almost lost you! My family, my wife, my life; I almost lost it all! Do you want to know what was resonating in my mind ever since I had found you and you weren't breathing? Do you want to know what I couldn't get out of my head that whole time? All I thought to myself was my family is gone! My wife, my unborn..." Shaune became emotional and started to get choked up. "My unborn children. And you with your constant antics have almost cost US! Not just you. It cost us! I'm curious to know when will it stop? In France; Now here. God Torianey, when will it stop?" Tory reached her hand to wipe his tears away. Then he turned to her and said, "Do you want to know what my recent resonating thought is? That I ran out of chance to save you. Please baby, tell me something." Seeing Shaunes' greave stricken face, it became clear that she had to tell him the truth. "I promise I'll tell you the truth when we get home."

As they pulled up to the mansion, Tory didn't wait for Shaune or anyone to open her door. She jogged up the stairs and went straight to his den. She didn't even take off her jacket. As Shaune followed her to the den, he saw her go into his desk and pull out the photos that the PI gave him of his first wife's infidelity. In a shocked voice he asked, "How did you know about these?" "Look at the photos closely." She opened the envelope and handed the photos to him. "That's my ex boyfriend. The same ex boyfriend I ran into back in Jamaica; the same ex boyfriend that tried to kill me at my house. While we were dating he kept talking about him and his best friend and all the places they had hit up. But I never met him. He would tell me all the crazy stories about when they went to Brazil and went through a brothel of women in one night. I would listen to painful story after painful story of him and his sidekick best friend running through women. Then his best friend got married; he didn't like it. So he broke it off with me to pursue his wife. His plan was for his friend to catch his wife cheating and he would ultimately divorce her so the two of them could be besties again. See, there was not room for anyone else in his best friends' life other then him." "This can't be true. Marcus?" Shaune whispered. "I had followed him that night so I could try and talk to him. He went to this hotel over on Kenely. I watched him go into a room where there was a woman who was dressed in a pretty lavender robe. When I got to the door, I knocked and she opened it, but this time she wasn't wearing the robe anymore. I said, "My name is Torianey Heckstall; who are you?" She was more then happy to tell me she was Lisa Mills-Guadau. Then I asked her, "How come you're in a hotel room with my boyfriend and not your husband?" Then he finally came out and that's when he told me he never had any intentions on marrying me. So now in some strange twist of fait, I end up dating his best friend and yet again he doesn't like it. So there you have it; you best friend, my ex-boyfriend, my killer, your ex-wife's lover and the hitmen's client." "How do you know that?" "After the hitman said he found me, he said, "Mr. Swain sends his regards." Crazy how one man can cause such destruction in a matter of two and a half years." Eerily, the dots started to connect for Que'Shaune; but he needed to know one thing. "How come he didn't try to kill Lisa?" "She made it easy for him. You knew what she married you for; fame, money. He was just more money for her. The more you have the more you want. She got greedy and his plan was to expose her so she could be eliminated as competition for him. Now me on the other hand, you know me; you know how I love, and so does Marcus. He knows that I love with total commitment and I never deviate from that. He also knows he can't compete with that. He tried to bribe me with his empty promises of loving me if I left you. When I declined he tried to scare me, now that plan didn't work, the next step was to kill me." "And you would consider protecting him." "No not him. I wanted to protect you. Marcus is a crazy man. You said it yourself; he doesn't work for anything but thinks the world is entitled to him. He's a psychopathic sociopath with no heart or soul; and when he gets thrown overboard it's no telling who he might hurt next. I just didn't want it to be you." Shaune got mad and started to yell. "Tory I told you my job is to protect you not the other way around. And why should I be so concerned about protecting you? You're doing a bang up job as it is; emphasis on bang up." "I just thought that at some point he might go away." "Really Tory, and how is that working out? A man that tries to kill you twice is going to say, "Fuck it! I tried once, I tried twice, and that's enough for me." I think he's going to come in for a third round." Fearful of the unthinkable, she had to ask him, "You're not going to do anything rash are you?" "No, I'm too tired to continue on. I'm sure you would agree that the last few days have been exhausting. So why don't we go upstairs and put this aside for tomorrows discussion." Then he took her by her hand and led her upstairs to the bedroom.

The night was still early. However, while in a romantic embrace, Tory drifted into a deep sleep. But Shaune was wide awake. He couldn't sleep; his mind was reeling over the fact that Marcus put his hands on his wife and he could not let it go. More importantly, he was concerned that the third strike was sure to come since he failed twice. "I have to beat this motherfucker to the punch, literally!" He said to himself. He managed to unravel himself from her hold without waking her. Then he put his pillow in place of himself. He ran downstairs to his den and pulled out a black lock box. He opened it and pulled out a silver glock semiautomatic. He loaded his clip and cocked the chamber. He tucked it behind him and put on his jacket. When he got to the garage, he called Marcus. "He Marc, What are you doing right now? Great. Meet me at the cabin. Man Tory is a handful and I need some downtime seriously." The cabin was a place where they could kick back, relax and have fun; but this time Shaune wasn't going to meet Marcus for fun. He was going to kill him and bury his body in the woods. In Shaunes' mind the world wouldn't miss miserable Marcus Swain. He might even be doing the world a favor; most of all, his wife. "Okay man, I'll see you there in a bit." After he hung up his phone, he jumped into his car and sped off.

Que'Shaune had gotten to the cabin before Marcus. As he sat on the leather couch, his first thought was to put a bullet in his head as soon as he walked through the door. But like Tory, he wanted to hear his side if he had one; then he would kill him. Marcus had violated in so many ways and now it was time for payback. His phone rang; it was his wife. With a calm voice he said, "Hey baby." "When I woke up you weren't here. Where did you go?" "I'm just taking care of some business. I'll be home shortly." "Please tell me you're not going to do something crazy?" Shaune heard Marcus' car pull up to the driveway. "I'll be home shortly... I love you." "Que'Shaune please don't..." He hung up his phone cutting her off. As Marc walked in, Shaune changed his look on his face. He gave the impression that he was happy to see him, but deep down Shaune had pure murder in his heart. "Good to see you again Marc. It's been a while since we had some time to spend alone, you and me." "I agree; since the old ball and chain. I hear that she almost gave birth." "That was a false alarm. But she's fine now." "Glad to hear it." As Marcus went to pour himself a glass of scotch he asked Shaune, "You want one?" "Yeah, I'll take a drink this time." "So how has it been dealing with a woman like Tory in her pregnant state?" Shaune figured he would tell a few lies to see him sweat. "Well, let's see; there are the crazy cravings. Pickles and salami; she ate that every night and came to bed smelling like a raving Italian. Then there was the mood swings. One night I forgot to put the toilet seat back down and she threatened to give me a vasectomy." Marcus busted into laughter while he handed him his drink. Shaune felt it was time to stick it to him; so he concocted his own story. "Then there were those high sex drive moments." Marcus stopped laughing and cleared his throat. "It's 3 O'clock in the morning. We're sleeping in our bed as usual. All of a sudden, I feel her hands on me; and not just on me, she's moving towards my dick." Shaunes' plan was working; he could see that Marcus was starting to look uncomfortable. Then he felt it was time to torture him a little further. "So I asked her "what are doing Tory?" She said, "I want you daddy! I need you right now." That was all she needed to say. All I could do was turn on my back and let her take it; and she did. She rode me so hard and so good. I can honestly say those were the best moments in sex we had. It was memorable." Then Marcus looked uncomfortable. "She also loved when I pulled her hair when I was giving her the business." And out of nowhere, Marcus laughed and said, "Yeah she loved that didn't she." "How would you know?" Then Marcus stuttered. "Huh? I was… I was saying most women like that kind of stuff. That's how I know. Look Shaune, I didn't come here to talk about sex with Tory" "You mean my wife?" "Whatever. Either way, this is not the place." "Why not? When we're here we're either taking advantage of them or we're talking about them. What's so different now?" Marcus felt like the air in the room was getting thick. The more uncomfortable he got the more uncomfortable he looked. But Shaune kept his cool; and what better time to stick it to him then now. "Hey I remember you were dating this chic back when I was married to Lisa. You never told me here name, nor have I ever met her. What was her name?" "Oh I don't remember. I've been through so many since then." "You said she was special. How can you forget about those types of women?" Marcus got up to turn his back to Shaune. He didn't want him to see him unravel as he did. "I called them all special. What's one?" "I don't know Marc, Tory is a special women. I can't imagine letting her go. What would you do if you had a special woman like Tory in your life?" Still with his back turned Marcus felt that dagger hit his heart. Then he turned to face Shaune. Then Shaune said, "What's wrong? You got something you want to tell me Marc?" "What are you getting at?" Shaune got up and walked closer to Marcus. "I'm saying that you destroyed my marriage to Lisa all the while running Tory straight into my arm. And now she's my bride. Tell me Marcus, how does that make you feel to lose that big?" Then Shaune took a sip of his drink and continued. "I have to admit, that was one of the biggest favors you have ever done for me. You managed to help me get rid of a gold digger and replaced her with the best thing that ever happened to me. I really would like to thank you for that." Then Shaune swallowed his drink, put his glass down and finished. "But see, there is one problem I'm having with this whole arrangement. My wife just confessed to me tonight her ex boyfriend has been harassing her. She even told me that he tried to kill her. Twice! She said you were her ex-boyfriend. She said it was you trying to kill her. Is that true Marcus?" "Shaune... I..." Shaune punched him so hard; he flipped over the couch knocking down the lamp and table. He came around to him and commenced to kicking him about his face and stomach. Then he jumped on him and continued to pound Marcus' face with his fist. He even felt his nose break. At that point Shaune pulled out his gun and jammed it up against Marcus' chin and out of breath he said, "I invited you here to put an end to your miserable fucking life. You've been hurting my wife; and that shit is a total violation. You wanted to take away the one thing that meant everything to me. You just couldn't be happy for me and leave well enough alone. See, you may have her scared, but I'm not scared of you, you sorry son of a bitch." Then he took his gun and slammed Marcus in the face. "Please Shaune! Stop!" "Is that what my wife was screaming when you were beating on her?" As Marcus started to cry, he pleaded to Shaune, "I'm sorry. I swear I won't touch her again." "You damn right you won't." Then he shot Marcus in the palm of his right hand. After he shot him, he got up off of him and said, "The next time you think of harming another woman, this might serve as a reminder." Before he left the cabin, he turned to Marcus and said, "If you go near my wife again with the intentions to hurt her, I'll put you down like the rabid animal you are. So stay the fuck away from my wife." He left Marcus on the floor bloody and battered holding his wounded hand.

Shaune came home and rushed to his den so that he could hide his evidence and tell his wife what she needed to know and not the whole truth. But then it was too late. Tory came running into the den and saw Shaune trying to hide his gun and she could also see his bloody hands. "What happened?" "Nothing." He answered nonchalantly. "You killed him didn't you?" "No I didn't kill him." "Then whose blood is that all over you?" Tory ran back upstairs and locked the bedroom door. He ran behind her to try and get her to open the door but she was too scared. As he knocked on the door he pleaded, "Baby, please open the door. I swear I didn't kill him. I wanted to... I wanted to kill him but I didn't. All I did was beat him and I told him that if he ever went near you again, I would kill him." But Tory never did open the door. And poor Shaune had to sleep in the guest bedroom.

The next morning, Shaune was in the den having his breakfast. He had asked Marta to wake Tory so that he could talk to her and try and ease her fears. Tory came into his den and stood at the door. "Please come in and sit down. I really need to talk to you about this." "I want a divorce." "WHAT!" Shaune yelled. "Seeing you all bloody with that gun in your hand was too much for me to see. If you didn't kill Marcus, then I can't imagine what he must have looked like." "Baby..." Shaune tried to go to her but she screamed, "Don't! Please don't come near me." Tory was visibly scared of Shaune. But Shaune stepped back and said, "Tory I did what I had to do. My intentions were not to scare you. Be angry, be scared, be what ever you want to; but a divorce is not going to happen." Then he sat back at his desk and finished his breakfast.

Later on that day, Shaune walked into the bedroom and surprisingly, the door was unlocked. His wife was sitting on the bed waiting for him. "Are you ready to talk or are you still contemplating divorce?" "What happened?" As he sat down across from her, he said, "I called Marcus to the cabin because I was going to put a bullet between his eyes. I swear I wanted to. I vowed that no one would ever hurt you. Don't you remember my vows?" "Why was all that blood all over you?" "I beat him so bad and then I shot him in his hand. I told him that if he would ever go near you again, I would take him out like the rabid animal that he was." "So what stopped you from killing him?" "Before the fight I said to him that he managed to chase a gold digger out of my life and chased you into my arms. Somehow, in a weird way, he did us a favor. I told him that you were the best thing that ever happened to me. So I figured that sparing his life would serve as a favor to him. But if he ever goes near you again, I will kill him. And I mean it Torianey." As he rubbed her leg, he said, "Can I please kiss my wife? I miss you." She grabbed his hand and pulled him closer to her so she could hug him. Then he kissed her and said, "I'm sorry for scaring you like that. Only when it comes to your welfare I'd become a mad man." "You've been so intense lately since France. And I can't say that I've been helping much." "That's one thing you have right. It has been pretty stressful." Shaune was ready to get up and go to the shower but he became overwhelmed with emotions that he could not suppress himself. "You want to know what the problem I have with you? You never listen. I asked you not to leave this house; but just like back in Massongy, France you had to defy me just so you could prove that you're in control. Then when the dust settled, you ended up getting hurt again." Tory started to feel bad because he had a point. She hated the fact that he would give her a demand; and despite the fact that he may have been right or wrong; even for her safety, she saw it as him trying to control her and she couldn't stand for that. "Shaune I'm sorry, I wasn't thinking…" Then he snapped at her and said, "No Torianey, you never think. It's like you hear me speak and its fair game to you. You have been reckless; you put our unborn children at risk twice; and let's not forget that you knew who it was that was trying to do you in all along and you kept it to yourself. I'm beginning to think that you just might be enjoying this." "That's not true…" Feeling fed up with her, he didn't want to hear what she had to say anymore. "I'm going to take a shower." As he got up to leave, Tory tried to stop him; but he manage to shrug her off and slammed the bathroom door.

Marcus arrived at his home. His car and his close covered in his own blood. He had lost so much blood, he started to feel dizzy. As he stumbled into his mansion, his servant gasped in horror of his appearance. "Sir, are you alright?" Sounding out of breath he answered, "Obviously, I'm not. I need you to call Dr. Chase. Tell him it's an emergency." Minutes later, Dr. Chase showed up to his home with his bag of supplies. The process took about three hours to clean Marcus up. See, Marcus knew that if he had gone to a hospital, he would have to tell the doctors who shot him and then the truth would get out about who was trying to kill Shaunes' wife. Marcus couldn't risk that; which is why he called Dr. Chase. Dr. Chase, although he practiced surgical medicine, was a man on the take. If you had the ends, he had the means to supply whatever your medical need was. Marcus once paid him $500,000 to inject a woman with an abortion drug. Apparently, after four months of carrying his child, the woman threatened to sue him for child support when she would give birth. Marcus' plan was to make the baby go away by drugging the woman and when she fell asleep, the good doctor would inject her with the drug. By the time she had figured it all out, it was too late; and Marcus had managed to get away with murder. When Marcus finally woke up, the doctor had been gone and his servant was standing over him. "What the hell are you

Feeling in the Dark

doing here and where is Dr. Chase?" He left while you were sleeping. He left you these pills and said to take two every six to eight hours." He took his pills and he said, "Leave me until I call you again." As he limped his painful body over to his closet, he opened his hidden safe. In it were some papers, cash and a nickel plated magnum. As he put it up to his sight, he said, "I guess I have to do this the hard way then. No more mistakes."

Que'Shaune had emerged from the bathroom. He was wearing only a towel around his waist. His upper body still wet showing off his muscular, toned, caramel complexion. Tory was sitting across the bed. She had wanted to apologize to him, but of course he had heard it all before. While he was putting on his sweats and tee-shirt he couldn't help but see his wife's face through the mirror. She kept exhibiting that same look that always made him weak for her. After a couple more looks from her, he could no longer avoid her. As he turned, looked at her with a surrendered look and said, "I'm sorry I lashed out at you that way. It was out of fear that I overreacted. You need to understand that when I insist on something, it doesn't mean that I'm trying to take over you. I never tried to control you or stop you from achieving your goals. If you at least stop and look, I was always in your corner." "I'm sorry about this whole thing. I just wanted him to go away. I really did think that once he found out that we were expecting, he would stop." "That plan didn't work Tory." "And you rattling his cage and beating him to a pulp is a better one?" "When the woman I love is involved, hell yes. He's lucky I didn't kill him." "Now I have the sinking feeling that I'm just waiting for the other shoe to drop." Tory was becoming increasingly fearful of the fact that Marcus was somewhere waiting in the cut; waiting to pounce on her. She knew that the next time she'd see him it was going to be inevitably painful. She also knew that Marcus was the type of man one would have to kill to stop; and Shaune didn't do that which may have been his biggest mistake.

Chapter 23

Mamello

Shaune and Greg were interviewing perspective body guards for Tory. For the past three months they had been sifting through application after application trying to find the right fit for her. Someone who wasn't too old that they couldn't keep up with her; or someone that wasn't too young that wasn't experienced enough. The process was proving to be overwhelmingly challenging because they couldn't find the right one. They had decided to wrap up the final round of interviews and there were no more candidates. "We've been through this for three months and not one worthy candidate." "Shaune, there were a few that seemed to be on the level. What was the problem?" As he looked at the pictures and applications he said, "Let's see; this one here, he's fame struck. I saw it in his face when he walked into the room. And this guy here, he's trying to get laid. Did you see how he pulled up his shirt to flex his muscles? Not around my wife. And this guy, he's too short." Greg felt he needed to level with him. "Dude, it's been three months, your wife is becoming increasingly impatient. Not to mention she's got her classes coming up." "I know. I've been hearing her yell about it all week. I do have one last ditch effort up my sleeve. Tony called me the other day and said that he had a viable candidate.

He said he would be perfect for the job; he was supposed to be here earlier this morning." "So what happened to him?" "To hell if I know." Just as he got up to leave, Marta walked in to announce a visitor for Shaune. "Shaune, you have a guest at the door." "Tell him to come back tomorrow." "He says that Tony sent him here." As he looked at Greg, he said "Better late then never huh? Show him in please." When the man came in, Shaune and Greg both were mesmerized by his appearance. He was a strikingly dark skinned South African man in his mid 30's and he spoke with a heavy accent. Strangely enough Que`Shaune had a feeling about the man. When he shook his hand, he said, "Please have a seat." "Thank you sir." The man said as he took his seat. "Tony speaks of you highly. He also told me you are originally from South Africa." "Yes sir, I relocated from Lagos, Nigeria. It was Mr. Anthony who had referred me to you." "Yes, he works for me. He helps me out when ever I'm in France where my other home is." "It must feel so lucky to live that kind of life." "What do you mean?" "I mean sir; you have servants waiting on you hand and foot; from one house to another." Shaune didn't know whether to be offended or pleased by his comment. So he said, "Thank you, I guess." "I was not trying to pay you a comment Monsieur Guadau. In my country it would be a privilege to serve ourselves and only when we could not, would we require a servant." Now Shaune started to take offense and said, "I'm sorry sir, what is your name again?" "Monsieur Obdell Mamello." "Monsieur Mamello, I make no apologize for my great fortune. I, like my father happen to be able to keep my family legacy up and running through hard work. This life was not given to me. And as for my staff; through their own work ethic, will they reap the benefits of my hard work as well. To put it simple Monsieur Mamello, no one who works for me works for cheap or for free. Something you might find out if you're hired." "Then I guess we should get down to business shall we sir?" "Please Monsieur Mamello, tell me about yourself." Mamello sat back in his seat, took a deep breath and started. "Back in Lagos I was a policeman. I was also part of the Nigerian Military. I had to fight in the war to defend my country from rebel forces..." "Mr. Mamello, I apologize for cutting into your great story, but my wife is not fighting a war. She's trying to stay alive from another man who wants her dead at any cost. I'm trying to prevent that from happening. My question to you is how can you help me keep her safe and alive?" "If you would allow me to explain, I promise there will be a point to my story." Shaune realized that this was going to take more time then he had anticipated. All he could do was listen on. Then Mamello continued. "My wife, much like yours was due to give birth. A few days prior I was called away from her and my town to assist in the of the rebel forces. The Intel that I and my team had received told us that the rebels were miles ahead of us; that we had to travel north to catch up with them. Only to find that the Intel we had received was false. We were led away from our city and when we returned, we found our city in ravage. Our homes were burned to the ground; bodies lye dead in the streets." Suddenly, Shaunes' interest started to peak as he listened to the horrifying story that Mamello told him. "What about your wife?" "I found my wife's body laying ripped open and the body of my unborn daughter was dead, next to hers. The sight was unbearable and mostly unforgettable. So now you ask me how can I keep your wife a live? As a husband I feel as though I failed my wife and my unborn daughter. But I now understand the utmost importance of security as well as the necessity of the safety of your wife and unborn children; having been there one time before myself." Shaune realized his goal was driven by the need for redemption. Trying to choke back his emotions, Shaune reached out his hand and said, "You have the job Monsieur Mamello." "I appreciate it sir." Mamello said as he shook his hand. Shaune got up to leave because he needed to clear his head after that horrifying story. Then he said to him, "Marta will show you where you will be staying. I hope you find it suitable for your needs. If not then just tell me and I'll see about how to better accommodate you. If you don't mind we'll discuss your payment and everything else later on after you've gotten yourself settled in. I have to go and inform my wife of your coming." "That will be fine Monsieur Guadau. Thank you."

The next morning, Shaune was eager to wake his wife and have her meet Mamello. As he woke her he started to explain Mamello and his story. He was hoping that by the time he had gotten through with her, she was on board with meeting him. Before she could actually meet the man, Shaune felt he needed to explain Mamello to her. "Before I take you to meet him, I have to tell you something." "What is it?" "Mamello is a very intense looking man. He possesses a standoffish look that just might intimidate you. But he's a really cool man." Not really sure of what he was talking about; she didn't put too much concern in it. "Well, let's go and meet the man behind the story and I'll decide for myself." When they got downstairs to the den, Shaune introduced Mr. Mamello to his wife. "Monsieur Obdell Mamello, this is my wife Memoiselle Torianey Guadau." As he stretched out his hand to shake hers, she looked up at the tall, dark skinned, towering man. He had the hardest features on his face one man could ever have. He even looked sad. Fighting in the war in his country had obviously taken a toll on him. Tory was slightly taken aback by his appearance. She took his large hand into her to greet him. "It is a pleasure to meet you Mr. Mamello." "Please Memoiselle, if we are to spend time together, I must insist that you call me Obdell." "Well then Obdell, I have to insist that you call me Tory. My husband told me about your wife and unborn daughter. I am so sorry to hear that." He didn't respond to her statement which managed to make things oddly uncomfortable. Shaune broke the ice and asked him, "Have you had breakfast yet?" "No sir, I was coming to see if your wife had an itinerary today." "Well help yourself to anything in the kitchen. My wife and I will discuss her plans for the day and I'll get back to you." "Very well sir." After Mamello had left the den, he turned to his wife and asked, "What do you think?" "He's okay." Although she had tried to appear nonchalant, Shaune wasn't buying it. When they got to the dinning room, he closed the door and said, "Spill it." "What are you talking about Shaune?" "I'm talking about Mamello. I can see that you have a problem. Now what is it?" "I don't have a problem with him. It's just…" She tried to shrug the situation off, but he just kept digging. "Just what?" "I mean he's extremely tall and he looks really angry." "Baby, I told you that he had a standoffish look about him that might intimidate you." "I know but he also looks flighty." "Flighty?" "Yeah, like he could fly off the handle any minute." "Well, I'm not concerned about Mr. Mamellos' anger management issues. Your safety is; and unfortunately, you're going to have to deal with it. Now, what are your plans for the day?" Feeling offended by his comment, she said, "I'm not going anywhere today." "So what, you're going to avoid him now?" Then she shrugged her shoulders as she started to eat her breakfast. "Torianey, you and he are going to be around each other for a good while. I would like to see you get along with him." Then she shrugged her shoulders again and remained silent for the rest of the morning.

Shaune was in his den getting ready to leave when Mamello walked in. "Mr. Guadau, you requested to see me sir." "Yes, please have a seat." "Is there a problem sir?" "Not so much a problem, just a concern I have. My wife thinks that you and she might not get along too well." Mamello chuckled and said, "Why would she think that? She just met me." "Mamello, I'm not trying to get into a dispute with you..." "Are you firing me sir?" "No Mamello, no I'm not." Shaune started to feel uncomfortable; and although he liked Mamello, he started to realize what his wife was talking about. He felt he needed to take a different approach with him. "When you were married, what was your relationship like?" "I don't think I understand what that has to do with your wife." "Please Mr. Mamello; just indulge me for a minute." Mamello felt in his world, Shaunes wife couldn't hold a candle to his. "My relationship with my wife, she was my world. There's nothing she could ask me for that I wouldn't provide." "This is what I'm talking about. Now what if she was around someone who was making her uncomfortable?" "With a respect to you and your wife, I have no control over your wife's feelings towards me. I just got here." "And I know that. All I am asking is please try and bond with her." "I understand your plight, and I will do what I can to make this work."

With a sigh of relief, Shaune said, "Thank you Mr. Mamello." Then he picked up his brief case and left the house.

Later on that day, Tory was standing outside the balcony when Mamello walked out to her. For a few seconds the air had grown thick because Tory or Mamello didn't know what to say to each other. However, Mamello knew that in order for them to bond correctly, one of them would have to open up. "Today is a really nice day to go out don't you think so?" Mamello asked Tory trying to break the ice. But Tory easily shut him down and said, "It's just as nice inside." Mamello felt he should give it one last try. "Come on; I'm sure there is some place you'd much rather be." She only shrugged her shoulder to shut him down once again. "Fine, I tried." Mamello said as he turned to walk away from her. Then Tory said, "Obdell wait!" She yelled to him. As shocked as he was to see that she was willing to stop him, he was equally shocked that she called him by his first name. Then she grabbed him by his hand and said, "I know exactly what we could do today."

Que'Shaune was in his den that evening. He had checked his watch and realized that it was getting late. He also realized his wife and new body guard were nowhere to be found. Just as he picked up the phone to call his wife, he had heard their voices in the hallway. He heard them laughing. "Perhaps they had managed to get along after all." Shaune thought to himself. They were both carrying shopping bags; and Mamello was wearing a tailor made suit that had resemble on of Shaunes'. "Welcome home, where did the two of you go?" He asked sounding concerned. "We were out shopping. Mamello here needed some new clothes for his new job. I took him to your tailor." Feeling offended, Shaune shot back, "Really? And why my tailor?" "Well, I love the way you dress and since Mamello looked like the grounds keeper, I figured that if he's going to be my body guard he might as well resemble you." With his teeth clenched, Shaune said, "But he's not your husband. What does it matter who he dresses like?" "It's not what you think. We were bonding like you wanted us too. If you had a set of instructions on how you wanted us to get to know each other, then you should have written them out and posted it somewhere. The fact remains that he and I are going to build our own relationship in our own way. That is if we're stuck with each other." Then Shaune realized that he was the one who built that monster. So he had to live with the situation. "Fine, I'm happy to see you found so garments to accommodate you Mr. Mamello." Shaune clenched his teeth and squinted his eyes trying to hold back his anger. Brushing aside his attitude, Mamello responded, "Thank you sir. Now Memoiselle Guadau, I'll be taking my leave of you. Good night." As he grabbed his bags and left, Shaune walked over to Tory who was rifling through her bags. "What did you get?" "I got a few things for the babies and I got this." She held up a red lace teddy. "That sure is pretty." "Yeah, Obdell thought the same thing when I wore it for him." Tory started to giggle, but Shaune didn't find it funny at all. "Please tell me you didn't exhibit this in front of another man?" "No daddy, you'll be the only man that I would ever exhibit anything for." "You promise?" "I do." "So when do I get to see you in that?" "After the babies are born." "Why not now? You know I can't wait that long." "You'll have too. I'm sorry but it's not fitted for my frame now. I'm just too big." "You're always so concerned about your weight, but in my eyes, you've never looked sexier; especially when you wave something like that around and expect me not to want to peel into you like a banana." Then he held her from behind and started to kiss her on her neck. "I can tell how bad you want it, but you know that I have to study for next weeks tests. You knew that my finals were coming. The sooner I get this over with, the sooner we can plan for the babies. Isn't this what we discussed when you want to have "that talk" that we were supposed to have after the honeymoon was over. Can you just let it slide this time?" As he drew her closer to him he kissed her ear and whispered, "Fine, I'm going to let this slide this time. The next time it's going to me sliding between those thighs." Then he let her go.

The next week Tory and Shaune came downstairs to see Mamello in another one of his tailor made suits made by Que'Shaunes' tailor.

Although she was happy to see him in his new garbs, Shaune wasn't. "Good morning Obdell. Wow, you look really sharp today." When Tory hugged him, he looked up at Que`Shaune who wasn't as happy to see him. "Monsieur Guadau?" Mamello nodded. "Monsieur Mamello." Shaune nodded as he clenched through his teeth. "Have you had breakfast yet?" "Yes ma'am I did." "Oh that's such a shame, Shaune and I was going to invite you to join us." Shaune shot his wife a look like she was crazy. Clearly he had not intentions on inviting that man to his table wearing that suit. "Maybe next time; however, I will prepare the car for our departure." "That would be fine Obdell. I'll see you shortly." Shaune and Tory went into the dining room where Marta was setting the table. He helped his wife into her seat, and then he gave Marta a kiss on the cheek. "Good morning Torianey." Marta said. "Good morning Ms. Marta." Tory replied back. She saw Marta pouring Shaune a cup of coffee. The smell was intoxicating. Tory couldn't remember the last time she had coffee. "May I have just a half of a cup?" Then they both yelled, "No caffeine for you or the babies." "How about a quarter... How about a sip?" "No caffeine means none at all Torianey. And I told Marta to throw out that black picote tea you've been drinking." "What?" "It's loaded with caffeine. I don't want to raise hyperactive children." "And what makes you think that's going to happen?" "If you keep indulging in caffeinated products, we will. And I will be spending more time at the office." "Whatever." Tory huffed. "So how long will it take you to finish these finals you have?" "I should be done by two or three pm today." "Will you give me a call when you're done?" "I certainly will." As Marta came in to serve breakfast, she gave Tory her tray which contained grilled chicken and scramble egg whites. "Ms. Marta, what is this?" "That's your breakfast." "I didn't ask for this. Who told you I wanted this?" Marta glanced over at Shaune. Looking at Shaune, Tory asked, "Shaune who eats this way?" "You do until the babies are born." As she folded her arms, she asked, "I'm curious to know exactly what are you having for breakfast?" Marta lifted up the tray to reveal 2 eggs sunny side up, 2 slices of bacon, a slice of Virginia ham and 2 English muffins with a side of jam. In total anger,

Tory heaved, "UNFUCKING BELIEVABLE! How come I can't have that plate? I'm pregnant." "There's too much starch and the egg yolk aren't fully cooked. This wouldn't be good for the babies." What was so daunting to Tory was he actually looked like he had believed what he was saying. "You know what Que'Shaune? You are becoming a real package. This is why we can't get along. I have to go or you will be wearing both these plates." As she got up to go, Shaune said, "Wait, aren't you going to eat your breakfast?" While she came barreling down the hall, she screamed, "You eat it you slave driving jack-ass!"

As Tory got into the car, Mamello had noticed that her disposition had changed since earlier that morning. "Is everything okay Memoiselle?" Just before she could answer him, a knock came at the car door. It was Que'Shaune holding his plate. When she opened the door, Shaune sat in the limo with her. "Baby I'm sorry. You can have my breakfast." He had quickly made a sandwich out of the English muffins, ham and bacon for her. "What's going on with you?" She had a feeling that her husband was upset about something; why else would he act like an extreme husband? "I've been a little frustrated these days. You've been so busy studying and I've wanted some attention." It became clear that not only was Shaune backed up, he was feeling overwhelmed by missing his wife. Not to mention Mamello dressing like him. "Oh daddy, I'm so sorry that my neglecting you has caused you to have a man-tantrum." "You had to do what you had to do. I was just missing you a bit." Just as she started to eat her breakfast, Shaune started to kiss on her neck. But then he became too intense with his kissing; so much that he started to fondle her. "Daddy…" "Yes baby?" Shaune whispered while continuing to molest his wife. "I have to go." With a sad puppy dog look in his face, Shaune cried out, "Can't we just go upstairs for a few minutes?" He was trying his hardest to convince her to go with him; but then Mamello had to intercede. As he cleared his throat loudly to get their attention, he said, "Memoiselle will Monsieur Guadau be traveling with us? We are moving pretty late." "No!" Shaune clench out. Tory turned to him and said, "I have to go now or I will be locked out of my finals. The minute I'm done, I will call you." Then she gave him the plate back and watched him get out of the car. After he closed the door, the car pulled off. She turned to blow him a kiss goodbye. "Your husband really misses you." Mamello laughed. "I always thought he was too busy to miss me. Now that I'm busy, he misses me. I can't figure that man out.

Chapter 24
The Wrath of Swain PT II

ory was done with her last final. The time was close to 4pm. She was trying to say goodbye to all the people who made her journey possible. She finally ended with her psych teacher Dr. White. Dr. White was a certified psychologist. He used to have his own private practice at Lexington General, but decided that he was better suited for teaching his craft. After she hugged him, she said, "I will really miss you and your class. It has been an inspiration to learn from you." "I will miss you. You were one of my most intuitive students. Will you be coming back to visit?" "That depends on my husband and his state of mind about coming back." "I hope you always remember your roots. Never forget where you came from." "I promise I won't." Then they hugged one last time. Tory came out of the building to see Mamello sitting in the limo waiting on her. Just at that point a truck screeched up behind her. It startled her. As she turned to see who it was, she noticed that it was the two hit men. Mamello jumped out of the car to run to her rescue, but one of the men started to fire at him. Then one of the bullets hit Mamello in his chest. When he hit the ground, Tory screamed, "OBDELLE!" The other hit man managed to grab her and shove her into the van; then it sped off. While they were in the van,

Tory started to cry. Then she asked the men, "Why are you doing this? I know you don't want to hurt a pregnant woman." "No we don't. We were paid to deliver you to our client." "I know its Marcus Swain. He wants to kill me." "What Mr. Swain wants to do with you is of none of our concern." Then her cell phone rang. One of the hit men took her purse from her and looked at her cell phone. "It's your husband." "May I talk to him?" "No you cannot." "Look, my husband can pay you way more then Marcus can." Getting fed up with her, one of the hit man said, "If you don't shut up, I will be forced to silence you."

As Mamello lay on the ground, blood leaking from his chest wound; a man came running to him. "Oh my God, are you okay?" Then Mamello opened his eyes and breathed in deeply. Apparently, the gun man had only nicked him in the chest. He simply got up and jumped in the car. He pulled out his cell phone to call Shaune, but the call went to voice mail. "Monsieur Guadau! I need you to call me back as soon as possible."

Shaune was back at home in the dinning room. He was trying to call his wife on her phone, but it went straight to voice mail. He was going to surprise her with an intimate dinner setting just for the two of them. He also wanted to surprise her with a thin platinum pendant necklace that she had been hinting at all year. And for dinner, he thought he would reenact their first date. He wanted everything down to the meal to resemble the first time they met. "Baby, it's your daddy. The time is a quarter after 4p and I'm home waiting on you. I have a surprise for you. I can't wait to feel those thighs around me." He giggled, then he finished. "I miss you and I want you to always know that Daddy loves his baby." Then he hung up and noticed that Mamello had left him a voice mail message. As he retrieved the message he could hear the distress in his voice. Typically, Shaune had assumed that Tory may have gone into labor and he was rushing her to the hospital. Much to his dismay, things were progressively worse. "Mr. Mamello, I do hope that you are bringing my wife home." Mamello, sound rushed and out of breath said, "Sir, your wife has been taken." "What! How did this happen?" "I'm so sorry sir; I was waiting for her in the car when a truck came behind her. One man shot at me while the other man put her in the truck. I couldn't shoot back because I couldn't risk hitting her." "Do you know which way they drove off to?" "Negative sir; I was knocked unconscious briefly after getting hit." After he hung up the phone, he had to take a seat to get a grasp of where his wife might be. Shaune started to grasp that since the hit men were connected to Marcus, then where ever Marcus was, that was where his wife was being taken. Shaune figured he give it one last college try to call Marcus. He picked up his phone and dialed his number. Much to his dismay, he answered. "I'm guessing that if I am receiving your call, you know your wife isn't coming home." "Please Marcus what ever you want I'll give it to you. Just don't hurt my wife." "Wow! The great Que'Shaune Guadau II is actually begging me for something. He never begs for anything." "What ever you want Marc. Just tell me." "Why did you have to have her Shaune? She was my woman before you came along." "She doesn't want to be with you anymore." "And she shall pay for that. I'm sorry to say, but those babies have to go too. But just know that when the dust settles, we'll get through this together you and me." As he heard the truck pull up, he ended his call. "I have to go now. I love you bro." Shaune sat in his chair stricken with the biggest fear he could ever have dreamed of. His family was about to be murdered and he was all out of options of saving her. Then he thought to himself, "If I were Marcus Swain, where would I be?" He figured Marcus' home would be too obvious. Then he ran to get the photos.

The hit men knocked on the door; they had Tory in front of them. Marcus opened the door and dragged her inside. "Tie her up over on the bed." While the one guy tied her up, the other one approached him and said, "We would like our payment now." Marcus laughed and said, "But she's still alive." "We never signed on for killing her. You told us that you wanted her brought to you. We don't engage in murdering pregnant wives." Marcus started to laugh hysterically. Then he said,

"Tory can you believe this? Hit men with moral consciences. Go figure. Okay boys, then let me pay you and leave me to my own dirty work." He reached into his brief case and pulled out two large envelopes. He tossed it to them and said, "Count it as you will its all there." After the hit men counted their money, they didn't bother to say a word, they just left. "Now we're finally alone." Tory started break out into tears. "What is wrong with you Marcus? Why do you hate me so much? I never did anything to you. When we were together, I loved you, I never cheated on you like you did over and over again; and each time, I forgave you. When was I supposed to say when? Now that I'm living a happy life you can't be happy for me?" "Not when your happiness stems from my ending friendship with my best friend." "People grow up and change. When will you?" As he took out his gun from behind his back, he said, "When you and your hell spawns are six feet under." Just as he started to put the gun to her head, a knock came at the door. "Who the fuck is it?" "Marc, it's me Shaune." Then he whispered to Tory, "How the hell did he know where we were?" As he went to the door, he said, "Why did you come?" "I want to see my wife. I want to know if she's okay." Marcus realized that if he continued on with Shaune outside the door, he might draw too much attention. "I'm going to open the door; if you move too fast I swear I will shoot her where she sits. Do you understand?" "Yes I understand." Then Marc unlocked the door and eased back towards Tory with his gun on her. "Okay come in." As Shaune and Greg walked in with their hands in the air, Marcus yelled, "Easy, not too fast. I will explode her like a watermelon. Now close the door and lock it. Then stand over there." As they did what Marcus said, Shaune turned to his wife and asked, "Are you okay baby." Before she could answer, Marcus cut in and said, "You shouldn't have come here Shaune." "I had to; you have my family hostage." "See Shaune, before this tramp came along you and I was a family. Then when she took you away from me, she wouldn't leave. Nothing I could do would make this BITCH! Leave. But see Shaune, once she's gone we can make things like it used to be." Pointing at his semi bruised face and his still wounded hand, he finished. "Oh and this, don't worry. I know it wasn't your fault. She made you do it. I forgive you though. When she's gone we could put this all behind us." "Marcus you're not making any sense. My family is not worth jealousy. How long did you think we were going to parade around like we did? Two grown men running through woman like we did; you had to know that I wasn't trying to live like that forever. If you kill my wife, how could you assume that I would want to go back to that life?" "Sad to hear you say that." Then Marcus turned to Gregory. "I can't understand for the life of me why you wouldn't take me up on my offer. He obviously values his wife more then you." "I would never double cross my boss. I would never have another good day in my life if I did." Then Shaune turned to Gregory and asked, "What are you talking about." "See, I had tried to make a deal with him. That if he would work with me to get your lovely wife and you here, I would eliminate the both of you; and after your untimely demise, Greg would end up as the new CEO to Redliner. Let's just assume that Sr. would miss his son so bad that he would be forced to take dear committed Gregory under his wing as his illegitimate son. Nice plan if I should say so myself. But unfortunately for you…" Then he shot Greg in his thigh and said, "I'm going to have to kill all of you. And who knows, maybe the old man might see me as a potential son; and I might end up running Redliner." Then he walked over to Tory and pulled her on to her feet. Her hands were tied behind her back. He sat her at the foot of the bed. Then Que'Shaune had one last salvaging thought. "Marcus, I get it now." "What do you get?" "I understand how I have been neglectful towards you. I realized that all you wanted was my friendship. I was being too selfish to understand that that's all you needed right?" Marcus backed away from Tory and said, "Go on." "I'm saying can we start over? As I think of it, I know that there is still room in my life for you. Let's do it like we used to. Go to Cancun and hit up biblical style remember?" Then Marcus and Shaune laughed together. "But what about Tory?" "What about her? She's going be at home with two screaming babies; and we'll be nowhere to be found, why because we'll be too busy bouncing from country to country just like we used to." Shaune actually saw that he was starting to get through to Marcus.

His focus was no longer on trying to kill his wife. Then he continued. "Hey, remember that Villa we went to in Mexico? All that tail we went through; so much pussy we in that room; fucking all night only to wake up to getting head all morning long." Shaune was speaking his language. But what Marcus didn't realize was he was only trying to get close enough to him. Before Marcus could regain his thought, Shaune pounced on him quickly. As they started to fight for the gun in Marcus' hand, Shaune had slammed him into the wall. He managed to knee Marcus in the stomach which put him down; but not before the gun went off. Then Shaune had delivered one last blow to his face to put him down for sure. As he got up off the ground, he kicked the gun away from him reach. Then Gregory yelled, "Shaune!" while he was looking in Torys' direction. As he turned to Greg, he saw the look of horror in his eyes. Que'Shaune was reluctant to turn but when he did, he could see only his wife's legs behind the bed. And they weren't moving. He darted over to her and he could see that her eyes were open and she was breathing heavily. The bullet hit her in her right lung. As she struggled to talk, she said, "You need to call an ambulance, my water broke." Shaune could see that his wife was getting weak. Not only was she loosing blood, she was loosing fluids. Although poor Greg was facing his own dilemma, he managed to pull out his cell phone and dial 911. After he got off the phone, Greg spouted, "Their on their way Shaune." Shaune was working feverously to keep his wife awake. "Please stay with me baby. Do you know what I have for us back at home? I cooked your favorite dinner and remember that necklace you kept hinting about? I got that for you to wear with that red teddy you bought. I want you to wear that for me; will you do that for me?" Tory tried to answer him; she started to choke on the blood that was forming around her lungs. Then Shaune heard the sirens. "Baby their coming!" He yelled. He knew he was loosing her. "Please squeeze my hand Torianey." He whispered. Deep down, Tory was trying to bargain with God that if he just let her live long enough to deliver Shaunes' babies, he could do what ever he wanted with her.

As they pulled into the hospital doors, Shaune was ordered to stay behind due to the severity of his wife's injuries. Before the doctor went into the operating room, he turned to Shaune and asked him, "It appears your wife in running into complications. If in the event you had to make a choice, who should we focus on first?" "What are you talking about? Their all going to be fine right?" "Sir, your wife is at a critical state. Her current state is just barely in the survival stage. If I need to make a choice, I need to know now." Que`Shaune was faced with a dilemma. Ultimately, he had to make a choice. "If you have to make a choice… Save my wife." Just as the doctor started to run into the operating room, Shaune grabbed him and said, "Please doctor, try and save them both." "I'll do my best." Then the doctor left.

Tory laid on the OR table. She was disoriented but in so much pain. She had heard the doctor and the surgeon talking. "She's lost a lot of blood and fluid. Did you talk to her husband about advanced directives?" "He said that if we have to, we'll have to save her first and let the children go." Upon hearing that, Tory yelled, "No! You will take the babies first!" Mrs. Guadau, your husband said…" "To hell with what he said. I carried these babies this far and Goddamnit they will live. If my children die and I live, I will come back to this hospital and tear it apart. And when I find you doctor, I will literally rip your fucking heart out just like you did me… You take them first." Now the doctor had a problem on his hands. Should he handle a husband who will be missing his wife? Or should he wait in the cut for a woman with a vengeance? Then he looked at the surgeon and said, "Take the babies first. At least he'll have his family. After she's done we need to move on to her." "Smart man." Tory said as her breaths grew shorter. As they prepped her to give birth, the doctor tried to worked fast to help her give birth to her babies. "Mrs. Guadau, I need you to breath deep and push!" the doctor yelled. Tory gave all of her breath to get her babies out and one by one they came out. First was her daughter. "Torianey Guadau." She huffed out. Afterwards came her son. "Que`Shaune Guadau III." She named him. "Congratulations, your son and daughter are now born." She managed to crack a smile "My family… My husband has his family now. Can my husband see his family?" The doctor nodded to the nurse to let him in. As Shaune walked in, the doctor whispered to him, "We don't have much time. We need to move fast; so please make it quick." He sat next to his wife and he could see that she was in total distress. He could almost imagine the pain she must have been in giving birth with a bullet still lodged in her. "We did good didn't we?" She whispered. As he looked at his two babies in their separate cribs, he couldn't help but feel overwhelmed with happiness. Then he looked at her and said, "You did a wonderful job." "Now you have your family right?" "We have our family." He picked up his daughter and kissed her. "You know she's going to be a handful?" "Just like her mother. I'm sure she's going to call me a slave driving jackass; slam car doors and constantly defy my directions." After they both giggled, Shaune continued, "And that's why their mother will be around to save them from me trying to kill them." Feeling conflicted to answer; she said, "You have to go now." "Okay, I will see you soon?" Tory could only nod to him. He grabbed her hand and kissed it. After he left out of the room, he heard her flat line, and the doctor yelled, "I need a crash cart now." He tried to run back into the OR, but was immediately stopped by the doctor. "Mr. Guadau, you can't go back in there." He grabbed the doctor and threw him up against the wall. "I thought I told you to save my wife first. Why is that fucking bullet still in her?" "Your wife made it clear that she wanted the babies to come first. She wouldn't let up." "You heard my god dam orders loud and clear. All you had to do was sedate her. If my wife dies, you better eat your mother fucking scalpel. I'm going to come back here and by the time I'm through with you, you'll wish you had committed suicide." The nurse screamed for the doctor to come into the room; then Shaune let him go. Suddenly, the doctor started to feel that saving his wife over the babies wasn't such a bad idea after all.

Que'Shaune had went down to the babies ward where his daughter and son were take after they were born. As he sat down and looked after them, he had noticed that they both looked like her. He held his daughter in his arms and smelled her. He not only noticed that they looked like her, but they smelled like her too. Shaune felt that sinking feeling that he would feel when he missed her and he started to cry. There was a tap at the window. It was his father. "May I come in Mon Files?" "Sure." "These are my grand babies no?" "Qui` Pare." Then Sr. picked up his grand son and looked at his grand daughter while she was crying and said, "I have a feeling she will be running Redliner." "How do you figure?" "She has that determined scream." Sr. laughed but Jr. didn't feel much like laughing. "Would you be willing to come with me somewhere?" "Dad, I don't want go too far from my wife." "Don't worry, this isn't too far." They both place the babies back in their bassinettes and went off.

Sr. took his son to the hospitals cathedral. "Dad, why are we here?" He asked his father. Then Sr. took him by his hand and led him to the alter. He took a match and lit a candle. Then he started. "When your mom died, I was devastated. There was nothing anyone could say to change the way I felt. I felt guilt, pain, anger and malice. An old friend told me the road to redemption is often hard but if sought out, go to God. And when you go to him, go with an open heart." "What are you talking about dad?" Sr. gave him a match and said, "Talk to him son. He is waiting for you." Jr. took the match, lit a candle and knelt at the alter. As Sr. stepped back to give his son his space, he started to pray. "God I have never asked you for anything. Well, accept for when I was trying to find my way into Torianey's life; and you made it happen. I remember promising that I would never let her go. I would always take care of her. And I did God; I swear I did the best I could. I saved her every time she got hurt, I tried to protect her, keep her safe. That was my job." As Jr. started to sob bitterly, he finished. "God I love my children with all my heart and everything I have in me; but I would give them back to you just so I could have my wife back." After he finished, he collapsed and started to cry his eyes out. His father came to console him. He had no words because he had never seen his son fall apart like he did. Then the nurse came ran in and said, "Sir, the doctor will see you now.

As they ran to Torys' room, the doctor was by her bedside. He turned to Shaune and said, "We managed to stabilize her." Feeling like there was more to his comment, Shaune said, "So what's wrong with her?" "She's unconscious." "So what do we do now?" "We wait sir. But I'll be totally honest with you; she might not make it through." "So like you said we'll wait." "I'll be back to check on her periodically." The doctor left the room so he could be with his wife. Sr. turned to his son and asked, "What are you going to do?" "What do you mean what am I going to do? I'm staying with my wife. When I leave this hospital, she'll be coming with me." "But son, what if..." Then Shaune cut him off and yelled, "I don't want to hear it dad! My wife is coming home with me." Shaune was adamant about his wife and wouldn't accept any other form of reasoning. "Very well son. Please call me if you need me." Sr. then kissed his son on his cheek and left him alone.

Chapter 25

Anything Worth Having Is Worth Fighting for

Tory awoke to where she thought was the hospital. And although it looked like the hospital, it was empty. There were no people around and neither was Shaune. She started to feel scared because she had no idea where she was exactly. She got up to walk through the empty facility. She stumbled on to three doors. Not feeling like she wanted to open the doors, she turned to find another exit. When she turned around, she saw that there was a dead end behind her and there was nowhere left to go accept for the three doors. It now became apparent that she was in some kind of a dream. Tory went to the first door and opened it. It was dark inside but she could hear voices. The voices were faint and she couldn't make them out. "Hello? Who's that?" She yelled. Suddenly, the voices grew louder and she started to see the faint faces of people she knew. They looked angry at her. Then one person came up and said, "This is what your darkness holds! Come and accept your fait." Tory backed up out of the room and said, "This is not my fait. I don't accept this." As she backed away, the door slammed shut. Tory looked at the other two doors and opened the second door.

This time, the second room was filled with light. When she stepped into the room, she saw the face of the one person she hadn't seen in fifteen year. It was her mother. "Mom?" She whispered in shock. Her mother had been killed in a car crash years ago. It left her devastated and now she stood face to face with her. "Where am I?" "You're in the light. See, unlike the dark you can see everything here." "What am I supposed to do mom? I'm so scared." Her mother took her by the hand and said, "Don't be scared." After she took her hand, she started to feel better. She felt a sense of serenity. Then her mother told her, "This is not your time; nor the place where you're supposed to be. You must go through the door where your future lies." "I don't care about my future. I've done what I was supposed to do." "No you haven't. There's so much more." "What else is there to do mom? Shaune has his children. I wish you could have met him. He's the perfect man." "Then why would you want to leave him?" Suddenly, the thought of being in the light didn't seem like such a good idea to her. "My children and my husband need me. But will I see you again?" "I can't promise you that. Unlike the light and the dark, your future is a mixture of both light and darkness." "Feeling in the dark?" She asked her mother. Then her mother replied, "With your eyes open." It became clear what Shaunes' phrase of feeling in the dark was all about. Who knew it took her mother to help her understand what it really meant. "I guess this is goodbye." As her mother let her hand go, Tory started to become overwhelmed with emotion. Then she started to cry as she back away from the room. She watched the door close and proceeded on to the final door; her future. She reached for the third door. When she opened it, she could see her husband in his pajamas, sitting in his favorite chair at home holding his two babies in his arms. As she walked towards them, a shot ran through her that woke her up.

It had been three days since the delivery of the babies and her falling unconscious. She opened her eyes and looked around her. She was still in the hospital; but this time she wasn't in it alone. When she looked to her right, she saw Shaune sleeping cuddled next to her. He looked weary in his rested state. His grooming started to look off. She started to rub his face and whispered, "Why would I want to leave you?" She took his hand and kissed it. Shaune finally opened his eyes; and when he saw that Tory was awake and alert, they both embraced and started to cry.

Two days after Tory had waken from her unconscious state; Shaune had informed the doctors that he was ready to take his wife home where she would recuperate. As he was packing up her property, Tory was dressing the babies and securing them in their car seats. She had come up on a memory that she couldn't shake. As she turned to him, she said, "You had told the doctors that if you had to make a choice, you wanted them to save me first. You want to tell me why you didn't choose the babies?" He wasn't prepared to answer her. "Que`Shaune, you want to tell me why our children weren't a priority?" He still didn't answer her; so she yelled. "Que`Shaune!" "Damn it Torianey! Look, everybody is here. You're here, the babies are here. Just drop it!" "You don't get off that goddamn easy." "I don't have any answers for you right now." "What kind of a monster are you?" "The kind that loves his wife." "More then his children? I don't know who you are anymore." "Whoever I am, I'm taking the kids to the car." Then he grabbed both car seats and left the room. As they were walking towards the car, Tory saw a face that she didn't think she would ever see again; it was Mamello. "Oh my God, Obdell!" She screamed as she ran to hug him. "I thought they killed you." "It takes more then a .34 caliber to stop a war Vet like me. And you Memoiselle Guadau, it is good to see you on your feet and much lighter I see." "Thank God we all made it." Then Que`Shaune said, "Are you going to reminisce with my wife or are you going to help me with these seats?" Then Tory whispered, "He might kill them in the process, so please go help him."

On the way home, Tory and Que`Shaune never said a word to each other. He played with his daughter while she held her son. He didn't like the tension between the two of them; so he tried to break it. "My father said that Torianey will be the new face of Redliner. What do you think about that?" "What if they want to be doctors? Better yet, what if she wants to be a doctor and your son wants to be this new face of Redliner?" "That would be something to think about." "You know what I just realized? You just wanted to have children so you can have an heir to sit on your billion dollar legacy." "That wasn't my only purpose for having children. However, yes a legacy to Redliner would be a good thing. My father is on his way out, and then there is just me to run things. So who will after me?" "So you had children just to keep the family business going?" Feeling fed up with her being argumentative, Shaune huffed, "Oh God, here she is throwing words in my mouth again. For a woman with a new lease on life, you sure haven't learned anything." "Oh yes I did, I learned that my husband never really wanted kids; you confirmed that when you told the doctors to save me and not your children." "Torianey, I had to make a choice. And I'd do it all over again." "You're just full of truths today aren't you Que`Shaune. Fucking dirtbag." Yet again, trying to divert a crisis, he only managed to make it worse. As the limo pulled up to the driveway, the staff was waiting to meet the new additions to the family. The doorman opened Que`Shaunes door and he darted out with out saying a word. Marta tried to greet him, but he brushed pass her like she didn't even exist.

Later on, Tory was in the twins' bedroom. It was an adjoining guest room that was converted into a child's bedroom. The closet was turned into a mini kitchen where a small fridge was used to store her breast milk; and bottles of sterile water. Also, on the side was a bottle warmer for quick access. The closet was filled with other items she would need to cater to them. Tory had just finished pumping her milk for the next day. She had fixed her clothes back on and as she emerged from the closet, and guess who was in the room? It was her husband. "We need to finish our conversation." "I've said all I wanted to say to you." When she tried to leave, he grabbed her by both arms, and pressed her up against the wall. "So that means you're ready to listen." He held her arms so tight that she yelled, "Que`Shaune, you're hurting me!" "I just wanted to make sure I had your full attention. I don't know how long you're going to hold this over my head. I don't even care, because I'm going to say this once. The doctor asked me to make a choice. If in the event they had to save you OR the babies, who would it be? I didn't have time to dwell on it. I couldn't get to talk it over with you. You want to know why I chose you? Somewhere in my mind a single thought came to me that said at least if I had you, after we'd mourn the death of our children we could start over. I certainly wouldn't want to start over with anyone else; I wanted to rebuild with you. Despite all the tension between us, I'm happy the three of you are here. I'm happy that my wife is on her two feet sassing me and walking away from me like she always does. You could have been a fond memory of what used to be the love of my life." Then he let her go and backed away from her as he finished. "So you can throw as many darts at me. You can throw as many rocks at me; you can even spit all the venom you want all day long. I'll take it; all of it. The fact remains is I'm happy to see my family." Then he left her alone in the room.

Tory was in the dinning room eating her dinner alone. Shaune had never come home since the time he had left. She had felt bad about starting an argument with him. She saw in his eyes that he had a hard time trying to explain his actions. She realized that he had a point; although it would have been painful to lose their children, they still would have each other and they could rebuild their lives once the pain had subsided. As she took a bite of her food, she huffed, "Oh Torianey, you know how to drive a man away." Marta came in and saw Torys' mood. "I checked on the babies; their still sleeping peacefully. They look so precious, especially when their sleeping." "Yes, they do. Thank you for checking on them." "Is everything alright?" "Not really, I may have chased Shaune away." "You could never chase him away. He loves you so much." As Marta took a seat next to her, she said, "I remember when he told how he met you. He had such excitement in his eyes. I had never seen him talk about one woman as much as he did you. It was like he was already in love. Shaune never talked about his ex-wife like that at anytime; but you, you were special to him." She pat Tory on her leg, and as she got up to leave, she finished. "If I know Mr. Que`Shaune Guadau II, he's not going anywhere anytime too soon." "Thanks Ms. Marta." Then no sooner did she say that, she heard her husbands' voice down the hall. A feeling of relief and excitement came over her. He walked into the dinning room and saw Tory sitting at the table eating her dinner. "Are you hungry?" She asked him. "No, I'm tired. I'm going to check on my children, then I'm going to take a shower and go to bed; goodnight." Then he left the dinning room. Apparently, he was still angry with her.

Tory came upstairs to find her husband in the bathroom shaving; he was wearing just a towel around his waist. "Hey." She whispered. "Hey." He whispered back. She sat on the bed and watched him in his towel. "You know it's been a while." "Yes it has." Knowing exactly what she was talking about. "But we both know that you have to wait six weeks until." "But there are other things." Then Shaune looked over at his wife and thought to himself, "Wasn't she about to leave me a few hours ago? Now she wants to make love to me. I can't figure her out." Then he said out loud, "I guess there are." While he was still in the bathroom, she came into the bathroom and held him from behind. "What's going on with you Torianey?" "Why does something have to be going on with me?" "A few hours ago you were about to cut my dick off and throw it out of a moving vehicle; now you want to make love to it." "Look Shaune…" He stopped her and said, "Tory, please I don't want to argue about this anymore. Haven't we been through enough already?" "I don't want to argue anymore. I just wanted to say that I understand your side. Never did I stop to consider what it would have been like to be in your shoes. Frankly, I don't know if I would have made the right choice; but the fact that your daughter, your son and your wife are here with you says that you made the right one. Shaune you are a great man and for me to treat you the way that I did, it makes me feel terrible. So if you choose to stay angry with me, just like you've taken everything I've given you, I'll take that." Tory started to walk out of the bathroom, and Shaune grabbed her. "Now when have you known me to hold grudges like that? You're the one that likes to stay angry. You always jump to a conclusion, and I just sit back and wait for you to cool off." As they embraced each other, Tory said, "I love you daddy." "You're my rock star and I'll always be your biggest fan." "I really do appreciate you Shaune." After they kissed, Shaune said, "So, there are other things huh?" "Yes there are." "Can I see what they are?" Then she took him by the hand and led him into the bedroom.

Two month later, after everything was finally returning back to normal; Shaune and Tory were getting used to being parents. Tory and Marta were in the twins' room feeding the babies. "My they are growing so well." Marta said. "Yes they are. It's only been two months; where did the time go?" As they both started to laugh, a news flash came on the television. It was the verdict of Marcus Swain. Tory focused in to hear the verdict. Although the jury ruled in favor of him being guilty for attempted manslaughter leaving him with life in jail, the judge overruled the verdict to a felony misdemeanor and only gave him 30 days of probation. "WHAT THE HELL!" Tory yelled. She yelled so loud that she woke up her son that was in her arms. Then Marta asked, "Would you like for me to take him for you?" "Yes please, I need to go see my husband." Tory gave her son to Marta and darted down to the den to see Que'Shaune. When she got to him, she ran to his desk and said, "Did you hear about Marcus?" "No, what's wrong?" She grabbed the TV remote and turned it to the news. After hearing the verdict for himself, he said, "This can't be happening." He quickly picked up the phone and called his lawyer. Tory started to pace the room back and forth as she waited for him to get off the phone. Finally, he hung up. "What happened?" She asked feeling anxious. "His father paid off the judge." Tory was becoming increasingly concerned. Marcus swain was going to get out of jail in a few hours. And it was a matter of time before he would come for them. "We have to do something Shaune. We have to leave now. I'll get the babies together; you can get our things together…" Shaune could see that his wife was about to have a nervous breakdown. He knew that he had to do something before Marcus got out of jail. "Calm down Tory! I'll handle it." "What are you going to do? Beat him up again? He wants us dead; which means he has to be stopped permanently." He looked at Tory with a calm look and said, "I know exactly what I have to do." "You're not a killer Shaune." He kissed his wife on the lips left.

Shaune had arrived at his fathers' house. Sr. was in his den watching television when Shaune came storming in. "Dad, I need your help." "Am I to assume this has to do with the Marcus Swain verdict?" "Yes it does; and I want to... I need to kill him." "I can make some phone calls for you." "No, I need to do this myself." "Mon Files, you are no murderer. Let me handle it." "No, I want to watch that son of a bitch die!" "Que`Shaune, I am much better at this then you are. You don't want that mans blood on your hands." Shaune stop pacing the floor and walked up to his fathers' desk and said, "You are better at this aren't you Pare`? You planned a great murder, but fucked up and murdered the wrong person." Sounding in shock, Sr. said, "What are you talking about?" Shaune started to laugh like a mad man. "Who am I talking about...? Who am I talking about...? I'm talking about mom! DAD!" Sr. felt overwhelmed as the family secret was brought face to face from his sons' mouth. "Who told you about that?" "Did you think you could shield me from the truth this long?" "Who told you?" "Not the sick fuck that should have... PARE`!" Feeling taken aback, his father jump out of his seat and slapped his son on his face hard. Out of shock, Sr. put his hands over his mouth after he watched his son land on the floor. Sr. never once put his hands on his son until this day. Shaune picked his self up and said, "Look dad, I don't care how you've lived with yourself all these years. I don't care how you can sleep at night. I even don't care how you manage to allow Uncle Francois to sleep under a bridge every night since that day. I have a family to protect and you, you have two choices; either you help me get into that prison to get rid of the son of a bitch; or if you don't, you won't have to worry about seeing your son or your grand children again, ever!" Shaunes' father could see in his eyes that he was serious about killing Marcus. He had remembered that same flame he had in his eyes; a flame that would only be put out by satisfaction. "Fine, I'll need to make some phone calls first. I swear Que`Shaune, I don't know who you are right now." As he Shaune turned to leave his fathers den, he said, "Who ever I am, I'll be waiting in my car."

Marcus was being taken back to the facility where he would wait for his lawyer to post his bail. Of course he had that usual smug grin on his face every time he would get away with something. He had a private escort back to the facility. Since the judge was paid off so well, he made sure that Marcus would not have to travel back with the rest of the inmates. As he got out of the private car, the correction officer said, "I have to put the shackles on you." "No worries, I'll be out of here in a few hours. And I'll be paying a few friends a visit." Certainly in his mind he was going to pay Tory another visit. This time he would make sure he would finish the job. When he got into the facility, the guard led him down a hallway that he was unfamiliar with. Then he asked, "Where are we going?" "To a special holding cell until you meet bail." The Guard said. This particular unit was empty. Since he was with a female corrections officer, he felt it was time for him to show his true colors. "You know since it's just you and I, maybe we can share a cell together?" "No thank you sir." "Awe, come on; who doesn't want a piece of a millionaire? I promise I'll show you the time of your life. You can even leave the handcuffs on; it might make it more fun." "Again, I said no thank you." Then he stopped and became really aggressive. "When I get out, I'm going to speak to your boss, the warden and make sure that if you don't give me what I want, you'll lose your job." She grabbed Marcus by his arm and said, "I'm going to have to insist that you keep walking." "Wow, I love when a woman takes control." As they were coming down to the end of the hall, he could see two other inmates standing as if they were waiting for them; and they weren't shackled. Marcus started to feel concerned because they were carrying chains in their hands. They grabbed him and threw him up against the bars and started to lock the chains around him. He screamed for the corrections officer to help him. "Guard! Do something!" Then he heard a voice come from a dark corner of the hallway. "She is doing something. She's doing exactly what I instructed her to do." The voice came into vision. It was Que'Shaune dressed in an inmate orange jumpsuit with a do rag on his head. "Shaune?" Marcus said in amazement. "Oh shit, wait, you didn't think you would be seeing me again? And I bet you had plans to see my wife after you got out. I'm here to prevent that from happening. In fact, I'm here to make sure you never leave this place alive." Marcus started to feel scared and his fear started to show. "Shaune, I swear I was..." "Don't tell me what you weren't going to do. That doesn't even matter anymore. I warned you once that if you ever went near my wife again, I would put you down like the animal you were. You didn't listen Marcus. My wife and children will live without having to look over their shoulders for you." "Shaune, I promise I will go back to England and you and Tory will never..." Shaune ran up to him, grabbed his jaw and slammed his head up against the bars and said, "My wife! You mean my wife and I will never see you again. See, you always call her Tory like you had some kind of personal claim to her. Those days are over. Again, you're right; we will never see you again." The officer gave Shaune a large container which contained a flammable liquid. Then she and the inmates left them alone. "So what are you going to do?" Marcus asked with his voice trembling. With a content grin on his face, he answered. "I'm going to take pleasure in murdering your fucking ass." Then he started to pour the flammable liquid over his Marcus' head. "Can we talk about this please?" "I though we did when I warned you not to go near my wife again. Why so full of words now?" "Shaune, come on, you're not a killer man." Shaune started laugh as he poured the remaining fluid at him splashing it in his face. "You know me so well don't you? Hey, whoever I am, you won't be around to find out." Then he lit the match; and just before he tossed it, he said, "Go to hell you miserable fuck!" As he flicked the match, he turned to walk away from him. While he was walking, he could hear Marcus' horrifying, blood curdling screams. But hearing his screams only made Shaune smile harder. Marcus Swain was dying in a way that only Shaune thought he should. As he walked down the hallway towards the exit, Marcus finally stop screaming and Shaune turned around for one last look to make sure he was dead; and he was. His body was burning so badly that his arms had separated from his torso. Afterwards, Shaune had headed to the basement where the furnace was located. He stood in front of the furnace and removed his clothes one by one and threw everything in down to his kicks. Then he pulled out a garment bag which contained his original clothes. After he was completely dressed, he threw the garment bag in the furnace; closed it and locked it back so he could make sure all the evidence of his presence being in the prison facility would be burned up just like Marcus Swain. When he left the basement, he came to the staircase where he was met by the corrections officer. She opened the door for him to leave, and they both nodded at each other to say goodbye. The sound of the overhead alarms went off, and the officer told him. "You better go. That means lockdown." He came up to the first floor exit. He walked down the hallway just as calm as if nothing ever happened. He walked pass the wardens' office and saw his father and Gregory handing him a suit case which was filled with money. When he passed by, his father looked at him and nodded at him; then Shaune nodded back and proceeded on to his car.

Shaune, his father and Gregory met up at an exclusive location so that they could access how Shaunes' plan went. Shaune got out of his car and walked over to his fathers' limo. His father came out of his car and said, "I take it you were successful with your plan?" "I was very successful." "Are you at peace with your results?" "Yes father, I am. If you would give me a chance to apologize for my behavior this morning…" His father put his hand on his should and said, "Don't apologize. We are Guadau men; we don't make any apologies for loving our families. Perhaps, if I hadn't screwed up years ago, your mother would be alive today. Living all these years as I did with my guilt and shame, my only concern is can you live with what you have done for the rest of your life?" "When it comes to protecting my family, I will do anything. And yes, I can live with what ever means I have to take to do so." Sr. threw his hands up in truce. "So I take it we now have a cease fire? And you won't keep me from my grande bebies since I have done as you asked." "We have a truce. In fact, this year we are coming back to the States to celebrate my birthday at Carrapellies; and I was wandering if you would be there to see your grande bebies?" As his father smiled and hugged him, he replied, "I wouldn't miss it for anything in the world." Then Shaune opened the car door for his father to get in. "Gregory, take care of that leg. I'm going to need my VP in France when you're fully recovered." "Will do; be safe in your travels." Greg said. Shaune got into his car and headed home to tell his wife that she could finally be at peace.

Torianey was sitting in her husbands den; her mind was still weary at the fact that Marcus getting out of prison. Then the news flash came on. It was another "Marcus Swain verdict" update. This time the news said that Marcus Swain was found dead in the prison facility he was being held in. She couldn't believe it. "Marcus is actually dead?" She whispered. Tory couldn't fathom how he could be dead. "Did Shaune really take care of him?" Then a sense of pure joy and relief came over her. She jump up and started to laugh out loud. While she was enjoying her moment, she turned to the mirror and saw blood on her blouse. She had realized that she forgot to change her bandage where her bullet wound lie; so she ran upstairs to change it.

Que`Shaune came home and his first thought was to look for his wife. When he saw Marta, he asked her, "Have you seen Tory?" "She's probably upstairs with your children." He darted upstairs to the twins' nursery. But she wasn't there. He walked over to his daughters' crib and watched her fidget. As he picked her up, he whispered, "You will be the face of Redliner. Your mom just doesn't know it yet. You know though; don't you?" Then he placed her back in her crib. He picked up his son and said, "You're going to be a doctor; and that's okay, because I'm going to need one between your mother and your sister kicking my ass around." He kissed his son on the forehead and placed him back in his crib. He continued on to look for his wife. When he got to the bedroom, he could see his wife standing in front of the mirror struggling with the bandage. She was in a lot of pain trying to remove it. She looked at the partially healing wound and said, "This is going to be one ugly scar." Then Que'Shuane came up behind her, helped her apply the new bandage and secured it with the tape for her. After he was done, he held her tight and said, "You know, when this heals fully, we could have it surgically repaired." Tory looked through the mirror at him and herself together with the bandaged covered scar. "No, I don't think I will." "Why not?" he asked in confusion. She smiled and said,

From Airplane rides; and table time pies
This journey was no walk in the park.
Dealing with if, and or maybes
While giving birth to twin babies
We'll always be feeling in the dark!!!

FINE!!!

To my good friend Michael B.